NEFERTITI'S HEART

A. W. EXLEY

Be the first to hear about new releases, occasional specials and giveaways. My newsletter comes out approximately 4 times a year. Follow the link to sign up:
eepurl.com/N5z5z

Author's Note:
This book uses British English

THE ARTIFACT HUNTERS:

DEDICATION

To Rob, Thomas and Ethan.

I may be the only girl in the frat house, but I wouldn't have it any other way.

CHAPTER 1

Sunday, June 23

THERE was something cathartic about wielding a crow-bar. Cara used one end to loosen the tacks, before ripping up the expensive, patterned carpet. She tossed the strip in a growing pile by the wall. She never intended to remove all the carpet, but with the cool metal bar in her hand, she lost herself in the rhythm of tearing away a layer from her father's sanctuary. Pushing a deep auburn spike of hair from her forehead, she took a moment's break from the dusty work. As spring gave way to summer, Cara found the air inside the narrow terrace house stuffy and oppressive, a situation exacerbated by her current labour. She flung open the second-storey window, took a large breath of London air, and coughed. Coal smoke and steam belched from the horseless carriages below and spiralled past her window. The combination of the narrow street and tall buildings forced the vehicle emissions skyward.

She blinked the stinging smog from her eyes and leaned on the casement as she surveyed her work. She had taken up most of the library carpet, the floor underneath finally revealed. Coated in several years of dust and grime, the boards appeared dull in the morning light. Pacing the floor, she knew she was close; a spot to one side called to her. The hairs on the backs of her arms rose as she walked the bare boards. *Ah.*

There. She saw wooden planks stained a slightly darker colour. A maid spent hours on her knees there. With a scrubbing brush and bleach, she had tried to wash away the blood before the new carpets were laid.

There was an old saying: *blood will out.* Cara wondered if this was what her grandmother meant. *You can scrub as hard as you want, but you can never remove the taint, not once it leached into the porous fibres of the wood.* The stain became a permanent reminder of the violence committed.

Cara remembered as she lay on the floor; unaware her blood soaked the carpet and seeped into the floor beneath. Darkness crept over the floor and surrounded her numb body. Oblivion wove tendrils around her; sight the last sense she relinquished. Her vision turned black as her fourteen-year-old self watched her father. He took a book from the shelf and pressed the hidden lever, before the waiting darkness swept her into blessed unconsciousness.

Twenty-one-year-old Cara fixed her line of sight and walked to the bookcase. The book in question was *Justine* by the Marquis de Sade. She snorted at the irony. She and Justine shared a similar experience at a young age, but Cara was grateful she never followed the unfortunate literary heroine's sad path. She removed the book and balanced it in her hand. The leather was a dark red, soft and supple from years of hands caressing its surface. The book was a valuable first edition, as were all the volumes in the library. Her father had expensive tastes and a love for the finer things in life. He valued his material possessions above all else. Even his only child.

She hadn't been back to the house since that day seven years ago. She refused to return until he was dead. Otherwise, she would have been tempted to help him shuffle off his mortal coil.

She placed de Sade's book on the desk and peered in the gap on the shelf. Not seeing anything remarkable, she inserted her hand and pressed the wall beyond in an experimental fashion. The panelling shifted under her fingers. She pressed harder and heard a soft *pop*. Brushing the brown suede ends of her morning coat out of the way, she folded her long legs, resting on the balls of her feet to see what the lever activated.

A part of the bottom shelf jutted up and yielded its opening fully to her slender fingers. The shelf hid a small compartment, otherwise impossible to discern. Cara could have demolished all the shelving with the crowbar and still would have been lucky to stumble upon it. She briefly toyed with doing it anyway, simply for the satisfaction of destroying her father's sanctuary.

Crowbars are great for working out parental issues.

She tentatively reached into the cavity. She felt something square and squat. Withdrawing her hand, she held a small, fat notebook. The book bulged with extra inserts and cards, tightly tied with brown string. She had found her father's catalogue of antiquities. The book detailed everything he acquired and, more importantly, contained the vital details of where he secreted them. He had never been a man to share, and ensured he was the only person to touch his treasures. The notebook would tell her which bank vaults she needed to visit, and the required passwords and access codes for the safety deposit boxes.

"I'll take that, thanks," a husky voice announced from behind her.

Cara stood and placed the notebook on a shelf. She cursed herself for being preoccupied and not hearing the intruder. Composing herself, she turned and gave the stranger a deadly smile.

"I don't think so. This is my house, and you're trespassing." Her fingers went to the leather holster at her hip. She popped the metal dome and drew her pistol. Her arm was straight and unwavering as she aimed directly at the thug. "My friend here, Mr Smith, also wants you to leave."

"My master is very interested in that little book. And to make sure I get it, I brought my friend."

A second man stepped out from behind the first, a metal pipe dangling from his fingers.

The two men looked similar. Tall, with the muscular, powerful builds of those who spend a lot of time pounding and lifting heavy things for fun. They both dressed well, with fine pinstripe suits, custom made to wrap around their broad torsos, and black felt bowlers pulled low on their foreheads.

Not your average burglars. And judging by those arms, they could bend metal with their bare hands.

Cara's smile never wavered. "I've got you both covered." She drew another pistol from the holster under her arm. "Mr Smith has his own friend, Wesson."

The first man chuckled and raised his hands in amusement.

"Look, Bruce, the pretty lady has a couple of popguns. What are you going to do with those toys, darling?" He edged closer to Cara as he spoke.

She didn't have time for his conversation; she had other things to do. She moved her line of sight and fired. The man cried out as the bullet penetrated the centre of his palm, rendering his left hand useless. He swore under his breath as he shook a handkerchief from his pocket. He wrapped the square of fabric around the injured hand. He blocked the hole and stemmed the trickle of blood down his arm, but not before droplets landed on the pile of discarded carpet.

I see the library is up to its old tricks of demanding blood payment.

Cara adjusted her line of sight. "Get out of my house or the next bullet goes through your forehead and ruins that lovely bowler."

"Well, we have a problem then," he said between gritted teeth as he continued to fumble with the handkerchief. "'Cause if we don't return with that book, our master is going to kill us anyway."

"Who's your master?" Curiosity niggled at Cara; she didn't think anything could be more compelling than a hole in one hand and a pistol aimed at the head.

"Lyons," he grunted. He pulled the ends of the cloth tight with his teeth, sealing the wound.

Lord Lyons, the villainous viscount.

"You do have a problem." *Failure* and *no* were two words that didn't exist in Lyons' vocabulary. He also had the emotional range of a slab of granite. His underlings wouldn't receive any sympathy when they returned empty-handed.

"I'll help you out with your dilemma." While smiling at the first man, she shot the second in the shoulder.

He cried out as the impact spun him sideways; the iron pipe fell from his hand as he dropped to one knee. He keened to himself as blood splashed onto the floor. The library demanded a heavy toll today from so many unwelcome intruders.

"Lyons might be less inclined to kill you now you're both injured, or amused when you tell him a girl did it. And you can give him a message for me."

The two men exchanged looks. The second man groaned and swore in pain, as he bled heavily from the shoulder wound. His fingers scrabbled at his neckerchief, pulling it from around his neck to wedge between jacket and torn flesh.

"Tell your master I may be open to a business proposition, but he won't be taking anything from me." Cara's tone was flat, deadly serious, and bored.

The two men wavered. She cocked the pistols and lined them up with two foreheads, to help the thugs reach a decision.

"We'll deliver your message. Then we'll be back to wipe the smile off your face." The first man promised, helping his friend to his feet.

"I'll be waiting." She kept her pistols aimed on them as they backed out of the library. She stood immobile until she heard the front door slam. Going to the window, she checked they were indeed winding down the road before she relaxed her guard. Watching them weave haphazardly down the street, she fed the pistols an extra bullet each from her belt before returning them to their holsters.

The library timepiece chose to interrupt her thoughts with a single piercing peal. The ornate clock had been commissioned to commemorate Victoria's ascension to the throne almost twenty-five years earlier. Tiny mechanical people stood around the edge, each waving a Union Jack flag as a royal carriage appeared from the back and revolved around the central clock tower. Cara hated it. It sat on its shelf, haughtily look-ing down at her. From her recollection, it only ever chimed when she was in trouble or being beaten.

She picked up the fallen crowbar and smashed the dome. Glass shat-tered, raining over the shelf and the floor. The whirring sound trailed off, and the mechanism fell silent. With a grin, she tossed the crowbar to the ground and stepped over the glass.

Moving to the small liquor cabinet, she poured a finger of whisky from the crystal decanter, retrieved the notebook, and then seated her-self at the desk. Cara stared at the notebook, the formidable rival for her father's affections.

She took a swallow of whisky, letting the alcoholic warmth radiate through her. Brown string yielded to a tug from her fingers, and the notebook fell open. Lord Devon spent a lifetime, and a fortune, in pur-suit of unusual antiquities from around the world. Cara flipped the pag-es as details of her father's adventures spilled forth. He was meticulous in recording his travels, where he found items, and how he acquired them. He often utilised illegal or immoral methods, which in part added to his paranoia about protecting his acquisitions. And vitally, the notebook revealed where each priceless treasure lay hidden.

Lord Devon never liked to share, but he occasionally held private viewings of his latest acquisitions. Showing off his latest treasures sparked a corresponding greed and envy within Lord Clayton. Clayton pains-takingly collected her father's gambling chits until he held sufficient of them to demand either full payment or the artifacts. He underestimated her father's affection for his collection. He offered up to the cruel lord an item of lesser value. One he had no use for; his fourteen-year-old daughter.

A loud clanging alerted Cara to someone at the front door.

Don't tell me they're back and ringing the bell?

She walked to the window and then leaned out. She looked down on the top of a brown bowler hat and the shoulders of a plaid overcoat standing on the top step.

"What do you want?" Cara yelled down.

The bowler hat looked up at the sound from above. Gold frame spectacles regarded her, the light reflecting off them, hiding the eyes behind.

"Miss Devon?" He had a clipped accent, achieved through years at public boarding school.

"Yes. What do you want?" Cara repeated.

A hand reached into a jacket pocket and extracted a silver and gold badge, which he held up. Cara couldn't make out the detail from the second-storey window, but she recognised the shape and colour. The centre of the badge held the letters H, M, and E in blue enamel and entwined around each other.

"I'm Inspector Fraser of Her Majesty's Enforcers, and I require a moment of your time." He tried to keep his tone low, so the neighbours on either side wouldn't hear the exchange.

Cara gave a long-suffering sigh. "I'll be right down."

Darting out the library door, she skipped the stairs. Despite her father's repeated punishment, she rarely exhibited ladylike behaviour; she balanced on the balustrade and slid down the railing. With a practiced move, she jumped to the floor before she hit the ornate end post, and flung open the front door.

"I suppose you'd better come in." Cara ignored the offered hand, and waved the inspector into the foyer, then ushered him into the front room. He doffed his bowler to reveal sandy brown hair, an open, honest face, and grey eyes behind his spectacles.

Cute, for a copper. Shame he's wearing the coat. I can't check out the rear view.

Deep red paint covered the walls of the parlour. Cara thought it made the room look moody, although benign compared to the blood-drenched library upstairs. She stood by the window. She had no intention of sitting and letting him get comfortable. She watched him take up a spot next to the cold fireplace.

"What can I do for you, Inspector?" Cara had a pretty good idea, but wanted to see how the policeman broached the subject.

His hands played with the brim of his hat, rotating it through his fingers. "It's about your father's death."

She noticed he didn't offer condolences. She waited for him to continue.

"Your father's death was . . . unusual. We don't see many Egyptian asps in London."

Cara knew a snake inflicted the fatal bite, but the exact reptile had been kept from public knowledge.

"Are you implying some form of foul play?" She assumed someone else shared her hatred for Lord Devon and did her a favour. The snake was an exotic touch; a bullet would have performed equally well.

"We have interviewed the staff. Your father was alone the entire week preceding the unfortunate event. He received no visitors or unusual packages. And, as I am sure you are aware, his bedchamber is on the second floor, with no obvious means of access to his window."

She took that as Enforcer speak for the chances of somebody bowling up, pulling an asp out of a pocket, then lobbing it into Lord Devon's bedroom were considered remarkably slim. And no doubt, they were out of likely suspects.

"And we know where you were." He held eye contact with her.

She wondered how long it would take him to hint they considered her involvement in Lord Devon's untimely demise. "So it occurred to you the long-lost, and estranged daughter might have taken it upon herself to resolve her daddy issues."

He smiled; small dimples at the corner of his mouth made him even cuter. She couldn't find anything to dislike about the man; from his appearance to his manner, he radiated casual charm. All topped off with good breeding and education, but not so much of either to make him unapproachable or stiff. There was just the tiny fact of him being an Enforcer, and Cara's loathing for the way the force failed her.

"We like to be thorough. But in the absence of any evidence to the contrary, the doctor has ruled it accidental."

Cara nearly laughed aloud. "I'm sure he was bitten accidentally. It doesn't answer the underlying question, though, does it?"

She returned his smile.

He held out his hands in a gesture of helplessness. "You can see my dilemma."

"Let me guess. You'll be watching me?"

"I see we understand each other, Miss Devon. The case will remain open. You never know when new information may come to light."

He moved out of the parlour to the front door, saving Cara from telling him to leave. He nodded and replaced his bowler.

She closed the front door behind him and then leaned against it. Thoughts churned and jostled around her brain, like hungry fish after chum.

The sooner I clean up here and sell a few things, the sooner I can get the hell out of London.

CHAPTER 2

Monday, June 24

HER *eyes first attracted him and held him captive. They were a clear pale blue, like the sky of a crisp autumn morning. But night had fallen, and her eyes were wrong. He watched it happen. Her pupils dilated and chased the blue away and the colour didn't return. Now, empty darkness stared back at him.*

The eyes were the gateway to the soul. And the heart was the seat of the soul within the body.

Her gate was barred against him. She was the wrong one. Her heart wouldn't be his.

He was learning, the power only just awakening as his memories returned. He accepted he might make a mistake or two before he succeeded. He would certainly pay more attention to the eyes next time.

If the eyes were right, her heart would open, and he would claim what rightfully belonged to him.

On returning to London, Cara's first act had been to dismiss the household staff. Her father's brutality resulted in a high staff turnover, and she found the Devon family home full of strangers. She held neither loyalty nor ill will toward the staff; she simply didn't want them around her.

She ensured they were well paid, before watching them trudge from the downstairs entrance. She preferred to know she was the only person making noise and rattling around the Soho address. She couldn't abide the time she spent in the house. She endured its confines only while she searched for the notebook. She knew leaving the house unattended would be an invite to every questionable person in London wanting to track down her father's collection.

Every moment she spent under its roof was like drawing a knife blade down her arm. As she moved from room to room, the sharp tip caused her to draw in her breath as invisible steel carved into her skin. She imagined the phantom tears in her flesh leaving droplets of blood wherever she trod. She and the house hated one another. The terrace house had taken too much of her blood and life essence. If Cara possessed the ability, she would have torn down the building, brick by brick, simply to watch it suffer and diminish, until nothing remained but a pile of dust.

Luckily, she located the notebook, and would tell the family solicitor to advertise for a tenant. She only had to remove what few items she wanted and move to smaller rooms elsewhere, while she finished her business of breaking up and selling off the priceless collection. There was no need to retain staff to attend a non-existent resident. Certainly, the house wouldn't care, though Cara suspected it would sulk at the lack of attention.

She rose early, and dressed casually in beige, buckskin pants and brown, lace-up riding boots. Her corset was her only external extravagance; the rich brocade of swirling green and blue hues had laced ties at the shoulders and a short collar, echoing the tailoring of a man's jacket. The corset laced up the front, so she had no need for a lady's maid to pull the laces tight. The colouring of the corset perfectly offset her cream undershirt. She picked up her gun belt from the bed and slung the brown leather loosely around her hips. The shoulder holster went over the top of her corset, and the pistol nestled by her armpit. To complete her outfit, she shrugged on a dark brown, morning coat.

Having no staff cluttering up the hallways also made it easier to avoid the social callers; without a butler to answer the door and take cards, a plucky few thrust their cards through the mail slot. Cara duly ignored the multi-coloured pieces of heavy paper, as they piled up on the entranceway floor. She stepped over the confetti on her way out and locked the door behind her. The key disappeared into a small leather pouch hanging off her gun belt.

She stood on the bottom step, taking in the hustle and bustle of the late spring, London street traffic. Soon, a heat shimmer would rise from the cobbled streets. Horses pulling a variety of different carriages worked alongside the new steam-powered coaches, which puffed black smoke as they were fed coal to keep them moving. Cara didn't know which she preferred, the equine droppings on the road or the noxious fumes of their steam replacements. She glimpsed one of the rare, new mechanical horses, powered internally by batteries containing stored electricity. With an exorbitant price tag, they seemed mere playthings for the most wealthy. The metal horses, a beautiful sight to watch, glistened in the morning sunlight, with gleaming copper and brass accents. The horses silently passed by and were soon swallowed up from view by the natural equines and more economical steam counterparts.

Cara jumped off the bottom step, then headed down the road at a cracking pace. With several errands to run, she hoped to avoid the society gossipmongers. They were curious for a glimpse of her face and hungry for details of her scandalous life for the past seven years. Though, she doubted any would recognise her. She bore little resemblance to the fourteen-year-old who last trod these pavements and who had scampered in and out of the London shops.

"Cara!" a voice called. Familiar, it tugged a memory from the back of her brain. Cara halted and turned; her eyes scanned the multitude of people ebbing and flowing along the pavement.

She spied a pretty brunette, dressed in tonal greens and a hat topped with peacock feathers. The woman waved an arm madly and in a completely unladylike fashion as she pushed her way through the crowd toward Cara.

"Amy?" Cara said, as long dormant memories stirred and rose to the surface of her mind.

"Cara. It *is* you." Amy threw her arms around Cara. "I heard you had returned, but were closed to callers. I've missed you so much."

Cara stiffened; she disliked physical contact. She steeled herself before briefly returning the hug. This woman posed little threat to her safety, so she was able to endure the embrace. Amy had been her childhood friend, a lifetime ago, when she was once innocent.

Amy held her old friend at arm's length and scrutinised her face.

"Oh, Cara, your beautiful hair," she said on taking in the shorn locks. She reached out a gloved hand to touch an auburn tendril curling softly around Cara's ear.

"Don't," Cara said, pulling Amy's hand down. "That's what he said. My hair was the only part of me I could hack off and burn."

Amy swallowed her words, her eyes widened in distress. "I heard about your father. I won't say I'm sorry."

"You don't have to. I'm certainly not." She spat out the words. Glancing around, she noticed their conversation affected the flow of pedestrians. Their position in the middle of the pavement acted as a blockage. The foot traffic behaved as worker ants who found a leaf dropped in the middle of their track; they became frantic at the loss of their regular path.

She took Amy's arm and pulled her to the side, closer to the buildings and out of the way. The ants quickly resumed their original route, and their activity reminded her she had her own share of tasks to complete.

"I have to get going, Amy. It was nice to see you again." She turned, but Amy took her hand, forcing her to stay.

Amy held Cara's gaze.

"We were friends once." There was something imploring in her tone and in her large brown eyes. Amy had never been able to conceal anything on her face, always so expressive and easy to read. Amy's openness was probably why Cara ended up in so much trouble. Amy could never lie to an adult to conceal the mischief her friend sought out.

She shook her head. "We were girlhood friends such a long time ago, Amy, and much has changed."

Amy softened her tone. "I never stopped being your friend. I wrote you hundreds of letters."

Cara frowned. "I never received any letters."

Her friend coloured. "I couldn't get them out of the house. My father wouldn't let me contact you . . . ." she trailed off. Undoubtedly, her father hadn't wanted any taint of scandal to touch his daughter. It didn't matter that Cara bore no fault, and events were inflicted upon her. She was irredeemably sullied, just the same.

"I thought you didn't want to hear from me," Cara said quietly.

Amy retained her friend's hand, heedless of her discomfort at the contact.

Cara longed to snatch it back, but another part of her missed such a simple act. Her view of physical contact distorted, she had forgotten the gentle reassurance the touch of another could convey.

"Come with me for a coffee. You can't think you will escape me so easily after all these years."

She was torn. Amy had been her childhood friend, but there were so many things she would rather forget, and Amy reminded Cara of her previous life. "I don't know, Amy. I'm not here to re-establish my life. I don't intend to stay long in London."

Amy clutched Cara's hand like a lifeline, refusing to let her friend escape. "I lost you seven years ago, Cara. How long are you going to punish yourself for something that was never your fault?"

She fought an internal war, but given the early hour, the coffee houses would be full with the sort of bustle she could survive. The majority of aristocrats wouldn't even be out of bed yet, let alone ready to face the public.

"All right. But I'm starving, so food is a must. I'd kill for a bacon butty."

Amy laughed. "I know just the place."

"What are you doing out and about at this hour anyway?"

A broad smile broke over Amy's face.

"I am engaged and have much to plan." She squealed in excitement.

"Well, we do have some catching up to do," she said, allowing Amy to dictate their course through the morning crowd.

They strolled along the cobbled lanes and streets of Soho for some distance, before turning toward the square. Cara remembered the area; the face of London constantly changed, but a few things remained constant. The Soho Bazaar bustled with activity, noise, and aromas.

The heavenly smell of coffee and baking wafted down the street and resonated with Cara's stomach, which let out an impatient growl. *I need to stock the pantry*, she chided herself.

The two friends skirted the enormous building that housed the bazaar and, instead, headed for a smaller coffee shop on the southern end of Soho Square. Cara paused on the pavement; an urchin nearby held a wedge of papers under his arm and yelled the morning's headlines. A name caught Cara's attention. She stopped and fished in her pocket. Her fingers found a coin, and she tossed the copper to the boy. He caught it with a grin and in return, held out a paper. She flicked her eyes to the headline as she entered the shop behind Amy. She paused to raise her head and take a deep breath of the heady aroma of coffee and yeasty bread. Her stomach growled again, reminding her she hadn't stopped for breakfast.

The coffee shop bustled with noise and bodies, every inch of space occupied. Lower-class people queued at an open window to grab warm bread rolls before heading to work. Middle-class gents sat at round tables, loudly discussing the day's business or arguing over chess and backgammon moves. A couple of ruddy-cheeked girls in smart blue and white uniforms with matching aprons dodged amongst the patrons. They expertly balanced large trays on their outstretched arms as they delivered orders to those lucky enough to have claimed seats.

Amy spied a waitress cleaning off the table top of a booth and waved her hand to catch the girl's attention. The girl smiled and beckoned to the two friends, flicking her cloth to shoo away a young man who tried to steal the table first. Amy pushed a distracted Cara through the crowd, in the table's direction, and gave their order to the girl.

Cara scanned the newspaper headline: *Jennifer Lovell, beautiful debutante, found murdered.*

Recently stirred memories snagged on the name; Cara knew her. She was of a similar age to her and Amy. Cara would have come out with them, if she hadn't been ruined beyond redemption. She took a seat and flung the paper onto the table while she settled.

Amy shrugged off her jacket and dropped the expensive garment on the bench. Glancing at the paper, she raised a hand to her face in horror.

"Jennifer?" Lowering herself slowly into the seat, she craned her neck to read the article upside-down.

Cara nodded and scanned the rest of the article. "Scant detail. It just says she appears to have been stabbed. The Enforcers are making enquiries to find the person responsible, but appeal to anyone with any pertinent information to come forward."

"I saw her only a few days ago." Amy's brow furrowed. "She had so many suitors. We've all been on tenterhooks waiting to see who she would pick. My money was on the Bulgarian Prince hanging off her, so dashing in his Hussar's uniform."

"I remember her; a pretty little blonde with quite unusual eyes. They were a pale blue. We used to go to the same parties when we were all little." Cara had forgotten the tea parties and picnics they hosted to occupy their time between lessons. When Cara wasn't climbing trees or stowing away on boats and airships, or generally trying to escape her existence. She lost count of how many times either a governess or the Enforcers had to retrieve her and return her home. Those days seemed sunnier and easier, before dusk fell upon her and dragged her from the light into the dark.

"We debuted together nearly three years ago. All the eligible men chased her. They swirled around her like minnows after bread thrown in the water. The rest of us had to fight over her discards. She certainly had her sights set high. She wanted to snag at least an Earl." Amy dragged the paper around with a fingertip to read the article for herself.

Cara mentally blew dust off long-forgotten faces. "Her family will be devastated. If I remember correctly, she was an only child?"

Amy looked up and muttered thanks to the waitress as she delivered their coffee and food.

Cara fell on her bacon sandwich like a woman who kept forgetting to eat, which she did when preoccupied. She discovered the one downside to dismissing the staff: there was no cook to cater to her appetite. Or scullery maids to restock the pantry, ensuring there was at least bread and cheese to snack on when hunger reminded her to seek sustenance.

"Her parents doted on her. Gave her everything she desired. I think that's why she aimed high. She had a certain lifestyle she want-ed to maintain, once married." Amy poured cream into her coffee and spooned in sugar before stirring absentmindedly. "She ruled supreme these last couple of years, and she had every intention of continuing to dominate society after her marriage. She would only consider anyone lower than an earl if they had a suitably enticing fortune with which to support her."

So much for love; material possessions win every time for some girls. Cara took a break from her sandwich to lick the bacon fat off her fingers. The advantage of being scorned by society—she didn't care what they thought of her and she could lick her fingers in public. She added cream and sugar to her coffee before taking a large swig. She savoured the mo-ment as the sweet caffeine fix introduced itself to the bacon-y goodness waiting in her stomach. *Bliss.*

Cara let Amy's conversation wash over her, as she looked around the busy café and wondered if the rooms above were to let. Living in this area was an appealing thought, being lost in the surrounding bustle ev-ery morning. The bakery and coffee shop occupied the bottom floor of a three-storey building, and often the top floors housed small apartments. It would solve her problem of feeding herself in the mornings.

Although, if I start eating bacon and croissants every morning, I'll need longer laces for my corset.

Amy watched her friend polish off her sandwich and nurse her coffee lovingly between her long fingers. "Where have you been, Cara? No one has heard from you for seven years, apart from the odd rumour of you being in some foreign country or another."

"I've been travelling. Grandmother was rather indulgent, once I recovered. She sent me to Europe, Asia, and America. Wherever I wanted."

Large doe eyes regarded her over the rim of a coffee cup. "So many years of running and keeping everyone at a distance. Aren't you lonely?"

Cara stared into her coffee mug. The steam circled inside, trapped by the porcelain boundary until it rose high enough to escape, freedom coming at the price of evaporation. Watching the wisps of heated air reminded her of travelling. Roaming the globe, Cara felt free, but insubstantial. No one shared her travels.

Lonely? She pondered the word. She always thought loneliness implied being empty. Something that was empty could sit, passive, waiting to be filled. She wasn't empty; she contained a vacuum deep inside, spinning constantly with an aching hunger. Reaching out, desperately trying to pull something, anything, into the nothingness. But at the same time, terrified of what might draw near. The vacuum attracted and repelled at the same time, a never-ceasing vortex of constant activity, never resting. *No wonder I'm hungry all the time.*

"I don't know if I could trust anyone to let them close enough to relieve the pain." Cara raised her eyes to her friend's face. "It's too easy to be hurt."

She met Amy's concerned gaze.

"God never intended us to be alone, Cara, we're just not made that way."

She decided it was time to change the subject. Early morning in a coffee shop didn't seem quite the right place to become too introspective about the life-sucking black hole in her gut. "Tell me about Jennifer. Who was she seeing?"

"There were so many, and all so similar—handsome, titled, wealthy." Amy frowned, remembering something. "She was so secretive about it, keeping us all guessing. She knew how to play the game. But I just can't imagine anyone wanting to harm her, she was so beautiful."

Perhaps someone got tired of the game and being kept dangling on the line for so long. Cara didn't voice the thought aloud. "Well, I'm sure the Enforcers will figure it out." She dismissed the headline to move to more interesting matters. "What about your suitor? Who is this mysterious fiancé?"

Amy's eyes sparkled. "You'll have to meet him. Come for lunch with us, next Monday."

Cara raised an eyebrow. Society had turned on her, and the scorn was mutual. Front and centre at feeding time was the last place she wanted to be. Her friend must have read her mind.

"He'll love you as much as I do, and to hang with what everyone else thinks."

"All right." Cara was curious, and hoped any suitor of Amy's would be as genial and easy-going as her friend.

"And for goodness sake, wear a dress, please. Do try to remember you're a lady in London and not an adventurer exploring some remote corner of the world."

Cara resisted the urge to poke out her tongue. "Technically, that's all I've been for the last seven years." Seeing Amy's distressed look, she thought, perhaps for the sake of old friendships, she should humour her friend. "All right, if it will make you happy, but I'll have to *buy* a dress first."

CHAPTER 3

Tuesday, June 25

HAMISH Fraser took a slurp from his tea and scowled at the liquid.

Cold. When did that happen?

He remembered the piping hot brew being set down in front of him a few minutes ago. Or, was it an hour? He glanced up at the large, round clock on his office wall. Its gleaming brass face boasted a riot of gauges and dials. An enthusiastic creator had included temperature, barometric readings, seconds, and, somewhere, lost in the middle—the time, on a twenty-four-hour cycle. He squinted and changed the focus of his eyes after hours of reading fine print, to make sure he looked at the correct dial.

Oh, two hours.

He tossed the report he'd devoured onto his desk and sighed. Pulling off his wire-framed spectacles, he rubbed the bridge of his nose, trying to relieve the pressure building behind his eyes. He ran a hand through his hair before donning the specs once more and returning to the pile of reports scattered over his desk. For a methodical and meticulous man, his workspace was a disaster. His desktop included a disordered mess of paper, files, and the occasional paper-wrapped sandwich. He refused to tidy up; he always found exactly what he needed, despite the surrounding chaos.

Hamish had been an inspector with Her Majesty's Enforcers for only five years. He joined the ranks after college and a brief stint of military service. While the discipline and order of military life appealed, it lacked the intellectual stimulation he sought. The role of inspector seemed custom-made for him. He quickly rose through the ranks of the Enforcers with his keen mind and methodical approach. His gentle demeanour put people at ease. Many a criminal had been hanged by his own words, saying too much around the inspector, lulled by his genial manner.

The death of Lord Devon bothered him. Nobody stumbled upon an Egyptian asp in his bedroom unless somebody put it there first. Or they happened to reside in Cairo. It certainly didn't happen while living in London, three floors above street level. The dead ends in the case were frustrating and numerous. Devon's staff knew nothing, or they were too scared to talk, even in the wake of his death. His friends knew nothing, or so they said. And his remaining, and distant, relatives refused to say a word to the Enforcers.

The man had not been liked, with few friends and numerous enemies. The asp was a personal touch, a message and an executioner in one neat, reptilian package. The name *Cara Devon* occupied the number one spot on Fraser's suspect list. Any ill feelings she bore toward her father were entirely understandable. The brutality she suffered was before Fraser's time in the Enforcers, but he heard the rumours. Society liked to gossip about the misfortune of others, and her tale sent a frisson of horror through upper-class parlours. Occasionally, noble daughters were traded in marriage deals, to pay family debts. But never before had a father handed over his fourteen-year-old daughter without a contract to sanction the arrangement. He shuddered that the crime against her went unpunished. His position and wealth protected Lord Clayton, the villain, that and Lord Devon's refusal to press charges. The Enforcers were powerless to see justice done for the young girl in the face of aristocratic opposition and stonewalling.

Fraser pried a large amount of information from a talkative servant. The maid concerned had to scrub Cara Devon's blood from the library floor. No one ever knew the full extent of the injuries inflicted by Clayton and her father. The staff he interviewed were incredulous she survived the final attack in the library. No one had seen her since that day, when her grandmother took away the unconscious child's body.

The first thing he did was ascertain the whereabouts of Cara Devon at the time of her father's death. She had been as close as Leicester, at her grandmother's estate, where numerous staff attested to her presence. He knew well enough that didn't mean she hadn't committed the act; it only meant she was well enough liked by the staff that they vouched for her. He had no intention of letting sympathy for her history allow her to take the law into her own hands and deliver rough justice. Though he wondered at the symbolism of the asp; if he could discern that, he believed he could crack the case.

Or, if he could rattle Miss Devon's alibi, he could mark the case as closed.

Finding a receipt for an asp in her name would be highly convenient. The only way to get the snake from Egypt to England in a timely fashion, before the cold killed it, was by airship. And no legitimate carrier had any record of *Egyptian Asp x 1 for Miss Cara Devon*. That left only one airship company with complete disregard for the legality of its cargo—Lyons. And that was another dead end. No one in his company or service would ever speak a word against Viscount Lyons. Either loyalty or fear sealed their mouths tighter than a deep-sea diving bell.

With no obvious leads and any trail cold, his superiors wanted him to shelf his enquiries. To top off his week, a titled girl had been murdered. The death of a young and beautiful aristocrat in a brutal manner took precedence over the snakebite death of a shady, and reviled, lord. Death amongst the upper classes always put the Enforcers on edge. Their superiors would start yanking his chain for answers. Fraser got the call to investigate the scene of the girl's death. While only landed gentry, and not a member of the peerage, he was the closest thing the Enforcers had to an aristocrat. His quiet demeanour was far more welcome in the drawing rooms and salons than the hulking mass of the common-born uniforms.

His door cracked opened and admitted the bulk of Connor, his sergeant. He was Fraser's backup on the street, and commanded a unit of street-pounding Enforcers who did the donkey work for the inspectors. Connor served as Fraser's sergeant in the army and followed his lieutenant into civilian life, slipping easily from one role to the other.

He jerked his meaty hand toward the door. "Doc's finished examining the girl and is ready to talk to you."

The girl's mother had been bereft. Fraser had to employ his talent for smooth talking, before she agreed to allow an examination by the Enforcers' doctor. She had been convinced her baby would be served up on an altar of degradation, her cold form pawed over and defiled by licentious uniforms. Fraser reassured Lady Lovell that the doctor would only examine the wound and determine the cause of death of her daughter. And no uniform would gaze upon her child's naked form. Even in death, they afforded full dignity to the victims during their enquiries.

"Good. I could do with a distraction." Fraser tossed the report to the desk and watched it slide under several others. The entire pile was close to slumping off the edge onto the floor.

Connor wrinkled his nose.

"Only you could call a trip to the morgue a distraction." A shiver ran over his frame. "Evil place," he muttered under his breath as he allowed his inspector to precede him out of the office.

"No." Fraser corrected him. "The evil is what is done to those who end up there. Not in the victims themselves or the place where they briefly reside."

The morgue was housed down several flights of stairs, deep under the earth. An imposing metal structure with reinforced bands guarded the entrance. Connor pushed open the heavy door.

A familiar blast of cold air greeted Fraser as they stepped inside. A dual layer of metal lined the walls. A constant hum came from the mechanical motor in the corner, its job to circulate water continually between the two layers of steel to keep the room cool. The colder temperature was necessary to ward off decay from preying on the deceased residents.

One wall was lined with giant drawers, each able to house one cadaver, or several orphaned body parts. The previous summer, they'd experienced a killer in the grip of a butchering frenzy. He left bits of London's street girls strewn over the roads and stuffed down drains. Fraser laboured over the jigsaw puzzle from Hell, making sure the girls were buried with their correct limbs, or as many as they could match up. Not that his superiors cared; the victims were only lower-class girls. Fraser saw it as a point of honour, to give them the respect in death they never received in life.

Today the central slab was occupied, a pristine white sheet draped over the current subject of attention. The top of the slab angled by a few degrees toward one end, with deep channels chiselled around the edge. Any fluids evacuated during autopsy would be carried away by the channels and down through a connecting drain in the floor.

The Enforcer's resident doctor, known affectionately as Doc, looked up on Fraser's entry and moved to his charge. He picked up the top corners of the sheet and folded it down over the girl's waist, revealing only as much flesh as needed for the conversation.

Connor hung back at the entrance. For an imposing man, he suffered a weak stomach and delicate sensibilities, and he rarely ventured past the entrance to the morgue. Fraser smiled. Connor's reticence in the morgue seemed at odds with his formidable reputation on the battlefield. He was unstoppable in a fight, but hated to be confronted with the harsh reality of death, particularly when it touched the young or beautiful.

"She's a pretty thing," Doc said.

Her long, white-blonde hair swirled around her shoulders, as though she were swimming and the locks drifted on the water. Her face was heart-shaped, and would have been beautiful with life and gaiety animating her eyes. In death, her pupils were fully dilated. It unnerved Fraser, the strange black gaze, obscuring the original eye colour. An angry, raw scar marred her chest. The gash was the only visible sign of any trauma to her young body.

"Cause of death?" Fraser asked.

Doc laid a hand on the girl's shoulder. It would have been a reassuring gesture, if she still breathed.

"A broken heart," he replied.

"What?" He looked up sharply at the doctor, sure he was joking with him.

"She was stabbed in the heart. The weapon ruptured the muscle, made a bit of a mess internally. Poor thing never stood a chance." Doc walked over to the metal bench running the length of the morgue. He selected an item, dangling a cream-coloured evidence card secured by twine.

"I removed this from the wound." Fraser held out his hand and Doc placed the slender brass item in his outstretched palm.

"A key." Fraser stared in wonder at the object. The key was eight inches long, the bow picked out in ornate filigree work. The end was flattened where the killer had used another object to hammer it into the girl's chest. The bit looked similar to any other key used to open gates or large padlocks. Except when Fraser looked closer, he saw the ends chiselled to a point. In profile, the teeth of the key resembled the edge of a tiny axe.

"I'll ask a few locksmiths about it; the design is unusual. Let's hope it twigs a memory for someone."

"He didn't just force the key through her chest, into her heart, either." The doctor continued. "He twisted or turned it, as though he were trying to unlock something."

Fraser frowned. The imagery was potent, though rather literal. The killer made a graphic, and obvious, point. He bounced the key in his hand, thoughts running through his brain already.

"Did your examination reveal anything else?" He left the delicate question hanging, knowing Doc would understand.

The doctor shook his head. "No. He hadn't taken any liberties with her."

Fraser sighed in relief. He didn't have to tell her family that, apart from their child being murdered, she had also been defiled. He nodded his thanks to the doctor.

"I'll let the family know she will be returned to them now." He palmed the key into the inside pocket of his jacket.

"One more thing," Doc called out before Fraser left. "It's about the garment she was wearing. It's made of some form of linen. I have one of my squints analysing it under a microscope to determine its origin."

Armed with the additional information, Fraser headed for the door and slapped Connor on the arm. "Come on, Connor, work to do. We need to sniff out the wronged suitor, and from what I understand of Lady Lovell, we are going to have rather a long list to go through."

Connor jerked awake from his brief nap against the doorjamb. His mind latched onto the last words it heard. "What makes you so sure it's a jilted fellow?"

Fraser thought the answer obvious, but humoured his sergeant. "Who else would want to inflict a broken heart on a beautiful young woman?"

Cara rose early and disappeared into the morning bustle of London. She had an appointment with her father's legal advisor to finalise affairs. She hopped a ride on a new public steambus to the City district, then alighted on Fleet Street, by the Inns of Court, and walked along Chancery Lane to Furnival Street. She paused and stared at the small brass plate affixed to the brick wall of a nondescript building. In a discreet font, it stated *Doggart & Allan—Solicitors*.

She took a deep sigh. She didn't want to waste a morning trapped in a stuffy solicitor's office, but there was paperwork to be concluded.

I guess they are a necessary evil.

She pushed open the door, then stepped into the small reception area. The décor, subtle and tasteful, matched the sign on the front door. Dark, neutral colours tied in with the rich mahogany and walnut furniture.

Cara approached the main desk. An efficient-looking, older woman with her grey hair pulled back in a severe bun clattered away at a typewriter. She wore small gold-framed spectacles; a chunky chain, in contrast with the delicate rims, ran from the frames and dropped away around her neck.

"Excuse me?" Cara interrupted the secretary.

The secretary's hands paused mid-word, suspended over the keyboard as she swung her head and stared over the top of her glasses at the interloper. Her gaze swept up and down Cara, taking in her unorthodox attire.

At least I'm wearing a skirt today. She hated the stiff skirts and crinolines favoured, and expected, by the rest of society. Cara found they hindered movement. If she had to wear a skirt, she chose her fabrics for practicality, in case she had to pick them up and run for it. Today, she paired the fluid green skirt with a front-lacing corset in a soft dove grey. A swallow-tailed jacket, in a complementary shade to the skirt, hugged her form. The coat, cut short at the front to display the corset, dipped into soft tails at the back. She left her hip belt at home, choosing to wear only the discreet shoulder holster. She figured she'd need only one pistol as company to visit the law office. Cara could visualise mental cogs ticking over, but the older woman was too well trained to voice any disdain or curiosity about the visitor in front of her.

"Yes?" One syllable, dripping with superiority.

"I have an appointment to see Mr Doggart. I'm Cara Devon."

A well-plucked eyebrow shot up. "I'll tell him you're here."

She rose from her chair and disappeared behind a panelled door. She emerged a moment later and held the door open.

"This way, please, Miss Devon." She had dialled back the attitude, her tone more solicitous.

Cara stepped into the office beyond. A solicitor of indeterminate age sat behind an enormous desk. He looked anywhere between thirty and sixty, his breed seeming to age prematurely and then hold in stasis until retirement.

"Ah, Miss Devon, please be seated." Doggart waved her to a chair. "Tea, please, Miss Wilson."

He directed his comment to the efficient secretary as she made her discreet exit, then swung his attention back to Cara.

"Terrible business about your father—" He paused, about to offer his condolences, but the icy look on her face froze his words. He coughed and cleared his throat instead.

"Yes. Well. You need to sign some papers, to finalise the terms of your father's will. As his only heir, the house goes to you." He shifted in his chair uncomfortably. "As I'm sure you are aware, there wasn't much else, unfortunately."

Cara bit back a snort. He was trying to say, politely, the house was her father's only asset, unaware of the fortune in stolen artifacts hidden around London.

"I am aware of the state of my father's finances." Her father spent every penny he could lay his hands on in the pursuit of antiquities. Lord Devon dying impoverished was no surprise; she merely wondered how he survived so long.

Miss Wilson reappeared and deposited a teapot, cups, and a small plate of biscuits on the corner of the desk. Playing mother, she poured out the tea before handing over the cup.

Cara added milk and waited until the secretary had finished and closed the door before continuing.

"I have one small additional task for you. I need you to find a tenant for the house. I have no intention of living there, and have moved elsewhere."

"Of course," he murmured, taking a sip from his tea. "It's in a desirable location; it won't be difficult to lease. I'll take care of all the details."

Cara nodded; relieved to have matters settled and glad her father hired a discreet and efficient solicitor. "Thank you. If you will oversee the lease and collection of rent, then that probably settles everything."

Doggart walked to the bank of filing cabinets occupying one wall. Drawing on a chain hanging from his waistcoat, he extracted a bunch of keys from his pocket, instead of the expected watch. He selected a key and unlocked a drawer. He rummaged within and pulled out a slim folder.

Returning to the desk, he deposited papers in front of Cara.

"I just need your signature at the bottom of each copy." He handed her a slim, silver pen.

She signed her name in a firm hand, closing one chapter of her life.

"There is only one other thing." He withdrew a slender envelope from the folder and handed it to her. "Your father instructed me to give this to you, in the event of his death."

She looked at it curiously, turning it over in her hand, so flat it couldn't contain more than a single sheet of paper.

I'm betting it's not a heartfelt apology.

The back bore the family seal stamped in red wax over the flap.

Doggart held out a paper knife.

Taking the little, ebony-handled implement, she inserted the tip of the blade at one corner of the envelope and slit it open. She passed the knife back, before inserting her fingers to draw out the slip of paper.

Unfolding the heavy paper revealed only a single sentence: *Careful. They are more than they appear.*

Cara frowned. She had no idea what the note meant.

Who are more than they appear?

"He said the letter was important." Doggart tented his fingers, regarding Cara over the top. His eyes flashed, but his training was too engrained; he wouldn't ask about the contents of the note.

She chewed her lip in thought, and dropped the note into her satchel, something to puzzle over another day. Rising, she shook hands with the solicitor and left his offices, glad to be back in the morning sunshine and life of London.

.

Thursday, June 27

CARA'S long legs carried her at a brisk pace down the busy road. Today she wore a skirt in the same deep, earthy, green tone as her eyes. The soft wool skirts swirled around her legs like eddies stirred in deep water by an undercurrent. A matching tailored coat hugged her form and dropped over her skirts, stopping at mid-calf. The back of the coat was slashed to allow the train of her skirts to poke through. She wore nothing on her head, her close-cropped hair shining a deep auburn in the morning sunlight.

An elegant carriage approached and slowed its passage. The driver pulled the burnished horses short, to keep pace with Cara. She ignored it for a while, and then wearied of its constant presence. The time had come to confront the intrusive occupant and give him a piece of her mind.

Another nosy noble, wanting a look at the damaged Cara Devon.

Her father's funeral the previous week had contained more spectators than mourners. Those gathered exhibited no sorrow, but an abundance of eagerness as they sought to pick her out in the crowd. She attended only to make sure he was dropped in the ground, and kept at a distance. She was surprised anyone recognised her. Apparently, the season so far had been incredibly dull. Her father's untimely death, and her subsequent return to London, promised a temporary relief from the ennui affecting the ton. Now it seemed they were competing amongst themselves to be the first to corner her.

Having found the notebook, she knew nothing of value remained in the house. The flow of cards through her mail slot was unrelenting. She escaped the constant banging on the front door by taking rooms farther down the road. They could rap on the door and peer in the windows all they liked; she had slipped through their fingers unnoticed. Except for this one.

Whoever her stalker was, he displayed incredible wealth. The horses were the new mechanical equines, so expertly crafted they appeared alive, though armoured. Overlapping, riveted, and articulated plates of metal allowed the movement of their limbs. Even their tails were metallic, streamers of thin copper wire a pure indulgence, serving no purpose whatsoever that Cara could discern. The animals travelled with sublime economy; unlike their breathing counterparts, they didn't snort, toss their heads, or paw impatiently at the ground.

If you can make a mechanical horse, why wouldn't you make it a unicorn?

Only when she stopped to give the imposing black carriage her full attention did she notice the man riding up front next to the driver. He gave her a familiar grin as he jumped down to the ground, his hand heavily bandaged. He doffed his bowler to her, before opening the carriage door. A small set of steps automatically dropped down with a soft hiss.

"Our master wants a word with you." He waved his injured hand, inviting her to step inside.

"How's your friend, the one with the shoulder problem?" Cara asked of the other man she shot.

A shadow passed over the henchman's face. "He don't work for Lyons anymore."

Cara shuddered, wondering what that meant.

The blinds, drawn over the carriage windows, concealed the occupant. She stared at the open door, debating her course of action. This development wasn't unexpected; in fact, she invited it. But his timing was annoying. She had things to do and no desire to be in London any longer than necessary. Picking up the corner of her skirts, she stepped into the carriage and took the bench seat facing backward. The Villainous Viscount, known in society as Nathaniel Trent, Viscount Lyons, occupied the opposite side.

Cara guessed him to be approaching thirty, young for his position in the underworld, but he had spent ten years ruthlessly climbing to the top. He was reputed to be the head underworld figure in London and beyond. His family had no fortune to match their titles, so he set about acquiring one. With a formidable head for business, he established an airship cargo company. It generated a healthy income stream on its own, plus had the added benefit of providing an excellent front for his illegal activities, and extended his reach far beyond London. He simultaneously repulsed and attracted society. He was titled, rich, bad to know, and deadly to cross.

And he's handsome.

He was tall, his legs taking up an inordinate amount of room in the plush carriage. Her eyes ran up over highly polished, black boots and muscular thighs. Heading farther north, she took in his powerful torso in a formfitting, grey frock coat. He wore his black hair short and his sideburns narrow and long, emphasising his strong face and square jaw. A shiver ran down her spine as she met his steel-blue gaze.

"You shot my men."

At least he got straight to the point, no inane social niceties. She would never have to worry about inviting him over for tea, crumpets, and chitchat.

"They were trespassing in my house and tried to rob me." She undid the buttons on her jacket. The interior of the carriage constricted around her; the heat from his dominating presence caused the temperature to rise.

"I've killed men for doing less." His tone was well modulated, with no change in inflection nor any hint of anger; they could have been discussing the weather.

"So have I." She held his gaze. She could play this pissing contest all day if he wanted. He wasn't getting his hands on her father's notebook. Lord Devon sold her into slavery and nearly beat her to death when she escaped. Her father owed her a large debt, and with his notebook secure, she intended to collect a small portion of her due. She was going to enjoy breaking up his valuable collection of antiquities as much as she enjoyed smashing his stupid, precious clock.

"Keep your men out of my house, unless you want to lose them permanently." She shifted on the seat. Her jacket fell open to reveal the shoulder holster with the gun nestled close to her chest. A custom Smith and Wesson with a carved ivory handle, the delicacy of the bone co-ordinated with the cream silk lining of her jacket. She made her threat without blinking. Let him discover she was no blushing English rose. She had thorns.

His eyes flicked to her weapon. His gaze moved from her gun, burned up over her rounded bosom, accented by the line of the corset, then back to her face. His expression remained impossible to read. Not one iota of emotion showed in his eyes. Cara had no way of knowing if he was amused, or annoyed.

"Very well. If you'll come to my house and have dinner with me." He stretched out his legs and casually crossed his booted feet, encroaching further on her space.

Cara tucked her legs closer to the seat and away from him. She fought the urge to fan her face, growing warmer under his scrutiny. "No."

He continued talking in the same regulated tone. "I'll have my carriage collect you at seven o'clock."

"What part of *no* did you not understand?" Cara cocked her head, wondering if he was even listening to her. Perhaps he was actually an automaton, which would explain his rumoured inability to emote. In her brief acquaintance with him, she had yet to see any flicker of emotion cross his handsome face.

"I'll have a carriage waiting every night until you accept."

"You're in for a long wait." She was at enough risk sitting in a carriage with him; she wasn't venturing into the lion's den. There was no guarantee she wouldn't be on the dinner menu.

"I thought you wanted to discuss a business proposition?" The tiniest change of inflection lifted his voice, but she couldn't pinpoint what it meant. He could be curious, have indigestion, or feel a building crescendo of rage, for all she knew.

She'd hate to sit opposite him at the poker table. *You'd lose a fortune before you realise he has no tells.*

She sighed, and leaned her head back against the plush, blue velvet side of the carriage, letting the fabric caress her cheek. She forgot the small detail of the business she wanted to engage him on. She enjoyed saying no to him, repeatedly. Refusal was probably a new experience for him, too, but it was hard to tell. Given her father acquired most of his treasures illegally, she needed the assistance of someone with access to the underworld to sell them.

"Saturday," she reluctantly agreed.

He nodded, satisfied with her answer, then rapped on the roof with his cane, indicating to the driver to stop. The door swung open, propelled by the grinning henchman. Lyons leaned forward and took her hand.

Cara flinched at the searing contact, fighting her urge to recoil at being touched. She'd spent years training herself to endure such social contact, to shake a hand or take an offered arm without fleeing. His presence unnerved her, bringing her deeply hidden fear to the surface.

He arched an eyebrow at her reaction, but his face remained impassive as he let her fingers slip through his grasp.

Unlike his henchman, who gave her a wide smile. "I'll be seeing you Saturday, then, darling. Don't keep us waiting."

The door slammed shut and the carriage pulled away like a wraith. The metal horses wore thick felt pads on their hooves, muffling all noise, the only sound the turn of the wheels.

Cara stood on the pavement, letting London's spirit swirl around her. She stared at her hand, expecting to see a scorch mark where Lyons touched her; he radiated heat. She shook loose the tension and fear from the unexpected encounter, and physical exchange. Once again composed, she picked her moment to re-join the flow of city life.

The carriage discharged her on Queen Victoria Street. She headed deeper into the oldest core of London, the City district. Walking along Threadneedle Street, she glanced up at the three-foot-high names carved into stone lintels. She stopped in front of the institution bearing the name inscribed in the squat notebook. A stone monolith, the building had Greek columns holding up its portico, which sheltered those on its steps who either ran toward, or away from, their money and valuables. The bank had occupied the same spot for over three hundred years. Stepping over the threshold into the cool interior, Cara suspected the bank still employed the original staff.

Wizened men in identical black suits perched on stools at ancient desks. The wood of the table tops had darkened to black with the oil from thousands of hands passing over the surface, sinking deep into the grain. Bent by age and the burden of lending and protecting the fortunes of the nobles, the bankers toiled at ledgers with silver metal styluses, the scratch of pen on paper relieved only by the *clack clack clack* of shiny beads on multiple abacuses, flicking back and forth in rapid calculations.

Tiny steel train tracks hung from the ceiling. A diminutive engine pulled small carriages containing messages, bank notes, and valuables. The cargo whizzed over customers' heads and disappeared through miniature tunnels cut high in the walls, hurtling to places unseen.

The floor of the bank was cream marble, in a beautiful parquet pattern, leading customers toward the service counters. Cara dragged her attention away from the identical drones labouring at their sums, and stepped toward a bank employee. He peered at her from across a large expanse of polished wooden counter. He appeared marginally younger than the drones, and his suit was dark grey instead of black. The vast counter was designed to stop any budding bank robbers from vaulting over the top, although Cara suspected the small row of deadly spikes, embedded in the worktop, were a far more effective deterrent. At the moment, they lay dormant, their tips level with the surface, but the push of a panic button would send them leaping up to greet any assailant. Protecting the money and valuables of the aristocracy was a serious business.

"Yes?" Pince-nez perched on the end of his nose, making him look like a crane as he stared at her.

Cara wished he would sneeze; she bet they would fly off, if he did.

She cleared her throat. "I've come to access a safety deposit box, please."

"Hmm." He regarded her suspiciously.

She probably looked like a bank robber. She pulled her jacket closed to hide the shoulder holster. *At least I left my hip belt behind, or they'd be pushing all the alarm buttons.*

"One moment, please." He spun on his stool and gestured for another aged bank official to scurry over. A whispered conversation took place, before Official Number Two nodded his head. He disappeared, and reappeared a few seconds later, by means of an exit Cara couldn't discern. It appeared as though he simply stepped through the wall and materialised next to her.

"Vault number and name?" he asked.

"Vault six and I'm Cara Devon."

He inclined his head to indicate the information was stored. "If you'll follow me please, Miss Devon?" he asked in a quiet, lisping voice.

She shortened her stride to follow the employee. He remained silent, except for the clink of metal against metal from the keys dangling from a long chain looped around his waist.

He led her through a large double door, guarded by two enormous men in full body armour and holding small portable cannons with multiple barrels for volley fire. In silence, she followed him as he descended a set of stairs, leading them far below street level. The corridor split in two, and he took the left path. A short distance along, the passage terminated in a metal door with a number of dials. His fingers flashed as he worked. Following a faint *click,* he swung the central wheel and the imposing door swung open.

The vault was cold and dim, and lit by a scant number of electric torches along one wall. Wrought iron gates lined the opposite wall. Each gate had a different elaborate design and a large number. The employee stopped suddenly, silencing the multitude of keys that jingled with every step he took. Guided by touch more than sight, he unerringly selected the right key to open the door adorned with rampant iron ivy and a brass 6 in the middle, attached to the bars. Beyond, Cara could see the alcove walls lined with small tin rectangles, like tiny coffins lining a crypt.

"Box number?" he asked over his shoulder.

"Five-seven-three-one-four-nine," Cara replied, having memorised the number from her father's journal.

He disappeared into the darkened bay. Cara heard a metallic rummaging noise, and then he reappeared carrying a large safety deposit box. Glancing at the container, she saw the numbers she recited emblazoned on its steel lid. He placed it on a high, central table and pulled the chain of the sole overhead lamp so it descended, casting a brilliant circle of light in the otherwise dreary room.

"You have ten minutes, and then I will return." He bowed slightly and withdrew, leaving her in absolute solitude with whatever secrets the security box contained.

Cara ran a hand over the sturdy metal container. Reaching into the satchel hanging at her side, she withdrew a small brass key. She fitted it into the lock and turned, pausing when she heard one click. The other

lock consisted of a four-digit code. She spun the numbers on the dial to
the correct sequence and heard a satisfying second click.

She opened the lid and stared at the object within its safe nest. She
dropped a black silken handkerchief over the artifact, lifted the object,
then placed it in the satchel. With one finger, she dropped the lid and
spun the wheel of the number lock. She tapped her fingernails on the
table top to alleviate the silence as she waited for the attendant to return
and escort her from the eerie dungeon and back into the bright light.

C H A P T E R   5

Friday, June 28

HE *had the perfect location for his work.*
Nestled deep in the earth's embrace.
The insulation, impenetrable.

It had been easy to acquire the tools he needed. Money greased hands and kept mouths shut. Shelving containing books, bottles, and vials, all vital to his research, lined one wall. A metal table dominated the centre of the room, leather restraints attached at key points. The table's legs were deeply secured into the stone below, so the thrashing of its occupant didn't dislodge its position.

Saturday, June 29

Cara waited in the gloomy front parlour until she saw the mechanical horses glide to a stop opposite the Devon family home at exactly 7:00 p.m. She kept up the façade of living in the house, so where she slumbered remained a secret. She didn't want anyone to know where she laid her head at night. People were most vulnerable during the shadow hours, and she was dealing with those who would use that knowledge to their own advantage. She glanced up at the single light in the room and marvelled at the work of Scottish inventor James Bowman Lindsay. His incandescent bulbs were replacing unsafe candles and gas, if people could afford them. She pictured the vertical metal ribbons that adorned the roof, spinning in the wind to generate power stored in batteries in the basement. The generators were a new status symbol; one glance at a tiled roofline advertised who possessed the latest technology. She punched the switch to turn off the light. A tingle of surplus current brushed her fingers and gave her a mild electrical shock.

"Bitch," she growled at the house. There shouldn't be any charge emitted through the switches; the house simply liked to mess with her. She locked the front door, then bounced down the stairs. She wore her buckskin pants, having spent the better part of the day finishing her search of the top floor. Lord Devon secreted keys to his lock boxes in various hidey-holes and she hoped she found every last one. The tenant took full possession the next day and she wouldn't be back.

Reaching the carriage, she cocked her head at the well-dressed henchman holding open the carriage door. "Since we seem destined to keep encountering each other, you'll have to tell me your name."

"Jackson," he growled, but Cara could see the smile in his eyes, he was hamming it up. They seemed to be making amends for their rough introduction.

"How's the wound?"

He held up a freshly bandaged hand.

"How do you think, lovey? It's got a friggin' hole in it." Although, he wiggled his fingers at her just fine.

"Admit it, I'm growing on you, aren't I?" she asked, a smile on her face as she placed a foot on the bottom step to the empty carriage.

"Like a wart, darling," he replied with his accustomed grin, before shutting the carriage door after her.

They took Oxford Street from dusty Soho to immaculate Mayfair. The carriage turned off before Marble Arch and skirted the edge of Hyde Park, following the wide and picturesque Park Lane. On the corner of

Park Lane and Wood's Mews, the carriage slowed, then paused. Cara heard voices and a whirring noise. Peering from the window, she saw a wrought iron gate slide open to admit the conveyance. The house was a two-storey, sprawling mansion. Gated and set well off the road, its resident lived secluded from prying society eyes. Electric lights, hung from simple wrought iron posts, lined the driveway and dispelled the shadows.

Cara hopped from the carriage, and followed the henchman up the wide, stone stairs and over the threshold. She stopped in her tracks to stare at an enormous clock, the centrepiece of the restrained entrance-way. The face of the timepiece was two feet wide. Delicate filigree hands and dials showed the date, time, temperature, and phases of the moon. A beautiful, enamelled pair of peacocks sat on either side, tail feathers of rich blues and greens draped over the side of the clock.

Jackson cleared his throat, to attract her attention. Cara drew her gaze from the clock and remembered her purpose. She was shown through to Lyons' study, a room far simpler than she expected. Given the location and exterior of the house, she thought the interior would show similar excess. Instead, his sanctum was quiet, restrained, a reflection of the tight control Lyons held himself under. The walls were painted a rich reddish brown that reminded Cara of paprika. A fire enhanced the welcoming feel to the study, strangely at odds with the reputation of the occupant.

Or maybe he uses the blaze to heat up the irons for torturing people.

Piles of neatly stacked papers covered the large desk; a personal aethergraph unit hummed quietly in one corner, a ticker of paper sliding neatly into a nearby tray. Cara wondered if he used it to communicate with his fleet of airships, or their pirate commanders.

He looked up from his desk; his eyes swept over her before returning to the papers in his hand. "I've had the maid draw you a bath. Dinner will be served at 8:00 p.m."

Cara frowned; she was being sent to have a bath? Though, now he mentioned it, the idea of luxuriating in hot soapy water sounded remarkably appealing after a day wrestling with the hell house.

She cast a look down at her attire. "I didn't bring a change of clothes."

"I've supplied something that should prove adequate." He never looked up from his work; his pen scratched over a page in a large ledger as he tallied a column of numbers.

The dismissal couldn't have been clearer. It never occurred to her to change for dinner. She was sitting down with a renowned criminal figure; she thought her everyday attire appropriate, but apparently, he heeded society conventions closer than she expected.

He continued his sums. "And you'll need to leave your weapons here."

Cara arched an eyebrow; sending her to bathe and change clothes was one thing, taking her pistols quite another. He finally crossed the line.

"I don't think so." She crossed her arms over her chest, one hand tucked around the pistol under her arm. As a defiant gesture, it would work much better if he looked at her.

"No one will harm you here, and they will be returned to you when you leave."

Cara snorted. She had fallen for that line once before. He finally laid down his pen and met her gaze, and she wished he'd go back to his work. His eyes drilled through her. She dropped her hands, placing them behind her back, so she didn't fidget under his scrutiny.

"I give you my word; you are safe under this roof."

A chill shot down her spine. Lyons was a man of his word. If he politely enquired about the state of a man's affairs, it meant the unfortunate individual was marked for death by dinnertime. She sighed and undid the buckle on the belt around her waist, and draped the gun over a nearby chair.

"And the other one." He returned to his work, but apparently knew her armaments better than she thought.

She paused for a moment, quietly contemplating rebellion. She had a growing urge to do the opposite of whatever he directed, simply to try to make him react. But, she hankered after the promised bath. She pulled her jacket off, dropped it on the chair, then unbuckled the shoulder holster and laid it with its companion piece.

Jackson gave her a grin.

"This way, my lady." He swept his arm and made a mock bow.

Nathaniel walked across his bedchamber, discarding his jacket as he went. The door to the bathing room was ajar, emitting a sliver of light. Movement beyond arrested his stride. He leaned in closer to the small gap. The blue and green tiled room contained a great copper bath, set in front of a blazing fire.

There came the gentle murmur of conversation between Cara and the maid. As he watched, Cara rose from the bath, her back to him. He thought of Venus emerging from the ocean, as water ran down her limbs and spine, to fall in rivulets into the bath. The water glinted silver over her back, until Nathaniel realised it wasn't water. They were scars. From shoulders to the small of her back, someone had torn her skin so deeply she was permanently marked. Pale scar tissue showed where the lash laid her open. It looked as if she had been raked by a tiger, a single, large paw having drawn its claws through her flesh.

The maid held a large white towel for Cara to step into, and her slender form was obscured from his view as the cotton enveloped her.

He shook his head thoughtfully as he stripped to change for dinner.

Cara smoothed the rich teal velvet over her hips, took a deep breath, and stepped off the last stair. She was waved into the dining room and found Lyons waiting for her. He stood solemnly in front of the fire, his hands clasped behind his back. He had changed to a black evening jacket with a deep blue waistcoat, and tonal cravat.

He doesn't look villainous, he looks devilish . . . or delicious.

A long table dominated the room, and would easily have seated thirty or more. Tonight, layered plates and silver cutlery for two occupied one end of the table, Lyons at the head, and a place to his right. He moved to hold the chair out for her, waiting until she sat, before taking his place.

A footman silently appeared and produced a wine bottle from thin air, pouring the pale golden liquid to the midpoint of the heavy crystal glass. Cara took a hesitant sip. She had the uneasy feeling that alcohol and conducting business with Lyons did not make a good combination, unless she wanted to give him the upper hand.

She decided to launch right into it, over the soup. "Lord Lyons, my father—"

"Nathaniel," he interjected.

Cara paused.

"Excuse me?" She knew his name was Nathaniel; she wasn't dense. Why was he telling her?

"Call me Nathaniel. And I don't discuss business over dinner." His tone was low, the words carrying an authority to them. His face might remain a mask, but his tone conveyed volumes.

She blinked. She hadn't expected to be on familiar terms with him. If she couldn't discuss business with him, they would quickly exhaust conversational topics.

Perhaps we could debate the merits of Colt versus Smith and Wesson? Or the most effective torture methods?

"Nathaniel." She rolled the syllables off her tongue. They lingered in her mouth, making the sound of his name as appealing as his appearance.

"Or Nate, to more intimate acquaintances."

Cara choked on her wine and coughed to cover her slip. She was here to discuss business, not her personal price.

The discreet footman whisked away the empty soup bowls, then brought out the fish for his lordship's approval before serving. The salmon smelt divine, Cara took up knife and fork and dove in. Their conversation covered a range of topics. Cara learned the history of the ornate clock in the entranceway, made by an obscure Russian jeweller called Fabergé. They discussed the implications of absorbing India into the British Empire, and the growing unrest in America.

The meal finished and plates cleared away, Nathaniel pushed back his chair.

"Tell me what happened," he asked.

Cara froze; her hand hovered in the air, caught in the act of reaching for the wine glass, while her brain whirled. She wasn't going to entertain him with the lurid details. Was that why he invited her to dinner, for gossip? "I understand the whole of London talked of it for months, and still does at times. There's no need to repeat the story."

He took a sip of his wine, meeting her eyes. "I want to hear it in your words, not those of the gossips. I would know the truth of it, and it won't leave this room."

She was tempted to stand and leave, to tell him to go to hell. But a tiny part of her could sense a release in letting the story free. Her grandmother knew part of it and Cara never spoke of it to anyone else. To whom could she talk? No one in polite society would listen; they preferred their sanitised version of events. Her friend would be crushed to hear the truth. She doubted the man next to her could be shocked, and he didn't care about reputations or the thin veneer of appearances. She wrapped her fingers around the delicate stem of the glass and took a fortifying sip of wine. Then, two more gulps, before she began to speak.

She started with the easy part. "My father loved two things in life. Collecting antiquities and gambling. Both contributed to his ruin. He hit a losing streak and soon had a trail of chits from one end of London to the other. And Lord Clayton wanted the artifacts."

Nathaniel nodded, this part of Cara's story common knowledge amongst the ton.

"Clayton collected the chits and called in my father's debts, hoping to get his hands on certain pieces of the collection. He didn't know my father very well; he prized his collection highly. He spent all his time, and fortune, to acquire them. He would not be parted from them. So he gave Clayton something of infinitely lesser value. Me."

He leaned back in his chair. "Was he the one who beat you?"

A frown briefly flitted over her face. *How does he know that?*

"My father could hand me over, but he couldn't make me go quietly into slavery. I bit Clayton the first day, deep enough to draw blood. He thought the lash would teach me obedience. He believed, between the beatings and starving me, that I would become compliant." She took a hasty gulp from her wine glass. What happened to her wasn't a memory she wanted to revisit. She still couldn't understand why she was telling him. She stared at her wine glass, as though it were somehow responsible.

Why am I telling him? But the words continued to tumble out, needing to be free from the place where she imprisoned them for so long, no longer able to be contained.

"Every day he had his valet hold me down, while he raped me. Until I escaped." She hoped the glossed-over version would satisfy him, her mind still skirted around the finer details.

"How did you get away?" He revealed nothing, neither disgust nor sympathy.

"I tore at my corset until I pulled out the boning. I bound the pieces together and filed it on the hearth bricks to make a sharp point. I didn't stop until I made a weapon. Then I waited. After a week, he got drunk, and thought I was weak enough to rape me without his valet holding me. He was wrong." She closed her eyes.

She heard him approach in the dark, laughing and cursing her father for handing over his fourteen-year-old daughter instead of the artifacts. He vowed to make Devon regret his decision, by abusing his daughter until the distraught father offered up the treasure in exchange. He crashed through the door, and threw her to the bed, his breath hot and rank on her face. Her fingers reached under the pillow and curled around the bundle of sharpened corset boning while he tore at her clothing. She waited for her moment, waited until he was vulnerable to her attack.

"He put it about he let you go." Nathaniel broke the memory, and Cara opened her eyes.

She laughed. "He did let me go. After I stabbed him as hard as I could in the thigh. I twisted the boning, wrenched it as far as I could, while he screamed for a change. And then I ran."

"Did you return home?"

"I was still naïve enough to believe my father would protect me. I was wrong. He flew into a rage. He thought, since I returned, he would have to hand over part of his collection. He would have beaten me to death if my grandmother hadn't arrived on the doorstep. He left me bleeding and unconscious on the library floor. I vowed I would never be defenceless again." She stared at her empty wine glass, light reflected through the cut crystal turning the room around her into a kaleidoscope.

Nathaniel shook his head. "You were never defenceless. You're a survivor, a fighter. You didn't give up and let events unfold around you. You fashioned a weapon and escaped. Most girls in your situation would still be there, waiting for someone else to charge in and rescue them."

Cara never thought of it that way. Lying down and giving up never entered her head as an option. She fought, and would have kept on fighting, until either she broke free or he killed her.

Nathaniel pushed his chair back. "Shall we adjourn to the parlour?"

He rose and held his arm out for her. With the offer made, he waited, staying out of her space, letting her decide to go to him, or not.

She stared at his jacket sleeve. Something niggled in the back of her brain, when it hit her. No one in the house touched her. Even the maid had been careful in helping her dress; no one inadvertently made contact.

Mere coincidence, or an order given by Lyons?

She tentatively laid her hand on his arm, grazing the fabric with her fingertips. Her heart raced, and she drew a deep breath as they walked through the doors to the next room.

A restful taupe paint covered the parlour walls, the ceilings, and mouldings a deep cream, the furnishings rich browns and earthy tones in luxurious fabrics. The lighting came from several wall sconces, and not overhead chandeliers. The small lights mimicked candles and cast a comforting glow about the room.

Her mind flitted, wondering what game he played, because she was in way over her head and struggled to breathe. She allowed herself to be led to the rich brocade sofa, then Nathaniel continued to the side table. He poured two glasses of brandy and took one to Cara. Returning to the sideboard, he selected a cigar for himself from an open box. She watched as he cut the end and struck a long match on the fireside. The sweet smell soon drifted on the air as he drew on the expensive cigar, tossing the used match into the hearth. He watched her from the opposite side of the room.

Cara looked into her glass, concentrating on swirling the brandy, watching the heavy liquid move within the crystal. It formed slow-moving, amber beads that spun downward. She took a sip, letting the liquor calm her nerves, though it had a lot of work to do.

"You have a business proposition," he said after several quiet moments.

At last, a conversation her brain could engage in without faltering. "I need help finding buyers for my father's artifacts."

An inhale and exhale of dove-grey smoke. "How extensive is the collection?"

She smiled; she was keeping that information to herself. "There are sufficient items that I don't want to flood the market. One or two every six months should provide an adequate income stream."

He drew on the cigar and tilted his head, to blow smoke rings toward the ceiling. He watched their progress. "I'll find you buyers and the best prices, if you'll do something for me."

Cara heard he sometimes traded promises, always making sure the balance swung in his favour. A knot formed in her stomach. What could he expect to gain from her? She had very little of value to trade.

"What do you want in return?" her voice hitched on the words.

He turned his head; his look held hers and never moved away. "I want to touch you."

Cara's eyes widened; her stare flew to the door.

I knew this was a mistake. He's no better than Clayton.

"Why?" She stalled for time. Her throat parched as fear built in the pit of her stomach. She would never make it to her guns in the other room before he caught her, not with the long skirts hindering her. Her eyes roved the room, searching for makeshift weapons.

"Consider it an experiment. You've had something taken from you. I want to see if I can give it back."

Her brain tripped over his words, confused. She came here to discuss selling her father's treasures, not to dissect the emotional damage she suffered after a week of being raped and beaten. "No."

"Don't you want to know what it should feel like, to be touched?" After another long draw, he dropped his cigar into an ashtray and crossed the room.

She struggled to understand why he even cared, unless his sole purpose was to unbalance her, to gain the upper hand in their business dealings. A tiny part of her burned with curiosity. She knew others found being touched pleasurable. Could it really be like that?

"I've already promised no harm will come to you under this roof." He flicked out the tails of his jacket and seated himself next to her on the sofa. He held out his hand, waiting for her acquiescence.

She stared at his long fingers and blunt cut nails, before she placed her hand in his outstretched palm. Burning curiosity waged a private battle with fear and neither emerged the clear winner.

He turned her hand over. His skin was warm. It surprised and fascinated her. He presented such a cold persona she expected his skin to be cool; marble like his demeanour. He stroked the inside of her naked wrist with his thumb.

She inhaled sharply. The simple touch was such an intimate gesture, her brain threatened to shut down, unable to process the responses it received from her nerve endings. He created electricity within her, yet it didn't hurt.

He paused, his thumb over her vein, her pulse raced and thrummed beneath his light touch. He held her gaze, his eyes calm and patient.

Cara took a ragged breath, but remained still, unused to the feelings running up her arm.

He bent his head and placed a kiss where his thumb caressed. Her eyes widened in wonder as he moved up her arm, kissing the delicate skin, his lips whispering against her.

"Have you ever been kissed?" he murmured against the inside of her elbow.

"No." She could hardly breathe the single syllable. Her frantic heart burned all the oxygen in her lungs to keep pounding.

"That's a far greater crime than any I have committed," he whispered. He looked up and leaned fractionally toward her.

Cara instinctively leaned away and came up against the backrest of the sofa. Panic took control. She feared being trapped and had to stand and move her feet. She paced to the fireside. The long velvet skirts trailed behind and dragged at her steps. She didn't have butterflies in her stomach; she had unicorns. They ran in circles and charged her insides with their horns, gouging her as they rampaged.

He watched her, and let her settle, before he rose and drew near. He had the patience of a child trying to edge close to a feral kitten. He approached from one side. One quiet step at a time, and never placed himself between her and her line of sight of the exit.

They played advance and retreat, until she stood still, shaking with fear, but letting him move close to her.

He placed a single finger under her chin and tilted her head toward him.

She held her breath and closed her eyes tightly, bracing herself, but wanting it over and done with. Her adrenaline rush to fight and defend herself was mere nanoseconds from kicking into action.

His breath touched her first, warm and sweet from the cigar. His lips brushed hers. His tongue licked the seam of her lips, tasting her. She shivered at the sensation running down her body, so foreign to the painful memories, her only other experience of intimacy. She braced herself for something hard and cruel. She never expected him to display tenderness. The relief overwhelmed her. A single tear welled in her eye and rolled down her cheek.

He moved and kissed the tear away, a feather light touch on her cheek. When he returned to cover her lips, she tasted the salt of her tear. She breathed out a sigh. She parted her lips to move against him, curious to experience more, but he pulled away.

"I'll have Jackson see you safely home." She was dismissed, and confused. Fear, curiosity, and something completely new rolled around inside her. Each sensation fought the others for dominance and control of her body. Her eyes searched for any clue in his face. The hard mask he wore belied the gentle way he touched her.

He turned his back, returning to his brandy and cigar as he stared into the fire. If he was playing a game with her, it appeared to be roulette. Her head spun like the wheel; the small ball bounced round and round in her brain as she turned and left.

CHAPTER 6

Sunday, June 30

THIS *one was different from the other. So reserved, holding herself back. He had been patient, earning her trust little by little. Playing didn't come naturally to her, but she learned, enticed by his gentle teasing. She had a quiet, noble countenance, almost regal. It boded well.*

He chose the gap between the sole two gas streetlights. The small circles of light only deepened the surrounding shadows. He had selected a small lane, its cobbled and neglected surface not wide enough for even a narrow trap. In daylight, only foot traffic or the occasional horse and rider navigated the rutted path. The deserted alley served his purpose well. Quiet. Secluded. Wrapped in darkness.

He leaned against a stone wall, waiting.

The brisk click of her heels reached his ears before he saw her at the end of the lane. Her skirts rustled with every stride. She pulled her cape around her slim torso, fingers entwined in the rich red velvet as she kept the garment closed against the night chill. She stopped in front of him, breathy in the dark, as though she had run to meet him. Her eyes shone brightly; excitement tinged the air. The faint odour of soap and lavender hit his nostrils. She had bathed, before venturing out in the night to meet him.

"Are you ready?" he asked, taking her hands in his and leaning forward to brush her lips in a soft kiss.

She hesitated only briefly, her decision already made when she left the safety of her home. "Yes."

"Did anyone see you leave?" He tucked her hand under his arm, drawing her closer to him.

"No, I crept down the back stairs while all the servants were busy."

"Then adventure awaits us." He stroked her hand, about to walk off, but she remained fixed to the spot. He ran his fingers down the side of her face and smiled softly.

"We'll have you safely home before you are missed." He allayed her fears. "I promise to return you to your rose garden you love so much."

She smiled up at him, the last obstacle overcome. Tightening her fingers around his arm, she allowed herself to be led down the lane, as he whispered of what lay ahead.

Monday, July 1

Cara was supposed to be dress shopping in an aristocratic mall, like the Burlington Arcade in Piccadilly. Instead, she jumped on a public steam-carriage to the London Docks. She perched on a high wooden mooring bollard on the edge of the Thames, watching the bustle of activity surrounding the airships. It had been a jump and a scramble to her chosen spot, but the post was wide enough to be comfortable. Earlier, she stopped at the coffee shop below her new apartment, and bought paper-wrapped sandwiches and a pastry. The staff filled her metal thermos with coffee and the picnic was stored in her satchel. She munched on her breakfast as she surveyed the river, peering through the murky water looking for any sign of fish beneath the surface as she tossed crumbs down.

This area of the Thames was dedicated to airships; the more conventional ships docked farther down. Only a few brave boats circled near the hangars and private jetties, trying to stay away from the incoming airships. Occasionally, one swept in low, like a giant bird of prey, causing the boat to rock madly trying to steer out of the way. Some of the newer model airships could land on the water and glide into their moorings, blurring the line between sky and water as they moved in both realms. Others were tethered to high mooring towers, their bows attached to the structures so their passengers and cargo could be transferred within the metal holding structures. They moved and swayed, giant streamers floating on the air currents.

Cara was an easy hundred feet away from the Lyons hangar and private wharf, watching one of the vessels arrive. It approached the Thames at a sharp angle. It terrorised a fisherman in a small dingy as its keel sliced through the water. The captain dropped her lower and she turned from airship into ship, backwash peeling away as she cruised smoothly toward the jetty. Men rushed to throw ropes as she bobbed against the side of the wharf in a gentle, welcoming kiss.

The captain strode the deck; his arms gestured to the men securing the lines as he issued his commands. Without waiting for the gangplank, he jumped over the railing and onto the wharf. His hand outstretched in greeting to—

Nathaniel. Cara's breath caught in her throat, even given the distance between them. She was surprised to see him dressed casually. He had no need of a jacket on the warm spring morning. The white linen shirt hung open at his throat, the sleeves rolled up to his elbows, as though he had been interrupted in the middle of working in the hangar. The addition of black knee-high boots made him look similar to his captain.

If he wore a sword hanging off his hip, I would swear he was a sky-pirate.

The routes between England and the Orient were notorious for sky-pirate attacks. Rumour had it Lyons employed pirates to command his ships and keep the other marauders at bay. The romantic version said he started as a sky-pirate and earned his start-up capital by plundering the cargos of European airships. A task sanctioned by Queen Victoria, like a latter-day Elizabeth and Drake.

The two men bowed their heads together, captain and commander. Lyons looked up, directly at Cara sitting on the bollard. He gave a small bow in her direction and she saw him say something to the captain. The thinly disguised pirate turned and stared at Cara, before giving a salute. He passed a comment to Nathaniel and she saw the two men laugh.

They walked toward the hangar, leaving a hive of activity behind them. The vessel had few passengers, who quickly disembarked and dissipated into London. She watched the process of unloading the cargo; an enormous mechanical arm stationed on the wharf side lifted boxes and crates of varying sizes. The arm lowered a chain into the open hold and brought forth the payload. Smaller items were carried by hand, larger crates dropped onto a waiting train gurney, which rumbled up its tracks into the cavernous hangar. One man utilised a metal exoskeleton to give him the strength to carry an enormous crate into the hangar.

Cara wondered how much of the cargo was legal, and how difficult it would be to transport an asp, hidden in one of the smaller boxes. Unless her father had chosen a rather poetic way to commit suicide, somebody had gone to the trouble of acquiring an asp to kill him. Inspector Fraser could puzzle away at its meaning, but her money was on someone her father annoyed on his trip to Egypt. He journeyed to Thebes, and stole a very special artifact. If the previous owner wanted it back, he needed the notebook, another reason to move out of the Devon house. She had no intention of falling victim to an asp amongst her bed sheets and meeting an end similar to Cleopatra's.

What really bothered her was the timing. Her father had travelled to Egypt eight years ago; why wait this long? What triggered the murderous attack now? If the snake charmer wasn't the artifact's previous owner, then it had to be someone who knew of its existence. That left Cara with an unknown enemy. She shivered at the thought; she didn't know who to trust and there were too many people who would dearly like to lay their hands on Lord Devon's infamous collection.

Packing away the remains of her breakfast, she slung the satchel over her head and leapt down from her perch. *Time to brave the dress shops.*

Cara mentally kicked herself. Her brain rattled since returning to London and encountering Viscount Lyons. She couldn't believe she agreed to lunch with her friend in a favourite haunt of the ton. Sitting in the open while the nobility gossiped and twittered about her behind their fans. Not that she cared what they thought, but it took energy to remain stoic.

She eventually did as Amy requested and went shopping for a dress suitable for the occasion. She hated the crinolines and wide skirts currently in vogue. She followed the Artistic Dress movement, and favoured simplicity and flowing designs. Her mind kept drifting to the deep teal gown she wore when Nathaniel bent his head and tasted her lips. The dress evoked simple elegance in the way the lush velvet conformed to her body.

She arrived on the pavement outside the restaurant in Covent Garden at precisely 2:00 p.m., just as it started to fill with aristocrats venturing out to brave the day. A steady stream of fashionable carriages, both equine and steam powered, discharged nobles hungry for food and the latest gossip.

The dining room radiated light and noise. The walls lined with the palest cream silk, glittering white chandeliers hung low from the ceiling at regular intervals, and even the floors were whitewashed. The simple décor became the perfect backdrop to display the latest expensive fashions draped on the women, the venue large enough to seat hundreds at identically laid-out tables of pure white linen and transparent crystal. Luxurious booths lined the walls, giving privacy to those who could afford it. Surrounded by yellow velvet drapes, they were the only burst of life in the calm colour palette. The chatter of those assembled and the collective clinking of hundreds of teacups nearly drowned out the gentle music of the mechanical quartet occupying the central raised platform. Their metal limbs played their pre-programmed compositions, oblivious to the disinterest of the diners, the beauty of Mozart and Bach lost on those more interested in the rise of Charles Frederick Worth.

Cara made her way through the elegantly set tables, following the waiter who led her unerringly to Amy. She kept a smile on her face and feigned indifference to the diners she passed.

For the sake of her friend, Cara dressed as expected for her station. She wore a deep blue and brown striped taffeta gown, her bodice cut tight, with large silver buttons running up the left side. The top echoed a military jacket, except for the way it accentuated her slim waist and rounded bosom. She hated fussy clothes; no one could climb a wall in a crinoline, so the skirt was simple. Cut close, it rippled and swirled out behind her in a soft natural bustle and small train. A small brown top hat completed her outfit, perched on her head at an angle, with a tiny half veil and a couple of curling brown feathers as an accent.

Amy gasped on seeing her. "Lovely," she said, as she kissed Cara's cheek. "John is running late, some business meeting in the city. He's a banker, you know. But he'll be here as soon as he can. And it gives us a chance to catch up."

Cara settled opposite her old friend and sipped her coffee quietly as Amy launched into a rambling monologue detailing her life for the last seven years. Cara was required to venture only the occasional comment or monosyllabic noise to keep up Amy's momentum.

Halfway through their coffee and sandwiches, an elegantly dressed man approached their table. He wore grey pinstripe and had dark brown hair, matching eyes, and a dandified moustache with twirled ends. Amy broke into a rapturous smile and grasped his hand affectionately.

"Cara, this is Sir John Burke, my fiancé. John, this is my dear old friend. Cara Devon." Amy did the introductions.

He started to extend his hand, and paused. "Miss Devon?"

"Yes." Cara could smell the smoke as his cogs did overtime in his head. Her gut told her this introduction was about to detour off the rails.

His hand dropped back to his side, contact never made.

"Your father recently died?" He drew the words out, ending on a querying note.

"Yes." She didn't need the mental alarm bells screaming their warning to know the train wreck was imminent.

He narrowed his eyes and swung his attention back to Amy.

"Do you really think Miss Devon is an appropriate friend, my dear?" He took the seat next to Amy and farthest away from Cara.

"What?" Cara and Amy said in unison.

"Well, she is unwed, and . . . not a maid." He made vague hand gestures at Cara, trying to demonstrate his point without actually looking at the object of his contempt.

A flush ran up Amy's neck, matching the deep red of her afternoon gown. "Cara was a child. You'll not hold another man's act of violence against her."

"It's more than that." He coughed delicately into his hand, and twisted the end of his moustache into an even sharper point. "Lord Clayton said she was no maid when he had her."

What? Blinded by the light from the oncoming train, Cara didn't step off the track in time. The engine smashed into her, and sent her body hurtling down the rail. With a shaking hand, she tossed her napkin onto the table. She had lost her appetite. The air was stifling in the cool room, burning her lungs as she drew a breath, fuelled by her rising anger. She would not stay and be insulted by ignorant toffs who turned their back on her. None of them lifted a finger to help, choosing instead to gossip about her misfortune. Cara had a small Derringer hidden in her satchel and her fingers jerked over where it lay. She briefly toyed with shooting Sir John in the middle of the salon, and saving her friend from future heartache with such a shallow and vacuous man.

"It's all right, Amy. I'll go." *Before I'm tempted to spill his blood all over this lovely, pristine tablecloth.*

She stood; John turned in his chair, so his back faced her and refused to rise. Amy flushed a deeper red at the deliberate snub.

Cara caught her breath, but she refused to cry. Conversation around them dropped as curious eyes turned to watch the unfolding humiliation:

dinner and a show, centre stage. Mechanical tea trays continued to weave between the tables, unaffected by the imminent drama.

A firm hand took hers and squeezed her fingers.

"I was just coming to fetch you. I assumed you would rather join me." Nathaniel materialised from nowhere and saved her from death by social embarrassment.

There was a hurried scraping of a chair, Amy's fiancé caught in the act of having his back to Viscount Lyons.

"Yes." She stared at her hand in his; instead of her usual anxiety, she was surprised to feel calm, even comforted, by his presence and touch. His unflappable control soothed the shame and anger surging within her. He coolly ignored the other man at the table. His indifference delivered a death sentence to his social inferior, witnessed by a hundred eagle eyes.

"I'll talk to you later, Amy."

Her friend rose and kissed her cheek, an unspoken apology in her distressed eyes, before she rounded on her hapless fiancé.

Nathaniel drew Cara away as the argument rose behind them.

"I'm glad you resisted the urge to shoot him. I think even my influence with the magistrates would struggle to cover up the crime with so many witnesses. No matter how much he deserved it," Nathaniel whispered in her ear as he escorted her to his private table.

"How did you know what I was thinking?" Her anger rose and fell, leaving an empty hole in her gut. She hated such confrontations; they were exactly why she avoided any place the aristocrats frequented.

"Your trigger finger was twitching. If I'm right, you fired at least three shots into his body while he convulsed on the table." His booth was an expensive and secluded oasis amidst the noise and activity. The velvet, tasselled curtain was partially drawn and left only a small gap for the staff to come and go. They were segregated from the main dining room and as private as possible, when surrounded by a hundred other people.

"What brings you here?" Cara asked as he held out a chair for her to be seated. "Apart from stopping me from committing an act of murder?"

"I'm hunting a bollard bird I spotted this morning." He took his seat opposite her.

Cara was speechless, trying to read his face. "Did you just make a joke?"

His mouth twitched. "You're not the usual type of bird we see perched on the mooring posts. My captain and I agreed you were a definite improvement to the scenery."

"I wanted a quiet spot to do some thinking. I find it restful near the water, even if it is the dirty old Thames."

"What were you thinking about?" He poured coffee for her, before leaning back in his chair. His blue eyes were like the sky today, encompassing everything, observing every tiny detail unfolding under his reach.

"Egypt." She blurted the word without thinking. She saw the way his brows drew together before relaxing again, as though it triggered a memory. Reaching for the cream jug, she busied herself with cream and sugar. Stirring the elegant silver spoon, she created mocha eddies to distract herself from dwelling on what Egypt might mean to Nathaniel.

He took a sip from his cup. "Jackson tells me you didn't return to your Broadwick Street house last night."

"No. I have no desire to live there. I moved last week." Her solicitor advised her that the new tenant took possession on Sunday. *And he is welcome to the cantankerous baggage.* Cara idly wondered if the house had made its malicious side known to its newest resident yet.

"Where are you residing now?"

A slow smile spread over Cara's face. "I'll keep that information to myself."

There was a glint in his eyes. "I will find out."

He drummed his manicured nails on the table top before catching himself, and picked up his cup instead.

"We shall see, then." She was careful coming and going, never taking the same route. She also had a variety of shops and cafés she could slip through, if she thought anyone was following her.

His drained cup dropped back on its saucer with an undignified rattle. "You're on dangerous ground if you think to tease me."

She resisted the urge to laugh.

"Teasing you is akin to playing Russian roulette: both hobbies have a high chance of ending in a fatality." She closed her eyes and let out a sigh, far more at ease hidden behind the buttery swathe of fabric. *Let the matrons add this encounter to the gossip about me.*

Nathaniel shifted in his chair. "I wanted to ask if you could do me a favour."

She opened her eyes, listening, curious what he might want from her.

"My captain brought me a package today that needs to be delivered."

"Why can't you do it?"

"The lady concerned and I are not on the best of terms. She doesn't want to see me or my men." He ran a fingertip around the rim of his cup.

Cara watched him caress the porcelain and remembered his light touch under her chin before he kissed her. "I'm sure you can conjure up somebody capable of delivering it for you."

"It's of a personal nature. I need to know if my promise to her is fulfilled. I require someone discreet." His hand stilled and dropped back to the linen tablecloth.

Curiosity overcame her; she wondered if the woman concerned was a former lover. Perhaps she was being paid off for services rendered. "All right."

He put a hand into the pocket of his jacket and withdrew a small silver cardholder. He slid a cream card from the deck. Extracting a gilt pen from the same pocket, he wrote something on both sides, before handing the card to Cara. On the back he had written the name Countess de Sal and a Belgravia address, across St James Park from the restaurant. The front of the card bore an entwined V and L in the upper right corner, the bottom inscribed with Lyons Airship Cargo and Enterprises. In the blank space in the middle, he wrote her name in a large ornate hand. Her name on his card was a subtle sign and one that made her frown. She wasn't in his pocket.

Nathaniel held out a small rectangular parcel slightly longer than his hand and about as wide. The nature of the object lay concealed under layers of brown paper and tied with string.

Cara glanced at it and raised an eyebrow. Picking it up, she noted the package wasn't heavy, before tucking it safely in her satchel.

God, I hope it's not a snake.

"I'll have my carriage brought around." He gestured to the waiter hovering just beyond the curtain, eager to respond to any request.

"I'll walk. I could do with the fresh air." Cara rose, and Nathaniel fluidly rose in time with her.

"It wasn't a question. It's at least a thirty-minute walk."

"I know." She looked him in the eye. "Don't presume to give me orders. I'm not in your employ."

He took her hand and stroked her palm with his fingers, before kissing the top. With the first breath-stealing smile she had seen from him, he let her leave as she chose.

CHAPTER 7

CURIOSITY ate at Cara as she walked the pavement. Her body moved automatically, heading down the Strand and across Green Park to the address on the card. Her brain was free to concentrate on the spinning vortex of questions. Who was the woman? How did Nathaniel know her? What did he promise? And most intriguing, what was in the package?

On reaching Wilton Row, and the correct house, she paused at the bottom of the steps. The façade of the house gave a distinct air of dishevelment. Paint chipped and peeled from the windowsills. Brown grasses grew in the window boxes and tumbled their seed heads over the sides, as though trying to escape. Cara was grateful she was dressed appropriately for calling on a Countess, but wondered what she would find, given the neglected state of the exterior.

She rapped sharply on the knocker and waited. And waited.

An elderly butler opened the door. A long creak emitted from either the door or the butler; they both appeared to be in a similar state of disrepair.

She held the card out to him and he cautiously took it from her. He stared at it, blinked, held it at arm's length, and stared at it again. Cara had the distinct impression he'd misplaced his spectacles.

He showed her into the entrance hall. A thin layer of dust coated the skirting boards; the wood of the stairway balustrade was dull with grime. Despite the bright day outside, gloom ruled inside, even the air chill, like a mausoleum.

"One moment, please," he said before shuffling away, muttering to himself. He eventually returned and showed Cara into a decadent and decaying parlour. The walls were resplendent in duck shell blue and cream with gold highlights. It would have looked chic and slightly French, if the gold wasn't muted to a brownish yellow by the layer of dust. The silk cushions on the window seat were pale images of their former selves. The sunlight ate holes in the delicate fabric, so their stuffing spilled out of tiny evisceration slashes.

"The Countess will be down shortly." His job completed, he ambled away to whatever dark corner he emerged from, or off to find an oil can.

Maybe he could find a duster or a maid.

Cara entertained herself picking up the various objects scattered around the room. There were delicate porcelain figurines, decorative plates, and vases. After the third item she sensed a recurring theme, which involved a lack of clothing, a very special friend (or two) and rather athletic poses. The decorations gave an insight to the potential nature of Nathaniel's relationship with the countess and added fuel to her speculation.

The parlour door swung open and revealed the Countess de Sal.

Oh, lordy. Cara bit her tongue. The countess had long, greying locks in complete disarray, circling out from her head in a tousled, hairy halo. Her face had once been attractive, but time had rapidly stolen her beauty away. Her clothing was haphazard, mismatched, and buttoned wrong. Cara figured all was not quite right with the Countess de Sal. One look in her unblinking eyes told her the countess' cogs were seriously overwound.

"You have something for me?" She held out her hand expectantly, her fingernails cracked and torn, as though she had clawed her way out of the grave. Her fingers gestured to be filled, twitching and unfurling around an invisible object.

"Yes." Cara extracted the package and passed it to the countess.

The older woman turned her back, like a child jealously guarding a Christmas present. She pulled the string free, dropping it on the floor. The brown paper was eagerly torn off and discarded. Cara caught a glimpse of a small wooden box with brass corners. The countess ran a hand over the lid before cracking it open and peering within. She threw back her head and gave a deep, throaty laugh.

Cara was bursting to know what lay inside. Instead, she asked Nathaniel's question. "Lord Lyons wishes to know if his promise to you is fulfilled."

The countess spun around; the whites of her eyes showed as she stared not at Cara, but through her, at something in the middle distance. "Oh yes. Whatever else Nate may be, he is certainly a man of his word."

He did this to torture me. What the heck is in that box?

Unfortunately, there was no polite way to ask, unless she could get the woman out of the room and snatch a quick look inside. The countess stroked the lid of the box affectionately, as though a kitten lay curled in her hands and she caressed its fur.

She peered at Cara, seeing her for the first time with clear eyes. She cocked her head to one side. "Do you work for Nathaniel?"

"No." She made her tone emphatic, keen to hit that rumour on the head before it gained any momentum.

"Shame. There are matters, as I'm sure you appreciate, a woman cannot put in the hands of either the Enforcers or her family." She started dancing around the room with her box/kitten, singing it a lullaby in French.

Cara eyed up the door.

Time to leave before the crazy rubs off.

"I'm afraid I'm not following you." She edged toward the exit.

The countess spun her eyes lucid, in stark contrast to the rest of her appearance. "There are noblewomen who need your help. Women have problems, which can't be made public, but you could solve them, with a little help from Nate. You are one of us, and yet not, at the same time."

Cara laughed. "Why would I care? I'm out in the cold; to society, I am persona non grata."

She stepped close to Cara. "No. You're free." She tapped the end of Cara's nose, as though the action somehow verified her statement. "You just don't know it yet."

"You have the contact with Nathaniel, why don't you do it?" As soon as she said the words, she knew how ridiculous they sounded.

The countess laughed and muttered something in French to her small wooden box. "I prefer not to talk to Nate. He is a reminder of betrayal. And I no longer venture into society, I'm sure you can imagine why." Her hand swept down her body. "I am not long for this world. I have a bet with myself about which gets me first, the pox or the mercury."

Cara didn't know what to say. She heard syphilis killed just as horribly as the mercury supposed to cure it. Something was about to win the bet; the final stages of the disease explained the woman's appearance and erratic behaviour.

"I know a young woman in need. Her name is Isobel, and she has a rather delicate problem. Talk to her, make up your own mind if you will help. Many of the women are trapped in their lavish cages. Unlike you, they do not have the resolve to fight for themselves. You seem rather tailor-made for the role of problem solver." She extracted a card from amongst her ample décolleté and held it out toward Cara.

This is starting to feel like a bizarre treasure hunt, following clues written on little cards.

"I'll talk to this Isobel, then. If you will tell me something. What was Nathaniel's promise to you?" Cara took the card between two fingers and tucked it into her satchel without bothering to look at it.

"Long ago, he gave his word to deliver the source of my infection." Her eyes glazed over and peals of laughter bounced off the parlour walls.

High-pitched glee echoed around the room, as she danced with the wooden receptacle.

Cara shuddered, understanding what she cradled to her bosom.

"I'll show myself out." She backed out of the parlour, the twirling countess oblivious to her presence or departure.

She slipped through the front door, stood on the porch, and let out a deep breath.

Time for some fresh air, and a change of clothes to shake off the crazy.

Cara headed to her small apartment, taking a circuitous route, which involved a stop at a nearby bookstore. She paced the aisles, running a finger along spines, looking for a title that grabbed her interest to keep her company at night. She saw a familiar figure pace in front of the window. Jackson stalked the pavement outside. She smiled.

Game on.

Seeing none of the other customers paid her any attention, she slipped behind the counter and through the door to the back. The startled owner raised his hand to stop her, but Cara flashed him a beguiling smile.

"I'm trying to escape a boorish suitor; he just won't leave me alone. Do you mind terribly?" she said as she disappeared out the back door, and into the alleyway beyond, where she picked up her skirts and high-tailed it before Jackson realised she was gone.

Safe in her rooms, she slipped out of the taffeta bodice and skirt, hanging them neatly in her wardrobe. The little hat with the feathers sat on the shelf above its accompanying outfit.

Cara pulled on her usual outfit: trousers, front-lacing, collared corset, her two Smith and Wesson pistols, and a long swallow-tailed jacket over the top. She ran her fingers through her short hair after its confinement under the top hat. She stopped herself from messing it up too much, in case she started to resemble the loony Countess de Sal. She moved the rug in her bedroom. Prying up the loose floorboard, she retrieved the black silk-wrapped object and tucked it in her satchel.

She headed out into the late afternoon in a much better mood. She was surprised to see Jackson open the door to the Mayfair house and wave her toward the ground floor study.

Cara stepped into the entranceway, before turning back. "Did you not find a book you liked today?"

His eyes widened for a moment, before he growled at her. "You're not making my life any easier, you know."

She grinned. "I can be like that. But you could stop following me?"

"Not allowed to do that." He gave her a conspiratorial wink.

Cara wondered why Nathaniel had his men following her. To win the bet that he could find out where she lived, or to get his hands on the artifacts as she retrieved them?

"Since you're in a chatty mood, do you have a first name?" She was curious about her tail, and he seemed to have shrugged off their rough start.

"Yes." He leaned back against the closed door, his bulk blocked her only handy exit, but the restriction didn't worry her. Nathaniel promised no one would harm her under his roof, and she believed him.

"What is it? What's your name?" She nudged for more information. Two other men occupied the wide entrance hall. Tall and broad like Jackson, they looked more like bodyguards than footmen. They eyed her, and moved from their positions against the wall.

"Now why would I tell you?" He waved to the others, sending them back to their corners.

"I thought you had a soft spot for me." She stuck her bottom lip out, feigning a pout for effect.

He gave her his customary wide grin. "Jackson."

Cara smiled. "Seriously? Jackson? Your name is Jackson Jackson?"

He gave her a wink and she laughed. She wrapped the good mood around her, and bounced into Nathaniel's study. Her eyes shone with mischief.

His head shot up at the unexpected, and unusual, intrusion. He arched one black eyebrow. "You're in a good mood."

"Yes." *And I shouldn't be, standing alone in the lion's den.*

He wasn't only a lord by title, but by deed. He headed an underworld empire of unknown depth. Some said even the Rookeries deferred to him. Everything about him spoke of power, from the strong line of his jaw, to the broadly muscled shoulders under his expensive jacket, and the deference of people around him. He was dangerous, powerful, and utterly intoxicating. Especially to a woman who suffered a lack of impulse control and no respect for the mores of society.

He promised I'm safe here.

She flashed an impish grin. "The package is delivered and the countess is satisfied. And amused. And ever so slightly bonkers." She made circles in the air, next to her head. "When I left she was giggling over whatever is in that box."

She burned to ask the background to the story, but didn't fancy her chances of getting it out of him.

Nathaniel nodded in a noncommittal fashion. "Thank you."

"Are you always working?" She stopped in front of his desk, littered with reports, invoices, and accounts. The aethergraph ticked continuously, spitting its coded messages into the tray, where they lay patiently.

"There's always work that requires my attention." He dropped the paper in his hand on top of a growing pile on one side of the desk.

"You need a number two." She wondered if his legitimate or illegitimate business, kept him busy at all hours. She tilted her head, trying to read some of the dispatches upside-down.

"The problem with having an adequate number two is they usually aspire to be a number one. That's how I came to hold my position, and I have no intention of relinquishing it." He brushed the papers aside.

"So, assuming you have any non-work time, what do you do for recreation?"

He arched an eyebrow and leaned back in his chair. "It depends. I often go out at night to seek entertainment."

She shook her head, not satisfied with his answer. "That's a bit vague. With you that could mean anything. It could be stalking a ballroom or a bout of fisticuffs somewhere in Seven Dials."

He threw down his pen and gave her his full attention.

"You could come with me one evening and find out, if you wish." He made it sound like a challenge.

"Only if you promise it's going to be boxing." She changed her stance, dropped her weight, and gave a few experimental jabs at an imaginary opponent.

"You can box?" The corner of his mouth twitched.

She might have surprised him. Having seen him crack a smile at the restaurant, she longed to see another spread over his face.

"Yip." She took a few more jabs, putting the face of Sir John Burke, Amy's indignant fiancé, onto her phantom opponent. She finished him off with a right hook.

"But you don't like being touched." He pointed out the dichotomy in her behaviour.

"I'm used to being hit." She uttered the words before realising how pathetic they sounded aloud, and continued to cover her slip. "My grandmother indulged my desire to learn how to fight. You could make some money betting on me if they have lightweight fighters."

"You'd be bantam weight soaking wet." He raked his eyes over her form, making her skin prickle under his intense scrutiny.

"Apart from telling you I've delivered your package, I also brought you the first piece to sell." She dropped her arms and opened her satchel to withdraw the black silk handkerchief. She unwrapped the treasure, a solid gold cuff, encircled with green gems, five inches wide and covered in deep Gaelic images and runes.

"It belonged to Boudicca. Legend says it gave her good fortune and luck in battle. Unfortunately for her, a servant stole it before her last, and fatal, battle with the Romans." She dangled it from her fingers. "It's solid gold and edged with emeralds."

Nathaniel rounded his desk, perched on the edge, and extended his hand. Cara dropped the heavy piece of jewellery into his palm. He turned it over. Their current queen, Victoria, styled herself as the ancient Briton Queen

"And the provenance?" He examined the heavy item.

"There is a contemporaneous account describing the bracelet and how Boudicca hanged a servant for stealing it. The thing must be lucky, because she hanged the wrong servant. The cuff was passed down through various offshoots of his family, until my father stole it."

"It will fetch you a pretty penny, and whet some appetites for what is to come."

"Good." She needed the money, and the independence it would bring. She hated constantly asking her grandmother for funds, however willingly they were given. "And what's your cut?"

"Ten percent."

Cara gave an indignant snort. He was dreaming if he thought she would simply hand over ten percent of her father's collection.

"Five," she countered.

"Seven. And a favour." His gaze was steady and unflinching.

She knew the sort of favour he would demand. The unicorns pranced in her stomach again, their feet stomping up and down impatiently, but they hadn't started charging in circles yet. The monstrous fear lay in a corner, alert but watching. True to his word, Nathaniel hadn't hurt her, or pushed her beyond her comfort zone. He challenged her gently and showed her a glimpse of the sensations her body missed.

I want it, she realised. *I want him to touch me.*

"All right." She still had her guns. She hooked her fingers into the hip holster to give them something to do.

He took a step forward. She closed her eyes and inhaled his scent as he leaned close to her. He smelled warm and musky, with a faint tang of citrus. Her brain drifted on a current, wondering if he brought fruit in by airship. His chest was mere millimetres from her, but he held himself apart, not touching her. He bent his head and kissed the base of her ear.

She stiffened for an instant at the unexpected touch, before relaxing into the sensation. "What are you doing?"

His lips caressed her skin; heat flowed over her nerve endings, spreading from her neck upward and downward. Her hair follicles rippled and stood to attention, making her scalp tingle.

"If I'm giving up three percent, I'm going to make it worthwhile." His lips trailed down her neck; his tongue found the hollow at the base of her throat. She gasped as he licked the sensitive spot. She fought the urge to lean into him as a slow beat pulsed through her torso. Her mind wasn't ready to surrender yet; a part of her was constantly braced against the anticipated violence. She arched her neck, giving him better access as he kissed his way from the hollow, upward.

The fear stirred and stretched itself. Stimuli overwhelmed her brain, as the pleasure trying to take over her body registered as a threat. She had to protect herself, and took a step backward. Drawing in a deep breath, she let the fear resettle in its corner.

Nathaniel remained immobile, rooted to the spot. He didn't pursue her, he simply waited.

Under control again, she stepped toward him. The fighter in her needed to push herself, to find her limits. She needed to determine how much she could take before she fell. She tilted her head, reaching up for his lips. He took her bottom lip between his teeth, biting softly before letting go to claim her mouth, sliding his lips over hers. His tongue brushed against her teeth and carried on, finding her tongue and caressing it gently. Warmth radiated out from her stomach, as though she knocked back a hit of hard liquor. The same languid sensation ran through her limbs. She gave a soft cry, wanting more, but afraid of the pleasure running riot. She battled herself, trying to hold her ground.

Nathaniel stepped away, giving her room to breathe. Burgeoning desire ran through her body for the first time. He met her eyes, sucked in a breath, and turned his attention back to the gold cuff, still clutched in his hand.

"Word is spreading that you intend to sell off your father's collection." He brought the conversation to more conventional business matters.

"It should increase prices, then." The words came out breathier than she meant them; her body still battled her brain.

"It also increases the risk to you."

"I don't follow the connection?" Her brain only now turned from pleasure back to more mundane business matters.

"There will be others trying to lay their hands on Lord Devon's notebook."

"I can look after myself." She unconsciously traced a finger over the handle of her pistol.

"It would be safer here. I can keep it secure for you." He dropped the cuff into a drawer in the large desk.

She was silent. His behaviour made sense, his strategy revealed. She gave a short laugh. "So that's the game you're been playing. This whole gentle courting routine, asking favours, was simply a ruse. You've just softening me up to get your hands on the notebook."

She accused him, and herself. She had been so stupid; his tactic deceived her, and she responded so easily. She was so pathetically grateful to lap up his attention.

"You're wrong. I have my motives, but they are independent of your father's collection." He moved closer to her, but stopped a stride away.

"I'm not that gullible, but thank you for the education. I'll not be so foolish again." Her nostrils flared, and her voice came out harsh and clipped. Pacing to the door, she reached out for the handle.

"I want you." His tone was so low the words reached her ears only, and wouldn't carry to those listening beyond the door.

She froze, not daring to look over her shoulder. Her heart pounded, she was unsure whether to stay or flee. "You want the notebook. Don't confuse us."

"You."

One quiet syllable that arrested her headlong rush. A tiny part of her wanted to believe him.

"I have no interest in taking the frightened child to my bed, a girl whose only experience is pain and brutality. I want the spirited woman who shot two of my men to garner my attention. The strong woman who stepped into my carriage and didn't back down and who, apparently, knows how to box. She is the creature I want."

She turned to face him, a frown on her face. "If you think I'm going to fall into bed with you, you're mistaken."

His gaze mesmerised her, drank her in, possessed her. She swayed on her feet.

"Today? No. Tomorrow? No. But I'm a patient man and I always get what I want, in the end."

"No." She shook her head, breaking the visual contact. The flow of emotion was too much. Her body wanted to revel in his touch, but her brain couldn't comprehend contact without pain. Her mind screamed a warning and, turning, she ran out the study door and past a startled Jackson.

She hit the stairs at a run. Only the press of pedestrians on the pavement slowed her escape. Dropping to a quick walk, she let her body choose a random direction. She needed to walk. No, she wanted to punch something, hard, but walking would have to do. Her brain smoked with all the information thrown at her.

Part of her believed Nathaniel revealed his true goal, trying to get his hands on the notebook and through it, the collection of artifacts. Part of her desperately wanted to believe he was trying to get his hands on her. The second thought sent a frisson of fear up her spine and over her scalp, tinged with awakening desire.

CHAPTER 8

Tuesday, July 2

THIS *one lasted longer. He balanced on the point of hoping she was the one, when night descended over her face, and the darkness snatched her from his grasp.*

He didn't understand. He thought she was the one, so gentle and regal in her manner, such an echo of the other, millennia ago. He was tender toward her, his hand loving as he drove the key into her heart. Explaining to her that he did it so they could be together, forever. Unlocking her heart was the only way to reclaim their lost immortality. He thought she understood.

Why did she not return his love? Why did she deny him? How could they be together if she hid her secrets from him?

He was doing something wrong. Perhaps he was still too hurried, his excitement carrying him away. Certainly, she had been excited. Perhaps the anticipation of waiting for the key was too much? With the next one, he would move slower. He had all of time stretching before him. He could afford to exercise more patience.

He was learning and adapting; each failure brought new intelligence. Fierce hazel eyes beckoned him. Her eyes swirled to green with her desire for him. His groin tightened at the memory. It had been three thousand years since he buried himself in her.

Soon.

He already had an idea.

He needed chloroform. He would let the next one slumber and awaken her only when he was ready to turn the key. It would be a surprise for her.

Yes, the next one would be right. Then, all of eternity would be theirs.

Wednesday, July 3

Fraser frowned at his desk. He left a report there, and now couldn't find it. His desk comprised less than six square feet. How could a report simply vanish in such a small space? It didn't help he had approximately one hundred reports scattered over the desktop; he expected the exact one he wanted to be lying right on top. And it wasn't. He contemplated the pile. He might have to tidy something up, and such an action would disturb the delicate ecological environment he cultivated.

His door flew open. Connor's bulk appeared. His mass bounced over the sprung floor, and the vibrations jostled the desk's contents as he approached. A single file slid to one side, heading in a precarious lurch toward the edge.

"Ah!" Fraser lunged sideways and grabbed the thin cardboard about to make the last leap to escape. Just the one he sought. *No need to tidy up, then, the system still works.*

"Grab your coat, we're up." Connor gestured over his shoulder with his thumb in a *we're outta here* way.

Fraser frowned, briefly distracted from reviewing the report in his hand. "What's happened?"

"Another girl. Same as the first one. Them upstairs are going to yank your chain real hard on this one." The hand gesture changed to one pointing above their heads, indicating the offices above.

Fraser's frown deepened. "The same? What do you mean? Do elaborate." He tossed the file back into the fray as he retrieved his hat from the rack.

Connor continued talking as he flipped open his notebook. "Lady Abigail Swan, twenty-one years old, brunette, and apparently rather beautiful. Found dead this morning, with a brass shaft of some sort protruding from her chest. Sound familiar at all?"

Fraser swore under his breath. "Well, there goes our jilted suitor theory. Unless by chance, and happy coincidence, did this girl have the same suitors as Lady Lovell?"

Connor consulted his all-knowing notebook as they descended the stairs. "Nope. This girl only had one fellow courting her. We're back to square one, unless you come up with another theory."

They exited the Enforcers Headquarters at street level and climbed into the waiting steam-powered coach, which jostled and belched its way to the Swan home while Fraser ran through the Lovell case in his head. He re-familiarised himself with the previous case before stepping into the next one. The process ensured his brain would have the best opportunity to spot any similarities while the trail on this one was still warm.

Curtains in the surrounding houses twitched and shook on seeing the dark blue Enforcer conveyance in the quiet street. The neighbours would be well aware of the unfolding tragedy, but far too polite to gossip on a street corner. The news would pass lightning fast over back fences between servants, to be delivered upstairs in elegant rooms to eagerly awaiting ladies.

On ascending the stairs, Fraser found a house simultaneously in uproarious confusion and silent mourning. Many of the servants went about their tasks like automatons, devoid of all emotion, gliding about unseeing, deaf, and mute. At the same time, a high-pitched keening came from upstairs.

The mother, presumably. Maids flew up and down the stairs, trying to avoid the robotic staff as they responded to every shriek. The swift-moving women dashed amongst the solemn footmen, like wisps of mist ducking and diving amongst shadows.

Fraser flashed his badge at the sombre footman, although with Connor's uniformed and hulking presence behind him, his identity as an Enforcer was plain.

"This way, sir." He directed Fraser and Connor through the house and out to the rear garden.

The screaming diminished as they moved farther from the house. They walked a short distance down a terrace and over the manicured lawn. In the midst of the picturesque rose garden, circling dark blue uniforms indicated where the girl's body lay.

The unfortunate's father paced back and forth, futilely guarding his child. Colonel Swan looked up as Fraser approached. Despite his red-rimmed eyes, his back was ramrod straight. He gave off a military air in both his posture and staunch demeanour.

"Inspector Fraser." He showed his badge by way of introduction. "I am so sorry for this terrible occurrence, Colonel Swan. Rest assured we will do all in our power to find the person responsible."

Colonel Swan nodded his head. "Do what you have to. And do it swiftly." His gaze raked the bobbies treading the gravel of his garden. "But I'll not have any of them touching her."

Fraser sighed. Righteous indignation was a common reaction of the aristocracy, their fear of the regular constabulary poking and prying into their business. Or worse, poking and prying about their children.

"Is there perhaps a maid who might be up to the task of assisting us?" The presence of a familiar female might move the process along. "I can assure you, Colonel Swan, if you let us do our job, your child will be treated with the upmost respect at all times."

Fraser was itching to examine the scene, to catalogue if the details were the same, or different from the previous case. His urge to begin his scene examination lit a fire under his feet. He shifted his weight back and forth, trying to cool his heels.

Another curt nod came from the grieving Colonel. "Her maid, Malloy. She's a country girl; she will want to see her mistress properly tended in death."

He waved over one of the footmen and instructed him to fetch the maid.

Dismissed, Fraser approached where the noble girl's body lay. He stopped a few yards away to survey the scene, to see what the choice of placement of her body told him.

Laid out in a grid of nine identical beds, tall yew hedges trimmed with military precision surrounded the garden. The trees were silent, verdant sentries, standing at attention around the fallen girl. The slain daughter occupied the central square of garden. Her form fitted diagonally within the frame of bright green buxus, encircled by roses on either side. Someone had draped a sheet over her, shielded her from prying eyes and further distressing the household. Bright red rose petals dusted the sheet, nature's blood spilt in sympathy.

Why here? What is the significance of the rose garden? How did the killer place her here, and no one saw him?

Fraser was ready. He lifted the corner of the sheet. Her expression was serene, her eyes closed, the muscles in her face relaxed. She looked like she simply fell asleep, except for her unusual pallor. Laid out as though for a viewing, with her hands crossed over her chest, the shaft and bow of a brass key jutted out from her heart. A slice in her gown allowed the ornate bow of the key to protrude.

"Bother," he muttered, dropping the sheet. Dealing with a murderous, jilted suitor was one thing; a deranged killer of noble daughters was an entirely different nightmare. And not just for the toffs who would panic about the safety of their loved ones. Fraser was about to be on the receiving end from his Superintendent if he didn't catch the killer, and promptly.

He frowned, and picked up the corner of the sheet again. Something niggled in his brain. There was an echo, more than just the key. There was something else about this case that reminded him of poor Jennifer Lovell. His mind compared and discarded the facts of the two cases, looking for the other point of similarity.

He paced over the gravel as his mind flicked from this crime to the previous one. Mentally, he put each scene under a microscope and compared the two images. He knew what bugged him. *The gown looks similar, possibly identical?*

Although it could be pure coincidence; he had no experience with the night attire of noble girls. His experiences were of a lower, and more salacious, level, where nightgowns were not required. For all he knew, the slip of linen could be a standard garment for debutantes.

The crunch of another set of feet on the path arrested his pacing. Turning, he saw a maid in the uniform of black gown and long white apron. With dark brown hair tucked up under her white cotton cap, a trailing tendril was the only indication of her rush to make herself presentable.

"Sir?" She dropped a hesitant curtsey.

"Malloy?" Fraser thought she was holding up well. Her eyes were red, but she had scrubbed the tears from her face before venturing out to the garden.

"Yes, sir." The tendril bobbed back and forth, as she nodded.

He gestured for her to come closer. "I need your assistance with your mistress. I realise you must be terribly upset, so I will keep this short." He lifted the corner of the sheet. "The nightgown your mistress is wearing, I need to know how long she has owned it, and if possible, where the garment was purchased. It may be important."

He dropped the sheet once the maid took a measured look at the garment in question.

The maid shook her head before raising wet brown eyes to his. "It's not her gown, sir. I've never seen it before, and I know all her under things."

"Oh?" *Not one clue, but two. The gown is supplied by the killer.* He jotted down a note to ask Lady Lovell's maid if the gown was a normal part of Jennifer's attire. *It may be a clue as important as the key.*

A uniformed bobby approached with a small metal bed on wheels, and coughed to attract Fraser's attention. It was time to remove the body. Doc would be waiting to tend her in the morgue.

"Malloy, would you mind doing one last thing for Lady Swan? Could you assist moving her body? We want to ensure the correct level of propriety is maintained."

"Of course, sir."

He left the maid and the uniforms to lift the dead girl gently onto the gurney and to wrap her in a sheet, safe from prying eyes watching from behind curtains.

Fraser had matters to discuss with her father. A silent footman showed him through to the ground floor library. Colonel Swan stood at the window, staring out at the street, a brandy in his hand at ten o'clock in the morning. The drink didn't look like his first one of the day, not that Fraser could blame him under the circumstances. He cleared his throat to attract the older man's attention.

"If I might have a moment of your time, Colonel Swan?" Fraser stepped farther into the room, waiting for a nod before continuing. "Malloy is seeing to her mistress, and I can assure you our doctor will accord her full dignity. But I need to ask about your daughter's last few days, and did she have a particular suitor?"

Colonel Swan tossed back the last of his drink. "There was only the one fellow courting her, polite young man, Bartholomew Clark. They live just along the street. His father's a good sort; we served together. When she went missing three nights ago, we assumed they had run off together. I stormed over there, only to find him more confused than me."

Fraser noted the suitor's details in his notebook, while Colonel Swan dropped his empty glass onto the sideboard.

"We were trying to keep it quiet. Clark said she had been cool on him the last week or so. Since Abigail wasn't with Clark, her mother and I assumed she met some new beau, who turned her head. I sent out discreet enquiries; we just wanted to bring her home before word spread of her foolishness. That sort of behaviour ruins a girl's prospects, you know."

"Who was he, the other fellow?" Fraser had an itch running down his spine, the one that told him he was onto something, but he was going to have to dig hard to uncover the lead.

Colonel Swan rubbed his forehead. "That's the thing. We don't know. Even Malloy doesn't know any details." He swung to face Fraser. "Did he kill her? This new chap?"

Fraser kept his face impassive and his words non-committal. With two dead girls under similar circumstances, his gut told him a peer hunted amongst the daughters of the aristocracy.

Thursday, July 4

CARA spread papers over a desk in the public library as she pored over her father's notebook. Deciphering his coded entries was laborious work. He had codes and red herring codes, and she didn't know if she used the right one until half way through any passage. She thought selling off the artifacts would be a quick and easy job, and she'd soon be on an airship somewhere else.

Anywhere else, she sighed.

Her father's paranoia showed in his meticulous notes. It took days to figure out where just one artifact resided, let alone the entire collection. She couldn't fathom why he took such extreme precautions, but then, she couldn't understand most of what her father did.

Her brain finally called a halt to the morning's work and chased her outside in search of coffee. She headed down the main steps, toward St James Square, as a voice hailed her.

"Miss Devon?" a clipped accent called. She recognised the voice and turned to find two official-looking individuals at the bottom of the stairs. The voice belonged to a man in a plaid overcoat with friendly grey eyes peering out from behind spectacles. Inspector Fraser. Cara thought he looked more like a trustworthy physician and wondered how many people dropped their guard and said too much around him. Today, he had an enormous companion who wore the dark blue uniform of Her Majesty's Enforcers. He wore an armoured and weaponised gauntlet and a utility belt with a multitude of dangling pouches and gadgets. He looked more like a mountaineer intent on tackling Everest than a street enforcer.

What have I done now?

"Good morning, Inspector Fraser." She stopped in her tracks, waiting for him to reveal his purpose.

He nodded his head politely. "Would you mind accompanying us to headquarters?"

"Yes, I would mind." She stopped one tread higher than the inspector.

He looked taken aback. "I'm afraid I'll have to insist, miss."

Cara let out a sigh. She rolled her head to release the tension in her neck from the morning bent over the desk, and spied the carriage and mechanised horses across the road. Three days previously, she had run, confused, from his study. She watched her back, vigilant for any sign of Jackson following her. How did he know she was at the library? She wondered how long he sat there, watching for her to leave. She didn't need to see his impassive face to know those eyes were trained on her. A flush crept up her neck as she remembered Nathaniel's touch, his lips brushing hers, his tongue exploring her mouth in a slow, sensual dance. Her body demanding more than her brain could handle.

"Miss Devon?" The inspector repeated, trying to gain her attention. Cara shook her head, trying to dislodge the memory that haunted her, whether asleep or awake.

"Yes. All right, then." She sprang off the last step and fell in beside Fraser.

The Enforcers had a steam-powered carriage, painted the same deep blue as the uniforms they wore. As she stepped up into the dark interior, she caught a brief glimpse of the mechanical horses across the road being urged forward.

The carriage jostled, bumped, and belched smoke on its way around the corner to headquarters in Whitehall Place. The odour of the coal fire permeated the body of the carriage. Cara sniffed and wrinkled her nose. She could see the advantages to money and cleaner forms of transport. Fraser, appearing oblivious to the smell, tried to engage her in conversation about the weather and the latest developments in airship travel. She resisted his attempts during the short carriage ride, her mind darting around as she tried to figure out what he wanted with her.

What has he dug up about my father now?

They stopped outside the imposing, four-storey brick building of the Enforcers Headquarters. Inspector Fraser jumped out of the carriage first and extended his hand to Cara, which she duly ignored.

She jumped free of the stuffy confines and looked up at the building. With a minimal number of windows, high surrounding walls, and patrolling guards in hissing exoskeletons, it looked more like a prison.

"If you would follow me, Miss Devon?" He sounded like he was escorting her to a tea table, albeit a tea table in an isolated interrogation room.

He mounted the steps and crossed the dark slate floor of the atrium. He took a stairway on the left. Cara followed behind. His sergeant, Connor, flanked her, perhaps ensuring she didn't turn tail and run back to the street. Impending dread settled in her stomach.

Fraser led her into a small office, every surface crammed with files, papers, and books.

Connor quickly uncovered a chair and held it out for Cara. She sank into the threadbare seat, while the inspector went to stand at the window. She was in his domain, so waited for him to lead off. To distract herself, she stared at her fingernails and contemplated luxuriating in a hot bath, if only her small rooms had one. She hated dressing like a girl, but she loved to bathe like one.

"Have you thought any further as to who might want to harm your father?" Fraser asked.

Why would he haul her in to talk about her father? There was something deeper at play here. "No. I had no contact with him over the last seven years, except through my grandmother. I'm sure you came up with a much better list than I could."

Cara watched his posture by the window. He appeared distracted, gazing out onto the street, but his eyes kept flicking to her. "Is this solely about my father's death?"

His placid grey eyes were full of warmth and understanding, as he turned them on her. "In a way."

She held her tongue, waiting for the kick to his statement. She wouldn't let his personable nature fool her.

"You have perhaps heard that two young noblewomen have been murdered?" He sounded almost apologetic for broaching such ugly news with her.

"Two? I saw the newspaper article about Jennifer Lovell. I vaguely recall her from years ago." Cara's brain tried to leapfrog over Fraser and see where he was heading.

He moved from the window, halting next to his desk. "There has been another. Lady Abigail Swan. I'm sure the newspapers will be full of her sad demise by this afternoon. She was the same age as you. Did you know her, also?"

Cara turned the name over in her head. Abigail Swan didn't trigger any but the vaguest memories. She certainly couldn't conjure up enough to put a face to the name. She shook her head.

Fraser spread his hands wide. "There is a . . . tenuous connection to your father."

"Oh?" She was all ears, wondering what he saw in the disparate deaths.

He dropped his hands to clutch the back of his chair. "As you are aware, your father was killed by an Egyptian asp."

Cara remained silent, though alarm bells sounded in the back of her head.

"The two women were wearing an undergarment made of Egyptian linen." He looked embarrassed to discuss night attire with her. "From my enquiries, such a robe is not available here, in London, but must have come direct from Egypt."

A laugh burst forth from her throat. "Are you seriously telling me you think the murder of these women is somehow related to the death of my father because of a chemise?" The inspector's theory was too incredible to give the idea any credence. "So what is your hypothesis? That someone imported a load of Egyptian linen, containing an asp to murder my father, and then, what? After killing my father, did he cast around, looking for ideas of what to do with his surplus garments?"

He spread his hands wide and shrugged. "I don't like coincidences, particularly when they concern non-accidental death."

"And if you don't believe in coincidence, what exactly do you think is the connection?"

"You." He took his seat at the desk, rummaging he came up with a small notebook and a mechanical pencil. He looked poised, as if anticipating some big break in his case.

Cara frowned. *What on Earth is he getting at?* "That's a bit of a stretch."

He flipped through his notes. "The women were a similar age and status to yourself, and, as they say, *in your circle.*"

"Circle?" She choked on the word. "I don't have a circle, in case you hadn't noticed. I was raped seven years ago and the ton consider me damaged goods. And that's putting aside the fact I've only been in London for a couple of weeks, hardly time to establish *a circle.*"

She crossed her arms over her chest, staring at him through narrowed eyes. He was pushing all her buttons today.

"Funny how society blames the victim, but Clayton walked free while his chums slapped him on the back. Out of curiosity, where exactly was the force while I was being raped and beaten?" She threw her own accusation at him.

The anger welled up inside her. She tasted bile at the back of her throat with each shortened breath. Due to his high position, no one intervened or stopped Lord Clayton. He was never charged, or even censured. And now, she jumped to the top of the Enforcers' suspect list when girls of her age and status were murdered. No doubt he thought she harboured sour grapes that they got to do the season and wear pretty frocks, while she had to stick to the shadows. *Screw you society, I've had a gut's full.*

Fraser shuffled his papers and didn't meet Cara's eyes. "What happened to you was unforgiveable. But so is what is happening to these young women. They're not killed straightaway, you know. He keeps them alive for a couple of days; for what purpose, we do not know. Can you imagine their terror while they wait?"

She shuddered. She spent a week locked in a room, and knew exactly what it was like to be trapped. At the sound of footsteps outside the door, her heart would stop. She would freeze, balanced on the knife-edge of panic, as she waited to see if the doorknob turned, if the monster would enter. She screamed, but no one came to rescue her from the unending nightmare.

"Yes, I can well imagine their terror," she whispered.

"The link back to Egypt is too compelling to ignore, and you're the only connection I have who can answer my questions. The other three are dead." He held up his fingers, counting the digits as he recited the names. "Your father, Lord Devon, was the first. Then, Jennifer Lovell and now, Abigail Swan."

"So you think I'm on some sort of murderous rampage?"

He gave her a gentle smile. "I'm not accusing you of anything. But you certainly seem to be in the middle of something. Perhaps there is information you know, but are not sharing? Perhaps there is something that touched you and these girls? Some common occurrence, which may have originated with your father?"

He sounded like a psychiatrist, asking her to tell him about her child-hood. He used a gentle, probing tone.

She'd be damned if she was going to wear the blame for the deaths, just because he couldn't come up with his own suspect.

I should have stayed away. I should have taken an airship to America, or Australia.

"If you have any evidence, charge me. Otherwise stay the hell away from me." She pushed her chair back so violently it toppled over.

"Don't go leaving London, Miss Devon. I require you to stay here until my investigation has concluded."

She shuddered; bile rose from her stomach and her fingers itched to hold her pistols. Without casting a backward glance, she stormed from the room and down the stairs.

Ranting at Fraser, she hit the street and kept on going. Pedestrians, sensing her mood, automatically parted for her, letting her cut through the traffic unimpeded.

Fraser removed his spectacles and tossed them on the mound of paper. He rubbed his temples.

Some days, I think I should have gone into banking, as mother wanted.

"Well, that didn't go quite as planned." Connor piped up from his corner, where he tried to blend in with the bookshelf, although an elephant would have been as effective trying to hide in a small office. "Feisty thing, isn't she?"

"Hmm . . . might try a slightly different approach next time. I don't think softly is going to get us anywhere." He returned his specs to his face and left his chaotic desk.

"Do you really think she knows anything?" Connor couldn't see the invisible path Fraser scented.

He gave his sergeant a surprised look. "I'm sure of it. I just don't think she has made the connection yet. Anyway, I'm going down to see Doc."

Connor held his hands up in horror. "You're on your own. Yell if you're heading out. I'll be down in the weapons range."

Deep in the bowels of the Enforcers' building, Fraser stepped into the chill air of the morgue, the hum of the mechanical water circulator comforting, like having a nanny hum as a baby drifted off to sleep.

Abigail Swan held the central position and Doc talked to her softly, as he went about his work.

"Tell me the bad news, Doc." He approached the central slab, with Abigail exposed from mid-chest upwards. A sheet concealed the majority of her slender body.

Doc looked up. "Same as the other poor wee thing, I'm afraid. Key looks identical." He paced to the workbench to retrieve the item.

Doc handed it over, and Fraser weighed it in his hand. The key found buried in her heart certainly looked similar, but a microscopic comparison would confirm his suspicions. "I've been interviewing locksmiths, but they all swear they've never seen the likes of this before. Although they tell me it wouldn't be terribly difficult to make; you just need some basic equipment, time, and patience." He gave a wry smile. "They all thought a loving hand crafted these."

He stared at the young girl, once so full of life and potential. Now her silent beauty would cause panic and unrest amongst the ton. Fraser waited to be hauled upstairs and grilled by his superintendent. He needed to find this mysterious suitor, quickly, before he stalked his next prey.

If he hasn't already chosen her.

Time for a change of tactic. "How long has she been dead?"

"A few hours, a day at most."

Fraser chewed his lip. "She'd been gone for a couple of days, same as Jennifer Lovell. She spent two days with him, before he killed her. What do you think he does?"

Doc raised his bushy eyebrows. "That's a question for the living. I can only answer questions for the dead."

This is going nowhere.

The name Cara Devon nagged at him as he made his way back upstairs.

Tuesday, July 9

CARA leaned against her upper story window, sipping coffee as she watched the bustle of activity in the street below. Events from the previous few days played over in her head. Thinking about Nathaniel sent a shiver of electrical current skating over her skin, akin to playing with the light switches in her cantankerous house. He was as enticing as climbing out of her bedroom window late at night. Part of her brain knew she shouldn't do it, but another part is lured by the appeal of unknown adventures in the dark.

Doubts nagged at her. What were his true motives? He sent two men to steal her father's notebook and then attempted to make her hand it over. Was she playing into his hands? Cumulatively, the collection of artifacts was worth a fortune. Selling it would ensure her security and more importantly, her independence. The objects were a tempting fortune and she would have to guard closely their location, until they could be sold.

No wonder father was so paranoid. A country estate would be much easier. You don't have to worry about someone nicking one of those in the middle of the night.

She needed a distraction. Remembering her interview with the mad Countess de Sal, she retrieved her satchel and rummaged through the contents to extract the cream card. In a shaky hand, looking like a spider had some form of epileptic fit while covered in ink, the countess had sprawled a name and address.

In a neat, pragmatic hand, Cara added her own name to the back of the card.

Time to play tea parties with our dollies.

She remembered pretending to make social calls as a child. She and Amy would line up their dolls on a manicured lawn and wait for other neighbourhood girls to visit. Although usually, Cara disappeared up a tree instead, armed with pockets full of pebbles she used to aim at the delicate porcelain teacups below.

She quickly swallowed the remaining coffee before dressing in the blue and brown taffeta outfit with the little feathered top hat. She twirled in front of the mirror, and adjusted the angle of the hat, then headed out the door into the warm, nearly summer day.

A newsboy on the street caught her attention with his cry of, "Beautiful debutante horribly murdered!"

People rushed to grab their edition and morning dose of titillation. Cara joined the mob and purchased a paper. She scanned the article as she walked. The details were scant and told her less than what Inspector Fraser revealed. The article stated Abigail Swan was found, murdered, in her backyard. Then there was a load of rampant speculation connecting her death to that of Jennifer Lovell. Not that they were wrong in their speculation, unfortunately.

This will send a shiver through society. Brutal murder is so lower class.

At least the newspapers hadn't yet got wind of Fraser's suspicion, that the murder of her father was also connected. Cara would be pursued more feverishly than the fox at the hunt if they caught that scent. She finished the article and tossed the unwanted newspaper in a nearby bin. She picked up her pace, keen to get the impending visit over and done with and discharge the obligation that passed to her with the small card.

The neat and tidy house teetered on the edge of Mayfair and Soho. Clipped topiaries stood guard on either side of the door. She hoped the orderly exterior was a reflection of the residents and she would be met with polite civility. Her skin still crawled when she remembered the scene in the restaurant.

She rapped on the door and almost simultaneously it swung open at the hand of an efficient butler. She extended the card and a terrible silence loomed between her and the servant. The butler raised his eyebrows, but remained silent. He gestured, indicating she was to wait; he left her standing on the porch with only the topiary for company. She was thinking about bolting back down the stairs when he reappeared, waved her inside, and ushered her into the parlour.

Cara stood on the threshold and blinked. Several times.

Whoa, there must be a lot of women in this household.

She wondered what sort of household she had stumbled into this time. The parlour was resplendent in shades of pink, purple, and cream, from striped wallpaper to cushions looking like enormous sweets and swagged curtains in the same bilious shades. Cara felt a headache coming on just looking at the confection surrounding her.

A petite woman bustled into the space, practically invisible but for her frantic movement, camouflaged against the candy cane walls with a dress the same vertical shades as the wallpaper. Her pale hair was devoid of its own colouring, instead reflecting the purpleness of whatever she stood near.

"Countess de Sal sent you?" Her eyes darted around the room, and she licked her lips. She closed the parlour door, cutting off Cara's exit from the screaming girliness.

"Yes. I'm Cara Devon. The countess believed I could be of assistance to you." Cara progressed cautiously, not sure what lay ahead and trying to watch her step.

The other woman gave a start on hearing Cara's name, as though she hadn't paid much attention to the card. She looked Cara up and down.

"Everyone is talking about how you have returned to London. You're so brave to come back, after . . . ." She gestured futilely with her hands, before dropping one to her hip, and pressing the other to her forehead.

Cara arched an eyebrow.

What's that supposed to mean? Is it solidarity, or is she about to die of embarrassment that I might be seen here?

"I think Lord Clayton is the brave one, if he ever dares come near me again."

The other woman's eyes widened. Cara wondered if Isobel knew of her tendency for roaming the streets with her pistols for company.

"Yes, well, good for you. Shows them at least one of us has teeth." Isobel ran a hand down the purple drapes, flicking at invisible dust spots.

Solidarity, then.

"I find myself in an awkward situation. And I cannot turn to my family for help." The young woman abandoned the curtains to torment the folds of her skirt, wrapping the fabric around her finger and pulling tightly. Her digit turned the same shade of purple as the enveloping taffeta.

Cara waited for Isobel to continue.

"I have written some rather foolish letters to a young man, which I want back. I believe you may be able to assist in retrieving them?" Hopeful expectation flushed her face.

"I require the gentleman's name?" Cara probed as politely as possible; this wasn't really her calling, but a part of her said the simple task was easy money. How hard could it be to play postman?

Particularly if Nathaniel delivers—

"Joshua. Joshua Denver. He lives in Whitechapel. He works as pit crew at one of the airship hangars." She released the skirt and turned her attention to fluffing up the already oversized cushions. "I have asked. Repeatedly. But he is refusing to hand them over. Naughty boy."

The way Isobel breathed *naughty boy* spoke volumes. Cara resisted the urge to raise her eyebrows and mutter *tut tut*. Now she wondered what was in the letters.

My money is on Isobel writing something rather saucy to naughty Josh.

"I have a fiancé now, you see." She blurted out the words, unnerved by Cara's continued silence. "And it wouldn't do for him to know the intimate details of my friendship with Joshua. I was so much younger, and impetuous. I did things without fully thinking through the consequences." Isobel wasn't one to hold anything back, apparently.

"Of course," Cara murmured.

So she slept with Joshua, but wants the fiancé to think he is buying a pristine product.

"It shouldn't take too long to have the correspondence back in your hands." Given Joshua worked at the docks, she could probably have the letters by dinnertime. Or, she could let Isobel stew over how foolish she had been for a bit longer.

Isobel let out a sigh of relief, no doubt glad to hand over the recovery of her dirty laundry to someone with an equally grubby past. Her family, and more importantly, society, would remain none the wiser of her behaviour. She resumed darting around the room, straightening pillows she encountered in her path.

Isobel needs to get out more, she's all pent-up energy.

"Is it true? About these girls being killed? Jennifer, and now Abigail?" She pummelled a delicate throw pillow before dropping it back on the sofa.

Cara frowned at the abrupt change in the topic of conversation. "Yes. Though I'm sure the Enforcers have it well in hand."

She omitted to mention Inspector Fraser believed she was central to the unfolding tragedy, and through her, linked Lord Devon's death to the other two. God help her if that titbit ever got out. Society would erupt in a frenzy more spectacular than a warehouse of Chinese fireworks hit by lightning.

Isobel dropped on top of the freshly plumped pillow. She looked younger; her eyes brimmed with tears. "I'm so worried—"

Emotion spilled over and she sobbed into her hands; large heart-felt tears rolled down her face and escaped between her fingers.

Cara looked around, hoping someone would spring to the rescue, perhaps a pink-clad knight lurking amongst the gay wallpaper. She had no experience of tearful women, and Isobel didn't look the type to respond to a punch in the shoulder and being told to buck up.

She decided on a more diplomatic approach.

"Whatever is the matter?" Her brain screamed at her, *don't ask and don't get involved.* If only she knew, when she held out her hand for the small package Nathaniel needed delivering, she was stepping into an infinite vortex that would keep sucking her down.

Isobel extracted a handkerchief from within her bodice and blew her nose loudly in a key that would make any trumpet player proud.

"She's run away!" She sniffed.

The hair on the back of Cara's neck prickled in warning. "Who? You need to give me a bit more detail, if I'm going to be of any help to you."

Another heartfelt sob and blow into the handkerchief, which was doing a sterling job, all things considered. "It's my friend, Beth. I'm sure she's just done something stupid. But she's been gone since yesterday. She swore me to secrecy. And then, the newspaper article today—" Her fingers clutched the brave hanky as it withstood another onslaught. "I'm ever so worried."

God, I hope I've got an alibi, if this goes where I think it's heading.

"Was she seeing anyone?" Cara wondered how to get herself out of the rabbit hole she appeared to be wedged in.

Isobel nodded with sufficient force to dislodge the soft bun at the back of her head, tendrils of blonde hair tumbled around her ears. "She wouldn't say who. He was ever so secretive. That's why I'm sure they've just run off for a week of passion and fun before settling down. We all do it, don't we?"

She tried to laugh, but it rang hollow.

"Isobel, what's Beth's full name?"

"Beth Armstrong. And she's not a high-ranking noble. Her father is only landed gentry, and they say the killer is only after peers, so I'm sure she's all right." She tried to convince herself, but didn't do a very good job of it.

Cara had no words of comfort to offer. "First things first, I can certainly retrieve your letters for you. And I'll put word out about Beth. Let's see if we can find her naked and covered in honey with her lover in some pub in Cheapside."

She tried to cheer the other woman up and was rewarded with a weak smile.

"Covered in honey," Isobel repeated with a breathy sigh.

I think I have an inkling of what's in those letters now.

"Thank you." Isobel pressed Cara's hands to her bosom before wiping away her tears and pinning her escaped hair.

Once again, Cara was out on the street with information ricocheting around her brain. Where to turn? Nathaniel or Inspector Fraser? Certainly Nathaniel would be able to lay his hands on the missing letters; that was a simple matter, and probably what Countess de Sal intended. But what to do about the missing girl? How was she caught up in this?

Maybe I should just jump an airship and leave this mess for Fraser to sort out. But that would mean running. Again.

She wandered down the road, mulling over her options. Her gaze caught the unmistakeable hulking mass and dark blue uniform of an Enforcer. Fate provided at least one solution, and Cara bee lined for him.

"Can you get a message to Inspector Fraser?" She accosted him before she had a chance to change her mind.

He looked around behind him, unsure whether she was addressing him or not.

Lordy, they must employ them based on mass, not intelligence.

She snapped her fingers in front of his face to attract his attention back to her. "Inspector Fraser? Can you contact him?"

He nodded slowly. "Yes, ma'am. I can. We have an aethergraph in the wagon." He gestured to the steam-powered carriage idling at the end of the street.

"Good. Tell him to meet Cara Devon as soon as possible, in Trafalgar Square, by the monument." She gave him a push in the direction of the wagon and headed off. Trafalgar Square sat halfway between her current location and the Enforcers' headquarters. If the uniformed Neanderthal lurched into action, and passed along the message promptly, Fraser shouldn't be too far behind her.

The large square held as many people as pigeons. Both species rushed about their business, congregated in groups, and squawked when surprised from behind. Cara threaded her way to Nelson's Column and sat on the stone step. Nelson kept watch on the horizon far above her head. She toyed with passing the time by chewing her fingernails, but suspected if she ever started the nervous habit she wouldn't be able to stop.

"Miss Devon? You're obviously still in London."

"You told me I couldn't leave. Or did you think I would slip aboard one of Lyons' airships?" She turned to face Fraser, the sun ringing him from behind, caused her to raise a hand to shelter her eyes.

"Well, I appreciate you didn't take the opportunity. I have heard you've been seen out with Viscount Lyons. I would caution you about him, but I suspect you didn't ask to see me urgently to discuss your social calendar?"

"No." She chewed her lip, wondering how much Fraser knew about Nathaniel. "You have a problem, and I suspect it's about to get bigger."

He arched an eyebrow at her; his eyes burned with curiosity behind the glass lenses. He seated himself next to her, so she no longer had to squint, but ensured he was not so close he would encroach on her personal space.

"Oh?" Another polite noise.

"I have learned of another missing girl. Beth Armstrong. Her father is landed gentry, not a peer. But—" She couldn't explain the way the hairs rose on the back of her neck when Isobel mentioned her missing friend.

"But?" Fraser removed his specs and extracted a small cloth from his pocket. He busied himself cleaning the lenses while she gathered her thoughts.

Cara exhaled slowly. "It's too similar to Jennifer and Abigail to dismiss. She was seeing someone new, someone secretive, and now she's up and vanished. Her friend thought she had run off for a week or two of pleasure. But, with the news of Abigail's death hitting the streets, she's not so sure."

"Ah." He replaced the cloth and hooked the ends of the frames around his ears. He was keeping up an excellent line of non-committal, monosyllabic noises.

"And after our conversation yesterday, I don't want this one pinned on me."

He laughed. "Perhaps I might conclude you are trying to throw me off the scent by delivering this information."

She shot him a look; she didn't see the humour in his comment. Perhaps she should up and leave.

"When was the young lady last seen?"

"Yesterday. The information was passed to me today. Her friend is worried about the similarities."

He stood. "Thank you, Miss Devon. I'll start enquiring as to the young lady's whereabouts. Let's hope she is found safe, but slightly embarrassed."

He gave her a polite bow and headed back across the square.

CHAPTER 11

THIS *one had taken him longer. She was jumpy and suspicious. He had needed many days to orchestrate the accidental meetings. The gentle brushing of their hands in bookshops and cafes. He hunted her like a cat stalking its prey. Silently, patiently. He knew he had won when her breath hitched when she saw him. Her heart fluttered, in anticipation of his touch. She leaned into his caress.*

Getting her away from the watchful eyes of her family had taken planning. The ton was shutting down, daughters under strict parental supervision, as fear rippled through the upper classes. They didn't understand his work. They didn't understand what he sought. Their minds were too small to comprehend him. Their fear wasn't their fault; they were simply inferior. He would be benevolent when he ascended, when he held their small lives in the palm of his hand.

This little one knew. She understood. She crept out her bedroom window in the heart of darkness. Knowing he would catch her. She ran to him. She was the one. He knew it deep inside. He tried to contain his excitement.

"Nefertiti," he murmured, brushing her hair away from her face. "Love me once more. Make me immortal."

Black, terrified eyes stared back at him, the whites in vivid contrast to the wide pupils. Her head shook violently from side to side, rubbing against the restraint over her forehead. She made little mewling noises against the mouth gag and a single tear welled up and rolled from her eye.

His hand reached out to the small, wheeled trolley. He picked up the key, and lovingly stroked the length of its shaft. He raised the object to his lips and kissed the cold brass reverently, before replacing the key on the trolley amongst gleaming surgical blades.

His hand reached for the bottle, which he held up to the light. The glass was a dark amber colour, making the contents look like mead for the gods. He unstopped the bottle and held the cloth over the neck. He tipped the bottle over and back, before quickly replacing the cork.

He draped the cloth over her mouth and nose. She flailed back and forth, making gurgling noises against the cloth biting into the sides of her mouth. Tears streamed from her eyes, ran down her temples, and disappeared into her hair. The tang of urine hit his nostrils, as she lost control of her bladder. Her desperate protest became weaker and fainter and then stopped altogether.

"I know you're excited, little one." He stroked her cheek, removing the tears, wiping away the stains with the cloth. "Soon we will be together, as we were meant to be."

Dropping the cloth onto the trolley, he picked up a stethoscope. He inserted the earpieces and pressed the trumpet end to her skin. He listened, and made minute movements with the instrument, until he found the right spot. With a pen, he made a mark on her chest. He worked quickly and efficiently, as he sliced through flesh and muscle with the scalpel. The necessary incision was only a small one, but its placement was pivotal. He cut deeper, revealing the ribs he needed to avoid. He took up the key and guided the slender shaft into the incision, turning the blade so the teeth fitted through the gap. Closing his eyes, he let sensation guide him. The gentle pulse of her heart resonated along the key's shaft when nestled close to its objective. He smiled; the two were in perfect unison with each other, beating as one.

Breathing a sigh of relief, he closed the wound with small, delicate stitches. He knew women were particular about their appearance and he wanted the scar to be as small as possible. He didn't want her to fret about an unsightly mark on her body.

The waiting was the hardest part. He occupied himself by tidying away the bloody cloths used during the procedure. He cleaned her body, wiping her limbs clear of the waste evacuated in her excitement. He dressed her in the simple linen shift she always favoured in the dry heat of Egypt. The gossamer fabric bunched around her leg restraints. He carefully drew the bow of the key through a small cut in the fabric. She was perfect, like a porcelain automaton, waiting for him to turn the key and awaken her.

The sun was well past its zenith by the time Cara went in search of Nathaniel. She had changed clothes and grabbed her pistols. Drawn by the scent of danger around him, she exercised caution by donning the matched handguns, her definition of carrying protection. She hadn't seen him since running from his study a few days previously and was unsure of her reception.

His Mayfair house sat devoid of his presence. His staff informed her he was working at the docks. With a growing sense of agitation, she headed back to the main road and hailed a hansom cab. Her journey took her past an enormous hole in the ground, as though London suffered an attack by a monstrous mole. Workers laboured in the earth to build the new underground railway transport system far beneath the streets.

Cara alighted at Tower Hill and walked the remaining distance to the Lyons hangars. An airship tethered to the dock rocked as the mechanical claw removed the last of her cargo and dropped it onto the waiting trolleys. Cara paused at the edge of his territory, watching the well-oiled bustle of activity. One hand fingered a pistol on her hip, before she dropped her coat back into place, and moved closer. She spotted the ever-vigilant Jackson leaning against a stone wall, smoking a cigarette. He flicked the stub into the gutter with his good hand as she approached.

"I don't know what you've been up to, darling," he called out as she neared.

"Why?" She halted, and noticed he no longer wore a bandage on his hand. An angry scar showed where her bullet went through his palm, but he didn't appear to have suffered any permanent damage.

"He's been like a bear with a sore head the last few days. He's in his office at the back of the hangar, but tread lightly." He headed down the path to the airship.

A stone settled into Cara's gut and the constant fear climbed on top of it.

What the heck am I doing? Maybe it is time to get out of London. I could leave the solicitor to collect the artifacts, if I trusted him with the job.

She stepped into the dimly lit hangar. Scents from around the world flooded her nostrils while she waited for her eyes to adjust to the interior. She inhaled lemon grass, curry, and chilli. She could recognise them all from her travels, each one bringing back distinct memories of times spent in China, India, and America.

Boxes, crates, and urns of marvellous shapes and sizes were stacked in row after row, awaiting either delivery or dispatch. Men laboured back and forth, their efforts reducing some rows and enlarging others. Keeping out of the way of busy workers lumbering in exoskeletons and the fast-moving mechanised carts, she made her way to the office at the back of the hangar. From inside, lights blazed through the glass on the top half of the windows. Wooden shutters covered the bottom half, and the light contorted into silvers to escape the confines. The shutters obscured the office's occupants, though Cara could hear muted conversation through the wall.

She tapped lightly on the closed door.

"Come," an unfamiliar voice barked.

She slipped through the door and pressed it shut behind her.

Nathaniel stretched back in his chair, his long, booted legs propped up on the desk. His cream shirt lay unlaced to half way down his chest, and the exposed tanned skin drew Cara's eyes. In one hand, he held a cigar; in the other, a glass of brandy. Opposite him lounged his pirate captain, his hands similarly occupied with cigar and brandy. They exuded the casual camaraderie of old friends, catching up on events since their last meeting.

"Why, if it isn't your bollard bird," the pirate commented to Nathaniel.

"Cara." Nathaniel dragged on his cigar, tilting his head back to blow smoke at the ceiling. "I thought you were busy with Inspector Fraser today."

"Are you following him or me?" Annoyance briefly flared in her face. She thought herself adept at losing the tails Nathaniel put on her. He very seldom sent Jackson now, changing faces to try to throw her off what he was doing. Though, Cara was confident he still hadn't succeeded in discovering her new residence.

"I've learned the wisdom in keeping track of the inspector's movements. You're proving a more challenging prospect." Another draw on the cigar; smoke circled the high ceiling from the two men.

The pirate laughed at some private joke. He had sandy brown hair draped around his face, and piercing black eyes set in a tanned angular face. Stretched out beside her, his body was long and lean, like his face.

Nathaniel waved his brandy in the pirate's direction. "This is an old acquaintance, Captain Lachlan Hawke."

Fitting—a bird of prey, raider of the skies.

He rose and took her hand. She pushed down the urge to panic. Even though her body started to relish Nathaniel touching her, this was someone unknown. Her brain screamed a danger warning and she stiffened as he kissed her skin.

"Loki, to my friends." He released her hand, watching her reaction as he sank back into his chair. A waft of salty air drifted over her, tangy and pleasant, making her think of sitting by the ocean, with the sun warming her back.

A smile came unbidden to her face, as her body relaxed. "Loki? God of mischief? I think I might like you."

He gave her a dark wink.

She swung her attention back to Nathaniel and promptly wanted to drown in his eyes. A crystal, clear blue today, they invited her to immerse herself and let him wash over her. With a sigh, she tried to drop her eyes downward, and ended up fixated on his lips. She remembered how they travelled down her neck to the base of her throat, sending ripples of pleasure through her body.

He coughed and Cara blinked. She resisted the strong urge to pummel her fist into her forehead.

I need a better distraction. Whatever I'm doing, it's not working.

"Joshua Denver," she blurted.

Nathaniel's face remained impassive. "And the relevance of this gentleman is . . . ?"

Oh, hell.

"He has some rather intimate letters from one Isobel Johnson. The young lady is rather anxious to have them back. The young man is not co-operating. Countess de Sal thought you could help and asked me to act as go-between." The words came out rushed and garbled, but she managed to get the message across.

Nathaniel sat silent for a measured moment. "I'll send word out. It won't take long to track them down. She'll have then back within a day or two."

"Thank you. He works at one of the hangars, so he shouldn't be too hard to find." Cara flicked her gaze back and forth; two sets of predatory eyes watched her intently. Her brain advised her the time had come to get the hell out, before she ended up as dinner, being fought over like a downed zebra with a couple of lions hanging off her rump, intent on ripping out her entrails. She backed toward the door.

"Care for some entertainment this afternoon?" Nathaniel changed the subject and halted her backward movement.

Curiosity flared within her. She swallowed, wondering if he was going to suggest something involving all three of them.

"I've had enough paperwork for the day. Loki and I were about to head downstairs to the Pit. We thought a spot of sparring would burn off some energy. Are you game enough to join us?"

She cast her gaze from Nathaniel to his captain, sure that there was some undertone at play, but not able to place her finger on it. She brushed her coat aside and unconsciously rested her hand on the pistol butt. She traced the design carved into the ivory with a finger, while she turned the prospect over in her mind.

"You did say you could box?" Nathaniel placed his empty glass on the desk and scrunched the cigar into an ashtray, waiting for her reply.

Maybe that's what I need. To beat something and burn this distracting taint out of my blood.

"All right. It's been awhile, but I'm game to go a few rounds."

He nodded and shared a look with Hawke, before the two men rose from their places. Nathaniel led off, while Cara followed. At the back of the hangar, Nathaniel pulled on a shelf of small boxes. The shelf swung outward, revealing a dark and narrow staircase. Hawke and Jackson trailed them.

Far beneath the ground, the small stone hallway opened into a large and softly lit room.

She understood why they referred to it as the Pit. Large carved blocks of stone fashioned the walls. Given how deep they were under the ground, she suspected the room was completely soundproof. The electric lights gave off a muted glow behind their heavy glass coverings. Tiny iron bars covered the glass and Cara wondered what happened in the room, that the lights needed protecting. A large, square, black padded mat dominated the middle of the room. The walls of the room held aloft swords, daggers, and staves. Weapons or instruments of torture were used as decoration in nearly every available space.

The wall opposite the entrance contained a double steel door. The already imposing frame bore multiple rivets from the attachment of extra layers of steel. Two large bolts at top and bottom secured the doors to each other. Two equally large padlocks secured whatever lay behind.

Given the Pit was far below ground, hidden behind a secret staircase and already soundproof, Cara could only imagine what lay behind the reinforced door. Her curiosity finally found a line it refused to cross. The chill down her spine told her she didn't want to know what the door hid.

Punching bags hung from the ceiling in one corner. Four of Nathaniel's men either sparred or watched. She headed to a wall with a gleaming wooden bench and a row of coat hooks. She quickly removed her jacket and unslung her gun holsters, hanging them above the bench. The men turned to watch the impromptu striptease. She saw raised eyebrows as she unlaced her corset and draped it over the bench. Raised eyebrows turned to slack jaws, as she pulled her shirt loose, and undid the bottom few buttons. Grasping the two ends, she slid the fabric up her back, before tying it tightly beneath her breasts, exposing her midriff.

Jackson approached her with a roll of white cotton, and methodically bandaged her wrists and hands to protect against repetitive blows. She flexed her fingers and took a couple of jabs. She rotated her neck, wondering who she would be fighting, as she moved onto the mat.

One of the smaller men—

She gulped. Nathaniel had stripped to the waist. Her eyes widened, and her gaze roamed all over his naked torso. She drank up the hard flesh, finely etched abdominal muscles, and faint lines of long faded scars. A jagged, angry stripe looked recent, as if a knife grazed his ribs not too long ago. A thin line of dark hair ran downward from his belly-button and vanished into the top of his trousers. It took a monumental effort to drag her eyes up to his face. The ghost of a smile lingered over his lips at her intense examination.

"When you're ready." He raised an eyebrow.

He's going to drive me loonier than de Sal if I don't clear my head soon.

They circled each other on the large mat. Cara gave a couple of loose jabs at his head. He didn't even bother to defend, leaning away from her blows. She hadn't been serious, only judging his reactions, testing him. She didn't take long to ascertain he wouldn't strike at her; he only defended. She put more effort into each jab and uppercut, determined to make him react. He blocked efficiently, and she couldn't lay a hand on him. He batted her away as if she were a dragonfly hovering around his head.

They sparred for several minutes. Nathaniel absorbed each blow she threw, while Cara tried to clear her mind by achieving exhaustion. It didn't work. She bounced on her toes, thinking.

Time for the unexpected.

She spun and delivered a roundhouse kick to his torso. He blocked and rocked back, the power of her kick far greater than anything she could deliver with her fists.

His eyes narrowed as he reassessed her. An approving roar went up from his men present.

Their support buoyed Cara. Another lightning kick and she knocked him back again. A slow smile spread over her face. She might be a woman, but she knew a few things about using her legs.

Now Nathaniel worked harder, her blows more fierce than he anticipated. She alternated her jabs and uppercuts with front kicks. The moves faster, she was determined to show him what she was capable of, before she burnt through all her energy.

Another kick and he pushed past her leg, and then lunged as she spun past. He grabbed her, and pulled her tightly to him.

"I think it's time to end this. I don't think it would do for my men to see you defeat me, or to even entertain the idea that defeat might be possible." His breath was hot behind her ear, his arm wrapped around her stomach, with a large hand spanning her naked flesh. His hard body pressed into her from behind, and a thrill shot through her at the strength of his hold. His thumb brushed the underside of one breast, making her bite her lip to stifle a groan.

He let her go. Jackson threw his shirt at him. Nathaniel shrugged on the garment while regarding her. "Well played. Perhaps I would place money on you."

His face was impassive, but his eyes devoured her. "Have dinner with me tonight. I'll take you to Bonnui." He threw out the name of the most exclusive dining establishment in London.

She wrinkled her nose. "No, thank you."

He arched an eyebrow. "Other women would be ecstatic to go there, to be seen. Would you rather go for a pint of ale, and to watch some sport in the East End or Whitechapel?"

Interest sparked in her face. "Yes. I wouldn't have to wear a fancy dress or worry about being snubbed by the other women."

Hawke burst out laughing. "If it's a lowbrow adventure with this little one, I'm definitely joining in."

Cara's eyes roamed the room, taking in the ever-watchful men. Their numbers had swollen while she and Nathaniel sparred. The air seemed stifling, hot, and sweaty, making her suck in every dry breath, the atmosphere charged, like before an electrical storm. The image of lions on the zebra fled her mind, replaced by a hungry pack of hyenas, with eyes glowing yellow in the dim light. She realised how deep she was in over her head, in a hidden room, surrounded by ravenous predators.

She pulled an edge of bandage and began to unwrap her hand, rolling the cotton as she went, buying herself time to think through her predicament. "No, thank you, I have other plans for this evening. Another time, perhaps."

Hawke elbowed Nathaniel. "She said no to you."

"She does that a lot." He kept his position by her side as she finished rolling the bandage and tossed the bundle to Jackson to put away.

A commotion from the hallway caught their attention. She glanced up to see two miserable-looking men pushed through the door. With their arms tied behind their backs, and unable to put a hand out, they fell hard onto the stone floor. A group of men piled in behind them. Picked up roughly by their forearms, the pair of bound men were dragged to the middle of the room, rudely deposited on the mat, and forced to their knees. The pack scented fear in the air; men circled the two unfortunates. Tension rolled around the room, while they waited for a cue from their leader.

"Cara," Nathaniel breathed her name quietly. Her wide eyes flicked to him. "Gather your things and go upstairs, use my office to get dressed."

With one finger under her chin he kissed her lightly, his lips brushed against hers in a brief taste before he released her. "Go, now."

For once in her life, Cara fully intended to obey a command. She swallowed and complied, quickly skirting the growing crowd.

Nathaniel rolled up his shirtsleeves and walked to the middle of the room, Hawke at his shoulder. One of the downed men started sobbing, his tears falling onto Nathaniel's polished boot. The other whimpered *I'm sorry* over and over in a chilling litany.

Ice water ran down Cara's spine. Grabbing her pistols and the remainder of her clothing, she headed for the exit. She didn't run, in case she caught their attention, but adrenaline pumped through her legs, ready to be utilised in an instance if necessary.

Hitting the corridor, she heard a cry go up from those assembled. The hyenas bayed for blood, moments before tearing their prey to shreds.

Thursday, July 11

HE struggled to contain his anticipation as he went about his business. Interacting with people, he carefully hid his emotions behind a mask, until the moment he could return to her side. She needed time to gather her strength.

Two days had passed, and now he could interrupt her slumber. He stopped the slow drip of chloroform. He stroked her forehead. "Everything is all right. You're safe with me."

She stirred, disoriented, and turned her head. Relief written in every pore, she believed his words, until she locked eyes with him and knew the truth. He caressed the key.

"We'll be together for eternity. I'll not lose you this time, Nefertiti." He twisted the bow, once, twice, three times.

Her body arched up off the table; only the restraints held her in place. Her eyes widened, blackness wiped over them. The sob in the back of her throat changed to small gasps; the convulsions timed with the cries until she dropped back to the table.

He undid the restraints. His fingers were clumsy with his eagerness as he freed her. He called her name, waiting for her to sit up and greet him as her *lover. His brow furrowed. Why didn't she sit up? He shook her shoulder and called her name.*

Brushing away the hair from her eyes, he looked into the face of his love. Empty black eyes stared back at him.

"No!" He screamed his rage at the stone walls.

Friday, July 12

Despite the bright sunshine, fresh breeze, and cheerful company, Cara's thoughts dwelled in a dark, underground pit with hot, dry air and a naked torso her fingers kept reaching out to trace. She shuddered at the pack mentality of Nathaniel's men. She knew she courted danger, but for the first time, menace took a visible form and threatened to touch her. Nathaniel had sent her from the room before peril wrapped around her. The logical part of her brain urged her to flee before she got burnt, and another part wanted to move closer and embrace the heat.

Amy tucked Cara's hand under her arm, physically pulling her thoughts back to her present location. "I've missed having you to talk to."

"I'm sorry, I'm not very good company these days." She tapped the side of her head. "Too much going on in here. Everybody seems to be talking at once." She offered an apologetic smile and tried to concentrate on Amy's monologue about her wedding dress fittings and the finer details of cake decoration. Although her friend omitted all mention of her fiancé's name.

They strolled along the tree-lined paths next to the Serpentine in Hyde Park. Nannies pushed prams with enormous rubber tyres and spring suspension, to give a cushioned ride to slumbering infants. Other children rattled past in the new mechanical prams, clockwork movements powering the light, steel wheels. Governesses puffed to keep apace of the fast-moving buggies containing their charges. Cara liked the park with its ancient trees. It reminded her of her grandmother's estate and childhood summers spent running barefoot through fields, or catching tadpoles in the lake.

A young man hurried along the path toward them, halting a few paces away, to tug off his pork pie. "Pardon, miss, but I have a message for you."

"Yes?" Cara had a pretty good idea who the message was from. "Miguel, isn't it?"

She was learning the faces and names of Nathaniel's men. Knowing the identity of who followed her made them easier to spot in a crowd. Two could play the intelligence game, and she did not intend to let Nathaniel gain the upper hand.

He tugged his cap again. "He has those letters you were wanting, if you are free?"

He gestured across the road, to where the carriage sat on Exhibition Road. With its blackened windows, no one could see inside. The mechanical horses gleamed in the sunlight, like precious objects created by some bizarre jeweller rather than a mechanic.

A chill shot down her body, as she wondered what became of the two men she encountered in the Pit. *I'm playing with fire while dousing myself in kerosene.*

"I won't be long, Amy. Why don't you go ahead and order us tea?" She gestured in the direction of the outdoor tea stand, their ultimate destination.

Amy hesitated and cast her friend a worried look.

"I'll be fine." Cara reassured her and gave her a gentle push. "Order sandwiches, I'm famished."

Amy laughed. "You're always hungry," she said, before strolling away.

Cara followed Miguel across the road. He held the carriage door open for her. Picking up her skirts, she stepped in, and took the seat opposite Nathaniel. His legs sprawled, his physical presence and personality dominated the small interior.

He held up a bunch of letters, secured with a bright pink satin and lace garter. "Rather racy. No wonder she wants them back. They would fetch good money if she submitted them to a gentleman's magazine."

"You read them?" It hadn't occurred to Cara that Isobel's correspondence would be open to his scrutiny. Although, she had promised herself a tiny peek, just to confirm her suspicion about the contents. She rationalised the difference: she was a woman and would understand Isobel's emotional outpouring. Nathaniel would be looking for the business angle.

"Of course. The young man had intended to use them for blackmail, and I like to keep abreast of such things. Aren't you just a little bit curious?" He waved the package back and forth.

She bit her lip. Curiosity seemed to be getting her into a lot of trouble. Maybe the time had come to curb her meddling. Perhaps a better way to keep occupied would be to take up knitting or needlepoint.

"There's a particularly fascinating letter involving a swing, and a rather enthusiastic description of the young man's appendage, that is my personal favourite. Although I think Isobel engages in rampant poetic license in her writing." He levelled his eyes at her and a slow thrum pulsed through her body. "I could read the passage to you, if you'd like to offer your opinion?"

She held out her hand. "Thank you, but I don't need to know the intimate details. I'll drop them back to her today. I'm sure it will be a weight off her mind to have them returned."

He raised the letters higher, out of her reach. The tiniest smile twitched the corner of his mouth. "Two things. Firstly, tell the young lady she owes me a favour, to be repaid at my convenience."

"All right." She had expected some such arrangement from him. "What's the second thing?" Her heart crashed against the lining of her corset, waiting for the expected answer. He patted the seat next to him. Cara hesitated, knowing what he would demand. She made up her mind before changing sides, unable to speak with the blood pounding in her ears.

With his free hand, he reached out and cupped her neck, pulling her toward him. There was no gentle prelude or teasing. He crushed her mouth. His teeth nipped her lips before his tongue drove into her mouth, seeking her out, giving her nowhere to hide. She couldn't even gasp as he sucked the very air from her lungs; her breath became his. His tongue slid over hers as he explored her mouth. When he released her, she collapsed against the side of the carriage. Her eyes closed as she caught her breath, her pulse rampaged under her skin. Once under control, she opened her lids to meet his pale gaze.

"The letters?" She held out her hand. The air crackled and sizzled between them.

He handed the small bundle over. "I enjoy doing business with you, *cara mia*." He turned her name into an Italian caress as his eyes lingered on her heaving breasts, highlighted and displayed by the cut of her corset.

She tucked the letters into her satchel and tried to appear business-like, while her fingers struggled to obey simple commands like *do up the damned buckle.*

"I get the feeling you don't trust Loki." He changed the topic abruptly.

Cara's head shot up and a frown creased her forehead. "I don't know him well enough to make that judgement. But my gut tells me not to trust the two of you together."

She compared them to plotting schoolboys, about to dip a girl's plaits in an inkwell, except, they were far more dangerous, and exhilarating.

"We have shared a woman before. But I have no intentions of sharing you." He held her gaze as his tongue ran over his lips.

Something deep inside Cara tugged and stirred.

"Is that supposed to reassure me?" A thrill shot through her body, regardless of what her mouth said.

He kept her eyes captured, holding her in thrall. "He's a friend. Come out with us."

"No," she managed to whisper. "What happened in the Pit the other night?"

His eyes flicked down briefly, releasing her. "Consequences."

"Care to elaborate a little more?"

He shrugged and stretched, a feline lethalness in the movement. "My business dealings aren't always as pleasurable as this."

She was in deep water again, treading to keep her head from disappearing under a wave. "I have to go. My friend is waiting for me."

He kissed her hand before releasing her.

Cara stood on the path watching the glittering horses leave. Part of her brain screamed, *yield!* The other half yelled, *run!* Neither was winning. Not yet. She shook the thoughts from her body like a dog shaking off water after a bath, before striking down the path.

Amy had commandeered a table under the dappled shade of a horizontal elm.

Cara brushed the swallowtail of her corset aside, before dropping into her chair. She closed her eyes and leaned back. A gentle breeze stirred the leaves and refreshed the languid summer air around them.

"Do you want a lecture about the dangerous path you are on?" Amy's voice came from the other side of the table, accompanied by the clinking of china.

"No." Cara was doing just fine lecturing herself.

"Then drink your tea."

Her lids flew open and with a grin, she reached out for her teacup and a delicate cucumber sandwich. "I missed you. This. Having a friend."

Amy flushed. "Then don't you dare disappear for seven years again, or I might have to track you down."

Cara took a bite of the crustless sandwich. "Did you know them? Jennifer and Abigail, the two murdered girls?"

"Oh yes. We were often at the same parties. Jennifer was big game hunting, Abigail completely different. She only ever had the one suitor, and she seemed devoted to him, though he was rather dull." Amy picked over the delicacies, before selecting one to add to her plate.

"Were they friends?" She pushed for more information, trying to see the connection between them. She vaguely knew Jennifer, but had never met Abigail. *What does Fraser see, drawing us together?*

"Not that I ever saw. What is your interest?" Amy paused and looked at her friend. "You're starting to sound like that Enforcer."

She shrugged. "Speculating, that's all. I've been away for so long; I don't know who the players are anymore." She turned the conversation to the other girls they had played with as children, and Amy updated her on who was married and who had been shelved.

Afternoon tea finished, they decided to walk the edge of the lake before parting company. An angelic-looking man approached them. He was tall and slender, with soft, dark blond curls falling around his oval face and framing pale amber eyes. He quickly doffed his top hat and licked his lips several times. His Adam's apple bobbed up and down under his cravat.

"Miss Devon?" He stuttered over her name.

"Yes." Cara eyed him; he didn't look like any of Nathaniel's men, he had none of their brashness about him. Rather, an aura of bookish innocence clung to him.

"I'm Weaver. Weaver Clayton."

Cara recoiled as though struck. Involuntarily, she reached out and grabbed Amy's arm.

He held out a hand, as though to stop her from running away. "I'll only take a moment of your time, Miss Devon."

Cara glared at the young Lord Clayton, failing to see how he could have anything to say that would be of interest to her. "Say your piece quickly, Lord Clayton, I have no tolerance for your family."

Weaver shuffled from foot to foot and swallowed compulsively. "I wanted to apologise."

Cara's eyebrows shot up.

He has to be kidding.

No apology could ever make up for what his father did to her.

"Not for that," his words tumbled out, as though hearing her inner thoughts. "What my father did is beyond redemption, and he will have to reckon for his crime in the underworld. I wanted to apologise for not being home from Oxford that week."

"I'm not following your point."

"I believe if I had been home, I could have stopped what occurred. I owe you an apology for not being there, to save you." His large amber eyes darted around the park, as though expecting someone to intervene.

She cocked her head; no one had ever apologised for failing to help her. On the contrary, they looked at her as though she were culpable. He showed a certain amount of bravery in coming forward and approaching her.

"Thank you. You're the first person to ever say that." She meant it; for his part, he looked genuine.

The young man gave her a shy smile. "Thank you for listening to me. I have wanted to apologise for a long time. I'll leave you in peace." He nodded and replaced his top hat, before turning, and heading back down the path.

"Well," Amy said, confusion written all over her face. "What do you make of that?"

Cara let out a breath. "Gutsy move. If I had my Smith & Wesson handy, I would have shot him on the spot."

"You're unarmed?" Amy teased.

Cara laughed and patted her thigh. "Derringer. Damned nuisance to reach, though."

"Well, since you can control your itchy trigger finger, you are definitely coming to dinner with me tomorrow night. It's only a small gathering and you need to dip your toe back into the social pond."

"No, I don't." She was distracted and Amy saw an opening.

Amy pouted. "Well, come for me, then. John is busy working and the Ambrose family have acquired an Egyptian princess who I am dying to meet. And I simply cannot go alone."

Cara resisted the urge to wail, *but I don't want to*. And possibly stamp her foot, for good measure.

"It's a small, intimate gathering. You'll be fine. And did I mention I will just die if I miss out?" Amy pleaded.

Cara laughed at her friend. "All right, I'll go. I guess I can't have your death on my conscience."

CHAPTER 13

Saturday, July 13

I hate you, wardrobe. But here is what's going to happen. I will close the doors, say a magic word, open the doors, and you will present me with a suitable evening gown.

Cara shut the door and leaned her forehead against the dark polished walnut. "Work, dammit."

She flung open the doors, and stared at the same two dresses. The blue and brown striped, taffeta day outfit and the deep teal, velvet gown Nathaniel provided the night she dined with him.

I wonder if I was supposed to return that? Too bad.

She pulled the teal gown off its hanger and threw it onto the end of the bed. Formal clothes without an extra pair of hands became a personal battlefield. She struggled with the corset laces and the yards of fabric in the skirt and train. Eventually, she managed to encase her body to her satisfaction, which meant there were no obvious draughts. She would leave it to Amy to tighten and fasten everything on the way to dinner.

A short time later, she sat in the carriage, her back to Amy, as her friend laced her corset tighter and tackled the tiny black buttons holding the dress together. One-sided conversation washed over her, while she tried to figure out how the last few weeks had gone so catastrophically off course.

She had planned to be in London for a week, at most. Collect her father's artifacts, dump them with someone to sell and *bam,* be gone. Instead, she was drawn into a bizarre business deal with a viscount, in which he bartered for the right to touch her. Enforcers were circling her, thinking she was central to their investigation of three deaths. She had been corralled into helping noblewomen with their seedy problems by chasing a trail of little cream visiting cards. And now, she was laced into a gown to attend an evening soiree with a bunch of toffs she couldn't stand, all so her childhood friend wouldn't expire.

"Don't even think of escaping," Amy said from behind her.

"How do you know what I'm thinking?"

"You're twitching all over the place and your hand is edging to the carriage door." Amy tackled the last button and declared her friend fit for company. "Plus, I was your friend for fourteen years, before you disappeared. I learned a thing or two about you in that time."

Amy dropped a gossamer-thin wool shawl over her shoulders.

"For example, I know you are poking your tongue out at me."

From Cara's bolt-hole in Soho, they detoured to Isobel Johnson's home to deliver the bundle of letters into her thankful hands. She hugged Cara in gratitude, at having her saucy missives returned, her relief tinged with worry about her missing friend, Beth. Cara shook her head, having no news to impart. She left the woman with one problem resolved but another still pressing on her mind.

The carriage arrived at a Mayfair address. The two women alighted, and stepped into the plush mansion hosting the evening's entertainment. The butler escorted them through to the parlour, where the other guests drank champagne and exchanged small talk, while waiting for the call to dinner. Amy drifted over to gossip with the hostess. Cara stayed to one side, contemplating hiding behind the tall indoor palm. Her heart skipped a beat on seeing the darkly handsome man engaged in conversation across the room. Tonight was a formal night, and her heart sank that he wasn't in pirate attire, but he was equally handsome in tails and waistcoat, with a cravat so sharp it could draw blood.

His head swung around and fixed on her, causing her to grab a passing flute of champagne a little too hurriedly. She looked down as a small amount of liquid sloshed over the rim with the sudden movement. She switched hands, wondering if she could risk licking the fallen alcohol off her hand when someone beat her to it.

Nathaniel had her hand, raised it to his lips, and kissed away the spilt champagne. His tongue snaked over her fingers, causing her to hold her breath. He lingered over her in an entirely inappropriate way. She fought the impulse to pour the expensive fluid down her décolleté and mutter *oops*.

"You've been avoiding me." He relinquished her hand.

"You've been crowding me." She couldn't think when he was near her. His presence made the blood pound so loudly in her ears, thought became impossible.

His eyes roamed the room before returning to her. "Nice dress. Suits you."

"I've been meaning to return it to you." Her hand stroked the lush fabric. The cut of the dress was so different from what the other women wore. Cara hated the crinolines the other women had under their skirts. They were iron prisons, hampering movement. The dress Nathaniel provided for her was more fluid, and she wore it with nothing underneath. The dress covered, yet revealed; with each step she took it clung to and displayed her curves.

"I could always take it off you tonight." He said it deadpan, no hint of emotion on his face.

A blast of heat burst through Cara, and he left her in a whirlpool of swirling emotion as the dinner announcement came. As one of the highest-ranking aristocrats present, Nathaniel walked through with the hostess. Amy and Cara linked arms; being at the back of the row of diners, they were among the last to take their place.

When they approached the table, she found Nathaniel holding out a chair for her, before sinking down on her left.

"What are you doing?" she whispered as she took her seat. "You should be up by the hostess."

Nathaniel flicked out his white linen napkin. "I will not endure this evening surrounded by bores. With my reputation, I can sit wherever the hell I want."

She saw the discreet and furtive looks shot in their direction. "If the company is so boring, why on earth are you here, then?"

He caught her hand under the table and stroked her palm. "Because you are here."

She paused, not sure how to respond. *Damn him.* "Well, behave yourself, or I'll be forced to jam my fork into your thigh."

His mouth twitched. "I promise to be on my best behaviour. For dinner."

She did a double-take, wondering what he planned for after dinner. His thigh rested close to hers under the table and she could feel his heat through the velvet of her dress. True to his word, he was an entertaining, and thoughtful, dinner companion.

Once the servants cleared away dessert, the group passed into the front parlour, where an ancient sarcophagus dominated the room. Intricate hieroglyphics that described the life story of the occupant dominated the limestone exterior. The host told an outrageous story of how the coffin contained one of the most beautiful princesses in all of ancient Egypt. Cara doubted it very much. The final resting place of royalty was a secret guarded all the way to the underworld. Far more likely, the heavy coffin was the final resting place of someone middle-class.

Displaying artifacts was all the rage among the upper classes. They scoured the ends of the earth to find ancient and exotic mummies to display after dinner in a hideous game of corpse one-upmanship. The unravelling of the poor unfortunate turned into a grown-up, and gory, version of Pass the Parcel. You never knew what lay within or whether you had a good prize or not. Paying top dollar for your desiccated corpse didn't always translate into the best entertainment.

Nathaniel stood at her side; his formidable presence deflected the curious looks and comments of the other diners, for which Cara was grateful. However, he also constantly inhaled her air, making her struggle with his proximity and a lack of oxygen.

Four footmen entered the room and took up positions at each corner of the stone coffin. At a nod from the host, two pushed and two pulled. A loud grating noise preceded movement, as the lid slid sufficient for the staff to wrap fingers around the edge and lift the heavy cover free. They leaned it against the wall, before silently disappearing, their work done.

Three women rushed forward, eager for the first glimpse of the long-dead princess.

Cara hung back. She had spent several months in Egypt. On her rides through the Valley of Kings, she saw the discarded corpses left by the tomb robbers. She did not need to rush and be titillated. She once stood in their defiled tombs and saw the beautiful stories illustrating the walls in rich, vibrant colours. She had no desire to disturb someone's long slumber. The story of the woman's life was far more interesting than her body, a mere dry husk, discarded millennia ago.

The women diners gripped the edge of the coffin with eager fingertips as they peered into the depths, and promptly gave a range of ungodly screams. Two fainted straight away, hitting the floor before anyone could intervene. The third staggered backward to swoon into the arms of a convenient suitor.

Screaming and fainting? I have to look now.

Inquisitive as ever, Cara stepped over the minefield of lesser constitutions littering the floor. Nathaniel held her hand, his eyebrows raised as chaos erupted around them. The host called for water to revive the fallen. Their bodies were cradled into sitting positions, like giant porcelain dolls, handled by the men in the room. Amy stood wide-eyed and out of the way, fanning herself frantically at the unfolding excitement.

Approaching the sarcophagus, Cara looked over the edge and into the last resting place of someone who walked the Earth before Christ rose and died. Except it didn't contain the body of a princess, or even a middle-class lass. Not even the body of someone who had been dead for three thousand years. Perhaps closer to three days.

A crude attempt had been made to mummify the girl. Multiple layers of fine linen, wrapped around her limbs and body, skimmed the edge of her face, leaving her identity exposed. Her eyes were closed, her lips tinted blue and eerie against her pale skin. Black hair swirled around her face and tumbled down her shoulders. She could have been Sleeping Beauty, awaiting the kiss of her prince, except for her hands clasped over her chest. The bow of the key protruded from amongst her fingers, as though she held it in place. A red stain crept away from the brass shaft.

"Beth Armstrong, I presume," she whispered. This was the third one, but the first so publicly displayed. "How did you end up in there, I wonder?"

"You know her?" Close behind her, Nathaniel caught the name on her lips.

"No, but I was told she had gone missing. Somebody better contact the Enforcers. Fraser will be all over this one. And me, when he finds out I'm here."

After a single glimpse from the host, no one else dared approach the sarcophagus. Accustomed to obedience, Nathaniel took control and issued orders. He sent the host to the library to call for the Enforcers and Inspector Fraser. Other men led the women from the room, to recover from their shock away from the fresh corpse. No one touched Cara. One look from Viscount Lyons made it clear no one was to interrupt her thoughts.

In the unfolding chaos, she stood calmly, contemplating the dead girl and her gruesome end. A life taken far too soon. Something nagged, and refused to sit in the back of her mind, discordant words that belonged together. Her eyes widened.

Egypt. Heart. Key. The words jumbled in her brain, crashed into each other, and fell back, making a perfect mosaic. A picture she recognised from long ago. She gasped and took a step back, straight into Nathaniel.

"What is it? Have you seen something?" He caught her before she toppled over, his strong hands wrapped around her shoulders, steadying her.

"Yes and no." She shook her head. "The elements. I've seen them before. They spark a memory."

Nathaniel spun her around to face him, and she fell silent.

"Not here," he said, glancing around them at the men still present, watching their every move.

He drew her through to the empty dining room and closed the doors behind them. He grabbed two clean wine glasses and an abandoned bottle of white wine. He poured the golden liquid into the glasses, letting his silence indicate she should continue with her train of thought.

Cara clasped and unclasped her hands, waiting for the tangle in her brain to settle. "What the killer is doing, the keys in their hearts, the reference to Egypt, it reminds me of an artifact called Nefertiti's Heart."

He raised an eyebrow and handed her a glass. He took a deep drink from his own glass.

"It's an artifact from the reign of Akhenaten. He ruled Egypt in 1,400 B.C. Some say he was the first messiah, since he preached there was only one true god and that all others were false gods. He proclaimed himself son of the true god. At Akhenaten's side ruled Nefertiti, the most beautiful woman in the world. Only he held the key to her heart. Legends say possessing her heart made him a god and gifted him with immortality."

Cara took a long drink. Letting the liquid settle in her stomach, she contemplated the stirred memories. They were happy ones, for a change. She rode fast Arabs across the desert, revelling in the movement of silken muscles under her body. She explored tombs and ruins, running her hand in wonder over hieroglyphics thousands of years old. She spent hot, languid days swimming in cool green waters with local children. Her father, preoccupied with finding the artifact, left her free to roam.

"Going to Egypt was the only trip father took me on. We spent over six months there, while he tracked down Nefertiti's Heart, and then he stole the artifact from its resting place. He squirrelled the thing away somewhere in London." At times, she wished they'd never returned to England; the brief spell of happiness was over too quickly.

"It sounds like the killer, with his keys in women's hearts and the obvious Egyptian touch." Nathaniel picked two leftover chocolates off the central plate. He offered one to Cara and popped the other into his mouth. "Do you think the killer is searching for his Nefertiti?"

Cara took the sweet, lingering over the contact with his fingers, before chewing the chocolate. "No. I think he's a whackadoodle. But throw in the asp that killed my father, and it's too much of a coincidence. I think the killer, whoever he is, knows about the Heart. And that should narrow the field of potential murderers down considerably."

"Do you know anything else about it? Why would he be so obsessed with it?"

"I don't know. I'm scratching for memories. We went to Egypt eight years ago, and I was more interested in the horses and swimming holes, not old relics. I need to go through father's notebooks and read his notes. I have no idea where the Heart is, or how the killer knows about the artifact." She threw her hands in the air in despair.

The doors slid open, interrupting their conversation. Inspector Fraser regarded them, his demeanour calm, as always. Deep blue uniforms moved behind him, and the hulking mass of Connor, his sergeant, stood at his shoulder.

"Fraser," Nathaniel drawled. The temperature dropped considerably.

"Lord Lyons. I'd like to talk to Miss Devon. Alone," he added, seeing Nathaniel showed little inclination to move from her side.

"Why don't you interview the other guests first? We haven't finished our conversation." Nathaniel flicked the tails of his jacket aside as he perched on the edge of the table, his manner dismissing Fraser.

Cara sucked in a breath; a frosty history lingered between the two men.

Fraser flicked his eyes to Cara, before he nodded and shut the doors again.

She breathed out a sigh. "You did that on purpose. I could have spoken to him now."

"He needs to learn his place."

"And I've told you before, don't make assumptions on my behalf." She put down her wine glass and opened the doors. Inspector Fraser turned on hearing the movement and she beckoned with one finger. He muttered something to Connor before walking toward her. She retreated into the dining room.

She waited until the doors closed, before asking her question. Something nagged at her, since gazing down on Beth Armstrong's serene face. "How did she get in there? It took four men to remove the lid."

Fraser removed his small notebook from a pocket before answering. His eye flitted to Nathaniel. "An interesting question. I will be following the sarcophagus and its movements."

"I'll save you some time, then." Nathaniel ran his fingers down Cara's arm in a caress before moving to the doorway. "The coffin came in on one of my airships, just over a week ago."

Fraser arched an eyebrow. "I'll need the manifest of the shipment it came in on, and details of everyone who had access to the sarcophagus."

"Of course." Nathaniel gave a sardonic smile and Cara wondered if the information he gave Fraser would bear any resemblance to the truth. He slipped into the parlour and closed the doors, leaving her alone with the inspector.

Fraser directed his full attention to Cara. "Imagine my surprise on finding you here."

"Really? Because you don't look surprised."

"No." He frowned and looked flustered, actions out of character for him. "I was trying for irony. Obviously, it fell flat."

She filed his reaction away to examine later and moved on to more pressing issues. "I assume the girl is the missing Beth Armstrong?"

"I will have to ask her family to be sure, but the description fits. How did you come to be here, Miss Devon?"

"My friend, Amy Hamilton, was invited. I came as her plus one. I didn't volunteer to come." She would rather pull her toenails out with a pair of pliers than rub shoulders with the ton, but she did what she had to, to make her friend happy.

He wrote in his little notebook with an equally petite pencil.

Cara drained her wine glass and wished for Nathaniel, and not just to top up the glass. She had a desire to lean against him, and have him fold his arms around her, and make everything else disappear.

"So why did the killer utilise this gathering to display his latest victim?" The inspector voiced his internal dialogue.

"So you don't think it's me?" She grasped the tendril of hope in his statement and use of the male pronoun.

His calm manner washed over her. "I never said I did. But I still believe this is drawing around you. If you would only confide in me."

"Why here?" She changed tack, uncomfortable with the intimacy Fraser sought to establish between them. "The other two were found in their homes. Why change, all of a sudden, to something so public?"

Fraser looked at her steadily, as though trying to see through her soul with his pale grey eyes. "Perhaps the killer is trying to get your attention."

His words cut through her. "I never asked for this," she whispered.

"I have other guests to talk to. Please excuse me." He left her alone.

Her mind raced. Amy entered the room at some stage. Cara didn't know if she had been turning events over for minutes or hours.

"I'll ask for the carriage to be brought around. We can go now. They are done with their questions," her friend said, rubbing her arms to dispel a non-existent chill.

She nodded and followed Amy back through the house to the entranceway. Amy sidled up to the butler to ask for their carriage. Cara leaned her back against the wall, closing her eyes, trying to remember her trip to Egypt as a child and any detail that may now be relevant.

Nathaniel approached her, and stepped close, one arm resting on the wall by her head. His warmth and musky scent enveloped her. Opening her eyes, she found herself partly trapped. She could duck to one side, if she wanted to.

"Tomorrow night, *cara mia*?" He drew his knuckles down the side of her face, and she leaned into the caress. Her body ached for the physical contact.

"You'll have to try hard to top tonight's entertainment. Murder. Screaming. Fainting. Police brutality. What are you offering?"

His lips twitched in his almost-smile. "Me, Loki, beer, and boxing."

The offer sounded fun and distracting, if only she could trust him. If only she could trust herself. She decided to go with her gut and told her brain to be quiet for once. "Bring Jackson as chaperon and I'll say yes."

"You trust Jackson but not me? You remember he works for me?" He looked amused, and curious at her logic.

A smile touched her lips. "I've shot him. We have a working relationship now."

"Tomorrow, then. Come to the house, since you won't tell me where you lay abed at night." He dropped his tone to something husky; the words caressed her body.

"Does it worry you, where I lie to sleep?" She gently teased.

"Not where, as much as *how* you sleep." With each word, he leaned closer to her.

Cara trod a knife-edge, remembering that playing with Nathaniel was Russian roulette.

"Naked. Does that ease your curiosity?" she asked, fanning the fire growing between them.

A low groan escaped his throat. He dipped his head, his lips millimetres from hers, as their breath mingled.

She closed her eyes and waited, the slow tingle spread through her body in anticipation. After a moment stretched into an agony of longing, she opened her lids, and locked gaze with him, his eyes a cloudy day of drifting blues and greys.

Damn you, kiss me already.

Unable to wait any longer, she stood on tiptoe and stretched up, brushing her lips against his, needing to taste him. The urge to have his skin pressed against hers grew with each encounter. He slid his lips over hers, the kiss languid and unhurried. Their tongues played, brushing one another, chasing back and forth.

He pulled back and lifted his head fractionally. "Your carriage is waiting."

He inclined his head in the direction of the doorway, where Amy tapped her foot and drew her stole around her shoulders, waiting for her wayward friend. He didn't move, but let Cara slip away from under his arm and out the door.

Fraser stopped her on the steps, just as she and Amy headed out into the darkness and their awaiting carriage. "Lyons is not the man to trust, Miss Devon. If you would listen to my humble opinion, I would advise you to tread very carefully around him."

She flicked her gaze beyond Fraser to where Nathaniel stood immobile in the entranceway, waiting for his own carriage. Too proud to admit Fraser might be right, she did wonder who to trust?

Monday, July 15

YET again, the wardrobe door hung open as Cara considered her choices. Beer and boxing with two pirates. She would need something she could run in. And possibly climb fences. Preferably, a robust fabric, with a dark pattern, to hide any bloodstains.

Or whatever else the two naughty schoolboys get up to tonight. What am I doing? She berated herself. Her brain argued with her instinct. One told her to stay home and stay safe. The other yearned for the danger. Her skin tingled at not knowing what the evening would bring, and she was utterly alive at the prospect.

She dressed carefully. Pants, lace-up boots, brown and grey collared corset with a cream shirt underneath. A tailored, grey wool jacket went over the top, with a small Derringer tucked into her boot, *just in case.* She paused before she headed out the door, rethought several potential scenarios for the evening, and went back to the wardrobe. She re-emerged several minutes later, a short blade strapped to her upper arm and hidden under the fall of her shirt. Feeling prepared, she stepped out into the cool of the evening.

Full dark had descended by the time she jumped up the steps to the Mayfair house. The doors swung open before she reached them.

Brilliant yellow light illuminated the stairs and half the driveway, from the enormous chandeliers hanging in the entranceway. Miguel was on door duty this evening.

"Evening, miss. They are waiting for you in the parlour." He gave an impeccable impersonation of a majordomo.

The next set of doors swung open on the taupe-coloured parlour where Nathaniel had first kissed her. The men stood at the fireplace talking; their heads turned as she entered. They were both dressed casually, tall boots, buckskin pants, simple waistcoats over plain shirts, and no cravats this evening. Nathaniel wore dark tones of grey and blue, Loki in earthier tones. Hungry eyes raked her body from top to toe and Cara belatedly thought perhaps this wasn't such a good idea after all, the three of them pressed into a carriage. Not that the Lyons carriage was small, but Nathaniel hadn't kept his hands off her in one yet.

"Shall we?" he enquired, one sardonic eyebrow raised, as though he read her thoughts.

Or perhaps I should stop staring at him like a lovesick puppy.

Heading outside, relief washed over her when Nathaniel entered the carriage and decided to take the seat opposite her, leaving Loki to sit next to her. Though, her relief was short-lived; Nathaniel fixed his eyes on her and his gaze never deviated, for their entire journey. By the time they reached their destination, every pore in her body hummed like they were all playing little harmonicas.

Loki jumped out first and stood, with a roguish look and hand extended, to help Cara out. She hesitated, before curling her fingers around the outstretched palm for the few seconds it took to step down from the carriage. Not that she needed any assistance, but curiosity barged to the surface and wanted to touch the pirate, to gauge what her gut would say of the encounter. He lingered over her, earning him a scowl from Nathaniel.

Warm. And beguiling, her instinct reported. Cara looked down the street and saw a tall monument in the middle of a busy intersection, where multiple roads converged. The footpath teemed with life, while the gutters stank of death. She turned her gaze to Nathaniel.

"Seven Dials?" She arched an eyebrow.

"I thought you wanted somewhere far from the strictures of society." His face remained passive, but Cara caught the hint of an amused twinkle in his blue eyes.

The pub was small and cheerful; blazing lights and raucous laughter drifted from within. The sign over the door declared *The Prick & Rose* in colours that would be gaudy in the daylight. Cara's stomach constricted and did a flip-flop.

Make up your mind, do you want this or not? Do you want excitement or quiet nights with a banker, like Amy?

Nathaniel stepped forward and took her hand, and then he squeezed her fingers gently. "Nothing will happen to you. We'll keep you safe." He gave her one of his breath-stealing smiles and a wink.

I don't want safe, I want excitement.

She made up her mind, and damn the consequences.

The inside of the pub was a seething mass of primarily unwashed bodies. Cara noticed a few better-dressed patrons seeking their entertainment in the riskier section of the city. A boxing ring took up the central position in the middle of the establishment. The mat, a dirty, off-white shade, showed multiple clean splotches where bloodstains were washed off at the end of the evening. Two rows of ropes hung around the mat, all that would contain the opponents and separate them from the eager spectators.

They found a table close to the ring and the upcoming matches. There were no chairs, the tables of a height to lean on. By unspoken agreement, the men placed Cara in the middle, Nathaniel on one side, Loki and Jackson on the other. A few eyes were cast in her direction, but there were sufficient women circulating the crowd to keep interest away from her. Moreover, she was overdressed; the other women present wore only corsets and tiny bustles. The skirts barely touched mid-thigh, the expanse of their legs fully exposed at the front, the bustle dropping to knee height at the back. Their garters highlighted an enticing area of flesh between skirt and stocking. The corsets amply displayed what the women had on offer, and Cara saw coins change hands, and men led away to cheers from their companions.

Jackson disappeared for several long minutes, and reappeared with a tray laden with dented, tin mugs and pitchers of beer.

"Food's on the way," he said as he laid out the items and politely filled Cara's mug first.

She had no intention of getting drunk and every intention of making the one drink last all evening. She listened to the warning from her pragmatic brain, which told her letting alcohol drop her guard, and impair her reactions, would be a fatal error in this situation.

A waitress dropped bowls of hot chips and fish bites on their table. Cara caught her arm and ducked under Nathaniel for a quick conversation with the woman. The call came for opponents in the first match, a fight for the women. Loki gave Cara a speculative look as she returned to the table.

She scowled at him. "Don't insult me."

She poked him in the ribs.

The women competitors wore corsets and hot pants, the fight designed to have the men ordering more beer, as they sought to whet their thirst. The women grappled and grabbed each other in a display more erotic floorshow than fight.

"If I said please, would you join in?" Loki's hungry eyes swept from the scantily clad women rolling on the mat to Cara.

She bounced a hot chip off his nose in response, earning her an earthy chuckle from the airship captain. "Perhaps later? A private show for just me and Nate?"

Bantamweights were next, and still she took small sips of her beer and stayed quiet. She wanted a hard fight, to push herself to the edge of her limits. These fighters, mere youths, did not look even old enough to have stubble darkening their chins. The roar and cry of the men washed around her as they placed their bets and screamed when they won, or lost.

"Next round," the ref hollered. "Lightweights."

She took a slurp from her beer and waved her hand.

"Me!" she challenged. The room fell silent for a moment as the crowd took in her slim form, barely bantamweight, and no match against the larger contenders. She shrugged off her jacket, and nimbly unlaced her corset, passing her clothing to Jackson. He wore his usual amused grin as he held her discarded clothing. The crowd went mad; a hundred voices yelled as they placed frantic bets, for and against Cara.

Nathaniel put out his hand, stopping her at his side. "Do you know what you're doing? You're fighting way above your weight class."

"Don't worry about me. I have a few tricks, remember?" She gave him a cheeky wink.

She finished tying her shirt tightly around her middle and pushed through the ropes into the ring. Her opponent grinned, imagining an easy victory. He turned to his friends and raised his hands, eliciting a roar in response.

She raised an eyebrow and let one of the staff tape her hands and wrists. This would be a tough bout. Her opponent, heavier, taller, leaner, looked scrappy, with a hungry glint in his eye. She didn't expect any leniency for being a woman. If she wanted an easy round, she would have joined the farcical women's fights at the start of the evening. Or even the bantamweights, comprised of juveniles burning off the extra testosterone of puberty. She needed to go hard, for her muscles to burn and ache, and to take a punch or two.

Cara knew she had to get a certain distance into the bout before using her feet, particularly if she wanted to earn a tidy profit from asking the waitress to bet on her. She had slipped the woman money, and instructions, earlier.

The other fighter threw his opening punch and she dodged under, relieved to discover his reflexes were slower than hers. He overextended, and she ducked close to deliver an uppercut. It landed, but he sneered at her effort. He whipped out his own shot, missing his mark by the tiniest margin and his bound fist grazed her cheek.

They each got in a few more blows before she decided to mix it up. Plus, she was enough of a girl to not want her face smashed. She bounced and a slow smile crept over her face.

I know something you don't know, she sang in her head.

She spun and delivered a roundhouse blow to her opponent's torso, knocking him back against the ropes. The spectators went wild; frenzy ripped through the assembled masses. Now her opponent looked pissed off; the idea of losing to a girl didn't sit well with him. *Luckily,* Cara thought, *angry fighters make mistakes.* He lunged violently with short, punchy jabs. Only a couple hit home on her torso, as she ducked and weaved and followed her first kick with two more. A straight kick to his face flung him over the ropes, grasping the coil for balance as he spat blood onto the floor.

Come on, come on, she taunted in her mind, waiting for him to turn. He leapt from the ropes straight at her, hoping to catch her off-guard, thinking she would lower her defences if she scented victory. He was wrong. He ran straight into her booted foot. The blow to his head sent him backward and to the mat.

The crowd erupted into louder jeers, catcalls, and whistles as the ref held up her hand, declaring Cara the winner of the match. She ducked under the ropes. The fallen man's friends dragged him over to the side, patted his face, and pushed a mug of cold ale into his hands. She made her way through the press of bodies as hands patted her on the back and offered congratulations.

On reaching their table, Nathaniel reached out one hand and grabbed her nape, his fingers pressed into her hair as he drew her into him. She went to him, willingly, excitement pounding through her body. He kissed her fiercely, stamping his possession on her for all in the bar to see. She entwined her hands in his hair, increasing the approving roar from the crowd. When he went to pull back, she held him, diving into his mouth. Her victory made her bold as she sought him out, drawing him into her.

For the first time in her life, Cara took what she wanted from a man.

Breathless, she pulled back. His eyes blazed, but he didn't let her go, keeping her within his grasp.

Grabbing the mug of beer, she took a quick swig, the malty fluid adding much needed moisture to her mouth and throat. Her eyes shone; she would have a few bruises along her ribs in the morning, and an impressive one on her cheek, but the exhilaration was worth the aches. Life pumped through her veins, painful memories retreated and became faint line drawings in her mind. She breathed, she lived, and her actions reaffirmed her decision to seek out excitement, regardless of the risks.

"How much did you make?" she asked Nathaniel.

"Enough to pay for more beer than you can drink."

He stood protectively behind her, one hand on the table, the other wrapped around her exposed waist, shielding her from the crowd with his body. Jackson and Loki on either side kept away the well-wishers and those with darker intent in their eyes.

She leaned into him, resting her head against his chest. The heat from the contact spread through her body, gradually replacing the heat from the physical exertion with something more primal. Need pulsed through her, threatening the long-held fear for control over her body.

"Who's next?" the organiser yelled over the noise of the crowd.

Loki jumped to his feet. "Me!" he bellowed in response.

"Can't let you have all the fun." He winked at Cara as he unbuttoned his waistcoat and tossed it over his chair. He fluidly pulled his shirt up over his head. Cara's eyes went wide, but it wasn't the golden rings through his nipples that caught her attention. A row of tiny scars dominated his right side, front and back, both sides covered in an identical, graceful arc.

"What gave him that?" she tilted her head and asked Nathaniel.

"Shark." He leaned down and brushed his lips over hers, testing her internal state of mind.

Curiosity rose to the bait. "How does a hawk get a shark bite?"

"Fishing where he shouldn't have been." Nathaniel's lips twitched in silent laughter at a private joke.

Loki strode over to the ring, his back emblazoned with his namesake, its wings outstretched over his shoulder blades. His skin darkened by years of living outside and scars showed it wasn't an easy life. Each jagged line made Cara wonder at the story or encounter behind it.

The ref barely stepped to the side when both men lunged at each other. The bout was fast and brutal. Blood flew in all directions as the two opponents pummelled one another. Cara winced every time Loki took a hit, his body absorbing the impact and rocketing back into action. Long years of fighting for his life were evident in every strike he made.

Equally matched, the fight drew on. Men cheered at fever pitch for their favourite. Cara found herself yelling Loki's name each time he landed a blow on his opponent. Finally, the other man fell backward over the rope, tumbling at the feet of a passing waitress. She squealed as his fingers laced around her ankle. She kicked him with her high-heeled foot and stepped over him, much to the laughter of the crowd.

Loki wiped sweat and blood from his face with the back of his arm as the ref announced him the winner. He returned to their table triumphant, although far more battered than Cara. He downed his beer in several thirsty gulps.

He thumped his empty glass on the table and gestured to the waitress to refill their pitchers, before turning to Cara. "How does this evening compare to last night's entertainment?"

She munched on a deep fried fish bite, a stark contrast to the prime fillet served the previous evening. "Not as many people have died."

Jackson laughed. "Not yet, but give them time."

Tempers were starting to flare around them, as those who won on the fights taunted the losers. Small skirmishes erupted here and there, most quickly broken up by other patrons and the few large bouncers circulating. Cara could well imagine more heated disputes were settled outside in brutal fashion.

"Did you know her, your fresh mummy?" Loki asked.

Cara shook her head. "No."

"But you're on the trail of something, yes?" He cocked his head, looking from Cara to Nathaniel behind her.

"I think so. This killer is driving keys into women's hearts, and last night he left Beth in a sarcophagus. The image reminds me of something my father retrieved from Egypt, a relic called Nefertiti's Heart." She unconsciously rested her hand on Nathaniel's arm, playing with the cotton of his shirtsleeve. "I think it's connected somehow. I just don't know how."

She saw the path her mind wanted to follow, but didn't know how to get there, the missing route beyond her reach. "But how do you research something that was created three thousand years ago?" Cara let go of Nathaniel's sleeve to clasp her beer mug and stare into the amber depths.

"What you need is a reference book, like they have in the big libraries, where you could look up Nefertiti's Heart." Loki joked as he popped the last chip into his mouth and licked the salt off his fingers.

Connections jolted in her brain.

"That's it." She slammed down her drink. "Loki you're a genius!" On impulse, she leaned forward and kissed his cheek. His dark eyes flashed and he raised his fingers to where her lips touched him.

"That's enough of that," Nathaniel said. "Or he'll start getting ideas." He bent his head close and whispered in her ear. "Remember what I said about not sharing."

His arms tightened around her waist. A blush crept up Cara's neck and she fought it down. Loki's comment triggered an old memory.

"There's a book. I remember my father talking about it now. He used to mutter about it at night." A frown creased her brow, her mind trying to draw the tendrils of memory nearer. "I just have to figure out how to find it."

"Give us some sort of clue about the type of book and we might be able to point you in a direction," Nathaniel said.

She concentrated on a long forgotten conversation. "It's old, possibly medieval? It contains oral histories and legends of many artifacts. I know father tried to get his hands on it, to complement his collection, and was thwarted."

Nathaniel rested his cheek next to hers. "You want a rare book dealer. If such a book came back on the market, they would hear about it. There are only two or three who would carry anything medieval. I can give you names in the morning."

"Thank you." She gave an unexpected yawn. The excitement of the last few days had exacted a toll. The adrenaline of the fight slipped from her body and left fatigue and aches in its wake. "I'm going to leave you boys to it."

Nathaniel tightened his grip around her. "I'll have you taken home."

"No." She broke free from the circle of his arms and collected up her discarded clothing. "I'll grab a cab."

"Are you going to constantly defy me?"

"I will, if you word it like that. You don't own me." Sleep called her name and shortened her temper. Touching her didn't give him the privilege to dictate how she lived her life.

A dark eyebrow shot up. "Then I'll walk you out, at least, and see you safely in a Hansom cab."

They wound their way through the other people. She approached the exit and their waitress caught up with her.

"Your share, love," she said, thrusting a wad of notes into Cara's hand. "Find me if you ever want to do it again." She gave Cara a wink before disappearing back into the crowd.

Nathaniel gave her an amused look as she pushed the money down the inside of her corset. Cara gave him a smile as they headed out into the night air.

CHAPTER 15

Tuesday, July 16

Aquick visit to Mayfair the next morning and Cara held a list of three rare book dealers to visit in the greater London area. The first one was a dismal failure. The owner gave her a haughty look and treated her like an imbecile for not knowing the name of the book she sought.

I thought they were called rare books because there aren't many of them. You should have known which one I meant.

She trudged through the dark and narrow back streets of Soho to find Goslett Yard and the second on the list. The little shop was ancient, the timber façade blackened by centuries of grime and filth from the London streets. Soot coated some of the uprights; scars showed the building survived its battle with the Great Fire while the flames razed other structures to the ground. The glass of the windows was so thick, light ended up distorted and refracted on the journey through the panes.

She pulled open the heavy door and stepped back in time. Candles burned in wall sconces, shedding little light and a gentle, warm radiance. The smell of melted beeswax, books, and lavender oil permeated the air. The ceiling soared higher than the width of the shop, making for a strange visual illusion, as though she stood at the bottom of a book-lined well. Surrounded by the words from a thousand pens, peace settled over her. The rows of books enticed, and she longed to run her fingers over their spines in a whispered caress.

She reached out a hand; her finger hovered over a tiny gilt hummingbird. A sharp memory stilled her hand. Her father had always been angry when she touched his books, berating her about their worth and complaining about the oils and dirt on her hands. She turned her hands over and stared at her fingers, then risked a stroke. She caressed the little bird, indulging in the contact with the unusual, small tome.

Emerging from the tall stack of books, she approached the counter. An elderly man perched behind a high desk, a peacock feather quill in his hand, as he laboured over an illuminated manuscript. A pot of liquid gold paint stood open in front of him. A small electric lamp lit up his workspace, the only modern concession in the shop, the book too precious to risk an unguarded candle so close to the fragile paper.

Looks like the original shop owner.

She cleared her throat, and he looked up at her with a gentle smile on his deeply etched face. His eyes were milky with cataracts and she wondered how he fared in a bookshop, or how he could labour over repairing a book. Or, perhaps his love for the written word drove him onward, despite the impending blindness.

"I'm looking for a book—" *And I'm incredibly stupid,* she thought as he immediately smiled indulgently at her.

"It's oral histories from the ancient world. It's a very old book, possibly mediaeval in origin." She had no idea what she was doing. Her father's notes were frustratingly vague and her memory hadn't been particularly helpful. Not that she ever paid much attention to her father's work; she was too busy keeping out of his reach. Here she was, assuming a bookshop owner would know exactly what she was talking about. She wracked her brain for any more detail. "There were particular myths from Egypt, and items of power . . . ."

He cocked his head; she had a brief mental image of a much smaller version of him running around in his brain. The miniature version opened, and then slammed shut hundreds of filing cabinet drawers, looking for the correct piece of information.

"*Magycks of the Gods*," he said.

Cara exhaled a sigh of relief. She wasn't mad; it did exist. "Yes. Can I purchase it please?"

He shook his head. "No."

Oh, hell.

He looked wistful, as though remembering a favourite student from long in his past. "The book went to a new owner some years ago, I'm afraid."

Double hell.

"Are there any other copies? Reprints, perhaps?" She grasped for straws; the book was from hundreds of years ago and related stories thousands of years old. It probably hadn't been serialised in any of the newspapers.

He gave his indulgent smile again. "No. There is only the one. And the book did not want to be copied."

The warning chill shot down her spine at his last statement.

The book didn't want to be copied? I should introduce it to the house that doesn't want any occupants.

"Could you at least tell me who purchased it?"

He gave the same slow shake of his head. She resisted the urge to kick her toe against his desk in frustration. "Thank you for your assistance."

At least she knew the name of the book. She just didn't know where to find it. She headed back out the door, as a figure slipped from between two of the shelves and followed her. He hailed her on the deserted pavement outside the shop.

"Miss Devon?"

Cara froze. Weaver Clayton. She didn't like to be reminded of his family, or to find him creeping around behind her.

"Yes, Lord Clayton?" Her tongue struggled over the surname.

He quickly removed his black silk top hat.

"Weaver, please. Let's avoid unnecessary unpleasantness for both of us." He gave her a shy smile. "I often spend my mornings here; rare books are something of a passion. And I couldn't help but overhear you are looking for a particular old volume."

"Yes." She was unsure how much to reveal. "I'm doing some research and my father used to mention the book. I would love to read the old stories. A shame it's gone."

"Well it is, and it isn't." He tormented his hat while talking to her, his fingers nervously reshaping the brim. "I may be of some assistance to you."

"Oh?" She was prepared to listen to him if he had information.

"I studied ancient literature and civilisations at Oxford, you know." The way his fingers tortured the expensive silk hat, it might soon be beyond redemption. "I became aware of that particular book myself."

She held her place, despite her brain urging her to run away as fast as possible. Curiosity would get her into trouble one day. *It already has,* she chided herself.

"I believe I know who purchased the book some years ago."

Bingo.

"And you're willing to share this information?"

"Yes, if only to be of assistance to you." He nodded, eager to please. He was a wee puppy trying to earn favour in its new home, desperate for a kind word or look. Given what Cara knew of his father, she wondered at his childhood; they might have more in common than interest in a rare book.

"It would be of a great assistance to me." She waited for him to fill in the vital details.

"I'm not sure how co-operative the new owner will be. You see, the book was acquired by Countess de Sal."

Cara's face fell. *That means another visit to crazy country.*

"Thank you, Weaver." Her thanks were genuine, but she was loath to be indebted to him.

He gave her a small bow and replaced his deformed top hat, before walking in the opposite direction.

Cara struck out for a dishevelled house in a once well-maintained street in Belgravia.

She rapped on the door several times and waited so long she wondered if she was too late. Perhaps de Sal had moved on, to either another address or another dimension, or maybe the ancient butler expired before he made it across the entranceway. Succumbing to her vice, she reached out a hand and tried the doorknob. The door gave and swung inwards, revealing the elderly majordomo.

His hand outstretched to the door, he peered at her in a somewhat confused manner. "She's not receiving anyone."

"It's important." Cara figured the normal rules of house calls didn't apply. Making use of her age advantage of at least ninety years, and fully functioning knees, she slipped past him into the entranceway.

He looked around, somewhat confused, and closed the door. Turning on creaking legs, he gave a start to find her behind him.

"She's not receiving."

"Yes, we have had this conversation already," she muttered. "Is she upstairs?" she asked in a louder tone and pointed to the floor above.

"Yes," he replied automatically. Then his brain caught up with his tongue. "No, she's not receiving."

Too late; Cara was already halfway up the stairs.

She stood at the top, wondering which way to the master suite, when she heard an odd crooning noise. The hair on the back of her neck rose, but she followed the sound anyway. She crept down the threadbare carpet, floorboards creaking under her weight. Paintings of grim ancestors lined the walls. They all stared down elongated noses with looks of haughty disdain. Some had round holes in their foreheads, Cara leaned closer to inspect one and discovered it was a bullet hole.

She drew away from the executed portraits to track down the singing. The lullaby came from behind panelled double doors that stood partially cracked open. *Like me. I'm cracked for being here.*

She rapped lightly with the back of her knuckles. "Countess de Sal? It's Cara Devon."

No answer. She knocked louder, then slid the doors apart.

Countess de Sal sat up in an enormous four-poster bed. An ancient tapestry of earth tones hung around the bed and dropped down in swags at each corner. Embroidered leaves, vines, and tree branches clambered over the tapestry. The countess lay surrounded by numerous cushions of matching shades of brown and green. She cradled a pug dog dressed in a green gown, as she sang a lullaby. The dog looked as desperate to escape as Cara felt.

The countess looked up and stopped singing. "You."

"Yes, me." Cara's eyes swept the room. The heavy drapes were closed against invading sunlight. Coal burned brightly in the large fireplace, despite the fact they were fast moving toward July. The fire heated air already overwarm and stifling.

The countess captured Cara's attention again with a thump.

"Have you slept with Nate yet?" She burst into laughter, and waggled her finger at Cara. The dog took its opportunity the loosened grip afforded, and shot from her arms like a cannon ball from the barrel. In a blur of green taffeta, the little canine was out the door and gone. Without missing a beat, the mad woman picked up a cushion to clutch to her bosom instead. She stroked the tassels, as if the cushion was a longhaired cat. "A little birdie tells me you are resisting his charms."

Cara thought certain little birdies needed shooting, if she ever found out who they were. "I need to talk to you about a book. Not my love life."

"And not about love letters, for I hear they have been returned to Isobel's hands. If you change your mind, I could lend you books on love. I have many illustrated ones on the physical aspect. I'm sure Nate would prove a most enthusiastic tutor." Laughter rolled from her, thick and fast, the crazed sound too loud in the stuffy bedchamber.

Cara needed to get the conversation moving in the right direction, before she dwelt on what exactly Nathaniel could teach her. "I'm here about a book. *Magycks of the Gods*. I believe you purchased it some years ago?"

The countess threw her head back on the pillows and stared at the ceiling. She remained immobile for so long, Cara worried she would have to reach out and give her a quick poke, to see if she still breathed.

"Why do you want it?" her voice sounded calmer, less strident.

"Call it research." Her eyes roamed the room, lingering on the small wooden box with brass corners on the bedside table.

"I need a better answer than that, if you want me to part with a valuable mystical book."

Cara blew out a snort of air and took a punt. Anything to escape the melting heat; sweat tried to trickle down the inside of her tightly-laced corset. "I think there's something in the book that is connected to the murdered girls."

The older woman sat bolt upright, the corpse struck by lightning and springing to reanimated life.

"Really? Why didn't you say that first?" She leapt from the bed and grabbed her dressing gown off the floor.

"Come on." She beckoned, stuffing her arms through the gown, then vanished out the bedroom door. The gown trailed behind her, swirling with the movement as though on unseen winds. She looked like an apparition, haunting her own home, moving silently on bare feet.

Cara didn't need to be told twice. She bolted out the door as fast as the little pug. The countess drifted down the stairs, disappeared off to the left, and headed along a dark corridor. Then she vanished, slipping through a wall. Still several paces behind, Cara was relieved to see a door and she wasn't chasing a spectral entity down into the pits of Hell. Rather, over the threshold, she found a thoroughly modern heaven—a well-outfitted library.

Two dark brown, leather wing chairs occupied the central space, sharing an overstuffed ottoman. The walls were floor to ceiling books of every imaginable shape, thickness, and colour. A gleaming brass rail ran around the entire room, supporting a narrow library ladder on wheels, secured by its casters. Soft electric lights lit the room, turning it into a secluded cave, where anyone could escape the harsh realities waiting outside the front door.

The countess stretched out her arms and spun round and round, absorbing the comforting atmosphere of the library. When she opened her eyes and looked at Cara, she seemed calmer and more lucid. Rubbing her hands together in anticipation, she stalked to the shelves. She peered at the book titles, hands ran along spines, as she muttered words under her breath.

"You want to know, don't you?" The question was unexpected and directed at Cara.

"Yes." She knew it wasn't polite to pry, but screw it, she really wanted to know how the other woman had spiralled into madness. Cara thought her behaviour was more than the effect of the pox on her mind. Part of Cara hoped she would learn enough to stop her taking the same plummet off the deep end.

"Curiosity killed the cat." De Sal watched the play of emotion over Cara's face.

"And satisfaction brought it back." *Or, at least, let it die with a smile on its face.*

She went back to examining the books. "I was his mistress for nearly twenty years."

Cara frowned trying to connect what few facts she knew. Nathaniel was approaching thirty, and unless he was a very precocious child, they were talking about someone else.

"His uncle. I was a girl of fifteen, escaping France, when he introduced me to the pleasures of the flesh and took me as his mistress." The countess gave a small sigh, and reached above her head to pull out a dull grey book. The covering on the spine had come loose and it dangled free, like a flap of skin exposing the vertebrae beneath.

"The Lyons family closed ranks and protected their own. Nate's father knew his brother had the pox, but no one stopped him, or warned me. He had already infected his wife and child. And they let him take up with me. Then, after twenty years as his faithful lover, he simply walked out on me. He left me to fester in my own rampaging symptoms, with only the mercury to comfort me."

An awkward social situation loomed before Cara, one never covered in etiquette class. She certainly would have remembered the day they practiced *What To Do when someone reveals a lover infected them with the pox, dumped them after stealing their youth, and left them alone to slide into insanity.* She chose silence as the more appropriate response.

"I was there when Nate was born and watched him grow up. We were close once. Then he changed. He shut his emotions away and became like them. He did promise me revenge on his uncle. And he honoured his word." She held out the book, *Magycks of the Gods* stamped in large black letters across the front.

Cara took the book. "What was he like? As a boy?"

A broad smile split her face. "As charming as he is now. But so open. As he grew older, he threw up his defences, to protect himself. His relationship with his father was not a happy one."

She snorted. "I know what that is like."

De Sal tilted her head. "You are not so different."

Her fingers trailed along the shelf, stopping at a large red spine. "Are you sure you don't want a book?" She drew her nails down the spine, revealing one ornate letter at a time. K. A. M. A. S. U.—

"I know that book." Cara halted the finger's progress; heat climbed up her throat. "I have spent time in India."

The countess clapped her hands together, delighted with the gem of knowledge. "Excellent. You will be a surprise to Nate, then."

And somehow, we have detoured back to my love life.

She tapped a fingernail on the ancient book in Cara's hands. "Let me know what you find. I expect to hear all the gory details. I like your visits. No one else is brave enough to cross my threshold, apart from my little songbird who trills information. You must call me Helene. I have been too long without a real friend."

Dust motes rose off the old cover. Helene flicked a hand to brush one away, and grazed her nose. She gave a startled cry as the organ slid down her face and hit the carpet. Wide eyes looked at Cara. Two metal prongs glinted, showing the exposed artificial nose attachments. The pox had eaten away all the gristle, and left a gaping, open hole in her once beautiful face.

A flash of green and the small pug dog dove on the nose and darted from the library with its trophy.

"Minnow!" Helene shrieked and ran in hot pursuit.

Wednesday, July 17

THREE keys sat on the corner of Inspector Fraser's desk. Amongst the chaos, they were a sliver of order, with space neatly cleared around them. Each key was an identical distance from its companions. Teeth faced inward; ornate filigree bows touched the outer edge of the desk. Through the bows, and attached with twine, cardboard labels dangled over the side. Inscribed in black ink on each label was the name of a girl. A dead girl. Three lives locked, never to be opened again.

Fraser stood and touched the closest key with his fingertips. *Beth Armstrong.* He walked with leaden feet up the stairs to the superintendent's office. Taking a deep breath, he rapped sharply on the door.

"Enter," barked an order. The super occupied an entire corner on the top floor, with a picturesque view of the city. He stood at his window, a dispatch dangling from his fingers. He looked up at Fraser's entry.

"Ah, Fraser, what progress have you made?" Clipped tones indicated another military man. A colonel in a former life, he was used to having his orders obeyed and never questioned.

Fraser halted in the middle of the room and coughed to clear his throat. "I believe I am starting to discern a pattern among the victims—"

"Starting? You're *starting* to discern something?" His superior swung to regard him, a thick red vein pulsing in his temple. "We have three dead young women. Gentlewomen, Fraser. Do you understand? Three dead ladies, not your common street tarts. How many have to die before you find him?"

Fraser hated this bit. The victim's place of birth should have no influence over how much effort he expended to find the killer. Street girl or noble, they both deserved the same level of attention from him. Although given a choice, he would rather seek out a street girl for comfort than any highly bred, nervous creature. "I'm sure you appreciate, sir, we need to examine all the clues to find the monstrous person responsible."

"I need you to appreciate that I want to be able to enjoy a quiet brandy in my club without being accosted by anxious aristocrats!" the superintendent bellowed. "London is in an uproar, we have some chap stalking and killing the daughters of the nobility. You cannot begin to appreciate the pressure I am under, or how many irate questions I have to field while at my club." His voice rose and fell with his anger, his cheeks and nose turning beetroot red.

Fraser remained calm; he had weathered such storms before. Better to let the superintendent's rage buffet about him, bend under the pressure, and remain standing in its wake.

"I believe we have a strong lead with Beth Armstrong. The sarcophagus she was found in came from one of Lyons' airships." He stood with his hands behind his back. Threads were beginning to draw together, the picture revealing itself.

"Viscount Lyons? Be very careful of your facts before you go after him. Just because the coffin passed through his hangar doesn't mean he's involved. Any one of his crew could have had access to it." The superintendent tossed the dispatch on his desk and sank into his upholstered leather chair. "He's one of us. Be sure of your evidence."

"Quite," he agreed with his superior. *But not only did he have access to the sarcophagus, he also fences valuable and exotic items, and has a strong interest in Cara Devon.*

The superintendent waved his hand, dismissing Fraser from his presence. "Let me know if anything else comes up. Otherwise I expect progress by the end of the next week."

He bowed his head and remained silent, lest he say something out of turn. Today was Wednesday; his super expected him to solve the murders within the next ten days.

Back in his office, he flung himself into the chair and stared with unseeing eyes at the chalkboard that covered one wall. To one side was the name Lord Devon, and next to it the names of the girls, their addresses, and what slim correlations he could find among them. Arrows and question marks flew back and forth, but none hit their target. He was so close, if he reached out his hand, he should be able to grasp it, yet when he opened his fingers, his palm was always empty.

Connor appeared in the doorway carrying a mug of steaming tea. As he approached the desk, he passed too closely to the chalkboard, his massive shoulder brushing one of the names.

Fraser uttered a groan of frustration. "You rubbed out her name."

Connor plonked down the tea and looked from chalkboard to his sleeve.

"Aw, she's all over me." Using one meaty hand, he brushed the remnants of Abigail Swan's name from where it clung to his dark blue jacket.

Rubbing his hands over his face, Fraser looked up at the chalkboard, now minus one surname. He was running out of leads and accumulating dead girls.

Connor cast around, looking for a piece of chalk. Finding one, he approached the board.

"Names, names, and family names," Fraser muttered, contemplating the lonely Swan, bereft of its forename. Now, instead of representing a beautiful young debutante, it could mean her family, her estate, or her father. *Click.* A cog turned in his brain, a wheel fell into place, and a previously hidden door swung open.

"Stop!" he cried.

Connor froze. Fraser once saved his life by halting him as he was about to step on a land mine. Now he stopped instantly whenever Fraser used a certain tone of voice. Connor's eyes rolled downward, as though expecting to find something deadly attached to his leg or under his foot.

"What is it?" he whispered.

"It's the names." Fraser pushed himself away from his desk.

"What?" Connor dared a look over his shoulder, a frown creasing his normally smooth brow.

"I've been looking at the names all wrong." He pounced on the small duster sitting on top of a filing cabinet. "You can move now, preferably out of the way."

Connor exhaled and gingerly stepped backward three paces.

Fraser took his place in front of the board and rapidly rubbed out Beth and Jennifer. He left only three surnames—Lovell, Swan, and Armstrong. Above the surnames he wrote *Lord, Colonel,* and *Sir.*

Now the board read *Lord Devon, Lord Lovell, Colonel Swan,* and *Sir Armstrong.*

He turned to face Connor, the chalk still clutched in his fingers. "We've been trying to connect the girls back to Devon somehow. But what if the connection isn't the girls, but their fathers?"

His sergeant blinked. "They're of an age. Seems the four chaps would have more in common. They probably socialised at the same clubs."

Fraser nodded. His excitement building, his skin itched for him to move, hunt, to follow the scent. "Exactly. What if he selects the daughters because of their fathers? Maybe the killer is trying to send a message."

Connor was not blessed with Fraser's intellect. He struggled to keep pace with his superior. "What about Cara Devon? Why is she alive then?"

Fraser frowned. "That doesn't make sense to me either. Except she hasn't lived in London for seven years. Only the death of her father brought her here."

"So why doesn't he go after her now?" Connor scratched his close-cropped head.

Keen intelligence lit in Fraser's eyes. He was on the brink of solving the puzzle. As he suspected, Cara Devon was proving the linchpin. "An interesting question, is it not?"

Stepping back from his handiwork, Fraser took a drink from his tea, spat it out—the liquid far too hot—and abandoned the mug. He grabbed his bowler and jacket from their stand behind the door. "Come on, Connor. We need to revisit the grieving fathers. This time we need to ask them what they knew of Lord Devon."

Their first stop was the home of Lord Lovell. Fraser stared up at the imposing, cream brick, multi-storeyed façade.

"Better you remain here, I think, Connor." He politely informed the sergeant, as he grabbed his bowler. The other man blew out a snort and climbed into the front seat next to the driver, leaving Fraser to tiptoe delicately through the social minefield awaiting him.

He politely enquired of the butler if Lord Lovell could spare him five minutes of his time.

The butler looked put out to see him at the front door, making it clear he thought Fraser's sort should be using the back entrance.

Unperturbed, he refused to budge from the front step, forcing the butler to usher him in so he could close the doors on the ever-watchful neighbours.

The butler disappeared down the wide hallway and then silently reappeared, thanks to soft-soled shoes. "His lordship can spare *five minutes*, Inspector."

Fraser smiled and followed the butler down the darkened hallway. He imagined the servant would have his pocket watch out as soon as he crossed the threshold into the study.

The tense atmosphere in the study hit him the moment he entered.

"I hope you are here to inform me of an impending arrest." Lord Lovell bristled with anger. The passage of three weeks had done nothing to diminish his anguish at the loss of his daughter.

"Unfortunately, no," Fraser was forced to admit, doffing his faithful bowler. "But I am following a promising line of enquiry."

Cold, hard eyes regarded him, questioning his ability.

Extracting his notebook, he launched straight in, not wasting any of the precious minutes allotted to him. "Did you know Lord Devon?"

Lord Lovell straightened under the question, his eyes narrowed. "Yes, we were acquainted."

"And Colonel Swan?"

A long pause, before he answered. "I am also acquainted with the Colonel, and with Sir Armstrong, before you ask. What exactly are you getting at, Fraser?"

He trod carefully with his next words. "Might I enquire as to the nature of your association?"

"We attend the same club, share a few drinks, cigars, and talk as men do." Watchful eyes and measured words; there would be no full disclosure here.

"Is that all?" He knew he faced a tough incline ahead of him. He needed to get to the root of their association. Nobles always guarded what they did behind closed doors, even if it ended in murder.

"I'll tell you if I recollect anything relevant." A dismissal, his five minutes up.

Fraser sighed. He was on the right path now, he only had to undermine them to find the information he sought. Lord Lovell halted him at the door.

"There is one thing, which we believe requires an answer."

He turned. "Yes, milord?"

"If this all ties back to Devon, why is his daughter, Cara, still alive? She's damaged, that one. No one would miss her. Why didn't the killer go after her and leave our daughters alone?" His words betrayed the men had discussed the connection to Devon.

A frown touched Fraser's face. "Unfortunately, I don't yet have a satisfactory answer."

Thursday, July 18

TIRED of the silent and gloomy library, and her cramped apartment, Cara took the pragmatic step of invading Nathaniel's luxurious home. Armed with a satchel full of books and diaries, she commandeered the ornate conservatory, the staff too startled to stop her. When Jackson appeared, he simply told them to leave her to it, after they provided a pitcher of lemonade and a plate of scones.

The conservatory was the closest she could get to Egypt, yearning to immerse herself in the brief happy time and entice the last few memories to the surface. The room had soaring indoor palms and a humid interior. She hoped the atmosphere would put her in the right mood for her work. Small mechanical butterflies swept around the space of all different iridescent hues. They flew from palm to palm, before resting in the sun's rays. Their brightly enamelled wings pulsed back and forth, catching and deflecting the sunlight. They were beautiful and an unexpected touch of whimsy to the house of a criminal overlord.

A white, painted daybed covered in brightly striped calico stood under one expanse of glass. Lined up with military precision along one side were numerous cushions. Cara threw herself upon the daybed. She extracted *Magycks of the Gods* from her satchel and dropped the leather bag back on the floor. A maid entered and deposited the tray of refreshments on the wrought iron table next to the daybed. She gave Cara a wordless curtsey before retreating.

She lay on her stomach, pulled several throw pillows around her, and read in the bright light. Rays poured in through the glass and lit up her body, as she reclined with the medieval book propped up on a cushion. Today, she wore a halter neck corset, with her chemise pulled down her shoulders, leaving an expanse of her back naked. The scars became silver chains in the sunlight; running between her shoulders until they disappeared under the rich, brocade fabric of the corset. She looked like a larger version of the petite butterflies, radiant beams dancing over her body.

Cara spent the previous week searching amongst her father's notes for any references to Egypt and Nefertiti's Heart. Although he went to great length to describe his chase and ultimate possession of the artifact, he clammed up when it came to saying what he did with the relic. Much to Cara's dismay, the Heart appeared to be the only object without a definitive resting place. She had compiled a list of banks, security houses, and a few country estates to visit to amass the remainder of the collection.

The book from Helene proved slow going. The ancient English and tiny script gave her headaches after only a short time of study. She read a passage numerous times before the words slowly made sense. Flicking through the pictures at least yielded the correct section to read.

She heard Nathaniel's boot heels as he entered the lush garden room. The daybed dipped as he sat. With an arm on either side of her, he leaned over to trail kisses along her exposed shoulder blades. His kiss was a sensual greeting, far superior to any handshake or polite bow. A shiver ran through her body, followed by a deep sigh.

"You're blocking my sun." She rolled onto her back to stare up at him. He trapped her within his arms, his eyes locked on hers. Heat spread over her torso and her breath hitched in anticipation. The fear in her gut stretched and extended a sharp claw, reminding her it still dwelt inside. She wondered what she would do if Nathaniel lowered himself onto her—panic and knee him in the groin, or dissolve into a puddle of gooey longing?

He brushed a fingertip over the blue-black bruise on her face, courtesy of her bout in the pub earlier in the week. The tiniest fragment of worry flickered behind his eyes before it disappeared. "You seem to have made yourself at home."

"I thought I would save Jackson or Miguel from sitting outside the library all day. I figure if I'm here, you know exactly where I am."

"How's the research going?" He sat up, breaking eye contact and rendering her internal question hypothetical, at least for the moment.

"Slowly. According to the oral histories, when Nefertiti died, her heart was removed as part of the normal mummification process. Instead of the expected organ, they found a gem." She clutched the ancient book to her bosom like a protective talisman. "The legend says the purity and strength of her love for Akhenaten was such that her heart turned into a diamond. Showing their love was eternal, enduring forever, like the gem."

Nathaniel raised a sceptical eyebrow. "Sounds like a cold sort of love, if she had a diamond instead of a heart."

She blew a raspberry at him. "Men. Obviously the romance of the symbolism is lost on you."

"Not at all."

His low tone vibrated through her body. She dropped her eyes back to the book, which proved rather ineffectual as either talisman or shield.

"Then what happened?"

"Anubis was touched by the strength of their love. He said he would release Akhenaten from the Underworld, and if he could find Nefertiti in the next life, he would grant them life, eternal as the diamond heart. He offered Akhenaten immortality."

Nathaniel trailed his fingers down her arm. "So where do the keys fit into all this?"

Cara exhaled a held breath, while trying to marshal her thoughts, a difficult task with Nathaniel so close, and stroking her.

"The heart is part diamond, part mechanical, with gold cogs and gears. Lapis lazuli and heliotrope veins run through the middle. From what I remember, father could never get it to work." She tapped the closed book. "According to this, Akhenaten is Nefertiti's true love. Only he possesses the key to her heart, which will allow him to claim their immortality. He must unlock the heart, which, I assume, requires some form of a key."

"But it's just a story, an oral folktale." He took the book from her grasp and set it on the daybed, leaving her with nothing to shield herself from him.

"I've seen the Heart. I wouldn't have a clue if it really is a diamond or not. Gemmology didn't interest fourteen-year-old me." At fourteen, she had more immediate concerns, like how to escape her weekly beating. She saw the artifact the week before her father gave her to Clayton, occupying pride of place on his desk in the library. He would spend hours staring at it, trying to figure out the mechanism. Cara thought it gruesome; who would want to fashion a gem into an organ? The Heart sat on his desk that final day, when everything faded to black.

"I wonder if it truly is a diamond. A gem that size would be worth a small fortune, without the added provenance of the murders." The treasure-hungry pirate glinted in his eyes. "You'd be a very wealthy woman. Have you found it yet?"

"No." She chewed her bottom lip. A diamond the size of a fist, and she couldn't find a single clue to its whereabouts. "Given the thing was stolen from its original owner in Egypt I would need to use your services to offload it. And I assume you'd still want your seven percent? So you stand to earn a tidy sum as well."

His eyes roamed over her reclining form. "You could try to haggle me down to five if you want?"

"What would it cost me?" She could barely ask the question, before the answer blazed in his eyes and singed the clothes from her body, leaving her exposed. "Nathaniel—"

He bent his arms on either side of her, lowering himself, but keeping his weight on his hands. "Nate. I want you to call me Nate."

"I thought that was only for intimate acquaintances?"

"Perhaps it's time we fixed that?" He bit her bottom lip, making her gasp, before dropping his head to cover her mouth. His kiss was unhurried, slowly possessing her, letting the heat build between them. His tongue explored every surface of her mouth, claiming its territory.

She curled her fingers deep into the calico cover of the daybed, clutching handfuls of fabric as his tongue danced with hers. She was scared if she put her hands on him, touched him, she wouldn't be able to stop.

Releasing her mouth, he moved to her throat, licking and kissing the delicate skin down to the base of her neck. He followed the line of her collarbone with his mouth, gently nipping the bone.

"Nate." His name became a cry on her lips. She arched her neck off the pillow, the heat he invoked pooling in her centre. One of his hands stroked up her side, reaching for the underside of her breast, but frustrated by the thick brocade and boning of her corset. The fear stretched within her.

Nate stopped and sat up, surveying the damage he wreaked on her self-control.

Cara breathed hard. *Guess the answer to my question is, dissolve into gooey puddle of longing.*

"How is it you have travelled the world without a chaperon? You move about London with no one to watch your every move." The change of topic gave her a chance to catch her breath.

"You've tried, remember?" She chided him of his attempts to tail her. "My grandmother always gave me a considerable amount of autonomy. And it's not like we have to worry about my reputation being ruined."

"I only watch you to ensure your protection, same as any chaperone, and to ascertain if you have any suitors." He sat next to her so composed, but she noted his chest rose and fell faster than usual.

As much as he created turmoil within her, she affected him too. She tucked the titbit of knowledge away as she stroked the cover of the ancient book. "I don't need protecting. Or any suitors, I'm not the marrying kind of girl."

External dangers didn't concern her, except for the one right in front of her, capable of stealing her breath. She'd made up her mind days ago to follow her fascination for him, regardless of where the allure led her. She had shut herself away in a tower for too long. "My father tried to marry me off in absentia once, not a hugely successful endeavour for him."

A smile twitched the corner of his mouth. "Who was the poor unfortunate you scorned?"

"I have no idea. It was a couple of years ago. I was in America when Nan forwarded his letter. I refused to return to England. Apparently the solicitor wouldn't proceed without some indication of consent from me." A mischievous glint shone in her eyes. "Or perhaps he forged my name, and I am married, but just don't know it?"

"And now? Don't you want to regain your place among the ton?"

She threw up her hands; a darting butterfly settled on her outstretched limb. The insect's red and gold wings glinted and winked before it took flight, heading back to the protection of the shrubbery. "I'm twenty-one and my father is dead. Countess de Sal said I was free and I intend to remain that way. Besides, no man would dare try and claim me."

"I would dare." His face was dead calm, with no hint if he joked or was serious.

She held her breath. Her stomach flip-flopped at the thought of him in charge of her life, of waking every morning to his intense gaze over the breakfast table, or finding his head on the pillow next to her. "My grandmother would never agree. Nice try. You won't get your hands on the artifacts that way."

"You still think that's my motive? I thought I was plain in my attempts to get my hands on you? Perhaps I need to be more obvious." He made to lean toward her again and she gave a yelp and sat up.

Their attraction wasn't a line of conversation she wanted to pursue. Certainly not while she lay on a bed in the sun, breathless from his passionate kiss. An idea chewed its way through her brain. "What if these artifacts aren't just ancient objects?"

"What else would they be?" He rose from the daybed and moved to stand amongst the greenery, putting physical distance between them.

She watched him lean against a palm so tall its fronds pushed against the glass roof of the conservatory.

"What if they actually did the things the oral histories purport they do?" She voiced the thought that itched in the back of her brain for days, ever since taking possession of the book.

He frowned. "That would be impossible."

"Is it? What if Boudicca's Cuff really does give the holder success in battle?"

Nate was silent, giving the idea some thought, rather than dismissing her out of hand. "Business is a type of battlefield. I can enquire as to the investment success of the person who purchased the cuff. It will be easy to chart the course he has taken and whether he won or lost."

A small measure of relief crept into Cara. The effect of the cuff was something they could quantify. The note from her father gnawed at her: *careful, they are not what they seem.* Cara initially thought he referred to an enemy, perhaps the person who delivered the asp. A friend or acquaintance who masqueraded and hid their true intent. But with each passing day, she became more convinced he meant the artifacts.

"Maybe that's why my father was so paranoid. He knew. It would explain the extraordinary lengths he took to acquire the artifacts. And the layers of security he maintained over where he hid them." She still didn't know where to look for the Heart, his prized possession and his biggest secret.

Cara packed away the books in her satchel, her mind too fragmented to carry on with the intense study. Something else ate at her, something tied to the brutal deaths of three girls. "What if Nefertiti's Heart really can confer immortality?"

He let out an appreciative whistle. "Then it's not just incredibly valuable, it's priceless."

"How do you tell if someone is immortal?" she whispered.

"You kill them, and see if they get up again," he answered, always pragmatic.

CHAPTER 18

Saturday, July 20

THE small millinery shop had called Cara's name from the very first day she strode past its window. Numerous gaudy hats in riotous colours stocked the bay window. To one side of the display hung an elegant little dark green number; it looked plain and unadorned next to its excessive companions. Unlike the other hats, some of which sported at least half a chicken, this one had only three peacock feathers curling over the large brim. She didn't normally succumb to girlish frippery, but, very occasionally, the need for something pretty crept up on her. Today, she finally gave in to temptation and entered the store.

The shop buzzed with a multitude of women trying on hats, stroking feathers, and playing with chiffon ribbons while keeping up constant conversation. Cara eyed the little felt hat in the window, wondering if the colour would reflect the tint in her eyes. The hat had a restrained style. A wide brim gave quite a different feel from the bonnets or miniature top hats, which covered every surface in the store. Cara reached out a hand, about to lift the hat off the hook dangling from the ceiling, when a hiss from behind froze her fingers.

"My daughter would be alive if not for you," a loud voice accused her.

All thoughts of the hat fled her head. After a brief check of her mental armour, she turned. A tall, angry-looking woman glared at her. Four women surrounded her, and nodded their heads. The group was all draped from head to toe in black, indicating recent loss and full mourning. They gripped a variety of black hats with thick, concealing veils, and all eyes narrowed to examine her.

"Excuse me?" Her eyes swept the small shop. Along with the group dressed in black, the other shoppers turned to gawk. Cara hadn't expected a showdown at the milliner's; she wasn't dressed for the occasion. With the advent of the warmer weather, she'd left her jacket at home as well as her shoulder holster and hip belt. A Derringer nestled against her thigh, but she would have to lift her skirts to reach the tiny gun. The only other weapon on her was the blade concealed under the fold of her sleeve. Knives were messy, and she hated to splash blood on her corset.

"These murders only started when you came to London. Our daughters would be alive if you had stayed away." The woman's tone climbed toward hysteria. Her friends patted her arms and made agreeable noises while shooting Cara deadly looks.

"I think you have me confused with someone else." Cara kept her tone calm. She never suspected hat shopping would be so fraught with tension. No wonder she normally avoided the girly occupation; this could turn her off shopping for life.

"The Enforcers say you are involved. They have been asking questions about you and your father. My daughter died a matter of days after you appeared." The woman swayed on her feet, and grabbed her supporters. They lowered her onto a seat placed behind her.

She placed the hysterical woman now: Lady Lovell. Her daughter Jennifer was the first victim of the mysterious killer. Or second, if he started with Lord Devon. The Enforcers' interest in Cara was now out of the bag. A shiver ran down her spine. *And so it starts, the stares and taunts and outright hostility.*

"Beth Armstrong was found in a stone sarcophagus that took four strong men to lift the lid. If I am responsible, how do you think I achieved that on my own?" Cara thought it funny how hysterical people ignored logic. However, they obviously decided as a group she was the scapegoat. She got the distinct impression the only way to prove her innocence to these people would be to get herself murdered.

"You're not wanted here. You're an unwelcome taint in the air." Lady Lovell narrowed her eyes and shot her words like bullets.

She hoped the woman's grief spoke, but she saw the nods and murmurs of agreement from the other noblewomen in the shop. She straightened her back and maintained her dignity. She refused to crack in front of them. She would never give them the satisfaction of knowing how deeply they cut her. "When they catch him, you will realise how wrong you are."

"We're not wrong about you."

Cara refused to debate her suitability as a murder suspect, and slipped out the door. She thrust a sob back down her throat. Eyes downcast, she all but ran along the pavement.

She burst through the doors to the Mayfair address before she knew what she was doing.

Jackson gave her a startled look.

"Is he free?" she demanded.

"No. But he'll see you, darling." He gestured with his head and another imposing bodyguard swung the study door open to admit her.

Nate looked up from his desk at the intrusion. Brief curiosity crossed his face at her obvious agitation.

She paced in front of his desk.

"I thought you didn't need my protection, but you look like you wished you had it today."

She halted mid-pace and scowled. *Damn it! I've run straight to him.* He was a magnet and she was a piece of metal. In her distress, it seemed natural to run in this direction. She needed his calm presence to wash over her and soothe her anguish.

"Weren't you toying with leaving London?"

"Inspector Fraser told me I'm not allowed to leave until he has completed his enquiries." She waved her hand, trying to dismiss Fraser and his investigation from her mind.

He made a discreet snort, which sounded like disdain. "I can put you on an airship. Where do you want to go?"

She was sorely tempted; she could go anywhere. With a pirate at the helm, an incredibly handsome pirate. An idea crept into her head and erased the unpleasant encounter she endured in the hat shop. A sly smile spread over her face.

"Where's Loki headed next?" She tried to sound nonchalant.

Nate blinked and laid his pen down. She had his full attention now, his jaw clenched and unclenched. "Perhaps not with him."

She shrugged; she saw the reaction she was after. He appeared impassive, but she was learning to search his face for minute changes and clues to what was going on behind those pale blue eyes. "Does your offer of an evening's entertainment still stand?"

"Of course. What has happened?"

"I've just been accosted in a milliner's shop and accused of murdering those girls. I'm tired of two-faced nobles who throw baseless allegations about me." She resorted to more pacing, waiting for her agitation to run its course. Worn out, she placed both hands on his desktop. "I'm tired of hanging in the shadows, keeping out of their way and skulking as though I have done something wrong. It's time I confronted some demons head-on. And I think you're just the person to have my back."

The corner of his mouth twitched; she longed to see him smile again and was curious about what it would take.

An impulsive idea bubbled to the surface of her mind. "Will you take me to Su-Terré?"

She licked her lips as she spoke the name of the illicit underground club. As a child, she heard the name, whispered by adults in the same hushed, excited tone children used to talk about presents on Christmas Eve. The club only had one currency—escape. You went there to either procure it or provide it.

His eyes narrowed. "Not yet. To go there, you have to answer a question for me. Are you mine, or willing to be traded?"

Mine. His words washed over her. *Are you mine?* Her nipples tightened against the stiff fabric of her corset at the idea. She parted her lips, needing to moisten them again. His eyebrow shot up, waiting for her response. She let out a heavy sigh; she wasn't ready, not yet.

"I have some business to conduct tonight at Savage's. I can escort you there, if you wish to accompany me?" He offered Savage's, instead, a legitimate playground for the wealthy in fashionable St James, containing a ballroom and several gaming rooms.

"At the gaming tables, I assume?" She wondered who would be relieved of their fortune tonight by choosing to sit opposite him. It would be interesting to watch him play.

"No. The ballroom. It's a far better place to hold a civilised conversation, saves all sorts of unpleasantness from sore losers."

She was taken aback; the ballroom was a far more crowded venue than the quieter poker tables. She turned the idea over in her head. Most of society would be there tonight; they sought safety in numbers, and with high summer approaching, the season was nearly over. The next week or two would see them leave the city for country estates. It would be a very public stand. She wouldn't just be coming out from the shadows, she would be standing under an airship searchlight. "All right."

One black eyebrow arched. "So you'll be dancing?"

She stiffened; she hadn't considered that proposition. She thought to simply watch and annoy the ton by breathing or stealing the last smoked salmon canapé. Dancing meant being held. Close. The monster inside her stirred, and lifted its head, but held its place, Nate's touch becoming something she craved, rather than feared. She didn't have to go. She could turn and retreat back to her rooms, forget she ever mentioned confronting the ton. But she'd spent years running and she grew tired of it.

"Bathe and change while you think about it. I have a dress you can wear for the occasion."

"Show me." Her voice was hesitant. "Here, now. What would it be like?"

He rose from his desk and approached her in slow motion. The blood rushed through her veins and pounded in her ears so loudly it drowned out his carriage clock on the mantle. He stopped inches from her. He picked up her right hand in his, holding it high. He slid his other hand around her waist, his fingers resting in the small of her back. His gaze never wavered from her eyes as he drew her to his chest.

Cara gasped at the intimacy of the embrace.

"It's scandalous to dance so closely." She tried to make light of the anticipated panic. Her breasts grazed his chest. She wanted to close her eyes and surrender herself to his touch.

"Good. It will give society something to be jealous about." His voice was low and throaty next to her ear. With her so close, he could skim her neck with his lips.

She held her breath, waiting for the monster to protest, waiting for the fear to force her to flee, but it had diminished in size over the last few weeks and remained silent. Instead, laughter welled up. She thought how jealous the other women would be, if he did this in the ballroom. They would never dare to step into his arms. They could only press their thighs together and dream of his lips tasting their bare skin.

She smiled; she trusted him, at least this far. "Let's do this."

He kissed her, his lips as gentle as his embrace. She leaned into him, the hunger becoming more insistent, as she pressed against his body. Her growing need openly challenged the fear residing within her for dominance, and need was winning.

He withdrew and placed her at arm's length.

"Go change, or you might not make it out of my study." His voice was thick with his desire for her.

She realised how close she danced to danger and scampered from his arms. She flashed him a smile before ducking out the door and up the stairs.

The bath was luxurious, with its combination of steam and exotic oils. She could have soaked all evening, letting the hot water leach away her cares and the ugly confrontation in the shop. She poured the fragrant oil into her palm and slathered it over her body, watching her skin absorb the tiny beads.

All too soon, the maid coughed politely and held out a towel. She toyed with disappearing beneath the water, and pretending she wasn't there, but didn't want to risk Nate coming to retrieve her. *Not tonight, anyway.*

Once dressed, she twirled in front of the mirror. *What am I doing?*

She couldn't fathom how Nate commissioned the gown and had it completed so quickly. Breathtakingly unconventional, the dress was made to be worn with no crinoline, heavy petticoats, or bulky drawers. The delicate, grey, silk chiffon was scattered all over with tiny, silver embroidered stars, and a diamante winked in the centre of each one. Apart from the dress, he provided a diamond choker to encircle her slim neck and a diamond-encrusted pin to nestle amongst her hair. The maid threw her hands up in despair at Cara's closely shorn locks. She finally decided to slick it back, making Cara's hair sleek like an otter pelt, before tucking the jewels behind her ear.

She paused at the top of the stairs, taking a moment to stare down the stairs at him, conferring with one of his men. He was handsome in his formal tails, the jacket tailored to his broad shoulders and narrow waist. His waistcoat gleamed the same pale grey as her dress, also sprinkled with embroidered stars. They would complement each other this evening.

She tried to analyse the tug deep in her gut whenever she saw him. *Is that the appeal, purely his attractiveness? Or is it something deeper?* Love was the sort of thing a girl would discuss with her mother, if she had one. Hers had died in childbirth, giving her life for Cara's. There was a hole in her life, in her heart, where her mother should have resided. *I need to talk to Nan.*

With one hand on the balustrade, she stepped off the top stair.

Nate's head shot up on hearing her light tread. His eyes drank in every move she made in the sinuous dress, as she descended. He moved to the bottom step, to take her hand, raising it to his lips while his eyes locked with hers.

She held her breath. He made the formal gesture into something far more intimate. His lips brushed the back of her hand, a promise of so much more to come, if only she dared reach out and take it.

THE carriage came to a stop under the portico to Savage's, on King Street. Aristocrats of all different levels poured into the large entranceway, eager to commence their night-time entertainments, despite the growing fear of a madman stalking amongst them. Cara closed her eyes and took a deep breath.

"Are you ready? Or would you rather go somewhere quieter?" Nate asked from her side. "Boxing, perhaps?"

In high society, a woman's reputation was everything, the only jewel she possessed, and it had to be closely, and vigorously, guarded. Cara's reputation was permanently ruined. She never debuted. She wasn't fit to be seen with the chaste daughters who were once her childhood friends. She travelled for seven years, learning about herself, and now she would step into the centre of their territory and challenge their views openly.

She opened her eyes, wide and full of defiance. "I'm ready. They can't shun me anymore or gossip behind my back. Let's see if they are brave enough to do it to my face."

He leaned in and kissed her bare shoulder, sending a ripple down her spine. "I've got your back."

He helped her from the carriage.

A newsboy stood on the pavement, waving the evening paper, yelling in his clear voice, "Enforcers clueless in senseless murders!"

Some of the men stopped, tossed the boy coins, and took papers from his outstretched hand. She could hear the murmurs running through the crowd, repeating snippets from the article. Murder of the lower classes was entertaining news; murder amongst their set sparked discord and fear. Three murders of eligible girls put a dampener on the Season. Cara could see fathers and brothers closely watching their daughters and sisters. No one would slip unnoticed from the ballroom tonight.

She entered Savage's on Nate's arm. On the entranceway floor, terra cotta red, navy blue, and cream tiles spiralled ever outward in an intricate pattern. Overhanging the centre of the pattern, an enormous chandelier, several tiers high, threw light in every direction. Cara picked up the corner of her skirt as they descended the red-carpeted stairs into the lavish ballroom. Chandeliers hung every few feet; the crystals picked up each light and threw it back to play with the diamonds and jewels adorning the women. They sent rainbows of colour whirling around the room. The deep blood-red walls heightened the emotion of the room and projected it back on the occupants.

Mechanical waiters glided through the patrons, serene, like swans. Their movements were perfectly fluid so as not to disturb the trays of champagne flutes and canapés attached to their metal limbs.

Heads swivelled; opera glasses and pince-nez raised as the dowagers present sought to identify Cara's face. They tried to ascertain who got the jump on their precious daughters by appearing with the much-sought-after viscount. Murder aside, marriage was a serious business, and Cara, an unexpected intrusion. Nate was notoriously cagey. He never courted anyone openly and he was fast approaching the age all good heirs were expected to tie themselves down. The titter of gossip rushed through the crowd like a wave approaching the shore. The wall of chatter crashed against the sand, turning to gasps of shock, as the handsome couple descended farther into the room.

The light from the chandelier caught and played with the diamantes sewn onto Cara's dress. The stars glittered in the refracted light of the ballroom, clothing her in an early evening sky. The sensuous fabric clung to her slender form, the front a simple drape dropping straight to the ground. Sleeveless, the skirt spilled into a sinuous train behind her. The back cut scandalously low, a silver chain holding the two sides together across her shoulder blades. The effect highlighted the scars running over her spine and made them part of the dress design.

Society enjoyed gossiping about violence committed behind closed doors, but they didn't like to be openly confronted with the results of abuse. Or to see brutality as headline news. But, no one could deny what had been done to her, not when Nate so elegantly framed her scars.

The press of people surrounded them, and Cara saw the effect of the unsolved murders ripple through the ballroom. Daughters were closely guarded, potential dance partners scrutinised by male family members before releasing a delicate hand. Fathers prowled the edges of the floor, watching with eagle eyes and swooping down to reclaim loved ones once the dance concluded.

"Dance with me," Nate whispered. "Since they are all going to gossip about us anyway, let's make it completely scandalous."

The orchestra occupied one end of the cavernous ballroom, the music amplified and circulated around the room. As the opening refrain of a waltz played, he swung her into his arms. He held her far closer than acceptable, his chest millimetres from hers. His hand spanned the flesh at the small of her back. His fingers gently stroked her exposed spine.

She wanted to close her eyes and bask in the sensation as they moved to the slow music.

This must be what a cat feels like, lying in front of the fire and having its fur stroked.

A mental image flashed through her mind. She lay naked in front of a fireplace, the heat from the flames settled over her like a blanket. Nate ran his hands up her body, igniting an inferno. She flung her eyes open before she became lost in her daydream, to find his cool gaze washing over her face.

He drew in a sharp breath. "Whatever are you thinking about? I hope it's us doing something naked, because your eyes have changed from hazel to green, as they do when I kiss you."

She dropped her eyes, trying desperately to cool the heat rising up her neck. She looked around for a distraction, searching for an inane topic of conversation. They waltzed past a waiter circulating with a tray of hors d'oeuvres.

Canapés? Oh, hell. Her mental picture changed to one of his dark head bent over her as he licked a trail of caviar off her stomach. His tongue probed into her bellybutton, lapping every trace of the expensive delicacy from her skin, as fire stabbed through her core. She moaned and arched her back under his touch. She fled from the image; her mind returned to the ballroom and Nate's intense gaze.

The corner of his mouth twitched, as he held in his laughter. "Perhaps I'll torture the details out of you later. It certainly looks worthwhile, to know what occupies your thoughts and makes you blush."

She changed the topic, to save her sanity. "Any word about the person who bought Boudicca's Cuff?"

"A little. A business deal no one thought would succeed reaped him unexpected rewards. I intend to probe further this evening. Tongues are looser in this sort of environment." His eyes scanned the room, seeking out those he would subject to his scrutiny later.

As they danced, her line of sight caught a face burned into the back of her brain, a visage that had given her nightmares for more years than she cared to remember. The colour drained from her cheeks and she faltered.

Nate tightened his grip, lest she fall. Spinning her, he cast around for what caused her to miss a step.

"Remember who you are," he whispered. "You're a survivor, a fighter."

Her eyes narrowed, she remembered the dig Amy's fiancé threw at her in the restaurant. Clayton justified his behaviour by claiming she wasn't a maid. The implication clear—she either deserved her fate, or worse, invited his brutality.

"What's getting you angry?" his voice brushed over her ear.

She gave a start. Either he read her far too easily, or she was flashing her emotions conspicuously this evening. "Let's see how well you remember your history lessons. The Romans promised they would never throw a virgin to the lions. Do you know what they used to do, to ensure that?"

His eyes flicked to where Clayton stood laughing with his cronies, obviously sharing some joke amongst them, as they flashed looks in Cara's direction. His attention returned to her. "The Romans had their guards rape all the women first."

She nodded. "Exactly. So they could loudly proclaim no virgin was torn apart by the predators."

"Who?" The dance ended and he drew her to the side of the ballroom.

She tightened her grip in his hand, remembering. Clayton could make his loud boasts because he had had someone else defile her first. "His valet."

She shoved the memory back down again. "I need some air."

There were far too many people in the ballroom and not enough oxygen. Even though she ditched the corset this evening, she found her breath coming in shallow gasps.

They walked down the side of the ballroom, to where the doors to the wide balcony folded back upon themselves. Her tormentor moved, ensuring their paths would cross.

"Well, well. It's little Cara Devon," his familiar voice checked her step. "Haven't you grown into something rather interesting?"

Time froze. Those in the ballroom, riveted to the spot, could only swivel their heads to watch the confrontation. Every voice silenced so as not to miss the exchange; every syllable and nuance would be repeated a thousand times in parlours over the weeks to come. Cara had spent seven years trapped in a cold, black nightmare; she wanted to embrace the light. She needed a cleansing fire to exorcise him from her soul.

I want to be free.

She used Nate as her touchstone. He radiated power and she drew on him. She drank in strength through his touch. Once full, she untangled her fingers from his, and approached her rapist.

She looked him up and down coldly. "Don't dare to presume you have any right to address me."

He laughed. "But we're such intimate acquaintances." His words a taunt, he threw down the gauntlet, to see how she would react.

She toyed with wrenching an arm off the mechanical waiter and spearing the limb through Clayton's torso. She enjoyed the mental image of watching him writhe with the animated fingers waving from a gaping chest wound. His blood would spill over the floor, the colour mingling with the deep red walls.

"Old age has addled your brain. You're a rapist of children and no acquaintance of mine." Her voice strong and sure, determined this weak old man would never touch her life again.

"I'd watch this one, Lyons, she has teeth." Clayton laughed nervously. "I'd recommend the liberal application of the lash to bring her into line."

"You seem to have mistaken me, sir. I don't need to force a woman. Nor would I ever inflict violence on a child." His words were icicles, each one tossed at the older man with lethal accuracy.

Cara leaned close to her tormentor. "You're pathetic, trying to pretend you are something. You couldn't even get hard unless your valet had his hand on your shrunken member, and couldn't finish the job without his finger up your arse. You're a failure, both as a man and a rapist."

A titter ran around the room, as her every word was relayed. Titters turned into snorts and suppressed laughter.

Anger flashed in Clayton's eyes, but he couldn't silence everyone present. He leaned on his cane, his need for the assistance obvious in his awkward movement.

A cruel smile crossed her face. The blow that enabled her to escape years ago had caused his disability.

The colour drained from him; he stood before her in shades of grey, revealing his frailty.

"I maimed you when I was only a child. Touch me now, and I'll kill you." She turned her back to him, and holding her head high, she strode out to the balcony. Conversation rose behind her.

The evening air was cool, after the humidity of the ballroom. The gentle breeze refreshed her agitated skin, brushing over her in a soothing manner. She wanted to bathe in the dark, to wash away the memories and release them up into the night sky, leaving her cleansed. And whole, at last.

Nate approached her from behind; his arms slid around her waist as he drew her back against his chest. She leaned into him, absorbing his steady heartbeat, letting her own slow to match his pace.

"Are you all right, *cara mia*?"

She closed her eyes and let out a sigh, one she had held in for seven years. "Yes. It's done. He's a weak old man and has no power over me."

Silence. There was no need for words and she wondered about the nature of the strange relationship weaving itself around them.

What am I doing? She chastised herself.

Feeling, at last, a long-buried part of her answered.

"Cara?" The query came from Amy, seeking out her friend.

"Yes," she replied from within her cocoon of Nate's arms.

He kissed the base of her neck and she held in a cry, brief caresses no longer enough.

"I have some business to take care of; I'll leave you with your friend. I'll find you shortly." He released her and gave the briefest nod to Amy.

She kept her eyes fixed on the night-time streets of London. Small circles of light danced around the street lamps, but they were too far apart to join hands and push back the darkness. She tried to peer into the empty spaces between; somewhere in there dwelt a killer. Or was he prowling the ballroom, unseen amongst them, disguised as one of them?

Even now, did he kiss a hand and waltz with his next victim? Cara had drawn blanks in her search for a clue, to where her father hid Nefertiti's Heart, and she wondered if finding the gem would stop the killer, or attract his attention.

Amy watched Nate return to the ballroom, her eyes wary, before turning on her friend. "Oh, Cara, what are you doing with him?"

"Whatever do you mean?" Her eyes were still miles away and she had to drag her mind back to Amy's side.

"Viscount Lyons. He's so cold." Amy shivered, rubbing her hands up and down her arms.

Cara shook her head. She could never think of Nate as cold, not with the level of heat he provoked within her. "No. He's controlled. Don't mistake that for being cold."

"Well, he's . . . a criminal," Amy dropped her voice to a whisper, as though she thought he might overhear them.

That aspect of his reputation and business dealings didn't concern Cara. On the contrary, she found his underworld involvement made him more approachable, more open-minded. She merely kept a weapon handy.

"I think possessing both a title, and a fortune, trumps such a minor detail." She knew how society operated. A man could get away with anything, as long as he was wealthy enough, and a peer. "And besides, he doesn't hold my past against me."

Amy flushed, embarrassed by previous events.

"Did Clayton do that?" Amy gestured to Cara's back and the silver scars glistening in the subtle evening light.

"Yes." She closed her eyes, remembering how the lash ripped through her young body. She arched her back against the pain. Instead of making her compliant, each blow added to her resolve to survive, to fight back.

"Let's go have supper." Amy held out her hands, not knowing what else to say.

Cara smiled. She was hungry. She fought a battle and emerged victorious. "Let's find some champagne," she said. "When we were little, we were inseparable, and then our lives took wildly different paths. Let's celebrate burying the lost years and moving forward."

The two friends made their way through the buffet tables and laughed over long-forgotten memories. They snatched champagne from the passing mechanical waiters and toasted renewing their friendship.

Cara became an object of curiosity to the other men. She was free and unrepentant in her refusal to bend to society's expectation. She displayed her backbone figuratively by standing up to Clayton, and literally in the body-hugging gown. Spirit and beauty were a heady mix for some of the young bucks; she was an exotic creature amongst them.

Two separated from the pack, approached, and asked her to dance. She politely declined, although she found the attention flattering. They refused to budge from her side and she gave a frustrated sigh.

Across the room, she saw Nate look up sharply, then break away from his conversation and head in her direction. A foolish individual stepped into his path, and tried to engage him. The look he shot the man was more effective than any knife blade; the man fell to the side as though dropped by a physical blow. Nate reached her side, his mere presence shutting down the other men.

"You're out of your depth," he informed them, as he took her by the arm and led her away.

Cara stared out the carriage window, her back toward him as she watched the pedestrians. He liked her short hair; he didn't have to sweep it out of the way to kiss her neck. There was something about a woman's throat that he found infinitely appealing. He didn't know if it was the curve as it rose out of their shoulders, or knowing how extremely sensitive the skin could be. And she was constantly exposed to him. Leaning over, one hand on the side of the carriage for support, he kissed her nape. His lips followed the vertebra from her hairline down. She tasted of jasmine, the bath oil he laid out for her. He thought of her naked form rising from the water and suppressed his groan. He had been so patient, but every encounter tested him to his limit. Her mere presence heated his blood to boiling point. He often resorted to fisting his hands until his short nails dug into his palm, to stop himself from claiming her.

The dress revealed all of her spine to the small of her back. A sigh ran through her body, making her shiver and ripple like silk. She grew accustomed to his touch, no longer the bolting horse when he reached out a hand. Now she responded to him.

He longed to follow each scar with his tongue, to turn them into a map of desire coursing over her back. To watch them writhe under his caresses until she cried for a release only he could deliver. Her scent wrapped around him. She filled his mind, as he wanted to fill her, and his arousal strained against his trousers at the thought. His lips had progressed only halfway down her back, before she turned.

A seductive half-smile played across her carmine lips. "Nate." She breathed out his name as a sigh.

Resting her head against the back of the carriage, her eyelids were heavy as she tilted her chin to him. A subtle invitation for him to claim her lips, which he could not refuse. He covered her mouth, his tongue demanding as it sought admittance. A soft moan escaped her throat as she parted her teeth, allowing him entry.

His arms snaked around her waist. His hands brushed the naked flesh of her back as he drew her, unresisting, to his chest. For the first time, he truly held her, hard against him, as his fingers ran up her spine. His mouth crushed her lips, their tongues fighting for dominance that was part dance, part joust. She was mead, and he wanted to become drunk on the taste of her.

He picked up the hem of her skirt and reached under. He followed the contour of her leg, gliding over the silk stocking. With one hand on her knee, he pulled her onto his lap, so she straddled him. He ran both hands up her legs, bunching up the gossamer thin skirts, allowing him access to stroke the velvet skin of her thighs. Her moan became more insistent.

"What are you doing to me?" her voice husky with desire as she caught her breath.

"I'm setting you free." He pulled her head back down to his mouth, claiming her, wanting her. Her hips moved against him. He groaned and ached to be free of the impediment created by the layers of fabric. She was so close, the silk knickers no barrier; he had only to open his trousers. He could only think of being buried deep inside her and satisfying his burning need.

She froze, her breath hitched. "No." A sob of fear came from deep in her throat.

He had pushed too fast and demanded more than she could give. He bit back his frustration and lifted her off his lap and back on to the seat. Both of them breathing hard. A tear rolled down her cheek from between tightly squeezed eyes.

He caressed the drop away with his thumb. "I gave you my word. You are safe with me. I won't demand something you're not ready to give."

He pressed his head against the blue velvet of the carriage interior and rolled his eyes behind closed lids, not wanting her to see how close he was to the edge. Grabbing his cane, he rapped on the carriage roof. There was a slight jerk as their progress halted.

"Jackson will see you home safely, but I have to go." He slipped out into the night, needing to find his own release before he lost control.

CHAPTER 20

Sunday, July 21

STRONG hands and scorching kisses gave Cara a troubled night. Nate was a man of deep appetites, and she showed herself incapable of satisfying them. Waking before dawn in sweat-drenched sheets, she did something she vowed never to do again.

She ran.

Scant little belongings went into the ever-present satchel. She scooped her father's notebook from its hiding place, hooked the tiny Derringer under the brown string, stuffed in *Magycks of the Gods*, and fled.

She headed to a nearby livery and hired a horse. She briefly contemplated catching a train, but didn't want to be confined. She needed action. Sitting on a train was too passive. Horseback gave her freedom, despite the fact it would take her longer. She needed to ride hard, for her muscles to ache and strain with the effort, to gallop every stride with the horse until her mind pushed beyond exhaustion into blissful nothingness.

The flow of London traffic oppressed her, and hemmed her in on all sides and kept their pace to a walk. She thought she would scream with the effort of reining in both herself and the gelding.

Once they reached open road, she kicked the horse forward. She rose in her stirrups and urged the gelding onward. She pushed him, mile after mile. Her brain burned despite the cool wind battering her face. The horse's flanks heaved as he cantered. Cara dropped back to a walk only when she felt sure no one followed, either on the road by carriage, or above by airship.

She paced the horse, not wanting him to drop on her and leave her stranded by the roadside. When the sun reached the highest point in the sky, she found an inn off the road. She sat outside with the horse and ate lunch, sharing her bread with the hungry equine. She lay back in the grass and stared at the pale sky, while the gelding grazed. The swirling grey clouds kept turning into a pair of blue-grey eyes, penetrating her, questioning what she was doing. Unable to stand the silent inspection by spectral eyes, she threw the gear onto the horse once more. Back in the saddle, she urged him forward. The road stretched in front of them and Cara ran toward oblivion.

Dark rolled above her as she trotted up the green, rural lanes of Leicester. The muscles in her thighs burned from the daylong ride. Her back ached and her fingers cramped. She longed to drop into bed and let sweet unconsciousness carry her away. It beckoned to her from the edge of exhaustion. *Soon.*

The impressive Georgian mansion dominated its landscape. Lights blazed from the lower levels of the house. A footman walked the circular entrance driveway as she rode up. He paused in his task of lighting the gas lanterns. He extinguished his flame and hurried up the stairs, shouting the arrival of the lone rider.

More lights flickered and appeared in the windows and soon figures clustered on the top step, eager to greet the unexpected guest. Cara released the reins as a groom rushed forward. The gelding dropped his head, exhausted, but having faithfully completed his task.

"Good boy," she murmured, scratching his wither in thanks before leaping to the ground.

"You scandalous girl!" A voice shrieked from above her. An older woman pushed to the forefront; the staff peeled apart to make way for her. "The entire village is talking of nothing but your outrageous behaviour in London."

Cara dropped her eyes as she walked up the stairs to the doorway; she halted when she was level with the formidable matron. The older woman was as tall as Cara, with the same erect carriage, although the years had added a few more pounds to her frame.

"Come inside at once." She grabbed Cara, then flung her arms around her in an affectionate hug. "You must tell me every teeny detail at once. I am desperate to know if this viscount is as cold and delicious as they say."

"Hello, Nan." She leaned forward to kiss her grandmother's cheek. "And he is. Like Michelangelo carved him from the finest marble with pure lust guiding his hands."

"Good lord," her grandmother whispered, a hand going to her bosom. "Nessy!" she screamed back down the hallway. "Tea and biscuits. The little scamp is here with oodles of juicy gossip."

She turned back to her granddaughter. "Oh, do tell me it's juicy. It certainly sounds it."

She gave a wink as she drew Cara into the house and guided her toward the warm and welcoming parlour.

Cara laughed and cast her gaze downward again, at ease to be home. "You're not supposed to be encouraging me, you know."

She crossed the parlour and threw herself on an overstuffed chaise in lurid brown and orange paisley. She raised her weary legs and stretched out on the sofa's accommodating length.

Nan gave a snort of laughter. "My dear I'm past sixty. Encouraging you is the most exciting thing I get to do anymore. I understand the whole of London is talking about your tiger stripes. The aethergrams have been flying back and forth all day."

Nessy, her grandmother's long-time companion, bustled into the room with a tea tray. She deposited it on the low table and found herself a spot on the sofa, eager to hear all the news.

Cara screwed up her nose. It had been Nate's choice to expose her scars in such a public fashion, not hers.

"Fitting, though," her grandmother remarked as she poured tea.

"What do you mean?" Cara sat up and took the proffered mug. She cupped her hands around it and inhaled. The tea gave off a welcoming smell and a cautionary sip confirmed her suspicion. Nessy had laced the pot with rum. She sighed. *Home.*

"It would take a tiger to walk next to the lion."

"I don't think I'm walking next to him, Nan." She stared at her tea, hoping the amber liquid would hold all the answers to her questions. *What the hell am I doing?* "I'm so out of my depth, I'm drowning. I need you to throw me a lifeline."

"Oh, child, you never did take the easy route in life." Worry etched lines on her grandmother's face. "And you're certainly gambling with dangerous odds."

"Well, I did manage to stick it to Clayton. He was at Savage's last night, looking old and frail, so I kicked his cane away. He won't be haunting my dreams anymore."

"Good. Sounds like you have someone much younger and more virile chasing you at night," her grandmother innocently remarked, as she dunked a biscuit in her tea. Nessy snorted by her side.

"Nan!" Cara laughed at her grandmother. Nan and Nessy, in their youth, were far more scandalous than anything she could accomplish. The head gardener still blushed in their presence, even forty years after whatever the pair of them did to him. Heading into their sixties, they refused to tone down their antics, and still managed to horrify the locals.

"I've leased the house out." She changed the topic, before her mind lingered on what happened in the carriage. "The lawyer said he's a scholar of some sort, and loved the library. Hopefully he stays long-term, and we don't have to think about the house again."

"And your father's trinkets?"

"Nate will sell them as we require."

"Nate?" Nan's eyebrows shot up at the informal contraction of his name and she nudged Nessy.

Cara caught her breath, too tired to spar with her egregious grandmother. "Not tonight, Nan. He's sold Boudicca's Cuff and the cash is with the lawyers. I'm trying to find Nefertiti's Heart now."

She chewed on her lip, unsure how much to reveal about the Heart and her suspicions. She didn't want to burden the older woman, or worse, make her a target.

"Is it true you are tied up with those horrible murders?"

She shook her head. "Yes and no. I have Enforcers on my tail. I think the Heart is linked somehow and the killer is after it. I need to go over father's ledgers he left here. I'm coming up blank trying to find where he hid the gem."

"Popular girl," Nessy muttered, elbowing Nan with a wink.

"Inspector Fraser thinks it all links back to father, and I think the connection is the artifact." She grabbed a hard biscuit to drop into her tea, watching the hot liquid crawl up the savoury morsel.

"I never did approve of your mother marrying Devon."

"If she hadn't, she would still be alive." Cara would have loved the opportunity to know her mother, knowing nothing except the stories her grandmother told of a headstrong and impulsive girl.

Nan reached out and took her hand. "And then you wouldn't exist. And who would keep me entertained with scandalous tales?"

"I'm exhausted, Nan. Can we leave the rest until the morning?" She placed her tea mug back on the small table.

"Of course, dear. I'll schedule the interrogation for after breakfast. Nessy and I will sort out the questions tonight, so we'll be ready to start as soon as you rise." The older woman gave her a warm smile, as Cara kissed her cheek. "First on the list will be what has you so spooked you ran all the way home."

Cara groaned. She might yet have to give all the intimate details of her late night carriage ride, and how Nate stole into the darkness when she proved unable to satisfy him.

She slipped from the parlour and climbed the stairs to her rooms at the back of the house. Exhaustion threatened to overtake her, so she dropped her clothes on the floor and climbed between the sheets naked. A weight dropped on the blanket next to her.

"I wondered when you would show up." She reached out a hand. A large, ginger tomcat rubbed himself against her outstretched fingers. A locomotive engine started deep in his belly. He circled twice before settling in her armpit, his head resting on her chest. His eyes closed in contentment as her fingers automatically stroked his fur while her brain tried to settle.

Despite the deep ache in her body, sleep was in no hurry to claim her. She listened to the cat's rumbling purr. She could only replay events from the previous evening. She felt lighter, free of Clayton and the fear he planted deep within her. A frown creased her brow. She was still a prisoner, though; her brain played gaoler. She longed to surrender to her body's need for Nate. She had been so close last night, but when he pressed against her, she panicked and froze. Her brain remembered only pain and battled her body, to shelter her from the anticipated agony. A tear rolled down her cheek.

What will it take to be free?

CHAPTER 21

HE *watched her leave the shop, her pale pink parasol raised against the unrelenting rain. She waved to her chaperone inside, perhaps indicating she would only be a moment, her eyes drawn to the haberdashery next door. A riotous display of ribbons, silks, and veils in a variety of shapes and colours filled the shop window.*

The other one had gone. He had been so close, his hand reached out for her, but he grasped only air. She vanished into the night. This one would be a poor substitute. He feared in his gut it wouldn't work; the other called to him and invaded his dreams. But he had to try. This one's eyes were hazel, too. Hope flickered within him. The eyes were similar. Perhaps, when he gazed into their depths, he would find what he sought and she would know him.

The street was empty. The unexpected summer downpour scattered the few hardy shoppers. No one wanted to linger and risk being drenched. People raised umbrellas and pulled hats down low. Eyes kept down to avoid the rain, few people took any notice of their surrounds or the other pedestrians. He pulled the brim of his hat down farther, before stepping off the pavement toward her.

"Madeline?" he called softly, halting her progress.

She swung around to see who hailed her.

"Oh, hello," she replied. Her eyes lit up on seeing him, a good sign. "I can't talk for long. Molly is watching from inside the teashop and I just want a quick look next door. We're heading off to father's country estate tomorrow, and I want some ribbon for my new bonnet." She indicated the haberdashery display attracting her attention.

"Of course," he murmured in agreement with her. "I understand. Terrible business, what has happened, and we need to keep you safe. We can't be too careful." He walked with her a few strides along the street. "I'll not hold you up. It's just that I have a gift for you, and I wanted to give it to you before you leave."

Interest sparked over her face. What woman didn't love the prospect of a gift? He watched an internal battle rage across her features. To stare at the ribbons and parasol handles, or the prospect of a surprise present?

"I'll just fetch it from the carriage, if you don't mind terribly waiting?" He dangled his bait and turned. He walked toward his waiting conveyance.

She trailed behind him, curious.

He opened the carriage door and peered inside, reached for something that should have lain on the seat.

"Bother," he muttered over his shoulder. "It seems to have fallen down the back of the seat. You know what those little boxes are like." He gave a quick smile and hopped up in the carriage, his hand diving down between the seat cushion and the plush lined side.

Her eyes widened. A small box indicated jewellery. Everyone knew that. The fish bit down hard on the bait.

"I'll help you look for it." She quickly offered and stepped up into the carriage. The door swung shut on them.

Monday, July 22

Cara stretched languidly in bed, arms over her head and pushed her palms against the quilted silk headboard. The sun peeked through muted red and orange curtains, illuminating her childhood room. The items on her dresser remained exactly as she had left them on her last visit. Nobody ever disturbed her room, ensuring she had one small slice of constancy. The ginger tom still slept hard against her; then he opened one eye, daring her to move.

"Sorry, boy, my stomach demands I get up. And knowing you, you'll want feeding, too." She sat up and swung her legs over the side of the bed. The cat meowed and gave his own feline stretch before moving to the end of the bed. She prowled naked to the large window, while the cat took care of his own ablutions with meticulous care.

She flung open the curtains. A clear blue sky greeted her, and the clean, green vista of her grandmother's estate. Her room looked out over the rear gardens and potager. The river curled past the orchard boundary; ancient trees draped their limbs over the lush meadows. Her heart lightened; she loved it out here. Time away from the frantic motion of London would help settle her mind and allow her to sift through her thoughts.

She dressed lightly in a simple cotton shirt and high waist skirt. The day was already warm outside and she planned to go exploring. She wanted freedom to run, climb, and chase like the thirteen-year-old in her demanded.

"Come on, you." She picked up the cat and tossed him on her shoulder, where he curled himself around her neck, regarding the world from his accustomed perch. She padded down to the kitchen on bare feet. Life was casual at the Leicester estate; the family often breakfasted at the large table in the kitchen, while the servants went about their day. Or even, quite scandalously, the servants joined them. Eating together kept everyone abreast of village gossip, and what was happening farther afield, and tightened the bonds of kinship that bound the close-knit household.

She greeted the household staff by name as she slipped into the warm and busy kitchen. Cook oversaw the baking of the daily bread, and the divine smell wafted toward Cara's nostrils. She dropped the cat off his perch on her shoulder, and he made like an arrow to the plate of cream in one corner and the off cuts from the previous evening's beef.

She gave cook a bear hug from behind.

"The scamp has returned," the rotund chef boomed, as she turned to return the show of affection. "Take a seat; you look like you need feeding up. You're all skin and bone."

She pulled out a chair opposite Nan and Nessy. A plate of eggs, bacon, and hash dropped in front of her, quickly followed by a mug of steaming coffee. She inhaled the coffee fumes, letting the sharp aroma stimulate her brain, before she took the first glorious sip.

"Nobody makes coffee like you, Duffie," she said to the red-faced woman. "I searched the whole of London and nothing compares to your brew. I swear you are a magician with a coffee bean."

The cook beamed with pride, as she bustled about her domain.

Nan allowed her granddaughter one mouthful, before starting. "This is the moment where you spill what happened the other day."

"Me, Nate, and a steamy carriage ride I couldn't handle." She managed to talk between alternate mouthfuls of coffee and bacon.

Nan and Nessy exchanged raised eyebrows. "That's fine for a teaser. Now we require the blow by blow account."

Nessy giggled at Nan's choice of words.

Cara rolled her eyes, and spent the next half-hour telling her enraptured audience of the exchanges between her and Nate. Some points she glossed over, like how she straddled him in the carriage and froze when his erection pushed against her knickers. But she told sufficient detail to let her grandmother and Nessy help unravel the turmoil in her mind.

"You're young, you're beautiful, and he sounds ridiculously handsome. Enjoy what you have. If you don't jump him, someone else will." Nessy summed the situation up succinctly, to earthy laughter all round.

"It's not that simple." She appealed to her grandmother.

"I'm with Nessy on this one. Don't overcomplicate things. You're a smart girl, listen to your gut."

"You lot are incorrigible," she muttered as she left the table. "I'm heading out before you talk me into doing something even more stupid."

"Say my name," he whispered, as he stroked strands of blonde hair from her face.

She murmured something; he leaned closer to catch the faint syllables.

"No, not that one. My other name," he insisted, growing angry at her ignorance. "Say my real name."

Her eyes widened, the whites glowing in the dim light. Her head moved back and forth, as she sobbed and tears trickled down her temples.

He placed his hands, palm down, on the slab next to her. His eyes raked over her form, as she trembled before him.

"Say my name," he insisted, louder, firmer.

She cried. Tears ran freely, the girl unable to form articulate words due to the sobs issuing from her throat.

An acrid tinge hit the air around him. Fear. Sharp and crisp in his nostrils. She wasn't right. If she was right, she wouldn't fear him. He expected the opposite to happen: she should love and welcome him.

Why was it not working? He was doing everything right. The problem lay with them. They closed ranks against him, whispering and tittering. They played the coquettes but never delivered on their promises. She wouldn't do that to him. She loved freely, unreservedly. Her love for him was pure and eternal. He should never have let her run. He should have taken her when he had his chance.

This one wasn't right. The one he wanted had slipped through his fingers.

"You're not right!" he screamed, the frustration overwhelmed and overflowed within him. He picked up the key and slammed it into her body.

"Not right!" He yelled it over, and over. His arm rose and fell, keeping pace with the words. "Not"—hand up. "Right"—hand smashed downward.

Time wore on. Unaware of its passage, he worked out his rage. Finally sated, he thrust the key into her bloody chest and left it there. He gave a deep cry and slumped over her legs, with his arms outspread. Minutes passed in silence.

203

He pushed himself upright again.

He picked up a towel from the nearby trolley and wiped splatter from his fingers and arms. Methodically, neatly, he ensured each bright red drop disappeared onto the cloth. Calm and in control once more, he could have been wiping excess butter from the lobster off his hands.

She would come back to him. She had to return to London. She was drawn to him. They belonged together. Everything up to this point had been merely practice, the flexing of long-forgotten memories. He was complete and ready for her now. The time had come.

They had waited three thousand years to be reunited; he could wait a few more days.

THE copper beech had stood guard over the Leicester countryside for hundreds of years. It watched houses built, pulled down, and rebuilt. The tree oversaw the building of the mansion and now stood vigil on the edge of the big house's orchard. It had long been a favourite retreat of Cara's; high above the ground, the fork of its enormous branches cradled her like a giant hand.

Looking up from her book, movement attracted her attention and she saw the airship appear on the horizon. It seemed to flit amongst the green canopy, as she watched its approach. She could think of only one reason why an airship would be travelling to this corner of the English countryside. The ship was a small, sleek model, built for speed and lightning strikes. All too soon, it hovered over the formal gardens at the back of the mansion.

Her heart gave a leap, unable to decide if she was pleased or terrified that Nate pursued her. She watched from her comfortable spot in the nearby orchard.

A line was tossed over the side of the airship and a black figure slid down the rope. As he neared the ground, he let go and jumped the remaining distance.

She climbed higher in the tree to watch. She saw her grandmother, followed by Nessy and two footmen, rush out to greet him. The conversation appeared animated. Her grandmother waved her arms, then turned and pointed directly at the tree, hiding Cara amongst its boughs.

She saw Nate's head dip and kiss her grandmother's hand, before he strode in her direction. He wore black pants with knee-high, black boots. A short jacket with military frogging hung open, revealing the half-unlaced, white shirt underneath.

Cara gulped. *Hooray for pirate day.*

She climbed back down the tree to her previous spot and tucked herself against the coppery-grey trunk. She stretched her legs along the branch and took up her father's journal, hoping to appear nonchalant, while her brain tried to figure out what to do. Her heart raced; from her spot, she couldn't see how close he was without peering around the trunk.

He hailed her. "I know you're up there. Are you coming down, or am I coming up?"

Prepare to be boarded? The thumping in her chest became frantic. She realised hiding up a tree was a tactical error. She should have jumped down and legged it across the field instead.

She heard the scraping of boots against bark and moments later, his presence filled her eyrie. He radiated energy. Standing in the fork, with his hands on the branch above, he looked like a roguish pirate hanging from the rigging. His gaze swept over her reclining form.

Barefoot, no stockings, no petticoats, there's my second mistake for today. She felt naked under his scorching gaze, but refused to pull the skirt back down over her bare legs.

"I didn't pick you for the sort for a day out in the country." She pushed the journal into a crevice above her head and tried to engage in polite conversation. And ignore the fact she was scantily dressed and hiding up a tree, like a woodland sylph waiting to be ravished.

He tilted his head, and looked quizzical at her choice of opening statement, but answered politely. "I've lost something. I thought I would start my search in this area. How is your research progressing?"

He dropped down next to her. The branch was comfortable for one, and decidedly cramped with two. Cara inhaled as he settled, his side pressed to hers, making heat course through her torso. The aroma of warm male musk with the tang of citrus filled her nostrils.

"I believe I'm onto something. Father hasn't made a single reference to where he stashed Nefertiti's Heart, and I think it's because he didn't have to. He kept it near him. I suspect the gem is still in the house, somewhere."

He made a noise in his throat but remained silent. He picked up her hand, raised it to his lips, and kissed her palm. Further conversation shrivelled under the heat of his touch. She closed her eyes, the gentle touch of his lips a spark to her body, made of tinder. The slow burn headed up her arm, a lit fuse heading for her heart.

"You ran from me," he said.

"I needed to think. Where did you go, after you left the carriage?" A knife poised over her gut, ready to rip through her if he admitted to seeking out another woman to finish what they had started.

He stroked her palm. "To get drunk. Very, very drunk. I didn't realise until yesterday afternoon that you had gone."

"I can't give you what you need and I don't know what I want." She swallowed. The very air around them burned and scorched the inside of her mouth.

"I wanted you from the first moment I laid eyes on you, *cara mia*." His fingers stroked along her arm, feathering over the sensitive skin, causing her to inhale sharply at the stab of pleasure.

She shook her head.

"You wanted the upper hand in a business deal." She took her hand back, tucking it under a fold of fabric.

"No. I first saw you long before that."

"I doubt it. I left London when I was fourteen." She considered inching away from him, but that would put her perilously close to the edge of her perch and the risk of plummeting out of the tree.

"I've never had anyone doubt my word before."

"You're a lord, not *The* Lord." She struggled to bring her body under control; she was inches from surrendering everything.

He leaned over and caressed the side of her face, brushing his thumb down her cheekbone. She couldn't meet his eyes, too afraid of what her own would reveal.

"The day I turned eighteen, my father took me riding in Hyde Park. He was on the brink of bankruptcy, and he told me I needed to marry money, and save the family title and estates. As we rode, he pointed out various fortunes in the carriages around us, discussing the merits of property and stocks that each held. I was expected to pick one and do my duty."

He dropped his hand. She wondered where his story would go, as she studied his long fingers.

"To me, those girls all looked like timid house cats. With their eyes downcast, they never risked a glance at the world around them. All so meek, doing as commanded. They were all so similar and bland. There was nothing to distinguish them. They were simply different hues and stripes of grey. The only difference among them was the composition of their fortunes."

Cara was getting hotter. She fixated on his hands, resting on his bent knee. She had changed her mind about wanting to escape, and instead tried to mentally command him to touch her.

"We saw people gathered under a large oak tree and we rode by to see what the commotion was about. High up in the oak tree, clinging to a branch, was a ginger striped kitten. She was caterwauling and spitting venom on those below. She also had excellent aim with an acorn."

He gave her one of his rare smiles and she knew she would drown in him. He was the ocean, and she was a mere raft upon it at the mercy, or rage, of the surrounding sea.

She laughed softly, sharing this part of his story. "I got my governess right between the eyes, you know."

He grinned and continued his story. "The people muttered the child was out of control, but I admired her. No one was going to pin her down and turn her grey. She was fierce, spirited, and fascinating."

So many people gathered that day, to watch her shame her family name. She had no idea Nate was one of the youths on horseback, watching. *Has he always been watching me?*

"The spectacle helped me make a decision. I vowed to make my own fortune, so my path would always be my own. I wouldn't have a puppet master pulling my strings and determining the course of my life."

"Is that when you went off and became a pirate?" Cara hoped he was going to tell her tales of his adventures aboard the pirate airships. His eyes were serious as he wrapped his arms around her and drew her into his lap. She let out a sigh and lay back in his arms, her head against his chest as ripples of pleasure spread over her body wherever he touched her.

"I made another promise that day. When the time was right, I was going to find that ginger kitten and see what sort of woman she became." Cupping her face, he leaned down and kissed her gently, his lips tasting her, teasing, until she had to rise up against him and demand more. He smiled against her as he deepened the kiss, leaving her short of breath when he lifted his head.

Cara finished the story. "My governess quit on the spot, walked off, and left me up the tree. It took a few hours and three Enforcers to get me down." Her smile faded. She remembered the rest of that day.

"What happened afterward?" He nuzzled her neck, making it exceeding difficult for Cara to concentrate on anything except the path his lips were taking and the liquid heat starting to pool at her centre. With one hand he worked at the buttons on her shirt, and pulled the soft fabric off her shoulder, exposing her collarbone to his caress. She gasped when his hand stroked lower and cupped her breast.

She continued her story, before rational thought fled her mind. "I screamed blue murder all the way home. I knew what was coming. Father was not pleased that I publicly disgraced his name."

She remembered how she stood in the middle of his library while he removed his belt. She was riveted to the spot; her breath came in short gasps as she anticipated the blows to come. Only when Lord Devon had vented his anger did she crawl to her room and sob uncontrollably into her pillow. "I think that's why he gave me to Clayton. He thought, being my father, he was too soft on me, and that another man might beat the rebellion out of me."

Nate kissed her again, hard, his tongue probed her mouth as though he sought to find and destroy the painful memories contained in her head. "You are unique, Cara, don't let them turn you grey. Don't be a bland automaton like the others. Come back to London. Come back to me."

Her heart swelled and ached at the raw longing in his voice. "Won't it damage your reputation as the hardened crime lord, if word gets out you have a soft spot for treed kittens?"

Reaching down, he wrapped his fingers around her ankle, stroking over the bone, before progressing higher. She closed her eyes, on the brink of surrender; she luxuriated in his slow touch.

"Well, this is no kitten. This is something far more wild and dangerous. A tigress, reclining on her treetop throne." His hand reached her calf and headed for her knee, dragging her skirts up as he went.

Cara sucked in a breath, her head pressed against his chest. Her bones were melting under his fingers as he stroked the back of her knee.

"Which means you were never a treed kitten, but a tiger cub. I think being known as the man who dared to stroke the tigress will only enhance my reputation."

"You know I can't do this. The pain—" She ached for him and the emptiness inside her screamed to be filled. Her brain remembered only how much it hurt, how Clayton ripped through her young body, as tears of pain coursed down her face.

"You can. You just need to want it enough. You're like a steam engine without a pressure valve. Eventually, it will be too much for you to bear." His hands never stopped touching her. The one cupping her breast gently thumbed over her flesh until a moan broke from her throat.

She thought she would scream with her craving for more, already it was too much, her mind close to splintering with need.

"The desire won't let you go, but will crawl under your skin until need threatens to rip you in half. The agony will surrender to pleasure in your brain, and you'll have to seek release." His hand on her leg stole higher still and stroked her inner thigh, while his mouth claimed hers.

She moaned against him, the pressure within her skin intolerable. If she didn't have him, her heart would explode from the hunger.

"Not here. We can't," she whispered. *We're up a tree.*

The wicked smile touched his lips. "Can you think of any better place, than where you feel safe?"

He was right. The tree had always protected and harboured her from the world. This was her sanctuary, where nothing could hurt her. Turning, with a hand on the familiar ancient tree trunk for balance, she straddled him. Her knees were abraded by the rough branch, but she didn't care. He bunched her skirts up around her hips, as her fingers fumbled with the laces on his shirt. She was desperate to touch his skin, to run her hands over him. She wanted to trace the scars she saw when they had fought. Pushing the two sides of the fabric out of the way, she ran her fingernails up his chest. He inhaled sharply, and groaned when she leaned in to kiss his shoulder, her tongue darting over his flesh.

He tastes as delicious as he looks, salty goodness.

His fingers stroked her inner thigh and crept higher, pressing against the silken fabric of her knickers. She groaned and leaned into his hand, inviting the most intimate caress. He increased the pressure with the heel of his hand and her skin fractured, unable to contain the desire coursing through her. She gasped as he caught her, holding her in place.

"I promise you, *cara mia*, no pain," he whispered against her cheek.

He pulled a knife from his boot, the steel a cold, hard kiss as he sliced the silk knickers from her body and tossed the slip of fabric aside.

Her hands shook as she undid the buttons on his trousers.

Free at last, his arousal rose up between their bodies and grazed against her.

Her body responded; heat and longing flooded her body and spread to her limbs.

With his hands on her hips, he guided her closer so he could press up into her. Cara cried out, teetering on the edge between fear and desire. Nate stilled and waited. He stroked her hair, his voice gentle as he reassured her, calling her *cara mia* as she fought an internal battle, and won. With a sigh, she sank down and her flesh yielded to him. The sob of fear turned to a cry of yearning, the emptiness inside her filled at long last. The last shackles in her mind fell away and she gave herself to him completely.

Her hips moved against him, over and over. She revelled in the feeling of him deep inside her, as the wave gathered momentum. He dipped his head and his tongue drew patterns on her breast. Then, greedy for more, she pulled his head up to kiss him, raw and hungry. Sensation overwhelmed her and the wave crashed through her body, the orgasm swept into every fibre as she cried out his name. Nate buried his groan in her neck. His arms wrapped tightly around her; his teeth grazed her skin as he was racked by release.

Cara pressed her forehead to his, trying to catch her breath. She was afloat on an ocean with a current buffeting her body. His arms held her, as tears ran down her face. She was finally free. She stretched, relishing the answering twitch from deep within her body. She held him captive, unwilling to release him, the sensation too delicious to relinquish. She gazed at him with heavy lidded eyes, her lips swollen from his kisses.

"If you keep doing that, we're going to have to be up here for a lot longer," he said, running his hands over her body. "I'm surprised your grandmother hasn't come looking for you yet."

She drew her fingers down the centre of his chest, watching the way his muscles moved with an inhaled breath. "I think I have splinters in my knees."

"Next time there will be a bed, and a complete absence of clothing." His lips trailed along her collarbone, licking the thin sheen of sweat from her skin.

Cara sighed. "We should probably move, before Nan and Nessy turn up."

The sensuous smile on her face turned to a look of disappointment when he slipped from within her as they stood. She held the branch above, to give him room to stand, while they readjusted clothing.

His arm pulled her back to his chest and she sighed against him. His touch blew on the embers still glowing within her. "I have you now, and I'll not let you go."

CHAPTER 23

NATE dropped out of the tree and Cara climbed after him, her father's journal in one hand. He grasped her waist and swung her down the last few feet. His arms enveloped her, pulling her to him as he kissed her throat. His lips skimmed her skin as he moved upward to claim her mouth again.

She pushed against him, matched his hunger. With the dam broken, her body yearned for more.

"What will you tell your grandmother we were doing?" His eyes sparkled.

Cara laughed. "I won't have to tell her a thing. She'll take one look at me and guess. Next time you visit, there will probably be a small commemorative brass plaque attached to the trunk."

They walked slowly through the orchard, his arm around her waist, keeping her close. They passed through the yew hedge, into the formal garden. Nate stopped and looked up at the small airship hovering above. "I can't stay, unfortunately. Urgent work calls in London; I have to take care of something."

A swift chill descended over her; a shadow passed over her soul, raising goose bumps along her arms. She quickly rubbed them away, remembering the two men down in the Pit and wondered if they were the sort of loose ends he had to tidy up.

"I'll be waiting for you." He drew his hand along her exposed shoulder.

She leaned into his fingers. "I'll be another day or two. I'm going through some diaries father left here."

She pulled back to wave the journal clutched in her hand. "And it's easier to think out in the open. I find you too distracting." Her heart still hammered against her ribs.

He nodded, satisfied with her answer. "Two days, at the most. Then, I come looking for you again."

He claimed another hungry kiss, and then strode off in the direction of the airship and the dangling line. He hooked his foot into a loop at the bottom of the rope and they hauled him back into the sky. She watched his rising form and gasped. Peeking from his pocket, her cream silk knickers hung, with the distinctive green embroidery in the corner.

God, I hope Nan doesn't see that.

She watched until the airship disappeared over the horizon before continuing up to the house.

Her grandmother waited for her on a swing seat by the back porch. "Where has your delicious pirate gone?"

Cara sunk down next to the older woman. She pushed off with her feet to set the seat in motion. "He gave his apologies. He had to go back to London, some business to deal with."

Nan reached out and took her hand. "What do you plan to do with him?"

"Why? Do you not approve?" she asked cautiously.

Her grandmother burst out laughing. "Approve? My dear, as if you ever needed my approval. But that's not why I asked. Nessy and I are going to wrestle for him, if you don't want him. We're not so proud that we'd refuse your cast-offs."

Cara laughed. "Well, you can't have him."

"Yes, perhaps not. But it certainly looks like you just have."

Blushing, she jumped to her feet. Her centre pulsed at the memory of clutching Nate deep within. "I'm going to the library, before you and Nessy start hounding me for all the details."

"That's all right, my dear. We still have vivid imaginations; we'll fill in the blanks." Nan called out as Cara disappeared into the house.

Tuesday, July 23

For servants, the day started hours before their masters and mistresses ever stretched a toe out from under their silk coverlets. The kitchen maid had been up for over an hour already, creeping out of her narrow cot while full dark still blanketed London. She warmed water and stirred in yeast, waiting for the gooey mixture to froth and bubble before adding in the flour. She lost herself in the rhythm of kneading the dough before setting her loaves to rise by the fire.

She glanced out the high window. The kitchen was below street level; the window slit showed her the feet and wheels of the London traffic above her head, once the city rose from its slumber. She could just make out the faintest hint of colour on the horizon, dawn about to break. The hooves of the milkman's horse clattered past her narrow view on the world only minutes earlier. She enjoyed her pre-dawn flirting with the roughly handsome milky, but she was behind in her chores already and couldn't afford his distraction this morning.

Brushing the flour off her hands on her plain linen apron, she headed for the back door, keen to have the milk inside before any of the street kids nicked it. She pushed the back door and was surprised it wouldn't give. She pushed harder and it moved a couple of inches.

"Bloody kids," she muttered. They had probably tossed a drunk down the steep stairs and left him propped up against the door to sleep off his intoxication. She put her shoulder to the timber and forced the door open enough for her to slip through, intent on giving the hobo a piece of her mind.

She rounded the door and stopped. She stared at the bundle of clothes, trying to figure out how they could weigh so much. Reaching down with one hand, she was about to shake the person when some instinct froze her movement.

Something didn't smell right. Sharp and metallic. And the shape was all wrong.

She stood up and prodded with her toe instead, letting her boot connect with the blanket and draw it to one side. Her eyes widened, struggling to make sense of the broken pile of flesh and limbs. Then, she turned her head and retched into the gutter until her stomach crawled back up her throat.

Fraser held a handkerchief to his nose. Vomit, blood, and excrement combined to make a toxic nasal assault. The girl discarded like a piece of rubbish—the very act infuriated him. There was no care or attention, only disposal.

"It doesn't fit," Connor muttered from behind him. He stayed away from the sheet-covered object

"No," Fraser agreed. He lifted the corner of the sheet and said a silent prayer for the broken girl underneath. Her chest a mess of stab wounds, too many to count with a casual look, he would need Doc to verify the accurate number of blows.

He's angry. So much rage. But at what?

From beside him, Connor recited facts from his notebook. "Madeline Alcott. This is her home. Her father confirmed the body as his daughter."

Fraser forced his mind to block out the pale beauty of Madeline's face; it was the only way to do his job. To remain impartial and sniff out the minute clues, he had to shelve the emotion. He would return to the memory later, and the sight would haunt his sleep. Only the bottom of a whisky bottle would erase the sight of Madeline's broken body dumped on the back doorstep of her home. Her torso resembled a butchered carcass, and from the centre, jutted the ornate brass bow of a very familiar key.

Later that night, Fraser stared at the bottom of his empty beer mug. Ale was a poor substitute for the hard liquor his body craved, but beer would have to do. He would drink enough to dull the memory, not to erase it. He needed his wits about him until the murderer was caught.

"What's the word on the street, Frannie?" he asked their waitress as she dropped two more beers on to their table.

"That it's just a bunch of toffs." Her tone was bitter. "Last summer, when that nut was killing our girls, they didn't care. They laughed while we were butchered in the streets like old mutton. Let them see what it's like for a change."

Her sister had been one of the victims of that particular serial killer, hacked apart and her limbs left to clog up various drains. They nicknamed him the Grinder, because of what he did with the flesh he removed from the girls. Fraser had never eaten a sausage from a street vendor since that case. He had his work cut out for him over those gruesome weeks. His superiors argued to let the killer thin the number of street girls. Ten were taken before he caught the Grinder and ended his reign.

"You were the only one who cared. You fought for us. We don't forget that." She patted his shoulder before slipping away to tend other patrons.

"Any news from Doc yet?" Connor asked, taking a swig from his beer.

Fraser ran a finger over the condensation forming on the outside of his glass. "He's up to two hundred separate wounds and still counting."

Connor let out a whistle and dropped his beer. "Poor wee mite. What did she do to piss him off that much?"

"I don't think he was angry at Madeline." He took a deep drink, the ale doing nothing to stave off the darkness threatening to envelope him.

Connor frowned.

"He must have been angry to do that to her. Over and over, without stopping." A shudder ran through his large frame.

"Oh certainly, I agree with you there. But I think poor Madeline was the outlet, not the cause." He surveyed the bar; conversations rose and fell around them. The room was so full of noise and passion, but he saw only the evil lurking and waiting to grab any one of them.

"Who, then?" Connor asked.

"Who slipped from London a few nights ago?" He flicked his passive grey eyes back to his friend.

Connor concentrated before coming up with a name. "Cara Devon."

Fraser nodded, watching Frannie bat away the hands reaching for her bottom as she moved through the crowd.

"That means he must be watching her. Or, heck, must know her." The sergeant made the connection Fraser had known for a while. "You know who it is."

"I believe so." He dropped his tone low, keeping the conversation for their ears only. "But this won't be an easy collar. We need all the ammunition we can get our hands on, and even then, it might not be enough. We're big game hunting, Connor."

Connor's eyes widened and he took another quick hit from his mug. "You could get us both killed with this one."

"If we fail, I doubt anyone will ever find our bodies to be able to make that declaration." He thumped his friend on the back to reinforce his cheery thought.

Connor muttered into his glass. "So what do we do now, then?"

The investigation had stalled. While the fathers of the murdered girls admitted an association with Lord Devon, they clammed up about the finer details. In his interview, Lord Alcott let slip the men shared a common interest, then he too had fallen silent, lost in his grief. Fraser's gut instinct told him he was close, that the pieces would soon fall into place. With the target he had in his sights, he needed far more than a gut feeling. His superiors and the magistrates would stand against him, without hard evidence. His hands itched to close around the final piece.

"I need to crack Cara Devon. That should give us the evidence we need. That, and I intend to dangle her like an enticing piece of bait. I believe the killer has merely been practicing on the other girls, that Cara is his ultimate prize." He waved his empty glass at Frannie. "We're going to take her away from him. And hope he lunges after her, that he will react without thinking to get his hands on her."

"She could end up getting killed." Connor pointed out quietly.

Fraser's grey eyes glinted hard, turning to steel. "Sometimes the goat gets mauled when you try to catch the lion."

Wednesday, July 24

LONDON called, and two days later, Cara answered. She turned over the faithful
gelding to the local livery and took the steam train. Her grandmother
and Nessy saw her off at the station, waving as the mammoth black and
steel monster clawed down the rails.

She tried to occupy her mind on the journey by flicking through her
father's diary and *Magycks of the Gods*. Her tentative theory about the
true nature of the artifacts grew the deeper, she dug. She kept finding
objects in the ancient book that her father tracked down and concealed,
almost as though he used the oral legends as a shopping list of items to
steal and hide from the world. The idea nagged at Cara. *If he knew what
they were, why didn't he use them?*

She jumped out of her compartment at the Liverpool Street station
with pent-up frustration fizzing under her skin. The hours of sitting,
unable to move, drove her to distraction. She wanted to seek out Nate,
tossing up whether to try the house or the hangar first. She needed to
burn off excess energy and a part of her knew exactly how he would
suggest doing it. She had another reason for seeking him out; a tug on
her heart posed a question she needed to answer.

She decided to walk off the stiffness in her muscles, before catching transport to Mayfair, and headed down Bishopsgate Road. Heading along the main street, she caught sight of the familiar bronze and copper mechanical horses and the large black carriage they pulled. Jackson chatted to the driver as he smoked his cigarette. Cara glanced at the adjacent pale grey stone building; it contained the White Hart Inn.

She waved to Jackson as she wandered closer to the window. She scanned the assembled people inside, and her breath hitched. She spotted him seated at a table not far from the window, his face impassive as the gentleman opposite him gestured to emphasise his conversation. Nate's gaze flicked up and caught hers. The barest twitch of a smile pulled at his lips, before the mask dropped back. He glanced briefly at his companion and she saw him say something, sending the other man into a renewed arm-waving frenzy.

His attention returned to Cara. Holding her gaze captive, his fingers pulled a handkerchief from his pocket, made of cream silk. He ran the fabric through his fingers and brushed it against his cheek. Cara frowned, until she saw the green embroidery. She dropped her lashes, her mind raced as heat spread through her torso.

He's playing with my knickers. In a public house!

She dared to raise her stare, His eyes reflected his hunger. A slow twitch pulled his mouth into a predatory grin. A knot formed in Cara's gut; flames licked over her and she parted her lips in a silent cry. His fingers entwined in the silk, reminded her of how he stroked her through the fabric and touched her pulse.

Cara dragged her attention from Nate's strong hands and took a deep breath to steady herself. She approached Jackson. "Will he be long?"

The bodyguard shrugged. "He's relieving that other bloke of his fortune. He usually lingers over something like that. Or he might cut it short, seeing as you reappeared."

She bit her lip. "Can you tell him I'm at the hangar? I need to hit something."

Without offering any further explanation, and with the image of Nate playing with her underwear burned into her brain, she changed direction and took off down the pavement. Setting a brisk pace, she dodged amongst the numerous pedestrians clogging the footpath.

Down by the Thames, she entered the dim interior of the enormous Lyons airship hangar. She paused to let the smell of different lands and cultures roll over her. She spied Miguel in the back of the hangar. He was strapped into a metal exoskeleton, the steel claws unloading large crates from a mechanical trolley.

"Can you take a break?" she asked him. "I want to spar, and you're more my size than that lot."

She pointed over her shoulder to the other men. Most of them hit in excess of six-foot-four, and half as broad. She wanted to burn off energy, not wipe off her face.

He gave her a cheeky smile. "Sure. I'll just finish up here."

He unloaded the last crate, powered down the suit and then released himself. They struck off down the secret staircase to the Pit.

She removed her jacket, pistols, and corset and hung them above the oak pew. Miguel bandaged her hands. She returned the favour, winding white cotton over the wrists and knuckles of the young man.

At first glance, they appeared evenly matched. Only a close inspection showed the youth pulled his blows, ensuring he wouldn't fully strike his opponent. The bout wound on, both fighters breathing hard after twenty minutes of strikes, dodges, and exertion. A light sheen of sweat was visible on Cara's forehead and bare shoulders. Miguel sweated openly, rubbing an arm over his forehead to clear his vision of the threatening liquid. He froze, his eyes focused beyond Cara's shoulder, giving her an opportunity to land a hard blow on his chin, sending him reeling backward.

She paused, slightly puzzled, wondering why he didn't bounce up. She swung around to follow his line of sight.

Nate stood behind her, his gaze swept over her body and his nostrils flared. He glanced to the other side of the Pit, to the heavy steel double doors, closed and padlocked.

Cara never asked what was beyond the door. Her curiosity fled at the idea of asking; a tingle in the back of her head told her she didn't want to know.

"Upstairs. My office. Now," he commanded, before spinning on his heel and stalking out of the room.

Wary and thrown off guard by his reaction, Cara picked up her discarded clothes. She toyed briefly with heading straight back to her apartment in defiance, but she longed to run her hands over him and finally have his bare skin next to hers. Heading up the stairs, she found the office door shut. She slipped through and closed it behind her. She tossed her outer clothing on a nearby chair, before unwinding the tape from around her knuckles.

"You shouldn't be here alone." He sat on the corner of the desk, his arms crossed over his broad chest.

"I wasn't alone." She tossed the ball of cotton bandage onto the chair with her clothes and started on her other hand.

"You know what I mean. You shouldn't be down there without me or Jackson." He clipped his words, holding his anger in check with each syllable.

She finished the second roll of bandage and threw it next to the first. Looking up, she caught his blazing stare.

"What is your problem? I thought you wanted me to come back to London. You told me if I wasn't back in two days, you would come after me. And just a couple of hours ago, you were practically sniffing my knickers in a tavern."

She was confused; after what happened in Leicester, she thought he would be pleased to see her. Her heart jumped into her throat at the sight of him, but he was angry.

"Just go to the house . . . please. You shouldn't be here, not today. We'll talk later," he said softly, running a hand through his dark hair. For the briefest moment, he looked overloaded, and vulnerable. The mask dropped back into place quickly. "I'm sorry. Of course I want to see you. It's just business, something unpleasant that must be dealt with first. I don't want it touching you."

A tingle shot down her spine and told her the unpleasantness was something to do with the double-bolted steel doors deep underneath the hangar. Something lurked behind them, and made his usual icy control melt just a fraction under its heat.

"All right, then," she agreed.

"Good. I'll have Jackson drive you to the house." He uncrossed his arms, a small amount of tension eased from his shoulders.

"No, thank you. I'll find my own way there." She still bristled at his tone. "I have some things to do along the way." She could be as equally stubborn, and for once, he didn't push for dominance over her.

"I expect to find you at the house when I finish up here." He dropped his tone lower, brushing a promise over her with his words.

She gave him a mock salute. "Yes, sir. But you could do something for me?"

"You're not getting your knickers back. They're my talisman. I intend to take them to every business meeting from now on." He gave her a heart-warming smile, but he looked tired underneath it.

She moved closer to him. "I just want one kiss, before I go."

His lips twitched, but before he could answer, she held up a hand.

"With one proviso. You can't touch me."

His gaze raked her instead.

"Very well. You have my word." He tucked his hands behind his back, an echo of how they started, almost a month ago. Only his burning gaze told her how much everything had changed. They had tasted each other, and Cara was fast becoming addicted.

Her pulse thrummed loudly through her veins as she stepped between his legs, her hip grazing him. Placing one hand on his thigh, she wound the other in his black hair, pulling his head down as she arched up to kiss him. His hunger was palpable, rolling off him as his tongue dove into her mouth. His warm scent filled her nostrils. She sucked on him, wanting more, and he responded by increasing the pressure and baring his teeth, nipping her lip until she moaned into him.

His arousal pushed into her thigh and she rubbed against the growing hardness like a cat, showing her own need and making him growl deep in his throat. She pressed against his chest, as a slow tingle spread over her skin. Her tongue played with his, then she pulled back, her heart pounded harder and faster than after the sparring bout.

His gaze was white hot metal, searing off her clothes. "I suggest you leave now, while you can. The business I have to tidy up won't take too long. Unless you want me to add another pair of knickers to my collection?"

She gave a shudder of anticipation, grabbed her jacket, and ran out the door.

The bath water was deliciously hot. Steam rose and swirled over the surface. Cara sank down and let out a deep sigh. The heat drew the stress of the last few days from her body. The water buoyed both her body and mind. The door to one side of the bathroom slid open and she glanced from under her eyelashes.

Nate entered and sat on the teal striped chaise in front of the fire. He pulled off his long leather boots.

Cara leaned forward and hugged her legs. Resting her cheek on her knee, she watched him for a change. His shirt came off over his head in one easy move. He tossed the garment over the back of the sofa. She let her gaze roam over the hard muscles of his torso. The finely chiselled lines made her fingers itch; she wanted to run her nails over him and find out how much pressure it would take to make him gasp.

Standing, he put his hand on the buttons of his trousers.

A smile curled her lips and she shut her eyes. Moments later, the water around her rippled and stirred. The level within the copper bath rose, accommodating Nate's bulk as he sank down behind her. Placing a hard muscular leg either side of her, he reached out and drew her through the water, back against his chest.

The steam enclosed both of them, moisture beading over their bodies. He tilted her head, so he could claim her mouth, his lips hard against hers. He took her breath into him, fanning the heat spreading through her limbs. His hands roamed her body, gliding over her skin slick with the oil she had poured into the bath.

Heat-induced lassitude freed her mind. She gave herself up to the languid sensations rippling through her at his touch. With one hand he thumbed her breast, sending delicious waves rolling over her. His other hand stroked lower. She arched her back at the exquisite knot building deep inside her. She moaned and writhed against him; her hands gripped his thighs.

His hand stroked her centre. Her fingernails dug into his legs as lightning flashed up her body, igniting her senses. A moan broke from her throat as his fingers played over the sensitive bundle of nerves. As he plied deeper, her body ached, screaming for more. Her hands clawed his thighs, unable to reach any other part of him in the confines of the bath and held captive by his body around her. He stroked her slowly, unrelenting. His fingers rose and fell as he nudged her toward the edge. She cried out; her skin on fire as the pressure within her built.

"What would it take to make you scream?" he whispered, his teeth grazing her neck. He rubbed with the heel of his hand as his fingers sent shockwaves through her body. He drove deeper into her, and her hips rose to push against him as she teetered on a precipice. With his free hand, he continued his assault on her breast and she cried out his name as release blossomed through her. It rolled from her centre outwards, arching her body out of the water as light sparked behind her tightly closed lids. Her body spasmed around his hand and she collapsed back against him, her head on his chest. Sensation lapped over her body with the water, as his hands soothed her. He caressed her while she came down from the erotic high. Her eyelids fluttered, not wanting to open.

"Don't go thinking I'm finished with you," he said. "You certainly don't get to fall asleep on me yet." His arousal pressing into her back emphasised his words.

She resisted the urge to pout; part of her wanted to lay in front of the fire and sleep like a sated cat. Part of her wanted more; she just didn't want to move too far to get it. He wrapped his arms tightly around her, and held her until the water started to cool.

He stepped out of the bath, grabbed a towel, and hooked it around his hips. He held out the other towel to Cara, and she stepped over the side of the tub, into the thick cotton folds. He took his time to rub her body, drawing the moisture into the towel, lingering over her breasts. He dropped to his knees to dry each leg, starting at her ankle and working his way up. He paused to kiss her inner thigh and she had to bite back the moan on her lips. Her skin was raw and each feather touch burned through her.

Satisfied she was dry enough; he tossed the towel to the ground, swept her into his arms, and carried her to the room beyond.

"This is your room," she whispered.

The deep green walls complemented the wooden furniture. The bedroom was luxurious and masculine. Small mementos from his travels decorated the walls and the mantelpiece. She saw a large and fierce tribal mask from Africa and a statue of Baast from Egypt. A richly coloured Persian rug spread over the floor. She wanted to study everything, learn where he travelled, and bombard him with questions.

He set her down next to the oversized four-poster bed. Barley-sugar twist posts held aloft a deep cream and green damask canopy. "You can explore my room later. Right now I want to explore you."

He discarded his towel, locked his arms around her, and tumbled onto the bed, rolling her under him.

"Oh dear, Miss Devon," he murmured hotly against the hollow of her throat. "You appear to have fallen into my bed."

She laughed at his line. "Was this a setup just so you could say that?"

"I have been waiting rather awhile. Ever since you stated so forcefully you never would." He made his point with her pinned naked under him. "Now roll over," he ordered, lifting himself enough to allow her to roll onto her stomach.

She complied and rested her head on her arms, the lazy cat waiting to be petted.

He straddled her thighs. Picking a scar, he traced it with his lips down her back, starting at her shoulder and moving down across her spine. He kissed, licked, and nipped at her skin. When he finished one lash mark, he followed the path of another. With his weight balanced on one hand, he used the other to caress her front as his tongue worked over her back. She was trapped between two layers of pleasure. Feline-like, her touch-starved body drank up every stroke and caress, all but purring under him.

Having tasted every inch of silken skin on her back, he rolled her over. He claimed her mouth in a hungry kiss; his tongue sought out hers. His lips were crushing in his need to possess her, to brand her as his.

She welcomed his weight on her, arching her body against him, the hunger within her desperate to be sated, now he had awoken it.

Breaking free, his lips trailed over her collarbone before heading south, down to her breasts. His tongue circled each in turn and drove her into a frenzy of longing. She reached out for him, desperate to explore and touch him, but he captured her hands and held them above her head. He tempered his strength, his grip strong enough to stop her distracting him, but loose enough she could break free. If she wanted to.

"When do I get my turn to be in charge?" She asked between gasps, wanting to reciprocate, to taste him and stroke him until he lost his icy control. She longed to see a rush of emotion across his face as she pleasured him.

"In case you haven't noticed," he breathed against the skin of her stomach. "I prefer to be in charge, and don't surrender easily." He continued licking wild fire down her body.

"I'll need handcuffs then," she gasped. His lavish attention made her writhe, her brain no longer able to function and form coherent sentences. She could only think of the ache inside her, needing to be filled by him.

He released her hands when his head dipped lower. His tongue explored her belly button as his hands feathered her thigh. His fingers pressed into her as his gaze sought hers. She moaned as he stroked her, the fire threatening to consume her again.

"No, Nate," she gasped. "It's too much. I need you, now."

He gave in to her demand, his breath short, and his eyes wild with desire to possess her. This was what she wanted, the freedom to give of herself and now she welcomed him. No space existed between them, as they moved together. He drove into her, each powerful thrust sending her spiralling out of control. She clawed her fingernails down his back, needing to be consumed by him.

Her heart ached to belong to him, and only him. His power and control made her safe; his strength matched hers and allowed her to be free. He was unrelenting in his rhythm, until she fractured under him, and screamed his name. Her powerful release was the trigger for his. Her body clenched around him and drew him deeper into her. He buried himself and cried out.

Careful not to collapse on her, he rolled onto his back, and gathered her into his arms. She nestled against him, her head on his chest, listening to the pounding of his heartbeat, smiling with the knowledge of the effect she had on him. Next time, she would cuff him to the headboard, and indulge every wicked thought she had about him. She would explore every inch of him with her lips, tongue, and fingers, until he broke and begged her to ride him to release.

Nate stroked her hair. He pushed his thigh between hers, an intimate embrace, securing her to him in all ways, as she drifted into sleep.

Early morning, with dawn still an hour or two away and there came a discreet knock on the bedroom door. Partially awake, Cara grumbled as Nate disengaged from her warm, naked form to answer the call. She heard a low, muttered conversation, followed by the door shutting. Rustling indicated he found clothes and pulled them on. The mattress dipped under his weight as he sat next to her, and kissed her bare shoulder.

"I have to go. There's an urgent situation I have to sort out. Stay here. I'll be back late morning."

She murmured agreement, not intending to move very far, except to give a languid stretch. Pulling his pillow to her, she inhaled deeply of his scent and curled back into sleep.

Thursday, July 25

CARA stretched her hands up over her head. Her muscles quivered at the memory of being used in new, and sensual, ways. She was disappointed to find the bed next to her empty, but vaguely remembered Nate leaving before dawn to attend urgent business.

Her stomach rumbled. She cast her eyes around the room and re-membered her clothes were in the bedroom on the other side of the bathroom. She was toying with a naked dash through the rooms when a soft knock sounded on the door.

She pulled the sheet up over her chest. "Yes," she called.

The door opened and the lady's maid entered, carrying a tray. Cara's stomach rumbled again on seeing the little triangles of toast in the silver holder, a soft-boiled egg, and smelling the glorious waft of crispy bacon.

The maid's eyes flitted around the room nervously as she set the tray over Cara's legs. Next to the breakfast lay a small, eggshell blue visiting card. A frown wrinkled her forehead.

"That came for you yesterday afternoon, miss."

Cara picked up the heavy card. The front bore a name and address. The back bore the inscription: *You helped Isobel. She said you would help me.*

Cara snorted out air. *Another one. This is starting to feel like a job.* Her attention drifted back to the maid, her eyes darting around the room.

"Are you all right?" she asked, propping the pillow up behind her. "It's Emily isn't it?"

"Yes, ma'am. And it's just I haven't been in here before," she breathed.

Cara arched an eyebrow. "Does he normally chuck women out during the night then?"

"Oh, no, but he never has them on this side. Not here, never in *his* room. Always over there." She gestured with her head to the room on the other side. The room Cara always used to change and where she dropped her clothing the previous night.

"Oh. So we are both invading his private domain." She chewed over the information as she munched on the crispy bacon. Although it made sense, he couldn't have made his point about her falling into *his* bed, if he tumbled her into the guest bed. But her heart skipped a beat, hoping it meant something else.

"Do you want me to fetch a dress for you, or do you want your own clothes?" the maid politely enquired.

"My clothes, if you don't mind."

Emily nodded her head and disappeared through the door to the bathroom. She emerged moments later with the clothing and folded them neatly on the end of the bed while Cara demolished the egg and toast.

Emily fussed over her like a woman with too much time on her hands and not enough to keep them occupied. Cara never thought why a house of men employed a lady's maid, but her mind skirted around how often Nate had guests in the other room, to warrant having a maid on his payroll. Eventually she managed to escape and left Emily to tidy up, while she darted down the stairs to freedom.

Miguel hailed her in the entranceway. "Where are you off to, miss?"

"Are you spying on me today?" She was in a good mood. If she closed her eyes, she could still feel Nate's naked flesh pressed to hers. The memory raised goose bumps along her arms.

"He's still busy with Jackson. Something messy blew up." His face pulled into a grimace. "He asked me to make sure you have everything you need."

He gave her a small bow and snapped his heels.

A smile tickled her lips. He reminded her of a gentleman's gentleman, not someone studying and emulating a crime lord.

"I have a visit to make to one of the neighbours." She held out the card for him to examine. "You'll be able to keep an eye on me from the end of the driveway. Then, I will go to my rooms to fetch some things, but I'll give you a wave before I do. If you're going to follow me, you may as well be useful and carry my bag." She gave him a wink. "I promise I will be sprawled in the conservatory by the time he gets back."

Her heart was light as she walked the short drive before hitting the busy main street. She waited for a steam-powered carriage to trundle past before darting across the road. Her feet quickly carried her along the pavement to a neighbouring house. She rapped on the ornate brass knocker and gave a wave to Miguel, who watched from the driveway. Waiting on the step reminded her, she needed to visit the family home and see if she could find where the cantankerous building hid the Heart. Preferably without the tenant breathing down her neck.

The butler showed Cara through to a woman's study. A deep yellow and cream pattern papered the walls, with matching heavy velvet drapes. The surface littered with letters, a small writing desk sat under the window. A piece of green ribbon draped over the edge, waiting to be wrapped around a bundle of correspondence. A cream chaise decorated with gold butterflies stretched by the fire. The room was small, quaint, and private. And a very definite indicator she was not considered a social visitor. The parlour out of bounds to her, this was strictly business.

I'm surprised I didn't get taken down to the kitchen.

A woman in her mid-twenties entered the room. Her dark choco-late hair coiled around her head with not a hair out of place. Her dress would have screamed money, if the construction weren't so subtle, so it coughed money discreetly, instead. Cut to fit like a second skin, the fabric emphasised every curve before flowing over her hips. Sara Collins, the name on the card, was a picture of icy control. Her black eyes regard-ed Cara in a predatory fashion, causing a chill to walk down her spine.

"I've lost my engagement ring." Her voice was as chilling as her gaze. *Straight to business, then.*

"Since you've asked for my help, I assume you didn't lose it picking roses in the garden." Cara noticed she wasn't invited to sit. She rubbed her hands over her arms, the atmosphere in the room frosty, despite the sunlight outside.

A momentary hesitation came before her next comment. "I lost it as a forfeit in Su-Terré."

Cara sucked in a breath; she was going to get her visit to the illicit playground, after all. She raised an eyebrow, wondering what escape the Ice Princess was seeking underground.

"I lost a bet to the Trickster. I was supposed to provide myself, but I panicked and gave up the ring instead. Now I need to have it back before my family discovers what I have done." She told the facts plainly, no rush of emotion, or embarrassment, marred her perfect face.

I can't imagine you panicking. "Why don't you tell your family you lost it in the garden?"

Sara's mouth twitched. "The ring is a very valuable piece. They would tear up every blade of grass to find it."

A warning prickled at the back of Cara's brain, the story not ringing true. "I'm no whore. I won't substitute myself for you. What are you prepared to offer for it?"

"A slight variant on the original terms. He can have me, but at my convenience, and for two nights instead of one, to compensate him for waiting. And you will be amply rewarded for fetching my ring."

The warning ice water turned to sleet as it ran down her back. *Something's not right here.* "I'll see what I can do, but I make no promises."

Sara nodded her head and walked to the door, when cold words halted her steps. "I wonder that you are still in London. The gossips say you will be the killer's final victim."

Cara eyed the other woman, weighing her words. "You'll be hoping I find your ring before he finds me, then."

Holding the door open, Sara waited for Cara to leave.

Practically turfed onto the pavement, she considered her next move. *She's not exactly endearing me to try very hard to retrieve her ring. And while I'm thinking of finding things, I think I'll pay the house a visit, on my own.*

Miguel lounged against the wrought iron gate farther down the road, his eyes fixed on Cara, even as he spoke to the bodyguard next to him. She gave him a wave and headed down the footpath toward him. He relaxed and turned his attention to his conversation.

A cab rumbled past, blocking the house from view. Cara used the opportunity, grabbed the handhold, and swung herself onto the running board.

The driver gave her a startled look from his position at the back of the cab.

She held out a coin to him, a smile on her face. "Soho, please, Broadwick Street."

He took the coin and shook his head. "Hop in, then."

Cara swung herself into the small interior and they chugged along the road.

Forgive me Miguel, but I have to do this without you shadowing me.

She disembarked down the road from her family home and approached it from the opposite side of the road, trying to discern if the tenant was inside or not.

Across the road, a hulking dark blue uniformed Enforcer climbed out of the steam-powered carriage. His eyes widened on seeing Cara and he strode across the road toward her, heedless of the oncoming steam carriages and horse-drawn vehicles.

Oh, no. Now what? She waited for the officer to reach her side.

"Miss Devon," he hailed her. "From Inspector Fraser. I was on my way to see if you were home." He gestured to the house across the road from where they stood.

She took the card from his fingers and stared at it. The Enforcers' blue and gold shield occupied one side. Next to it, the name Inspector Hamish Fraser appeared in neat, subtle type. On the back was a short, concise message.

CHAPTER 26

CARA reached Enforcers Headquarters and climbed the stairs to Fraser's office, her brain whirring with theories and information. She knocked and waited.

"Yes?" a voice came from within.

She pushed the door open to chaos. Files, reports, and tagged items littered every available surface. Some were stacked many inches high and resembled the paper equivalent of the Leaning Tower of Pisa.

"Ah, Miss Devon, have a seat, please." He stood up from his chair and indicated its companion on the other side of his desk.

She dropped into the chair with a heavy sigh.

He walked to the window and leaned against the side as he regarded her. "Does the name Henry Simons mean anything to you?"

She frowned; not the opening gambit she expected. "No. Should it?"

His placid eyes watched her carefully. "We pulled a man out of the Thames early this morning. He was identified as Henry Simons. He's been missing for a week now."

"Are you trying to find something else to pin on me now?" She snorted. She seemed to have moved to the top of the Enforcers' hit list for unsolved crimes.

"Not at all." He weighed his next words. "It's just that he was valet to Lord Clayton."

Cara was flash frozen, immobile as her brain smoked at high speed to connect the dots. "What?"

"He had been Clayton's man for several years, until he disappeared about a week ago. He met a very unfortunate end. And he was quite a large man, not the sort to fall prey to a lone mugger."

"Yes. I remember." She closed her eyes. One large hand held her down, another curled around her throat, and he eagerly did his master's bidding.

"It appears he was beaten and tortured over a period of time, possibly the time he was missing. Then he was gutted and dropped into the water. Rather careless actually, almost as if someone wanted him found." Those eyes watched her every reaction, weighed them in his mind.

Another memory tumbled into her brain. The night at Savage's, a week ago, she told Nate how Clayton had his valet rape her first, so he could proclaim she hadn't been a virgin when he took her. Then yesterday, unpleasant business distracted him. *I don't want it to touch you*, he told her.

She thought of his gaze darting to the heavy bolted steel doors down in the Pit. *God, I hope I'm wrong.* Her mind turned to what she endured over the eternal week she was held, beaten, and raped, repeatedly. *No. Rough justice is better than no justice.* She drew a deep breath, trying to keep her wits about her.

Fraser's chalkboard caught her attention, covered in notes, names, arrows, and question marks. Her name was circled over and over. She imagined his hand drawing the chalk around her name, concentric circles moving closer, pressing in on her.

He saw what drew her eye. "Four women murdered most brutally, Miss Devon. I take the responsibility of bringing the killer to justice very seriously."

He moved to his desk and drew a file off the top of the pile. It contained a wad of photographs. He extracted one off the top and tossed the picture onto the clear space in front of her. She glanced at the black and white image. Her breath caught in her throat, her mind struggling to determine what she was seeing. A mass of battered and abused flesh and from it reached a delicate bow suspended on its brass shaft.

"The fourth victim, Madeline Alcott. Different, as you can see; he appears to have vented his rage upon her." He paused, letting it soak in that the battered flesh had a name, and a life, once. "She was murdered while you were in Leicester."

"I'm sorry," Cara whispered, closing her eyes to shut out the image. She opened her eyes, and deliberately fixed them elsewhere, unable to look at the broken woman.

"I believe the connection is between your father and theirs." Fraser picked up the photo and gently replaced it in the file. He didn't toss the file back on the desk. Instead, he cleared a space for it in the centre. His fingers pressed the top, caressed each letter in the file name as though it were his rosary.

"Your father possessed something the killer wants, and these men knew about it. And you know what it is." He stated his theory simply, and waited. He stepped to the window, leaving her to mull over his words.

She couldn't do this alone. Not anymore. "Nefertiti's Heart."

Fraser turned, his eyebrows shot up, the very name an answer in itself to all the questions about the deaths. His hands curled around the back of his chair, expectant, waiting for her to continue.

"It's an artifact from the reign of Akhenaten in 1400 B.C. It's a diamond and mechanical heart. The myth surrounding it says it came from the body of Nefertiti, Akhenaten's wife. Her love for him was so pure and divine, it made him a god. The Heart is supposed to be able to bestow immortality, if the holder knows how to unlock it. My father went to Egypt eight years ago and hunted down the gem."

Fraser let out a soft whistle. "So the killer knows about the artifact. A heart-sized diamond would be incredibly valuable."

Relief washed through her at finally being able to discuss the topic, hoping Fraser would have answers to the questions that plagued her mind.

"My father used to hold private viewings of his acquisitions, for a select circle with similar tastes in illegally obtained objects. I believe you'll find all of them were invited to see the Heart." She waved her hand at the names of the men on the board. "But the killer has his facts wrong. The myth says to unlock the artifact, not a flesh and blood heart."

Silence descended, Fraser lost in thought, sorting through the puzzle pieces.

"And another thing: why kill my father and then the girls? If we assume their fathers all know about the Heart, why hasn't he gone after them? Why doesn't he kill them for their knowledge of the Heart, why kidnap their daughters and do . . . that?" She gestured to the file of photographs.

Fraser's grey gaze held hers. "Perhaps the killer thought it would be simple. Kill your father, and retrieve the object. Then his path either became more complex, or his mind became overloaded."

She tried to make sense of the killings. "How do you detour from trying to get your hands on a diamond the size of a fist and wander off and start driving brass keys through the hearts of debutantes? I don't understand."

A deep sadness dropped over Fraser's face. She wondered how he coped, dealing with an endless stream of cases like this. The onslaught of killers never stopped. He caught one and another simply popped up somewhere else.

"Killers like this, their minds are unhinged. Are we seeking an astute man who knows the value of large diamonds? Or, a deranged killer searching for immortality? What seems incomprehensible to us is perfectly logical to him. Perhaps something pushed him over the edge, and his mission to possess the Heart, for its commercial value, warped. His attention was already fixated on these families and became focused on their daughters."

One thing worried her, survival at the forefront. "Why am I alive, then?"

"Because there is something about you which marks you as special. I believe he has merely been rehearsing with the other girls, perfecting his performance for the finale."

Cara shuddered at the thought, and immediately dropped her fingers to the handle of her pistol, stroking the design etched into the cool ivory.

"You must know, he is descending into madness, if not already there. Impending insanity makes him imminently more dangerous to you. I believe he is simply saving you for last." He spread his hands in a helpless gesture. "And given what he did to poor Madeline, I think the end is very near."

She stiffened in the chair, Fraser's words sinking through, gradually realising *who* he was referring to.

"You're wrong." She shook her head in immediate denial.

"You're an intelligent woman. You know there is a connection. There is one man who has the means and motive. And, who would know the financial value of such an artifact."

She froze. *No.* One word repeated in her brain, a small bee hurling itself against the inside of her brain, frantically buzzing *no no no no . . . .*

"You must listen to me. You cannot deny the evidence any more. You place yourself in grave danger."

"You're wrong. The killer must be someone else." She swallowed, her gaze darted to his chalkboard. Next to her circled name was another. A name she cried in passion.

Who wanted the notebook? Who tried to steal it? Then, that day in his office, he suggested she hand it over for safekeeping.

No, her brain replied.

The sarcophagus came from his hangar. He had the manpower to lift the lid, and more importantly, the money to buy their silence and the position to enforce it.

No.

Who encouraged her to find the Heart? Who kept asking how her research was progressing? Asking if she'd come any closer to finding where Lord Devon had hidden it?

No.

Who knew the value of a diamond the size of a fist and had the contacts to sell such a gem to the highest bidder? Who had a double-padlocked steel door, deep underground in a hidden chamber?

Silence. The raging bee in her head battered itself senseless, her mind unable to keep defending him. A sob welled up in her throat as her heart broke.

God help me, I gave myself to him. I love him.

"You must stay safe, Miss Devon. Please don't go near Lord Lyons again. Leave this matter to the Enforcers. We will have you watched, until he is caught." His tone was gentle, her distress obvious.

She nodded, unable to speak. Tears built behind her eyes, the pain in her chest unbearable.

"Perhaps it would be better if you returned to your grandmother's estate? Where you have friends and family to support you."

"Yes." Her voice was robotic, a flood of emotion barely held in check. "I have to go."

The tears streamed down her face. She refused to believe any of Fraser's words, but the facts all fell horribly into place, the only explanation that made sense.

She ran down the stairs and through the mid-day traffic, uncaring of her direction. Her feet moved as the skies opened up. Mother Nature wept with her distraught daughter.

Her feet carried her through the crowds; people skirted away from the madwoman flitting through their midst. She ran until she found herself at the edge of the Thames, the water turbulent and grey, stirred up by the rain and wind, the perfect reflection of her inner turmoil.

Cara fell to her knees and let the tears overcome her, blending with the rain and river. She keened while her heart fractured. Time slipped by unnoticed. Darkness fell and blanketed her, protecting her from the prying eyes of those few around, rendering her near-invisible in her grief. Uncontrollable sobs and the pain in her soul exceeded anything ever inflicted on her body.

Laughter welled up in her throat and burst forth with a hysterical peel.

I've given my heart to a serial killer who destroys hearts. I've done his work for him. There's a story to entertain Nan and Nessy.

She changed position to hug her knees. Her tears now exhausted, the rain also relented, easing back to a steady drizzle. The water reflected the few lights from the surrounding warehouses. The workers left for their homes, and she was alone.

The noise came to her ears first, a quiet hiss and puff, punctuated by the zing of water hitting hot metal. The small steam-powered carriage drew near, strangely out of place by the docks, being more at home on the streets of Mayfair or Kensington. A new and expensive model, it could be operated from inside, and didn't require a driver.

She watched through red eyes as someone flung open the door. Soft light framed the sole occupant.

"Are you all right?" the gentle voice asked.

"I'm fine." She turned back to the river, hoping the carriage's occupant got the message and left her along. Water ran down her neck and disappeared between her shoulder blades, making her shiver at the cold touch.

"You're soaked to the bone. Let me give you a ride home." The voice was insistent.

Another shake of her head, conversation was too much effort. Her heart ached and emptiness leached back into her soul.

The rain parted above her head. Startled, she looked up.

Weaver Clayton held an umbrella over her. "Please, Miss Devon, you'll catch your death of cold. Come on." He held out his other hand to her.

She was cold, and shook, her teeth rattling against one another. The numbness soaked through her limbs and she didn't even want to contemplate the long walk back to her rooms. "All right."

She took his offered hand and stood. Her muscles protested at the movement after hours curled in one position. She quietly followed him back to the roadside and climbed up into the small carriage. She gave him a weak, apologetic smile. "I'm going to get your seats all wet."

His smile was warm and gentle. "It's only water. I have a towel here somewhere." He lifted the seat next to him, revealing a half-compartment underneath. With a quick rummage, he extracted a towel and passed it to Cara.

She muttered her thanks and started briskly wiping the water off her hair and face.

"This towel smells funny," she commented to Weaver.

A worried look crossed his face. "Really? It's been in there for a while; it might be a bit musty."

Cara took another deep sniff of the fabric.

"No. It's something else." She couldn't place it, but the odour tugged a memory somewhere in the recesses of her brain. A fog descended and clouded her attempts to recollect. She blinked; she hadn't realised how tired she was. *How long was I out there?*

"Do you mind?" He moved to her side, and held out his hand.

She shrugged, about to pass the towel over, when Weaver lunged. Caught unawares, with her reactions slowed by exhaustion, Cara found the towel wrapped around her face before she could react. Her fingers clawed at the fabric, trying to pull it away as he pressed it against her mouth and nose. The reek overwhelmed even as it swarmed into her head. She hadn't realised how strong he was. Or had she become weaker? Why wouldn't her body respond to her desperate commands?

Her hands slowed, her brain screamed at her to fight, her life depended on it, but she was incapable of answering. As darkness crept over her one horrifying thought solidified.

Fraser is wrong. The killer isn't Nate.

CHAPTER 27

Friday, July 26

CARA groaned. *God, this hangover hurts. I don't know what I drank, but I'm never touching it again.*

She rolled her head to ease the pressure headache, but something inhibited her movement. Something was wrong. Lightning seared through her brain as memories flooded back.

Weaver. He's going to kill me.

A sob of despair welled in her throat, but she choked it back down. A gag, pressed tightly through the corners of her mouth, blocked her cry. Her eyes flew open. The bright light directly above her head burned her retinas and she quickly closed them again. Red light flashed and strobed behind her lids. She took a deep breath through the fabric, willing the panic to settle and wait its turn. She needed her brain to function rationally, so she could evaluate her predicament.

She tried to rock her head, but something held her immobile, pressing over her forehead.

Can't move head.

She tried to raise her hands, but something tight pulled against her forearms.

Can't move arms.

An experimental move revealed her legs were strapped to whatever she lay on.

Legs also not moving. Well, it's confirmed.

I'm going to die.

She cautiously opened her eyes a fraction. The light seemed somewhat dimmer, and no longer seared into the back of her brain. She rolled her eyes, trying to make out her surroundings. By experimenting, she found, if she moved very slowly, she could rotate her head left and right a couple of inches. Through narrowed eyes, she saw grey stone walls. To her left, a wall of books, test tubes and jars. To her right, a trolley laid out with surgical equipment. The light glinted off scalpels, clamps, and scissors. There was a fresh roll of suture thread and a needle waiting to be used. She decided she preferred the view to her left.

She stared at the light fitting; the pounding in her heart kept pace with the heavy beat of the unseen clock. Each tick echoed through her body, reminding her time slipped by. Her gaze kept drifting back to the light fitting, an unusual wrought iron confection. There were five different branches, each holding aloft a small electric light. The arms curved and twisted into ornate patterns as they extended. *It reminds me of the one in the basement . . . at home.*

She twisted her head, trying to see, trying to make out any other distinguishing features. One cellar looked much like another. She never spent much time in the house, let alone down in the basement. The only distinguishing characteristic she could remember was the strangely out-of-place light fitting.

Cara tried to remember anything about her new tenant. She never bothered to meet him, leaving all the boring details to her lawyer. All she knew was that he was a scholar, doing some research. *And cutting up girls in the basement, apparently.*

"You're awake." The voice came from behind her, or possibly above her, and out of her limited line of sight. "You don't know how long I've waited for you."

She tried to turn to see where he was, praying he wasn't reaching for the tray of instruments. Her ears strained to catch the sound of metal scraping on metal. Her body was held immobile but her brain raced faster than light. She knew from Fraser that he didn't kill the girls immediately. He kept them alive for nearly three days, which meant he wanted something. She just had to figure out how to buy sufficient time. And pray Nate was looking for her. *I shouldn't have tricked Miguel.*

He leaned over so she could see him. His pale amber eyes, almost luminescent orbs, floated above her head. The flop of curls fell over his forehead as he peered at her. He reached behind her head and untied the gag. She took large, ragged breaths of air over dry lips.

"Say my name," he whispered against her cheek. His face brushed hers in a travesty of an intimate gesture.

It had to be a trick question. Her brain screamed at her tongue, *don't say whackadoodle!*

She scraped her memory and pushed down the panic.

"Akhenaten."

She could barely form the syllables. The name came out breathy, as though she infused it with desire, when in reality, fear constricted her breathing.

His eyes widened, surprise and satisfaction glinting beneath the insanity.

"You remember me." He drew his knuckles down her cheek.

She tried to nod, but couldn't with the band around her head.

"Yes." Her throat was so dry, her tongue dragged over her lips, trying to draw moisture from the air like a snake.

His gaze shone with joy and lunacy. "I knew it was you. I always knew you were the one. Father was so excited when he wrote me at Oxford, and told me he had found Nefertiti's Heart. I came home from college and you captivated me. So young, innocent, and beautiful."

Oh shit. That's why he thinks I'm connected. Clayton wanted the Heart and got me instead. And Weaver was there. Did he watch his father rape me? Sick bastard.

He stroked her face again. "It's your eyes. I knew you by your eyes. I had to kill your father to make you return to London. Then, I thought you didn't recognise me. That you didn't remember. And you've been hanging on to *him*."

"I haven't seen you for three thousand years. I didn't know if I could trust what the memories were telling me."

And if Nate doesn't rescue me, I'm going to be really pissed.

"It's been so long, Nefertiti. You promised me immortality." He sounded petulant, like a child promised a sweet if he behaved, who then didn't get one.

"You're the son of god, you were always eternal my love," she murmured gently, biting her tongue to keep the panic from surfacing. *God forgive me, but I need him to think I'm with him on this.*

"I want immortality." His tone became more strident. "Anubis promised me that if I found you, I would have eternal life."

He took to pacing back and forth next to her, drifting in and out of her limited range of vision.

"Soon," she whispered. "You're so close."

"The other girls, they weren't right. I kept trying, but deep down I knew they weren't you. I needed time to remember before I approached you."

"You need the heart, the remnant of our former lives." Cara scratched at her brain, trying to remember the story of Nefertiti and Akhenaten, so she could infuse her comments with sufficient details to make him believe her. "You need to remind these vessels of who we once were."

"Where is it?" He spun and returned to her side, peering at her intently. He waited for the answer that cost so many lives.

"It's here. Somewhere. But I can't—" The ticking of the clock was driving her to distraction, pulsing through her body, resonating with every beat of her heart. "Could you possibly stop that clock so I can think? I need to remember."

"What clock?" A frown marred his perfect, angelic brow.

"The ticking. It's so loud." The constant beat bounced off the walls and tore through her. "The noise makes it hard to think. I need you to stop the pendulum, for just a little while, please."

He laughed. "There's no clock here, I only have my pocket watch." He drew on the chain and held up a small gold pocket watch. He waved the timepiece back and forth over her head, as though he were going to hypnotise her.

"I don't understand." Her eyes widened. *The beating. It's the Heart. Here, in the cellar.*

How is it possible that I feel it? What has this conniving house done?

"The heart, it's here."

"Where?" He looked around, as though expecting to see the gem dangling from the light fitting.

"Buried. Under the floor. I can feel it." She laughed at him. "Don't you understand? The heart is linked to me. It used to be my heart. Of *course* I can feel the pulse. The heart beats within me and around me. It calls to me."

It wasn't taking much effort to turn on the crazy routine; her mind was halfway there with fear. "You need to let me sit up, so I can guide you to where it is."

He frowned again; he clearly didn't trust her. "I can't lose you, not after so long. I have searched through millennia for you."

She heard the sound of instruments rattling, metal clinking against metal. Her brain screamed and quivered in a corner at the noise. Tears welled up in her eyes. She hastily blinked them away. She had to concentrate. She had to live.

But how, when I can't move or fight? First chance I get, I'm beating him to a pulp.

She cried in pain as something jabbed into her arm. Ice flowed up her vein, spread over her shoulder, then wrapped frozen tendrils around her heart. The ticking slowed.

"What have you done to me?" A shuddering cry ran through her body, blind panic merely awaiting an opportunity to take over. Dusk settled over her brain, obscuring her thoughts in the half-light, making thought difficult.

"Something to relax you, that's all. I don't want you trying to escape. We're so close now." His hands undid the buckles holding her head and arms in place. He left her legs strapped to the table. With his arms around her, he helped her to sit up.

She groaned, vertigo threatened at the movement. The room spun at a leisurely pace, time slowed by whatever he had injected into her. She had no intention of vomiting in slow motion and struggled to stop her stomach from constricting.

She closed her eyes, concentrating on the beat pulsing through her body. She tried to touch it, to grasp where the sound originated. *Thump-thump. Thump-thump. Thump-thump.* Steady and rhythmic. She raised one arm and pointed to her right. "Over there."

He moved to that part of the room. "Where is it?"

Cara tilted her head. *I'm so tired. Let me sleep.* Her brain tried to bat consciousness away; it wanted to curl up in a corner and drift away. She took a deep breath, forcing oxygen up into her weary head. She tried to judge where Weaver stood, compared to the beat.

"Toward the door. Stop. Back this way. Stop." She directed him, until she gasped. A pressure descended over her, breath struggled to escape her body. He stood over the Heart, and *somehow*, his weight transferred to her chest.

"There. It's there. But you need to move." She gasped and slumped forward, her hands braced on her knees. He stepped back and the unseen force on her lifted. She turned her head, staring at him, willing him to stay off that spot.

The slate tiles of the floor looked impenetrable. Weaver cast around, then his stare fell on the three metal monsters slumbering in the corner. Two were automatons, macabre without their wax flesh to cover their steel nakedness, burnished heads with dull, vacant eye sockets. They slumped against each other, waiting to rise up and answer their master's demands. Next to them stood a metal exoskeleton, its dangling limbs useless, the creature's inner life missing. Made of gleaming steel with brass bolts and gears, a small, battery backpack provided the power source.

Cara now understood how he placed Beth Armstrong into the sarcophagus. The exoskeleton lent him the necessary strength to move the lid on his own.

He climbed into the metal armour, clicked his feet into the boots, then strapped the heavy leather belts over his chest. His arms slid into the metal sleeves, which curved down around his fingers. He flipped a switch within the arm mechanism, and activated the electricity backpack. The skeleton's limbs unfurled.

He moved slowly to the spot she indicated. He bent down on one knee with a click and a whirr. Sparks flew from the energy source, flashes of blue and purple against the grey walls of her prison.

He pulled back one arm, formed a fist and slammed it into the floor. Cara screamed at the hit, direct to her heart. She gasped for breath. Black stars sparkled in her eyes and darkness crept into the edges of her vision. She fell back to the table with a groan.

Bloody house is getting demolished for this.

Weaver's powerful blow cracked the floor tiles. He ripped them up with his monstrous claws, tossing them aside as he worked. He gave a cry of glee when he revealed a small compartment under the floor. He powered down the exoskeleton and pulled himself free of the metal housing. His hands scrabbled with the broken slate. She listened to the harsh clink as he dug his way in.

"I've found it!" he cried in triumph, pulling free the container.

She raised herself up, the length between her heartbeat and the echo reducing as he walked across the floor carrying his burden. By the time he placed the object on the trolley next to Cara, her heart pulsed in time with whatever lay within.

It looked like a small steamer trunk of aged tin. Rivets dotted the sides and the top. The lid curved slightly, as though fitting itself to whatever it contained. An old lock secured the latch. He went to the shelf, then returned holding a chisel and hammer. One strike and he removed the ineffectual lock. He cast a look at her, his eyes unnaturally bright as he lifted the lid.

He reached in and carefully withdrew a canopic urn. An unusual design, shaped in a womanly fashion, the head resembled the goddess Isis. Coloured paints on the body of the jar mimicked the cream linen folds of her gown. A small golden throne, fashioned into a crown, sat upon her head. The throne symbolised the power she conferred to the pharaoh. Gold bracelets decorated her arms, crossed over her chest. In her hands, Isis held an ankh and a short tasselled rod.

"The seat of the soul was normally returned to the body during mummification. But your heart, my love, was so special, it resides within the goddess Isis," he murmured as he set the jar next to the small tin chest.

He grasped Isis' head, the gold crown between his fingers. He twisted and wrenched, until he severed the beautiful face from her fuller body. He tipped the jar. A slow rattle sounded as something scraped down the inside.

He raised his hand, holding the diamond heart aloft. Light flared in the room. Rainbows danced and skittered over the walls, refracted from the large gem. Tiny brass cogs and strapping surrounded the priceless object. Red and blue veins ran over and under the brass additions, adding to the ghoulish realism of the artifact. A legendary heart, bound by strange mechanical workings, to make the gem beat and act as a valve.

"I still think it's gruesome," she muttered under her breath, her fingers creeping toward the straps holding her legs to the table. She tried to dance ahead of Weaver in her mind, devising a way to escape. She would not face death lying down, she would fight until her last breath.

Rapture spread over his face. His eyes widened in wonder as he held the heart in his hands. "I know what I have to do."

"What?" Cara swam through an ocean of treacle, her movements slow and arduous. Her brain struggled to stay awake. She was slowly going under and she desperately needed to stay conscious, to stay alert, and stay alive.

"It's so simple. I have to return your heart to you." He held the artifact over her body. The beat pulsed through her and the large gem simultaneously, although she couldn't discern any movement from it.

None of it made any sense. His words didn't make any sense. "But you have it now. The Heart is yours."

"No, silly." He smiled too widely, his eyes glazed over like Countess de Sal in the grips of her madness. "This has to go back in there."

He tapped a finger on her chest and carefully returned the Heart to the trolley. He rubbed his hands together gleefully, as he ran his eyes over his tray of instruments. He picked up a scalpel, holding the blade to the light. It glinted, light playing down the razor-sharp edge.

Terrible understanding shot through her. Her brain knew, but her body couldn't respond.

A tear rolled down her cheek. "Oh shit—" she managed to sob, before the injected toxin enveloped her and she fell back on the table, just as everything went black.

CHAPTER 28

NATE sat in his study, trying to work and failing, unable to concentrate on the papers in front on him. He looked up as the door opened, pen frozen in his hand.

"Well?" he demanded of Jackson the moment his bodyguard slipped through the doorway. He had returned home the previous day to find Cara missing. She had vanished into thin air, while within eyesight of two bodyguards and on a busy street. He hadn't slept; he couldn't, not when a piece of him was missing. He prowled his office instead, keeping an eye on the ticking aethergram for any news of her while his men scoured the city.

Jackson shuffled from foot to foot.

"We have a lead. One of the boys spotted her down at the shipyards last night. Before he could check if she was all right, a carriage came along, she got in, and disappeared." He paused and took a nervous swallow before continuing his report. "Plus, your Fraser tail checked in five minutes ago. He recognised Cara running from Enforcer Headquarters mid-day yesterday, but didn't think to relay the information until now; he figured she was heading in this direction, anyway."

They would all pay for that slip.

The pen in Nate's hand snapped under the pressure from his fingers. The two pieces fell to the desk in a torrent of blue blood. He pulled a handkerchief from his pocket and cleaned the ink off his fingers. His men were spread far and wide, searching for her. He hissed a name under his breath. "Fraser."

I'll snap his neck like the pen if she is harmed.

"He's at Headquarters, in case you want to have a wee chat with him."

Nate burst through the main doors into Enforcer Headquarters with Jackson hot on his heels. The rage rolled off him, sufficient to keep even the largest of the uniforms away as he barrelled up the stairs, his legs taking them two at a time, to Inspector Fraser's office. He didn't bother to knock; he flung the door out of the way, eager to curl his hands around Fraser's neck.

Jackson blocked the advancing Enforcers rushing up the stairs behind them.

Fraser looked up in surprise at the intrusion. "Lord Lyons—"

He got no further, as Nate rounded the desk and picked him up. His fingers closed around Fraser's throat as he dragged him from his chair and slammed him up against the wall.

"Where's Cara? She's gone. Someone saw her get into a carriage down by the shipyards and that's it. She has disappeared. My men can't find any trace of what happened to her." In the midst of his rage existed calm. His words perfect and clipped and full of bone chilling menace.

"I'm sure she has gone somewhere for her own safety," Fraser managed to stutter, despite the impediment against his windpipe.

The chalkboard next to Fraser's head drew Nate's eyes. Names and arrows radiated out from a central notation, *"Nathaniel Trent, Viscount Lyons."*

He dropped Fraser to study the diagram before his frozen gaze turned back to his prey. "You bastard. You told her I'm a killer."

"Aren't you?" He rubbed his throat and eased himself a step away from Lyons.

"I'd never kill a woman in cold blood." His fingers curled and uncurled at his sides.

Fraser huffed a quiet laugh. "Interesting choice of answer. You didn't say no."

"You're wrong. And he's taken her. So help me, if she is harmed—" Giving up on words to explain his gut-wrenching fear for Cara, Nate chose action to demonstrate his point. Drawing his arm back, he slammed his fist into Fraser's jaw.

The lighter man reeled from the blow and toppled over, then hit the wall. He slid down to land in an undignified heap on the floor.

"Get up," Nate snarled. He wanted the satisfaction of doing it again, but couldn't hit a man on the ground. He intended to beat Fraser repeatedly, until Cara was returned to him safely. He would tear the city apart brick by brick to find her, if he had too.

"How do I know this isn't just an act to throw me off the trail? Even now, you could have her trapped somewhere . . . ."

Nate grabbed the inspector's collar, hauled him to his feet and hit him again. A roar came from the corridor, as Connor tried to make his way past Jackson to reach his inspector. The two seconds were equally matched as they slugged it out for possession of the doorway.

Fraser stayed on the floor, rubbing his jaw. "I'm starting to suspect I may have been wrong in my initial suspicions. Although you have to admit, you fit the profile so splendidly, it seemed unnecessary to cast around for any other suspects."

Nate reached for the other man's collar again but Fraser held up a hand.

"You can keep hitting me, or we can find Miss Devon, and the real killer. Since, apparently, it's not you."

Nate backed off and gave Fraser room to stand and rub his bruised face. He waved his hand at Jackson to stop the feud outside the door. Uniformed Enforcers lined the narrow corridor, unable to gain access.

Connor rushed into the small office, placing himself between Lyons and Fraser, as the inspector regained his composure.

"Since it is obviously not me," Nate said pointedly, "who is next on your suspect list?"

"I initially thought Lord Clayton. He is the only other one with a connection to Lord Devon and the fathers of the dead girls. Plus, he knew about Nefertiti's Heart, since his obsession with the gem led to Devon handing over Cara." Fraser stared at his chalkboard, trying to make new connections under Lyons' enraged gaze.

Nate shook his head. "He's too frail after what Cara did to him."

"Yes, quite. And he doesn't fit with what we know of the killer: young, handsome, rich, and secretive." Fraser let the words hang between them. "What do we know of the carriage she got into this evening?"

Nate inclined his head to Jackson, indicating he was free to tell all he knew.

"Dark coloured, small, steam-operated vehicle. One of the new ones that can be worked from inside and don't need a driver."

The room fell silent, the occupants all considering how many such conveyances were in London and who owned them.

One person of interest sprang to Nate's mind. "Clayton owns one."

"We've already discounted him. Who else?" Fraser asked.

"But not his son. Weaver uses the carriage at times." Nate remembered something Cara had told him. "Weaver told Cara about the book, *Magycks of the Gods*. It's the volume she was reading to find out more about the artifact."

Fraser's face lit up, possibilities slotting into place. "I thought it was you, and freely admit I was wrong, but what if the killer is Clayton *junior?*"

He had a gleam in his eye, the bloodhound who had caught the right scent and knows in which direction to run. His hands flew over his desktop, pulling files and discarding them, before he held up one in particular.

His train of thought tumbled out his mouth. "We know what Clayton senior did to Miss Devon. What if Weaver had been involved?"

Nate ran a hand through his hair, desperately trying to put the pieces of the puzzle together. "He wasn't, though. He approached Cara a couple of weeks ago and apologised. He was away studying at Oxford."

"No." Fraser shook his head, his eyes scanning the report in his hand. "I've been doing a bit of digging about the original case. Seven years ago, he was put on academic suspension. He was sent home that week, suspended for *behaviour not becoming a scholar.*"

"He can't have been involved. Cara would have mentioned him being there." Nate paced the small office, the conversation going nowhere and not doing anything to find Cara. Pain shot through his chest at the thought of being too late and losing her forever.

Fraser tapped a fingertip on the file. "Just because she didn't see him, doesn't mean he didn't see her."

Nate stopped pacing. "You think he watched?"

"We can't discount anything. But imagine what effect seeing the young girl raped repeatedly by his father would have on a fragile mind. A mind that teetered on the edge of sanity?"

Nate turned over the idea. "Clayton senior would have been vocal about the Heart. He was desperate to get his hands on it. That's why he collected all Devon's chits, hoping to drive him to the brink of bankruptcy."

Barely suppressed excitement rolled off Fraser as he finished reading the report. "Guess what Weaver was studying at Oxford? Ancient literature."

"So he knew about the Heart and the book, was home the week Cara was raped, and has access to the carriage." Nate made a mental note to extract his own vengeance on Weaver. He would ensure he killed him particularly slowly. He'd prefer to do it twice, if he could lay his hands on a reanimator.

The inspector broke his murderous thoughts. "His obsession with her has warped over the years, become entwined with the legend of Nefertiti's Heart, and perhaps started this whole chain of unfortunate events. He probably murdered Lord Devon to draw her back to London."

"So where is he? We're running out of time. Would Lord Clayton be helping him, hiding him in the family's basement or something?" Nate's pacing increased with his need to do something physical in the hunt, to find the woman who meant the world to him. She was the blood that pulsed through his veins. Without her, he was merely a husk.

"Only one way to find out." Fraser grabbed his coat. The crowd in the corridor had dispersed; only a few uniforms lingered in case fighting erupted again.

"My carriage, it's quicker," Nate said as they headed down the stairs. He didn't bother to point out he wouldn't be caught dead in the noisy and smelly Enforcer vehicle.

The Clayton estate lay on the edge of London. The mechanical horses cantered unceasingly. They didn't require a break in pace like their mortal counterparts. Nate kept his calm exterior, but anger crawled under his skin, as his mind imagined what Weaver might be doing to Cara. Helplessness was a new emotion for him, and he didn't like it at all.

The startled butler bravely stood his ground and refused them admittance, for all of three seconds. At which point Jackson simply picked the man up and tossed him to one side. They found Clayton in the dining room, about to have his breakfast. He looked up from the buffet to regard the men who violated his privacy.

"Lord Clayton, where is your son?" Fraser asked politely.

Nate would have preferred a more direct, and physical, approach.

Clayton senior leaned on his stick, his fingers curling around the solid silver topped even as his lips curled in a cruel smile. "Now, what business do you have with Weaver?"

"You know damned well." Nate growled. "We will find him. The only question is how many pieces of him do you want back to bury? The longer you keep me waiting, the less of him will be found."

Clayton held his ground.

"How is your valet? I hear he disappeared." Nate stared at his fingernails.

Clayton's smile dropped and his face blanched. "Weaver is not here. He's playing house with that little hellcat."

Nate swore under his breath.

Fraser frowned and flicked him a curious look.

"Cara rented out her family home," he explained.

"You didn't know the tenant was Weaver?" An eyebrow shot up at a detail escaping Lyons' attention.

His hand balled into a fist, one misstep on his behalf had cost Cara so much. "I didn't bother to enquire. The house was of no interest to me once I knew she didn't reside there anymore."

"Back to town, then." Fraser, ever polite, nodded to Lord Clayton and left the room.

Nate paused on his way out, to step close to Clayton. "I do hope your affairs are in order, Clayton," he said, his tone so chilling the older man's eyes widened and his pupils dilated. From the ton to the rookeries, everyone knew what such an enquiry from the villainous viscount meant—ruin.

THEY halted on the pavement outside the terrace house and Nate glared up at the brooding building.

"Basement," he announced after a moment's reflection. "He won't want anywhere with a window, it's too high risk."

He looked over the railing at the stairway stretching to the kitchen entrance below the street. He placed one hand on the black wrought iron, and leapt over the side. He dropped to the basement level, landing on his feet like a cat. By the time the others clattered down the stairs, he had the door unlocked and pushed open.

With only a glance to check that the others followed, he crossed the threshold into the silent house. The kitchen lay deserted, although there were signs of recent activity. A half-empty tea mug rested on the bench. A bread-shaped lump sat under a paisley fabric cover.

"It's so quiet," Connor muttered.

"I would assume if the neighbours heard girls screaming, you lot might have made it here a bit sooner," Nate wrenched open the pantry door. Peering within, he found only silent rows of preserved fruit, bags of flour, and coffee beans. "We try lower. He'd want somewhere sound-proof and undisturbed. Look for the cellar door."

They fanned out and Jackson soon cried, "Here!"

A short corridor terminated in a solid door. Pushing it opened revealed a set of stairs disappearing into inky darkness.

Connor drew a short copper tube from his utility belt and shook it vigorously. Pale yellow light emitted from both ends of the tube, sufficient to light the way downward.

"Chemical reaction," he said to a fascinated Jackson. "Makes the stuff in the tube luminescent. We call them glowers." He led off down the narrow steps.

"The Enforcers still have one or two tricks you don't know about," Fraser muttered as followed his sergeant.

Nate and Jackson exchanged glances before hurrying after the others, lest they lose the dim light. The bottom of the stairs opened onto a small wine cellar. Hundreds of bottles lined the walls, gathering dust and spider colonies, now that no one entertained in the rooms above.

A large metal door stood opposite the steps, with no visible handle.

The four men stood and contemplated the silent obstacle. Nate's anger grew, hemmed in by the inactivity. He needed to do something. Anything. He charged the door, diverting his rage to his shoulder as he slammed into the steel door.

"Cara!" he yelled. The door remained immobile, his blow not even registering as a ripple across the surface.

"Excellent," Fraser muttered drily. "Now he knows we're here." He cast his analytical eye over the door. "Spike," he said to Connor and held out his hand.

Nate rubbed his shoulder and glared at the inspector.

The sergeant pulled a six-inch metal spike from his belt and handed it over.

"I assume you have a blade on you?" he directed to Nate.

"Whatever you are planning, do it quickly." He drew the knife from his boot and gave it to Fraser, hilt end first.

Fraser used the hilt of the dagger as a hammer. Coupled with the spike, he popped the bolts from the door hinges. "People invest in impressive locks, but always forget the hinges."

He pulled the bolts free and tossed them to the ground.

"Hurry up, Fraser," Nate growled. The white-hot agony of not knowing if Cara was alive or dead clawed its way through him.

Jackson and Connor pulled on the door experimentally, using the hinges as handgrips. They rocked it slightly in the frame, buying them valuable room to slide their fingers around the edge and get a grip.

Jackson looked at his opposite. "Ready?" he asked.

A curt nod in reply. The two strong men braced their backs.

"Now!' Jackson grunted as they wrenched the door forward. There was a sickening *snap* as the metal bolt barring the door on the inside broke. They bent the door around, giving them sufficient space to gain access to the room beyond.

Nate barely waited before he charged into the breach. His gaze briefly registered the scene within, before he was thrown back through the broken door. He landed at the foot of the stairs.

"We have a large, and metallic, problem." He sucked in a breath as he climbed back to his feet.

He saw enough to chill him. Cara lay immobile on a slab, blood spread over her chest and dripping onto the floor.

He charged again, ducked low and rolled to one side, avoiding the metal fist that slammed toward him. He came up behind the monster that winded him the first time. Weaver was in control of a dockside exoskeleton, normally used to shift large cargo, and not usually found in wine cellars.

Jackson and Connor burst through the wrecked door, followed by a more cautious Fraser.

The steel automatons rose from their corner, long limbs extended and flexed.

Weaver gave them their command. "Attack. Destroy the intruders."

He unfurled an arm and backhanded an advancing Nate, flinging him into the shelving. Specimen bottles full of formaldehyde crashed to the floor, spilling out their gruesome contents and spiking the air with a pungent aroma. From within his metal cage, Weaver roared over the squeal of metal, as his minions attacked in unison. "You'll not stop me. I will be immortal!"

Jackson and Connor threw themselves into fighting their metal equivalents. The glee shone in their eyes as they unleashed the full force of their blows. Intense grunts sounded as they smashed and dented the robots.

Fraser edged around the side of the room, observing and calculating odds. He kept his movements slow, so as not to attract Weaver's attention, while he inched his way closer to Cara's motionless form.

Nate pushed himself up using the broken shelves. He left Jackson and Connor to deal with the unflinching metal guards. His concern was for the unconscious form bleeding in the middle of the room.

"Cara," he called, refusing to entertain the idea they were too late and she might be dead. The steel arm swung for him, stopping him from going to her side. He grabbed hold of the limb and hung on, while he tried to find purchase for his feet on the cables running down the monstrous legs.

Weaver laughed from within his exoskeleton, the shrill noise combining with the grate and hiss from the metal armour.

"You're too late," he taunted. "Nefertiti is mine, she has always been mine."

Weaver caught Fraser's movement. With his other arm he swept away Fraser and tossed him at Connor's feet. The sergeant hauled his inspector up with one hand, while his other meaty hand was occupied squeezing a metal neck.

"No," Nate cried out, looking for some way to reach Weaver and wrench him out of the protective suit.

Weaver swatted at Nate. Fraser hit the frame from behind with a slate floor tile. It smashed and dropped to the ground, barely leaving a chalky imprint.

"We need something harder," Nate yelled. Fraser cast around for a suitable weapon, while Nate tried to reach the buckles holding Weaver into the framework. His fingers grasped one edge and started to pull.

"Oh, no, you don't." Weaver chuckled as he stretched out an arm, pressing Nate against the wall. He drew one metal finger down his opponent's forearm, playing with him as manic laughter burst forth. The metal tip sliced through flesh and sent blood running down, making his grip slippery.

Nate sucked in a breath as pain blossomed up his arm.

"Any ideas, Fraser?" he shouted from his position, imprisoned by the wall and dangling from the side of Weaver.

Fraser cast around, seeking a way to end the fight and pull Weaver from his metal suit.

Jackson and Connor were making progress in their private battle. Jackson wrenched an arm off his automaton and used it to batter the machine into the floor. Connor took a different approach; he dismembered a leg, sending his robot to the ground. He proceeded to jump on its chest, giggling like a schoolboy as he flattened the machine like a pancake on a griddle.

"The electricity source." Fraser pointed to the pack powering the suit, nestled between metal shoulder blades. "We need a way to route it to the skeleton."

Nate and Fraser both cast desperate glances around the room. Nate's gaze drifted back to the immobile Cara. She hadn't stirred, despite the commotion.

Fraser grabbed a piece of flexible copper tubing.

"Here!" He caught Nate's attention as he slipped out of Weaver's grasp, the blood working as a lubricant. Nate dodged under another blow as Fraser tossed the pipe.

He held the tubing one-handed and jumped onto the back of the skeleton, hoping Weaver didn't body slam him into the wall again. He bent the soft metal around the frame protecting Weaver's head. Taking a breath to brace himself, he thrust the other end into the battery pack, and jumped clear, even as he rammed the copper tube home.

Blue light flashed from the electricity source and raced along the copper conduit like ethereal fire. Flame touched the framework and flew along every inch of the steel exoskeleton. Weaver screamed as the entire structure came alive and turned on him.

His body arced and convulsed as the electricity flowed over his body and short-circuited his brain. The exoskeleton danced wildly around the room, crashing into the remains of the automatons. Sparks flew as metal grated against metal. Weaver's brain cooked and dissolved under the onslaught. He slumped within the framework and, without a living being to operate it, the entire exoskeleton teetered, before crashing to the floor.

Nate rushed to Cara. He put two fingers to her throat, feeling for a heartbeat. He breathed a sigh of relief when the faint *thump-thump* pulsed under his touch. He dropped a kiss to her forehead before turning his attention to the chest wound. He pulled back the edges of her sliced shirt. The cut was four inches long, but not too deep. Grabbing a wad of cotton from the nearby trolley, he pressed the bandage to the wound, stemming the blood loss.

The automaton soldiers continued to twitch and obey their programming, even as Jackson and Connor merrily dismembered them. Arms crawled toward legs, the individual pieces displaying a hideous intelligence to be reunited with their parts. Wielding torn-off arms, the men continued battering the parts into submission, until nothing dared move.

Fraser skirted around the twitching Weaver, the battery not yet exhausted and still powering the macabre display. He looked over Nate's shoulder to inspect Cara's wound. "It doesn't look too deep. We must have interrupted him, just as he started."

Nate shot him a hard look. "So, if I hadn't thrown myself against the door, and alerted him to us outside, he would have had time to finish slicing her open."

"Possibly." Fraser reluctantly admitted.

Jackson took over from Nate, putting his large hand over the bandage.

Nate picked up the ancient and valuable mechanical organ. Something red and circular, the size of a pinhead, pulsed deep within the centre of the object. He squinted to discern what lay in the core. *It looks like blood.*

The slice on his arm continued to bleed. A crimson trickle ran from his fingers to the gem. He watched, fascinated, as his blood soaked *up* into the diamond. It pooled in the delicate channels circling the heart. One of the tiny brass cogs gave a whirr, setting off its neighbours in a complex array. The movement of the mechanism sucked a drop of his blood into the middle of the gem. He saw his blood touch and swirl around the droplet already deep within the artifact. The two danced, before merging into one larger globe, suspended in the centre of the diamond.

Boom. A visceral beat shot through his body, rocking him back on his heels as though he took a cannon ball to the stomach. He gasped at the savagery of the blow. Before he could register what it meant, Cara sat bolt upright and screamed. Her fingers tore at her chest where Jackson tried to press the cloth to the open wound and simultaneously stop her frantic movements.

Fraser grabbed for her arms, before she hurt herself. She scrabbled to tear at her own flesh, her nails biting into the edges of the cut.

Nate's grip instinctively tightened on the diamond, even as he turned to help Cara and another pulse shot through his body.

On the table, Cara struggled to draw a breath.

"Heart," she managed to gasp, her wide hazel eyes locked with Nate's.

He stared at the gruesome relic in wonder. Her words about the true nature of the artifacts, that day in the conservatory, flooded back to him. *What have we done?*

He grabbed the canopic urn and eased Nefertiti's Heart inside. Taking up Isis' head, he wedged the lid back onto its body.

Cara drew a large lungful of air and fell back, lifeless.

"Well, that was unexpected," Fraser said. He opened one of her eyelids. "She appears to be unconscious again." He flicked his eyes to the urn. "Care to tell me what that was all about?"

"No."

"What about him, should he keep doing that?" Connor asked, pointing to the twisted wreck of metal on the floor. Weaver lay trapped within the exoskeleton. His eyes rolled back and forth, the lids fluttering as foam bubbled from his lips.

"Residual current," Nate replied.

"Can we stop it?" Connor edged around the twitching cadaver.

"We could, but we're not gonna," Jackson muttered.

"We shouldn't have killed him. Now he will never be brought to justice," Fraser said.

Nate gave a bark of laughter. "That is justice." He pointed at the convulsing figure. "I hope he's dancing in hell. Or we could increase the charge, reanimate him, and kill him again. Once just doesn't seem like enough for what the bastard has done."

He looked around the room. Apart from surgical instruments and broken specimen jars, containing Lord only knew what, there was nothing to show that four women lost their lives down here.

"I trust you will clean up. I have to get Cara medical attention. She's going to need stitches." With the leg restraints undone, he gathered her gently into his arms, and cradled her to his chest.

Jackson picked up the canopic urn and tucked it under his arm.

"You can't take that, the gem is evidence." Fraser protested.

"Your evidence is here, on the floor, laying in excrement and vomit." Nate's tone was flat, the time of mutual assistance over. He wouldn't forget that Fraser's actions resulted in Cara being hurt.

"You're safe, *cara mia*," he murmured, as he carried the unconscious woman through the darkness and out into the light.

Wednesday, July 31

FIVE days later, Cara unlocked the door to her apartment and pushed it open to find Nate sitting on her sofa, reading a book.

"And just how long have you known I lived here?" She shut the door and dropped her satchel on the floor.

"I will admit, it took me a couple of days to find out where *Arabelle Williams* pays her rent. Following the money was far more effective than trying to follow you." He closed the book and placed it on the nearby table.

Cara pouted. "You're better than I thought."

"You seemed to enjoy the cat and mouse. And you never asked outright if I knew." He softened his expression for a moment. "I was worried. You up and left. Again. You were supposed to be resting."

"Resting?" She snorted. "More like house arrest. You had me locked up in the spare bedroom, you weren't talking to me, and Miguel paced outside the door like some caged animal. I had to resort to climbing out the window."

She dropped onto the sofa and nestled into him, drawing her feet up under her. He wrapped his arm around her waist. Cara listened to his heart, beating in perfect rhythm with her own.

"I'm here now, to talk, if you want. And I knew you had gone. Did you notice? There was a slight echo to the beat." He tapped his chest, next to her ear. "It increases the farther apart we are and diminishes when we are close, until the pulse becomes one again."

She had noticed and that was part of the problem, her mind still tried to sort out the implications. "Are you saying you can use the beat as a locator beacon?"

He cocked his head, thinking on the possibility. "Yes, so no point in you running anymore, is there?"

Cara frowned, not sure if she liked him knowing where she was at any time. Although it would work both ways. And, he wouldn't be able to sneak up on her, but she had more pressing issues on her mind.

"You had him killed. Clayton's valet." A statement, not a question.

"Yes. I will not apologise for hunting those who hurt you." He was unrepentant.

"I hear Clayton is on the verge of bankruptcy." Another statement. "Rumour has it he will die in Debtors' Prison."

"Yes." He wouldn't be drawn on that subject either.

"When the nightmares woke me, and I couldn't get back to sleep, I used to pretend I had a knife and he was the powerless one. I imagined plunging the blade into him over and over. But now he is destroyed completely. He will be erased and forgotten."

He remained silent, but his fingers stroked her hair, the action giving her as much reassurance as any words.

"And Weaver is dead. So it looks like that chapter of my life is finally closed." She let out a deep sigh, glad to close that particular book and start a fresh, new one. "Fraser thought you were the killer. He intended to use me as bait."

"Yes." His arm tightened around her.

"And Weaver thought I was his lover who had been dead for three thousand years." She moved to straddle him, while her fingers undid his waistcoat buttons and pulled the sides apart, before starting on the smaller buttons of his shirt. She needed to place her hands on his bare flesh.

"Yes." He unlaced the front of her corset, pulling the ribbon through the eyelets until the garment tumbled to the floor.

"That boy licked one too many cane toads." She was victorious over his shirt and ran her fingers down his chest and around the waist of his trousers. She caught the quick gasp as her nails grazed over him. "Funny thing, honour. They all claimed to have it, but you were the only one who was true to me, who never lied."

He dropped a kiss on her forehead. He tugged the laces of her chemise free; his eyes flicked down to the small plaster between her breasts, covering the incision.

"What happened when I picked up the Heart?" He stroked her neck as he asked his question.

She didn't remember much. Darkness closed in after Weaver found Nefertiti's Heart. She drifted until intense pain ripped through her body. She screamed, believing Weaver was pulling her heart out of her rib cage.

When she remained silent, Nate continued. "I had blood on my hands, and I watched it get sucked into the diamond. At the centre was another drop of blood, yours. And when they mingled, I got hit, hard, in the stomach by something. Now I can feel you. Your wound has been like a tug on me, until now. It's nearly healed, isn't it?" His fingers crept to the back of her wool skirt, and worked the buttons loose, so the skirt would pool around her feet if she stood up.

"I had the stitches out this morning. It's healed faster than it should. Like your arm." She pushed his shirt over his shoulders and he tugged it free of his hands. She discarded his clothing on the floor with her corset. A thin red line ran down his forearm, all that was left of the slice from the exoskeleton.

"I think my blood came into contact with the Heart the day I escaped Clayton. The thing was sitting on father's desk in the library. When he beat me, a drop must have flicked off his belt onto the gem. It explains why I could feel a heartbeat; I thought the house had come alive. Down in the cellar, the pulse was so loud I thought I was hearing a malfunctioning clock. The ticking was driving me as batty as Weaver." She traced the lines around his abdominal muscles, marvelling at how warm his skin felt under her fingertips.

"What would have happened if Weaver's blood had flowed into the Heart?"

"Nothing." She chewed her bottom lip. "Love can only be given, not taken."

"You'll have to spell that out for me." His hands stroked up her bare thighs before moving to cup her bottom.

Cara ran a hand down the side of his face, meeting his intense gaze. A slight tremble in her fingers was the only sign of her anxiety at saying her next words aloud. "It only worked because I love you."

He took her palm and placed a kiss in the centre. His gaze never left hers. He didn't say the words, but they burned in his eyes and echoed through their strange new bond, *and because I love you.*

Reaching up, he drew her head to him and kissed her. His touch was gentle as he licked the seam of her lips before he claimed more. His lips and tongue tender, teasing, caused her to moan as the fire built within her. His hand on her bottom pulled her tighter against his hips as the kiss deepened. His tongue delved into her mouth as his arousal pushed against her.

"Come back to my house, my bed. Or were you planning on fleeing London?"

She drew a deep breath as heat flowed though her limbs. "I hadn't thought what I'm doing. I never intended to stay, but things have changed."

"Stay with me while we figure out what it means."

Leaning in, he nibbled the lobe of her ear, before he trailed down her throat.

She tried to clear her head before the pleasure rolling through her body, stole her ability to think. "I have no idea what exactly it means, except we're in tune with each other. You felt my injury and I, somehow, drew on your strength to heal faster."

"Are we immortal?" He paused in his exploration of her skin.

Mischief shone in her gaze. "Want me to shoot you and find out?"

"Perhaps not." He resumed licking her collarbone, sending her thoughts into a tailspin.

She shook her head, remembering what had been bothering her, a frown marring her brow. "And the blasted thing can't be sold now."

He halted his caresses. "It's safe, I saw to that. No one will be able to lay their hands on it."

She stood up and her skirt fell to the floor. Kicking her feet free, she resumed her place on his lap, naked except for a pair of silk knickers and a short chemise.

Hunger flared in his blue gaze as his hands ran up the inside of her thighs.

"I doubt any of the artifacts can be sold, if they're all like the Heart and Boudicca's Cuff. I'll be buried for months trying to figure out what each one does. And I was rather relying on the cash flow." Cara's lawyer was having difficulty leasing out the house where four girls were callously murdered.

"I can help you with that," he slid her hips closer, as her fingers loosened the fastening of his trousers.

She arched an eyebrow. "Oh?"

"I came to offer you a job position. You have certain skills and talents that could come in handy. I thought I would interview you for the number two spot. Someone once told me I worked too hard and needed a second." He gasped as her hand stole into his trousers and encircled him.

She stroked his hot flesh, running her hand up and over the sensitive tip. She marvelled at the size of him and wondered what he would taste like.

She smiled; she enjoyed discussing business with Nate, particularly when she had the upper hand, literally. "Aren't you worried I might have my eye on your position on top?"

"I was rather counting on it." He pulled her into a tight embrace, her hand trapped between them as he pulsed against her palm. His hands were possessive on her body as he claimed her lips in an open-mouthed kiss that melted her bones and moulded her to him.

"I'm in a delicate state, remember?" She pulled back a few inches, to tap her chest.

He took advantage of her distraction to lift her chemise up over her head, leaving her naked except for the silk knickers.

"You're nearly healed. But if it worries you, I promise to be very, very slow and gentle." He gave her a wicked grin. "I might add these to my collection."

He stroked her through the silk, causing her to inhale sharply.

"I don't think so. These aren't cheap, you know." She had a pretty good idea what going slowly would involve. "I think it's my turn to be in charge."

She picked up her satchel and extracted handcuffs. She dangled them from her outstretched hand. He gave a throaty laugh in response.

Nate picked her up in his arms and carried her through to the bedroom, slamming the door behind him with his foot.

THE MISSING MECHANICAL MOUSE

This is a short story I wrote for a magazine. I hope you enjoy this peek into Cara's life, after the events of Nefertiti's Heart

Six weeks later…

CARA pulled aside the green damask curtain. Taking a sip of coffee, she watched sparrows play on the front lawn, as they dive bombed each other and fought over seed heads. Their antics came to an abrupt halt when the gardener rounded the corner and the little birds all flitted to the protective hedgerow. Behind her, the aethergram ticked away on the corner of the desk, spitting a coded message into the waiting wicker basket and signalling the start of the work day.

With another fortifying java hit, she crossed the Persian carpet to the desk, and cast an eye over the message. The machine drew each letter from the aether with laborious precision. Sentences took long minutes to appear, and the cargo manifesto crawled along the ticker tape like a blind caterpillar missing half its legs. She wondered what contraband would soon arrive at the Thames airship dock, when the echo within her chest shifted, to beat almost in sync with her heart. She raised her gaze to the door just as it swung open. Nathaniel Trent, also known as the villainous viscount, the man who shared her heart beat and made her toes curl, strode toward her.

"Helene left a message for you, another injured bird needs your help." His lips twitched in amusement, as his fingers held out a small rose coloured visiting card. Cara was one of the few people who saw beneath his icy façade, to the dark depths swirling far below. Small ticks on the surface were a mere echo of deeper ripples, a tug of his lips meant he was amused as hell at her new role.

She blew a snort of air and dropped the coffee mug to the desk top. Society turned its fashionably clad back on her, but behind closed doors, many wanted her help. She never realised how many upstanding, virginal, young women of the *ton* concealed such sordid and grubby secrets. By some collective agreement, which nobody ever consulted Cara about, she had been nominated the problem solver for young ladies with indiscretions liable to tarnish their sparkling reputations.

She took the slip of heavy paper and glanced at the name and address. *Dianne Forsyth.*

Nate dropped his arm around her waist and pulled her close to the heat of his broad chest. His lips nuzzled up her neck and fire skated over her skin at the electric touch. A sigh broke from her lips, as she toyed with forgetting about injured birds and perhaps encouraging a lion back to bed instead. Running her hands down the soft linen shirt covering his torso, she hooked her fingers under the waistband of his trousers. Perhaps for once, society could await her pleasure, and not vice versa?

A growl rumbled through Nate's body. Even without her wandering fingers, her intentions leaked along their shared bond and flowed to him.

"Don't tempt me, I have work to do. A large shipment is due this morning of rather a fragile nature. I cannot be distracted or tired."

More kisses burned through her senses, the sensual haze fighting the coffee alertness, and she wondered who was distracting whom.

"Miguel wants to come with me," he murmured against her skin. "So Jackson will be your tail for the day, try not to lose him, he takes it rather personally. Tonight, *cara mia*, I will make it up to you." With a swift, hot kiss that stole her breathe, he unravelled his arms from about her, and disappeared from the study.

Cara took a deep breath, and tried to remember what she was doing before Nate muddled her thoughts. The aethergram gave a short violent cough, before falling silent. She ripped the ticker tape off and held up the message. One item caught her attention.

Three tonnes of rice flour.

She laughed when her brain decoded the true nature of the cargo. Explosives. No wonder he didn't want to be distracted while dividing up the shipment.

A short while later, with her immediate paperwork concluded and nothing urgent to attend, she left the calm sanctuary of the study.

"Come on, Jackson," she hollered like a barmaid down the hallway, as she walked across the marble floor toward the front door.

The large bodyguard stuck his head out the men's lounge and headed her way. His imposing mass intimidated everybody, except Cara. She knew his weakness for Belgian white chocolate, and if he got out of hand, she could always shoot him. Again.

"What about the carriage?" A frown fought for space on his scarred and lined face.

She shook her head. "We're walking."

The henchman regarded her as though she announced he was to don tights and take to the stage as Oberon, King of the Fairies. "You're bleedin' kidding me?"

She held the solid wooden door opened and gestured outside. "Chop, chop. Fresh air is good for you."

"You're a noble, love, you're supposed to take the flippin' carriage everywhere, not walk." He muttered, grumbled, and complained all the way down the curving driveway and along the street. He only shut up when he paused to light a cigarette and shoved it between his lips. The process of inhaling and exhaling distracted him from moaning about the enforced exercise. The glare he gave the other pedestrians ensured Cara walked in her own little unimpeded bubble.

She stopped outside her destination and Jackson took it upon himself to prop up a nearby lamp post, feigning exhaustion. He grumbled, but his immaculate suit hid hard muscle and old battle scars. All of Nate's men were fit, strong, and capable of fighting their way out of a myriad of situations. Jackson's complaints about tagging behind Cara were all bark, with no bite.

"I won't be long," she called, rapping on the dark blue front door.

Inside, the butler showed her through to a small parlour, decorated in tones of yellow and green. Books were scattered over sofas and end tables, adding a lived in touch. A cream coloured long haired cat occupied most of a sofa. The feline cracked one green eye open, surveyed Cara and promptly went back to sleep. She barely completed a circuit of the cheery room when the door opened to admit Dianne Forsyth. Her warm blonde colouring was perfectly offset by an outfit of pale green and the blush of new rose. Blue eyes held an open regard and the trace of a smile touched her pink lips.

"Cara Devon," she breathed, before holding out her hand to offer a steady handshake. "I never thought to meet you in person. You are so lucky."

Cara rocked back on her feet. Being called lucky was a new label. "Pardon?" she asked, sure she misunderstood.

"You and Viscount Lyons are so. . . open, about your relationship, you engage no subterfuge. The *ton* can talk of nothing else." The woman's smile broadened as she waved her hands about Cara to punctuate her words.

Three weeks ago Weaver Clayton attempted to carve out her heart. Two weeks ago, Cara took up residence at Nate's Mayfair home, only rarely venturing back to her Soho apartment. In the absence of any other scandal to relieve their boredom, society filled the void tittering about her comings and goings.

Cara blinked, unused to such a direct approach, the other woman's candour was as welcome as a spring breeze. "The worse has already happened to me. I stopped caring what society thought about me after that."

"While the rest of us fashion society's expectations into gilt bars for our pretty cages." Dianne gave a sad smile and Cara's heart melted round the edges.

I'm in danger of liking this one.

"You have a matter that needs my assistance?" She prompted with a soft tone.

"Yes." She sighed. "Samuel Denning courted me for over a year. We had an understanding; he wanted to wait until he came into his title, before making our engagement official. I believed his whispered promises, and gave myself fully to him. He recently became the Earl of Stoke, and found a far larger fortune than mine, with which to garnish his title." The other woman cast her eyes down and drew a deep breath.

In Cara's experience, an all to common refrain unfortunately. The man takes what he wants and leaves the woman to suffer the consequences of no longer being the virtuous paragon society demands. Cara moved closer, to lay a hand on her arm. "Do you still love him?"

Dianne raised her head, and rich blue eyes shimmered with unshed tears. "Yes. One does not simply brush aside such feelings. But he has chosen his path, and father has since brokered my marriage to an older noble, in need of a new wife."

"I'm sorry." A shudder worked down Cara's spine at the thought of being traded like cattle at market. *Bloodlines are so important in broodmares.*

Dianne drew another deep breath and clapped her hands together, dispelling the sombre air gathering in the gaily-decorated room, and startling the cat. "I will be content with the match. And perhaps love will grow over time."

Cara hoped so and the woman seemed resigned to her fate. A tiny part of her wondered if she would take some consolation in the passion she briefly shared with her suitor.

The noble woman patted the cat until it resettled. "Anyway, I have a small token of some sentimental value which Samuel is withholding. I wish to have it returned to me."

Cara's ever-present curiosity sat up, waiting for further details. "All right. What is it?"

The other woman fidgeted, her fingers tugging on the cat's ears, before a sigh worked from her chest. "A small mechanical mouse with my name carved on the underside. I believe Samuel keeps it about his person."

A mechanical mouse? Cara puzzled over the woman wanting a toy returned, the motives of other nobles were beyond her. Who was she to question what value they placed upon a wind up creature? "Where will I find him?"

Another tug on the cat's long fur. "His club, Red's. He has taken to spending most of his time there, so I cannot send a servant to him. They will not admit a woman."

A slow smile spread across Cara's face. *Challenge accepted*, her brain cried. "Won't admit women will they? Well, we shall see about that."

"Thank you," her new friend murmured. Her hand stroked down the long body of the cat for a moment, and then she turned to Cara. The sadness of a moment ago was now replaced by the hint of laughter dancing in her gaze. "Would you satisfy my curiosity? Is it true, the rumour that you reside under Viscount Lyon's roof?"

Cara laughed, she could understand curiosity and she liked the other woman's direct manner. She gave a shrug. "It suits me to live there. I have an office in Nate's house and I complete paperwork for Lyons Cargo."

Dianne fell back onto the sofa, a hand grasping at her chest. "Work?" She made the single syllable into an exclamation of surprise. "You mean like paid employment?"

"Yes."

The other woman's brows knitted together in concern. "Well, I never."

Cara guessed afternoon gossip in the salons and parlours would be devoted to devouring that little titbit. Who thought that her engaging in employment would be more scandalous than moving in Nate's bedroom. "I'll see myself out. I should have your mouse back by this afternoon."

Once out the front door, Cara tapped the top of Jackson's bowler hat to wake him up. "Come on, we're off to Red's."

Jackson scowled as he pushed off the post to fall in step beside her. He let out a long-suffering sigh as he corrected the angle of his hat.

Cara turned on him and threw up her arms. "All right, hail us a cab to St James, I can't bear the thought of you sulking all afternoon."

He flashed a toothy grin and promptly flagged down a chuffing hansom cab. The driver sat at the back with the controls and access to coal to fuel the fire, passengers sat with nothing in front of them, except the snub nose housing the engine.

The cab rattled along the road and they alighted in St James. Cara stared up at the discreet exterior of the building, built of soft grey stone with austere columns. The only extravagance to the club was the front door, painted a rich glossy red. The colour signalled the name of the club, without the need for a gauche nameplate. With an exclusive, and sought after clientele, Red's had no need to advertise its presence.

Cara bounced up the stairs and down the short hallway, which opened into a small and plush reception area. An ornate set of dark panelled doors occupied a large portion of wall space. Muted laughter and chatter could be heard from beyond.

An attendant in a black uniform stood guard, waiting to greet the members and turn away those bold undesirables who dared cross the threshold. He straightened on seeing her. His gaze narrowed as he, rather correctly, pegged her as trouble.

She fixed the man with a stare and cocked her head to the doors. "Is Samuel Denning within?"

"Yes, miss. But he cannot be disturbed."

"I'll only be a moment." She turned to her left and the entrance to the lounge beyond, only to find he moved fast, to block her path with his larger body.

He waved at the small brass plaque attached to the wall. "I am sorry, miss, but no women allowed beyond this point."

Cara's gaze flicked to the sign and read the three words embossed on brass. "You adhere to the sign?"

"Yes, miss. No women are allowed in Red's." A slight sneer pulled one corner of his mouth, as though he thought her intellect lacking.

She winked at him. "Humour, me. Read the sign aloud."

He shook his head, her request confirming his low opinion of her. Like a teacher at the head of a classroom, he pointed to each word and sounded out the syllables as he moved his finger. "Strictly no skirts."

"No skirts." Cara repeated, as her fingers slid under the back of her corset and found the hook and eye closure of her skirt.

"Well, it means no women, it's the same thing, isn't it?" He gave an indulgent smile, as though dealing with someone of diminished mental capacity.

Cara wrinkled her nose with laughter. "No, actually, they're not the same thing." Her fingers released the hooks and the soft wool skirt slid to the floor, pooling around her feet. She stepped out of the puddle of fabric and scooped it up, handing it to the stunned attendant. "Be a dear, hold that for a moment, would you?"

Pushing aside the double doors, she paused on the entrance. Heads swung at the intrusion and numerous wide eyes took in her attire. Someone started coughing, or possibly had a heart attack, while another hacked up a fur ball. Her brown-laced boots stopped just below the knee. Above, striped woollen stockings rose to mid-thigh to meet silk French knickers, the same dark chocolate brown as her stockings. Strapped to her thigh in a leather holster, she wore a four-inch blade.

Her swallow-tailed corset dipped to graze the back of her knees and obscured their view of her derriere as she passed amongst the assembled gentlemen. She smiled cheery greetings on her way through the mortified men.

One rose from his chair, nearly tipping over the small table holding an in-progress chess game. "Now just a minute—" he levelled a finger at her.

Cara waved a dismissive hand in his direction. "Keep your trousers on and don't get over excited. I have business to discuss with Denning, it shan't take long to conclude."

A man unwound himself from a fireside wingback chair, and turned to stare at her. "I say," he murmured, his eyes racking over her form. "I'm Denning and you can take as long as you please."

"We have a different sort of business, I'm here on a task for Dianne. You do remember her don't you? The one you set aside because you found her dowry lacking?" Cara hated men who couldn't stand up for the women they loved. Perhaps that was why Nate drew her, he knew what he wanted and had no intention of ever letting her go.

Denning's face flushed around his moustache. "You don't understand how noble marriages are arranged."

"No, for which I am grateful." Cara held out a hand. "Dianne's mouse, if you please."

"What if I refuse?" He ran a fingertip down the side of his waxed facial adornment.

A smile curled her lips, but never reached her eyes. She pulled the Smith and Wesson from the chest holster and aimed it. Low. "Do I look like I'm here to play games? You can hand it over, or you lose your family jewels. You have three seconds to decide which you prefer."

He laughed, a retort rising to the tip of his tongue.

"One." Cara cocked the pistol.

Frantic hand movements pulled the ivory mouse from his trouser pocket in under two seconds. He thrust the tiny object in her direction.

"Smart boy." Cara replaced the pistol and took the mouse, depositing the creature in the leather pouch hanging from her belt.

"You're not a law unto yourself, you know." Denning found his spine, now he didn't have a pistol pointed at his crotch. "You can't just march in here and do whatever you want."

Cara cocked her head to one side. "Given who has my back, I rather think I can."

A sneer touched the corner of his mouth. "He's not as untouchable as he thinks he is."

Cara frowned, about to ask what he meant, when a growing commotion echoed from the foyer. Filing away his comment, she walked back through the haze filled room, and past the slack jawed patrons.

Exiting the double doors, she found the small spaced crammed with the attendant, Inspector Fraser, and the hulking Sergeant Connor. Jackson lounged against the street side doorjamb, not allowed admittance any further into the exclusive club. He raised one eyebrow, shook his head and then returned to his cigarette. He obviously figured she didn't need any help.

Connor took one look at her state of undress, turned beetroot red and developed an instant fascination for the ceiling mouldings.

Fraser kept unwavering eye contact. "Miss Devon," he murmured, as though they met in the street on a Sunday afternoon.

She smiled at the dapper Enforcer. "Hamish. Here to arrest me?"

"Not at all, the attendant was concerned you may need assistance. He thought you were confused and had perhaps escaped from somewhere." Translation, the attendant rang for urgent help with the mad woman. Fraser plucked the skirt from the outstretched arm of the man and handed the garment to her.

"He thought I would require assistance to leave the premises?" Cara stepped into the skirt, flipped out the tails of the corset, and refastened the back.

He gave her a shy smile, which warmed his hazel eyes behind their wire-rimmed glasses. "As always, we understand one another completely." He gestured for her to precede him from the building, and Cara stepped outside to the amused gaze of Jackson.

"I trust you won't be returning to Red's today?" Inspector Fraser enquired.

"No, I don't think so." She winked and waited while Jackson waved his arm and hailed a steam powered cab. When it puffed to a stop beside them, he helped her up.

Once on their way, she extracted the mouse to examine it closer. It was made of smooth polished marble. The rough size and shape resembled a chicken egg, but with a more tapered, triangular end, forming the mouse's head. Delicate ears, eyes and whiskers were carved into the stone. An ornate curving pattern covered its body, instead of fur. A thin silver chain formed the tail, the end wrapped around a tiny key.

Turning the mouse over, its tummy bore the engraving *"to Dianne, always a pleasure."*

Next to the ornate lettering, Cara saw a tiny keyhole and succumbed to the constant curiosity. She inserted the end of the tail and turned the key several times. Once the key slid free, the mouse began a gentle pulsating motion. Cara stared at her hand, the small oval creature vibrating across her palm. She almost knew what it was, the answer so close that it danced just at the edge of her reach.

Jackson watched her with barely suppressed laughter. "Got it yet, doll? Figured out why a man would give such a toy to his lover?"

The words *toy* and *lover* buzzed around and around, until realisation slammed into her brain.

"Ewww! she cried, as her hand jerked, the mouse leaping for freedom to be caught by the swift reflexes of Jackson.

He burst into full force laughter and dropped the critter back into the pouch at her side.

Later that night, Cara lay on her stomach, reading, when Nate entered the bedroom. The tiredness vanished from around his eyes, as he drank in her sprawled form.

He sat on the bed next to her, and removed his boots. "How is your injured bird?"

He stripped the shirt over his head next, and Cara lost any pretence of interest in her book. She loved watching the muscles in his back bunch and stretch with each movement.

"Reunited with her mouse. Which, I suspect, she wants for when she is buried alive in the countryside, stuck in a loveless marriage with some decrepit toff." She rolled to her side and followed a faint knife scar with a fingertip.

Nate turned and captured her hand. "Well, if you ever find yourself buried in the countryside, or bored with your old toff—"

He pulled a small object from his pocket and placed it in her palm.

Cara recognised the shape and laughed. A retort rose to her lips, only to be swallowed down by her constant curiosity.

Perhaps, just this once…?

ABOUT A. W. EXLEY

BOOKS and writing have always been an enormous part of my life. I survived school by hiding out in the library, with several thousand fictional characters for company. At university, I overcame the boredom of studying accountancy by squeezing in Egyptology papers and learning to read hieroglyphics.

Today, I write twisted historical novels with heart. I live in rural New Zealand surrounded by a weird and wonderful menagerie consisting of horses, cats, a mad boxer, and chickens who think they are mini Velociraptors.

Web...www.awexley.com/
Facebook...www.facebook.com/AWExley
Twitter..@AWExley
Pinterest..................................www.pinterest.com/AWExley/

Be the first to hear about new releases, occasional specials and giveaways. My newsletter comes out approximately four times a year. Follow the link to sign up http://eepurl.com/N5z5z

HATSHEPSUT'S COLLAR
ARTIFACT HUNTERS BOOK 2

*Q*ueen Victoria is in the grips of an insatiable bloodlust thanks to an ancient Egyptian necklace, and it's the least of Cara Devon's problems.

Viscount Nathaniel Lyons has been thrown in the Tower. He has something the queen wants, and he has a week to deliver before his date with the executioner. Cara Devon isn't having any of that; she has her own axe to grind with the man who shares her heartbeat.

To save Nate, Cara must embark on a mission that will take her from the grim Tower of London to the opulent Winter Palace of St Petersburg and the frozen depths of Siberia. Along the way she must deal with a traitor, the mysterious contents of a tea chest and figure out how to wrestle Hatshepsut's Collar from around Victoria's neck.

Once Cara accomplishes those tasks, and assuming the mad queen hasn't plunged them into a world war, then she will have time to deal with Nate…

HATSHEPSUT'S COLLAR:
CHAPTER ONE

Mid-September, 1861.

FOR the first time in three weeks, the gossip columns remained silent on the subject of *"Miss Cara Devon, frequent visitor to a nefarious Mayfair address."*

Her stroll through the smoking room of Red's, sans skirts, sparked a furore across Europe and divided opinion. Gentlemen's clubs scrambled to either erect specific "no women" signs, or took them down; secretly hoping another fine form would be game enough to do a Cara Devon.

Tossing the paper into the trash, Cara dug her toes into the expensive Persian carpet under her desk, using the lush pile to work her digits back and forth. A stretch ran over the sole of her foot and into her arch and she gave a sigh of relief. The one drawback to her nocturnal activities with Nate, he made her toes curl so hard that by morning she had to work the cramp out of her feet.

More than three months had passed since she came to London to finalise her father's estate. She planned to stay a few days, a week at the most, and then resume her nomadic lifestyle. Then she tangled with Viscount Nathaniel Lyons and everything changed.

She took a deep drink from her fresh brewed coffee as the aethergram on the desk rattled into life. The machine spat out a steady stream of thin ticker tape, and it coiled into the wicker basket beneath. She cast a glance at the message, the cargo manifest for the incoming airship, returning to England after a long voyage in the Orient. She was coming to grips with her new role within the Lyons Airship company, where nothing was ever as simple as it appeared on the surface. The containers described as "Aunt Jemima's ikebana supplies" were code for Japanese contraband, usually pornographic prints, sometimes beautiful katanas, and last week, an exquisite Geisha.

Cara was horrified, until she learned the girl was there of her own free will. She bought her freedom from a secluded life by selling herself to the highest English bidder for one year. Unhappy with the arrangement Cara interrogated the hapless gentleman until she was satisfied he would treat the gentle courtesan with respect for the duration of the engagement. He appeared genuinely delighted with his acquisition and Cara extracted a promise from the woman to stay in touch, so she could keep an eye on the situation. She would play no part in the trafficking of women and made her opinion clear.

Opening a drawer, she took out a clean sheet of paper and grabbed the end of the ticker tape to write up the incoming cargo to satisfy the Customs officials. The paperwork a mere courtesy; Nate's influence so pervasive they very rarely examined the containers, and only the ones he pointed out they could open.

The door cracked open and Miguel, the youngest of Nate's employees, poked his head around. "Any plans for this morning?" he asked with a smile. With his auburn hair and hazel eyes, he looked like her younger brother, if she had any siblings.

"Yes." She looked up from her paperwork. "I need to take this manifest down to the hangar. Could you saddle a horse, please? A real one," she added in case he decided to be mischievous and throw a saddle on a mechanical equine instead. Miguel was her constant shadow. She gave him the slip six weeks earlier and ended up strapped to a deranged serial killer's table. The youth blamed himself, despite Cara pointing out she was the only one responsible for her actions.

His quiet spoken manner and unwavering loyalty to Nate piqued Cara's curiosity, and they settled on an arrangement. She promised to allow him to accompany her for a month and he would tell her how he ended up in Nate's debt and employ. With only a few days to go until he had to confess all, her curiosity started a countdown in her head.

Voices came and went in the entrance, the front door banging shut on some unknown visitor, as she finished her work. She grabbed her boots and laced the soft, brown leather over her shins. Scooping up the battered leather satchel, she shoved the paperwork inside and buckled up the flap. She slung the strap over her head and nestled it across her chest, pausing to pass her fingertips over the sensitive patch of skin next to her breast. Six weeks ago Weaver Clayton tried to cut her heart out. Within mere days, the wound had healed to a faint pink scar, thanks to the link she shared with Nate through the ancient artifact, Nefertiti's Heart. Not that either of them understood the bond forged between them that day in the cellar, except she could draw on his strength to heal faster. He could also track her whereabouts using the echo of her heart beat through his body, which made running away pointless.

Her boot heels clicked on the grey marble of the floor and she glanced at the ornate clock hanging opposite the main door. Its face was two feet wide, delicate filigree hands and dials showed the date, time, temperature, and phases of the moon. A beautiful enamelled pair of peacocks sat on either side, tail feathers of rich blues and greens draping over the side of the clock. The masterpiece told her it was 10:30 a.m., a week away from the autumn equinox, and a mild 15 degrees Celsius outside.

The bodyguard manning the door pulled open the heavy panelled barrier to the outside world and in his other hand, held out a grey wool coat. She gave him a nod of thanks as she grabbed the garment and bounced down the wide stairs to the driveway. Miguel waited in the paved driveway of the Mayfair mansion, a pair of matched bay geldings standing patiently beside him.

Cara shrugged on the jacket, over the top of her satchel, and pulled the collar up on the coat, when the deep frown in Miguel's face arrested her attention.

"What's wrong?"

He shoved a piece of paper into her hand. "These were just delivered to most of the men in the house."

Cara took the note and read over the few lines contained; it was a conscription notice. The named individual, ordered to report to a newly established training ground on the outskirts of London. If he failed to appear within five days, he faced either prison or the firing squad.

"Oh hell." If the notices were rolling out across London it meant only one thing——Victoria was raising an army from the youth of England. A shiver ran down Cara's spine as she wondered what fuelled the sudden recruitment drive. She reached out to squeeze Miguel's arm. "She'll not have you. I'll talk to Nate and see if he has somewhere we can move you with the other young men, until we see what is happening."

The open smile returned to his young face, such was his belief in his master's ability to sort the matter.

Cara placed one foot in the stirrup, swung into the saddle, and flicked the tails of her coat over the flank of the horse. Miguel passed up the reins before jumping on his horse. They headed toward the road at a slow walk on a loose rein. The sounds of voices and traffic wafted past the protective oak trees and down the drive, becoming louder as they rounded the corner and headed out the wrought iron gate into Wood Mews.

A woman in an understated lilac walking gown, with a matching tasselled parasol over her shoulder, raised a hand at the sight of Cara, waving her closer. She gave a sigh and nudged the gelding near the pavement and greeted Nate's neighbour, Sara Collins. "Lady Collins."

"Miss Devon. I am still waiting for you to retrieve my item." She stood close to the horse's neck so they wouldn't be overheard. The gelding sniffed at the parasol and snorted when a tassel tickled his nose.

Cara had become the go-to person for noble women with seedy problems they didn't want exposed to all of society. Only now did she remember her promise to Sara Collins, who had lost her engagement ring as a forfeit to a character called the Trickster. "Forgive me, no, the matter completely slipped my mind. I didn't want to be reminded of

Weaver Clayton trying to carve my heart out, so shoved that day to the back of my thoughts." She tapped a finger to her breast.

The other woman raised a dark eyebrow while her face remained impassive, an action reminisce of something Nate would do. "You appear fully recovered, and the matter is becoming most urgent. Questions are being asked of me and I can no longer avoid them."

Curiosity gnawed its way to the forefront of Cara's attention. "You know the person who holds the item and you've been to his domain before, why haven't you retrieved it for yourself?"

A chill wave flowed off the noble woman; Cara had over stepped a mark. "I was foolish once, I'll not make the same mistake twice. I may be seen or recognised if I venture there again. You will be handsomely rewarded. Please have the task accomplished by the end of the week."

Cara stiffened in the saddle. Being an impoverished noble she needed to find an income. She hated being reliant on Nate, even if she earned her keep untangling his paperwork. "Very well, I'll have it done in the next few days."

Lady Collins nodded, spun on her heel and with parasol over her shoulder, continued down the street.

Cara let out a breath of held air. She raised a hand and tugged her forelock in a subservient manner.

Miguel let out a snort of laughter at the gesture.

"Why am I helping her?" she asked.

He laughed, his eyes shining with mischief. "Because you are itching to go to Su-Terré and she gives you the perfect reason."

Cara shot him a smile. She was longing to visit the club and hoped the illicit playground lived up to its reputation as an escape for the wealthy and lost. "Ah, yes. That was it."

They trotted along Oxford Street and High Holborn, slowing as they approached the congested roads closer to the docks. As they rode toward the airship dockyards by the Thames, the slight echo through her body diminished, indicating she drew closer to Nate. The Lyons hangar was the largest structure, dominating thousands of square feet perched next to the Thames. Grey painted walls soared high above her head, the interior large enough to accommodate two airships in need of repairs.

Cara jumped from the saddle, and gave the gelding a quick scratch behind the ear before Miguel walked him away to the small stables at the rear of the main building. She turned her attention to the slip running from warehouse entrance, down to the murky Thames.

Nate and three of his men stared at the rail that hauled the carts from the airships up into the cargo hangar. A panel halfway down the slip stood open. Another man, only visible from the waist up, stood next to the workings. With his sleeves rolled up and grease on his hands, Cara thought Nate didn't look like any other noble she had encountered.

He looked up and said something to the workers before walking in her direction. He used a rag to wipe oil and grease from his hands as he approached.

Cara shook her head in amazement. "I've never seen a noble get his hands dirty before."

"You know I don't shy from dirty work." As a peer, Nathaniel was a lord above ground, but he also ruled the underworld with an extensive network of illegal activities. He earned a fortune through piracy and privateering that saved his near bankrupt titles and estates. He tucked the rag into the back pocket of his breeches, looking like a workman rather than a viscount.

"Not quite what I meant," Cara whispered as he hooked a clean finger under the satchel strap, running over her chest, and used it to draw her close. His mouth claimed hers in a languid kiss. His tongue licked the seam of her lips before sliding deeper to taste her. He sent fire racing through her limbs before he released her.

"The mechanism is getting worn. We've been increasingly busy. The men will need to use the exoskeletons for a day or two while it's replaced."

"You were gone early this morning," she murmured, waiting for her pounding heartbeat to return to normal.

"We had an early shipment." He wrapped an arm around her waist as they walked back toward the hangar, his warmth against her doing more to ward off the chill autumn air than the wool overcoat she wore.

She frowned. "No manifesto came through last night."

"Customs doesn't need to know about this one."

She sighed. His comment meant the entire shipment was illegal; probably one of his pirate airships, sneaking in with whatever it looted during its time aloft.

Startled whinnies came from the horses down the lane as a dragon-sized shadow swooped over them, accompanied by a low thrum. Cara stopped and raised a hand to shield her eyes, watching the blue and red painted airship glide overhead. Four spherical pods dangled underneath, looking like forgotten Christmas decorations. Each pod contained a soldier on lookout. She watched them spin their weapons toward the Lyons hangar as the airship did a lazy flyover. "There are more military airships around lately."

Nate's gaze flicked upward, tracking the military airship. "There's more of them circling. Victoria has her sights set on more jewels for her imperial crown." Her Majesty's Aeronautical Service expanded the Empire ever outward at an alarming pace, and their queen now styled herself as Empress.

"The lads at the house were served conscription notices this morning."

Nate nodded. "They came here last week. I've been shifting the younger lads to airship duties to keep them out of Victoria's reach."

Something else ate at Cara, not just the increased military presence, but the particular scrutiny over all Lyons holdings. "You would think she was expecting you to raise an objection, given the way they watch you. Or have you been up to something I really don't want to know about?" Cara searched Nate's face for any hint, but he remained inscrutable.

He raised a dark eyebrow. "Do you really want me to answer that?"

"No. Just keep Miguel and the other men safe." There were some secrets Cara wasn't ready to scratch open, like the enormous metal door padlocked shut, far under the ground in a hidden room. Instead she opened the satchel and extracted the paperwork. "I've done the Customs documents for this afternoon's ship. She's less than an hour away."

They entered the dim interior and paused, waiting for their eyes to adjust to the lower light. Cara loved the smell of the cargo hangar. The exotic aromas reminiscent of her travels around the world and made her wish for an adventure far away from the London smog. The numerous crates, boxes, and different shaped containers intrigued her and her hands itched to pull everything open to see what lay inside. They taunted her like mysterious gifts waiting under a Christmas tree.

They walked to the back of the hangar, where the office was located. Thin wooden shutters allowed the occupant to control the amount of light that could escape and also what the workers outside could see happening within.

Cara tossed the manifesto on to the desk and perched on the edge as Nate sunk into the black leather chair. "If you don't have any further work for me here, I'm going to visit Helene."

He ran a quick eye over the manifesto. "You two have become strange friends."

Cara shrugged. Helene, Countess de Sal was dying; having lost her mind, social standing, and her nose, to syphilis. Once the paramour of Nate's uncle, she supplied Cara with the rare books necessary for her research into old and mystic artifacts. "I feel normal around her, by comparison. Besides, she doesn't have much longer. I think it's important someone cares about what happens to her."

Nate tossed the paperwork to the desk. "This is the only ship arriving today, so there's nothing else that needs immediate attention."

"One other thing, do you have any plans for this evening?" she asked.

His eyes raked over her form perched on his desk. His desire burned in his gaze and along their common bond. "You mean apart from stripping you naked and licking honey from every inch of your body?"

"Apart from that," she murmured, her mind already drifting to the scene conjured by his words.

"Then, no. Unless you have something in mind you want to try?"

She had to blink to clear her mind from thinking of all the ways Nate drove her to oblivion with his strong hands and practiced tongue. "I need to go to Su-Terré. I told Sara Collins I would try and get her engagement ring back from the Trickster."

"Sara Collins?" A dark eyebrow shot up, exhibiting a life of its own. "She's a cold one. How did you get ensnared in her web?"

"I appear to have become the solution for noble women with indelicate problems." Cara straddled two worlds. She was noble born, but her association with Nate gave her access to the underworld. "I'm surprised you haven't snagged Sara. She's controlled, like you. Her family is well connected and wealthy. You'd make the perfect couple."

He ran his hands up Cara's buckskin clad thighs, his palms blazing against her body as his steel gaze held hers. "She's not my type. I wouldn't put anything near her I didn't want frozen off. I prefer something much warmer, and spirited, in my bed."

31041976R00176

Printed in Poland
by Amazon Fulfillment
Poland Sp. z o.o., Wrocław